Prince of Lions

E. Elizabeth Watson

To Vonder
Enjoy !

Candlelight Treasury

ISBN 10 0692609806
ISBN 13 9780692609804
Third Edition

To Emma Lucille and Donna Jeanne

In loving memory

Acknowledgements

Without my family, this work would not have been possible. I am forever grateful for my children who inspired me to start writing again, who accompanied me to cafes and libraries, who toured castles and churches with me, and who continue to be my biggest motivators. A special thanks to my husband who tolerates my writing habit and always offers honest critiques, and my extended family and friends for their encouragement and support. Another thank you to Cheeky Covers for the fabulous cover design. I am also appreciative of the writing professionals who have given great advice and guidance so that I can continue to grow as a medieval romance writer.

Translations

Ab imo pectore
From the bottom of my heart

Finis vitae sed non amoris, haec olim meminisse iuvabit
Love does not end with death, someday we will look back on this and smile

Alis volat propriis
She flies with her own wings

Pater Noster
The Lord's Prayer

Infinitus est numerus stultorum
Infinite is the number of fools

In inceptum finis est
The way you begin is how you end

In nomine Patris, et Filii, et Spiritus Sancti. Amen
In the name of the Father, the Son and the Holy Ghost, Amen

Discedere ad inferos!
Go to hell!

Cum larvis non luctandum.
One must not struggle with ghosts

1

The water steamed in the hearth and a raven cawed above the hut.

A bad omen, Gwenyth thought, wrapping her arm around her belly. The fear would soon be over with and she could begin walking the long journey home to Ballymead, the Lady Gwenyth, God willing.

Wind whistled across the foothills and rattled the door on its hinge. It blew open.

"Dear Iesus Christus," she muttered, crossing herself as she jumped to set the latch.

Slowly, she poured the broth and sipped it. Food had been little and what animal stock she had left, she could no longer ignore as her stomach protested its emptiness. She had used the last of it all at once. It was salty, hot and satisfying, and staved off starvation a little longer.

Then the pain came, a cramp at first that soon did not relent. She could feel the warmth running down her legs and soak into her slippers.

It's too soon! she thought.

But then she buckled over the flame. The pain grew. Her hands trembled and the cup dropped and cracked apart.

She groaned, then staggered, then fell onto the pallet as her groan grew into a scream. It wasn't supposed to hurt so badly, not right away. This was wrong, very wrong. She had seen it many times when she had helped Mrs. McIntosh.

Her head spun. She was sweating despite the frigid air. Her long, loose hair pasted to her neck. The wind rattled the door again but she was too delirious to take notice. It rattled harder. It banged. Her heart banged her ribs.

Forgive my sins, Father... She screamed loud and hard. *God is summoning me home!*

"Are you well!"

A man's voice was sounding through the rain that had begun to thrash the thatching and drip through the ceiling.

"Woman!"

The banging continued.

"Woman!"

With a crack, the door was breeched.

God has come for you, she consoled herself as the pain became too strong to remain conscious.

"Help me!" she wailed. "Please, God! Help me!"

It was bright when she woke. Her eyes couldn't focus in the sun that seeped through the window and it seemed like those summer days in the pond when she opened her eyes under water. Father had always allowed her to swim in spite of Mother's fears and superstitions. Beautiful Ballymead, blanketed with honeybees and flowers when the sun decided shining would suit it.

A cloud moved in front of the light and as her eyes found clarity she discovered it was not a cloud but a man, a tall man in a woolen surcoat the color of wine blousing over a leather belt. A chain hung across his shoulders made of golden links styled as lions gripping each other's tails. Against the door of the hut she noted a shield, divided with black and red the color of his tunic with the unmistakable profile of the black lion and the motto of the king.

Here Lions Rule.

A sword lay across it. Washing was hanging and a fire crackled in the hearth. She rolled her head and stared back at him. He was turned. All she could see was sable hair and sloping shoulders. He was washing his hands in a basin.

Water. She had thirst.

A horse whickered and thrust its black nose through the window, blocking the flood of sunshine. The man laughed a muted laugh.

"Away with you, Titan," he whispered and pushed its snout. "You'll break your fast as soon as the lady has broken hers."

His words were met with a defiant stomp of the hoof. He turned to Gwenyth, huddled in a ball beneath the warmth of a blanket that had not been there before.

"Now look what you've done, horse, you've woken her." He gave a courtly bow. "Sorry to disturb you."

She was too surprised to answer.

Manners Gwenyth, she chastised, but couldn't pry her lips apart.

He brought her water and she reached for it, but hesitated.

"Go on. You may take it."

She remained frozen.

"You've lost much blood and would do well to drink."

She looked away. Slowly he reached behind her head and tipped it up. He placed the quaich to her lips and she took a sip, then a swallow, then gulped it down so that water rolled down her chin. He took the cup back and stood before her.

"Are you well?"

The memory of the night flooded back.

The babe. There's no crying. "The babe," she croaked, bolting upright only to realize she was in her shift.

Gasping, she grabbed the blanket and wrenched it over her shoulders. The man turned around and without looking, handed a cloak back to her. When she was as decent as the scene would allow, he turned back around and knelt next to her. He looked grave and took her hand but she wrenched it back.

"Have you given a name?"

She hesitated to speak. "Amaranth...if it be a girl, William, if it be a boy."

His eyes, thoughtful, rested upon hers.

"Then I am sorry, My Lady, but your birth came too soon." The man bowed his head. "Your son, William, sleeps with God."

My son, William...

It should have been a relief and yet Gwenyth felt a tear. It rolled down her cheek and stained the blanket that the man had lent her. He reached forth with a kerchief to dab her eyes but she flinched. She looked back at him, suddenly realizing the oddness of his presence.

"I'm no midwife," his words whispered, though his face reddened beneath his stubble. "But due to your distress I hope you will see well that I had no choice but to assist."

Gwenyth's face turned as bright as his tunic.

"Lord in heaven," she whimpered and turned away, curling into a tight ball. "I should rather have died, My Lord."

"I should say you nearly did, Lady."

He said no more. The rustling sound told her that he had moved away. Water flowed freely from her eyes and she longed for childhood again, before any of this had happened. Those years had been wonderful when her brother William and her father would let her ride in their saddles while they tended to the reaches of Father's fief. Father had called her his butterfly.

'My little butterfly, so small and yet so curious...'

William had joked that she could outride the whole of King Bain's army with her love of horses. It had been the threads of Mother's patience to teach her to use the drop spindle. Mother had fought hard each night at the brambles caught in her tangled braid, scolding her for her wildness and scolding her father for teaching her to ride like a man.

'Ne'er a husband you'll get, my love, for a man doesn't look fondly on a wife who would rather stomp with the horses instead of embroider cloth...'

"I apologize, My Lady." The man was speaking to her again. "But seeing that there is no one here to introduce us, I'm Sir William Cadogan of Bain, champion of the court of the great King Bain and your humble servant. May I ask your name, My Lady?"

Him? Here?

She had heard of Sir William, everyone had, and recalled the poems written of him that the ladies sang during their needlepoint.

Sir William the Brave, to knighthood from knave, champion of Kings, and savior of slaves...but ne'er a husband will he be to you...

She had been on the verge of womanhood when he had earned his rank and fought in the Great War in Lispagne.

"May I ask what Sir William the Brave is doing alone in this rough country, My Lord?"

A smile shimmered across his lips though he stifled it.

"You may. And I thank thee for the hospitality I shared from your shelter." He bowed his head again. "I am on a quest and will take my leave soon, for by special orders of Our Lord King, I am to seek out whether someone lives or is dead and return them to their family. An uprising is happening on our Eastern Frontier, My Lady, and you are lucky to have avoided it in this remote pass. I fear it might be all out war soon if our king cannot tether down the dissenters." He looked back at her and then spoke again. "I should still like to know the name of my lady host."

"I'm no lady, My Lord," she lied.

"Are you not? You've very long hair for a peasant, and I would think garments like yours belonged to a ranking lady."

She rolled her head to see that her green gown with its gold embellishments and crisscrossed beadwork was hanging amongst the washing, and the bronze circlet with her veil had been retrieved from the basket in the corner.

"I thank thee for your kindness—" Her throat was so tight. "But you needn't waste time here when you've orders to fulfill." *Oh Gwenyth, only a lady of rank would think boldly enough to tell the king's First Knight what to do.*

"My time has not been wasted, Lady," he replied, persisting. "Your name, My Lady?"

"I'm sorry for my lack of manners." She sat up again, feeling her voice tremble. "It's been a trying time for me. I am Lady— I am wife to Sir William Feargach of Dwyre."

Sir William stiffened and the gentleness drained from his face so that she could see the hard lines of his skin. She looked down and twisted the blanket in her fingers, her forearms still yellowed and faintly purpled. She abhorred that title but her husband had taught her well to remember it.

"I apologize for your relation."

This was said with little sympathy. She pulled her knees clean to her chest and hugged them.

"My husband is dead, My Lord." The words barely made whispers and she could feel her face turning red all over again. "My father made the match, sir. He trusted William Feargach was an honorable man. But his family has discarded me for I didn't make the wife they wanted for their son." A trickle of tears began to roll on her cheek and she looked away with embarrassment.

"Who might your father be? Not another easterner?" His words had a tang.

"He comes from the highlands. He is Loddin of Ballymead, sir, and I am his only daughter."

His eyes widened. "Then you *are* Lady Gwenyth," he said. *How stupid of you, man. You should have known this was the one.* "I find it hard to match you to their description."

Gwenyth burned like fire and wanted for nothing more than the straw of the pallet to swallow her. How did Sir William Cadogan, the champion of thousands of knights, know her name?

"I'm thankful to meet you. You save me another trip into rough country," he smiled. "Our meeting has been fated. I was sent from His Majesty the king to assist your father in finding you. 'Twill be good news indeed that you live." He offered his hand. "Will the Lady Gwenyth of Ballymead come break her fast?"

She hesitated and looked at his hand as fear swept over her. He coaxed again and she didn't see many options, so slowly climbed off the pallet where he handed her more water and a cloth of powdered bread and cheese. Her stomach was flat again, as if no child had ever been there.

2

The portcullis thudded into place and the sentries pulled back their spears. Aindreas de Boscoe dismounted and handed his shield and reins to the late William Feargach's squire. He streamed across the bailey, muddy from horses trampling, and stinking in that acrid smell that typified a fortress preparing for battle. The fighting had been long already with very little success until now, and metal weapons were in short supply.

The yard bustled with servants and squires on errands, and the smiths were working day and night with what they had, toiling at their fires. All of Dwyre's fiefs had spared what they could.

Shea Feargach's metals won't be cut off for much longer, Aindreas thought. *Damn.* A corrupt soldier wearing the black lion at the outpost on the River Ruadhán had seen fit to turn his head with a bribe of coins. A few illegal shipments had been smuggled through.

He climbed the steps to the keep, an intrusive structure with sturdy bastions on each corner, pulling down his hood and jingling in his mail. Mud from his boots fell away in chunks and his cloak was heavy from the unrelenting rain that God saw fit to pour on them.

"What news?" Lord Feargach muttered as the guard opened the doors for Aindreas.

"My Lord, we have taken the mouth to the foothills. King Bain's men have all been slaughtered and the few that survive have fled with a message for their king."

"And that message?"

Aindreas summoned a disguise for his disgust.

"Lord Shea Feargach of Dwyre is rightful ruler over the lands east of the mountains and the bastard king will do well to remember that, lest we need to remind him."

"A good message," Shea chuckled. "Was that your idea?"

"It was, My Lord." Aindreas inclined himself and smiled, the sheath of his sword protruding out from his cloak.

"How did you manage?"

"They had not finished the masonry. Their enclosures were still made of wood, and wood burns when the doors become barred."

Shea nodded.

Clearly he is pleased for he is still sitting, Aindreas smirked.

"In addition, with the plundered Bainick weapons and supplies, I have ordered siege on the Bainick fort of Faulk to the south of us. Should Sir Iain and his men be victorious, which *would* be nice for a change, we will only have the port on the River Ruadhán in our way and if that should fall, you will no longer be barred from trade."

Shea closed his eyes and made a fist. "And then once we've re-supplied, we'll teach Our Lord King what it means to run. Well done, man. It only took you a fortnight to do what it has taken Sir Iain to *not* do in two months! I was afraid we would have to start using stones like our barbarian ancestors."

"If My Lord has no further requests, I should like to return to my men to rest."

"You may go." He waved his hand and Aindreas made a sweep for the door. "Oh, have you heard any news of the girl? Is she dead?"

Aindreas stopped.

So much for staying on subject. "Considering I have not been here to hear anything—"

"Just answer the question, man," Shea huffed.

"No, My Lord. At least, there's no knowledge of her."

"Just as well. If she lives, she'll run home to her father's estate and if she's dead, then praise the gods she's no longer our burden."

Stay true, Aindreas. He needs no cause to question your loyalty. "That reminds me. Did you know she was with child, sir?"

"What? What!" Shea slammed his fist upon the board and grabbed his tankard.

Here comes the tantrum.

"How many months was she? Why didn't she tell us?" He

hurled it against the wall and it shattered.

"I don't know, sir." Aindreas gauged the tantrum and decided it was safe. "I believe she is not yet due for another month, maybe two. Her maid just told of it to a stable hand who requested I inform you. Shall I fetch one of the women to explain?" Aindreas stood tall at the other end of the board while Shea flung his chair away.

Hopefully this fit will run its course soon, I could do with a wash and shave, he sighed. His sweat was rank from weeks without cleaning.

Shea threw back the fur draped over his shoulders.

"More ale!" he demanded. A frail woman skittered from the shadows and filled another tankard. "A child changes everything. I might have a grandson, another heir." He took a swig and rubbed his unruly beard. "Bring her maid here," he dismissed.

Aindreas bowed and strode to the door.

"Aindreas!"

He turned on his heel again. "*Yes*, My Lord?"

"The girl fancied you, did she not? Or should I say you fancied her?"

Aindreas stiffened. This was a double-edged question. It mattered not that he was Shea's top man if he answered it incorrectly.

He thought. "I believe she trusted me because of my friendship with your son, My Lord, him being friends with my squire as a lad."

Shea snorted at his tact.

"Good, that means she'll trust you now. Find the girl if she lives and bring her back. She's worth something after all. But mind you, Aindreas, just because she is widowed does not make her free for plucking."

Aindreas gritted his teeth.

"It's beneath me to do such a thing to any woman. And you know well that my ways are different than yours. Perhaps that's the reason she trusted *me*, My Lord. I bid you honor my loyalty and leave it at that."

Shea studied him for a moment then erupted into laughter.

"Oh! *Sir* Aindreas! A fine knight of Bain you would have made!"

The guards in the hall chuckled and the women in the corners were as stunned as roused quail. Their master hardly carried on in this way. Shea found his chair and plopped back in it.

"Away, man!" he waved between laughs. "And take your *noble* rest! Oh, one more thing!" Aindreas turned around once more. "You'll take Maccus and two others of his choosing with you."

Aindreas had always had a softness for the Lady Gwenyth. When she had first arrived, she was kind and very beautiful. William Feargach had fooled her and her entire family, playing the perfect gentleman until the gates of Dwyre clanked shut behind her and the men of the compound, warriors and laymen alike had boasted of what they should like to do to such a highland prize.

She had been gentle and had a way with animals, but grew quiet and pale from harsh treatment, sometimes remaining hidden for days, weeks, only to show up at board with welts and bruises when William had told her to join them. Aindreas had pitied her and when opportunity arose for a small act of kindness, he had shown it to her.

Let us pray you are dead, Lady, for if not, he could not disobey his lord, no matter how much he hated his orders.

Banging rang outside of the hut, slow clinks as Sir William worked at a craft. Gwenyth peeked through the crack in the door, but scolded herself and went back to her sewing. Not once had Sir William disturbed her despite it being their third day together. He didn't ask of her husband or pry for details about Dwyre and she was thankful for it. The year when she had turned six and ten should have been the happiest, for she had married a handsome man and fierce fighter.

Now, not quite eight and ten and I'm already a widow.

The dark knight sharing the hut treated her with all the kindnesses a lady was entitled. He was all but a shadow he kept so much distance, and would have slept beneath the stars and rain with his giant horse had she not bid him take refuge by the fire. The bleeding was subsiding bit by bit and the cramps that plagued her womb were dissipating. No mention had been made of her childbirth again. Sir William acted as though he knew nothing of it.

She placed the final stitches in the hem of Sir William's surcoat and listened to the clinking of metal. She tried to ignore the pounding. *Leave him to his labor, Gwenyth. Didn't William Feargach teach you well not to be curious?* She rubbed a scar beneath her chin and set aside the thread and needle. Moving to the window, she peeked out, but could only see an occasional bare arm swinging a mallet. Curiosity overcame her and she grabbed the surcoat, tying off the thread, snipping it with her teeth. She went to the door. His task seemed much more interesting.

Peering around the corner, she squinted in the light after so many days inside. He was a slender man with broad shoulders, toned no doubt from hard training and battle. He didn't look very old and yet his skin was tanned from the sun and wind. He had discarded his tunic on a stump and swung a mallet on a pike, fastening a wheel to a cart that had been abandoned with the hut.

Despite the crispness in the air, he was sweating. His hair as black as crows' feathers, mulleted in the champions' fashion was growing out and sticking to his forehead and neck. His muscles rippled across his back from his waist with every swing. A welt running from his trousers up beneath his armpit marred his side, an ugly burn had made his shoulder look wrinkled, and many slashes had disfigured his back. Aside from the blemishes, he was a fine looking man, if indeed poorly shaven from travel.

She stared at him, contemplating his presence. *Why would the king send the First Knight of his army to find me if the Eastern Front is rebelling?*

He swung the mallet again and struck, just as Titan stuck his snout in her ear and whickered.

"Oh!" she exclaimed, cowering beneath the warhorse.

He leaned down and lipped at her hair like spring grass.

"Titan!" Sir William dropped the mallet and moved to her in one swift motion. "Shame on you, man! It's a disgrace indeed to make such advances on a lady!" he jested and took his halter.

With a grin, he extended a hand to help her up.

"I don't know why I was frightened," she admitted. "I fancy myself a decent horsewoman."

"Do you?" He raised his eyebrow. "Then perhaps I've been wasting my time these past days. I should simply barter for an extra horse."

He let go of Titan and snatched up his tunic, letting it slide over him while a smile danced on his lips.

"My Lord?"

"Well, I'm no carpenter, Lady, but I feel I've made a good repair to this old cart, for your comfort during our journey of course. Though I'm afraid your notion of comfort might need to accommodate many bumps and ruts."

"I'm sorry, sir," she dropped down again and stared at the grass. "I am ashamed, I meant no insult—"

His hand reached back out to her.

"Please, Lady, I meant it only in jest." He was still smiling and a twinkle had lit his eye. "So you fancy horses. Do you also fancy spying on *humble* knights who are tempting their clumsy hands at a craft?"

Her face was burning and again she fell back to her knees.

"I wished only to tell My Lord that his surcoat is mended..." Her words were barely audible as she held out the garment. A smile consumed his face. "Do...do you jest again, My Lord?"

"Aye, Lady," he sighed. "You will do well to quit bowing, or you shall wear yourself out."

Titan lipped at her hair again. She stood and rubbed his nose.

"That is one unruly beast you pet," he remarked.

Titan tossed his head in disapproval while Sir William scooped up his tools and discarded them aside the hut.

"Oh, a magnificent creature, My Lord, if I may say so, despite his age," she murmured as she curled up his lips to see his teeth. "As black as night. He has, no doubt, a valiant record."

She let a timid hand rub his neck. Sir William raised his brows again and rested his hands on his waist. Titan nuzzled her. She tried not to smile but she did know horses and now the knight could see it.

"And he will become as soft as a songbird if My Lady spoils him with such flattery."

She walked around the animal like her father always did at the fairs each year when she would dance and sing and dance some more. Those had been such happy times.

'The sultans from the Land of Spices say that is the mark of speed, Butterfly...'

"Your Titan wears the mark of speed, Sir William," she noted, completing her circle and wrapping back around to stroke the horse's neck.

"My Lady?" Now he was intrigued.

Stop, you fool, she told herself. "That patch of white on his heel. He must be gloriously fast. Is he a mix with the breeds from the Land of Spices?"

"You do indeed know your horses, Lady Gwenyth of Ballymead."

"Oh, not knows, My Lord, loves, *ab imo pectore...*"

At a loss for words at her passionate statement, William stood quietly. She finally managed to wrangle her tongue.

"You're well-schooled for a woman," he remarked.

Her excitement drained away. If there was anything life at Dwyre had taught her, it was to know her place in the affairs of men.

'Men are talking, Gwenyth!"

A hand lashed her face and her skin smarted. William pulled her up by the hair while his father shook his head.

'You'll do well to remember that you are not in your father's house! Men don't wish a woman to be bold!'

'I'm sorry, My Lord...forgive me, please forgive me...'

He ran his hand through his hair. "Would you care to ride him—"

"I'm too bold. I shall tend to your supper." She hastened inside and heaved shut the door.

Of course I wish to ride him! she thought, but set to work cooking instead.

The rabbit that Sir William had caught lay skinned and ready. She set the pot over the fire and cut the meat off the bones into pieces, then dumped them in and turned back to slice the bread. She became lost in thought contemplating the knight, unwrapping the cheese and cutting out hearty wedges for him.

It was then that she smelled it. She whirled back around. Smoke was rising from the pot.

"No, no, no," she whimpered and dashed to grab the handle. "Ah!"

It burned her and the pot tipped over. The blackened meat rolled out.

"Oh you *fool*, Gwenyth, you fool," she muttered.

Her eyes filled with water and she scrambled to lift the pieces out of the dirt as her hand throbbed.

"Lady!" William slammed through the door. "What has

happened—"

"No!" she exclaimed and ducked into the corner.

William froze and stood puzzled.

"No...I'm sorry, My Lord, I'm sorry," she sniveled and fell down to her knees, clutching her burn. "I ruined your meal. I burned it. I forgot the broth, I am so foolish..."

William was too surprised to move at first but walked to her and dropped onto a knee.

"I know not why I startled you so terribly. I only heard you cry out and worried for you, that's all."

Worried for me?

He looked at her hand, clutched within her other.

"Are you injured?"

He reached for it but she held it fast.

"'Tis but a small burn and nothing more, for I was foolish and grabbed the handle."

"Please, Lady," he spoke even more gently. "Allow me to look."

He peeled back her fingers to reveal a welt rising along the length of her palm and fingers. The water sat beside them. He dipped a rag into it and let the droplets fall onto her skin, eyeing her carefully.

"I care not if the meat is burned, woman, only if I can put it in my stomach. Believe me, I have had to eat much worse. I am sure we'll be able to salvage it."

The coolness of the water was soothing and she tried to relax.

"There now. Are we feeling better?"

She nodded.

He took more water and caressed her skin with the rag. It rolled down her arm and soaked her sleeve. William pushed it out of the way and revealed a faded patch of yellow.

"That must have been an unsightly bruise. What caused it?"

She yanked her hand away and scrambled forward to finish collecting the meat.

"An accident, My Lord," she whispered.

"Do you have many accidents?"

She did not answer.

That night, he ate in silence while Gwenyth stood in the shadow and waited for him to finish. A jest about fine dining crossed his mind but upon glancing at her, he decided to hold his tongue. She still refused to sit and share the meal. She twisted a kerchief in her fingers and watched him, darting her eyes downward whenever he looked up.

Sir William took in her posture as he sopped up his broth with the remains of the bread. She was nervous, her face untrusting.

What has befallen this fair woman?

He made for the door so she could eat and change.

Those dark eyes, he thought as he went. *It's the fear I see in men who I am about to slay*.

"Lady Gwenyth," he turned to her before pulling closed the latch. "I hope you will know that you may speak your mind on our journey. You're not foolish, nor are you bold. I am not offended, merely surprised." He thought a moment longer. "To be honest, I should like it indeed if you kept talking."

3

She didn't look back on the fourth day as they pulled away from the hut, save for one last glance at the mound of earth that covered little William.

Kind Aindreas, she thought.

He had risked his life many times after smuggling her there so she might survive when Shea Feargach's men dumped her in the wilderness. Thrice he had brought her food and provisions as time would allow when he should have been leading his men. He had shown her a nearby mountain grove that had berries and had taught her to set a snare, so should he not be able to come back, she might survive. She knew he fancied her terribly. He was the one kind man of Dwyre and she knew that if he could have, he would have stolen her back to her father.

But the skirmishes along the Bainick Kingdom's Eastern Front had gone on for two months now as Shea, after months more of plotting, decided to begin taking back what had rightfully been his uncle's land. It was one of those very skirmishes that had claimed her husband's life. Aindreas had not come for nearly a month now.

Titan thrashed his head and stomped, fanning his feathery mane with a shake of her cart.

"I'm afraid my fearless warhorse is too proud to do the work of a mule," Sir William interrupted her thoughts. She smiled but remained silent. "I hope his conduct isn't making you ill. He is beyond discipline." Again, silence fell. "Were you married long?"

The question caught her off guard. It was the first talk of Dwyre that he had made. She had wondered how long he might wait before asking.

"No, My Lord, it hasn't yet been two years."

In truth, her stay at Dwyre had been just more than one year and five months before God had graced her with her abandonment in the mountains, but that time at Dwyre had felt like a lifetime of torture and the time pregnant in that hut like a prison sentence. She shuddered and soon realized he was staring at her.

"You must be grief stricken," he said carefully. "Do you miss him?"

She scrutinized him. "If I say aye, then I mourn for our king's dissenter but if I say nay, then I appear a heartless wife."

He turned back around as his jerkin creaked against the saddle.

"You are shrewd, Lady, but you mustn't think me the type who plays games with words to catch a misstep. Speak your mind. I wouldn't think less of you if you said no," he muttered, looking at the surrounding peaks as a storm moved in. "Are your bruises finally healed?"

His voice sounded cold. She looked down at her arms, now covered properly in their green sleeves. They had been so purpled that it had taken the whole of her abandonment for them to heal.

'Come here, woman!'

'No...no...please I beg you, My Lord—'

'Damn it! I said come here!'

He wrenched her forward and she ran from him. Instead, he whipped loose his belt. She felt it lash across her back and fell into the corner.

'What do you have to say, woman!'

'Please! Oh please!' she cried. 'I don't know what I've done!'

He was striking her again. She was crouched against the wall of the great hall, her arms thrown up to protect her head. She was closing her eyes now, allowing her arms to bear the brunt of his drunken strap.

'I'm sorry!' she screamed. 'I know not what I've done, but I'm sorry I swear it!'

He yanked her up from the lump she had turned into, but she collapsed once more.

'The men say you make eyes at them! They say you fancy Aindreas, that he gives you gifts! That you flirt with him!'

'Please, My Lord! He gave me but a flower!' she had begged, but he didn't hear her in his rage.

'I'll teach my wife what it means to be a man's whore!'

The thrashing continued and she prayed for it to be over as he threw her against the board and ripped open his trousers. He swept his hand across it and sent the cups and trenchers to the floor.

She fell to her knees and clasped her hands. 'I'm sorry, husband!' she whimpered.

'Get out! All of you!' William bellowed.

The women scattered away and the men made haste for the tavern. She saw Aindreas, his brow contorted as she screamed and tried to twist free.

'I'm sorry, Lady,' he mouthed.

Her eyes had welled with tears. She didn't notice Sir William stop the cart, nor did she feel his stare on her again.

"Have I offended you, My Lady?" His words were humble. "Are you well?"

She threw her face in her hands and cried. He dismounted and walked around, clenching and unclenching his fingers nervously, not knowing what to do.

"My Lady?"

She buried her face as the sobs fell forth. He sat beside her and peeled one of her hands away, holding it between his rough ones.

"Gwenyth?"

She looked up at him. His eyes were so green like emeralds beneath his black brows.

"I've, I've not known you long," he stammered. *You're the commanding Knight of Bain, man. Speak plainly before she thinks the King has sent a fool to protect her.* "I hope you'll do well to consider me a friend, to share your grievances with. Perhaps speaking of them will give you solace and your story can go before the king—"

"'Tis a man's right how he treats his wife, My Lord, and the king's law protects it," she whispered. "Rough handling is the way of many men." She gulped at the tears flowing into her lips.

"Not all men, Gwenyth." He ran a thumb under a tear and pushed it away. "Rough handling is the way of many fathers too, but some of us find a different path."

With that, she spilt her story right there on the side of the way with the mountain air blowing freshly.

"He was so handsome, William Feargach. He journeyed all the way to the highlands to ask for marriage," she cried. "His older brother was killed and it was up to him to carry on the family name. But he fooled me, he and his father fooled everyone..." She shook her head. "At first he used to apologize. He'd bend before me and take my hand...and tell me to learn to bite my tongue so he would have no cause for anger, but he never meant it...the lashings...they grew worse and worse and *worse.* I used to find any excuse to be busy, chores, the privy, whatever it took to keep clear of his path but even that was not enough for sometimes my absence angered him more."

"Did you not send word to your family?"

"I was forbidden to even write them. None of the other women were literate. And then, after a long time, a messenger came to tell that my mother," she gulped again, "she had finally passed away after years of illness. I couldn't go to her. He wouldn't let me go home to my mother. I screamed to the messenger for I knew him well. But the ladies pulled me from the window!"

Her eyes bubbled and William wiped the water away with his cuff.

"I begged him tell my father! That's when my father learned of my lot. He came to ask for me back and was all but fought off Dwyre land and when my husband was killed, they thought it best to just get rid of me."

She fell against him without thinking. He froze, unsure of what to do. Slowly, he wrapped an arm around her, still holding her hand in his clasp.

'You will know your place, William Cadogan, by Christ you will!' *The strap hit him hard as his mother and sisters cried. 'You are not a first son! And you shame my house with your presence!'*

He shook the words away for they had not cropped up in many years. In fact, he had done a good job of forgetting.

"Was it just beatings he dealt you, Lady? Did he abuse you?" he whispered.

She pulled herself from his embrace and looked away.

"I cannot speak of it, I...I was his wife, sir."

"But why not send you home?"

"It would have cost men and provisions to do so," she answered, not realizing she was clenching his fingers. "And Lord Shea needs them all to launch his rebellion against the crown."

Sir William stared blankly at the mountains. *You should be thinking of battle, William,* he scolded himself as he brushed her hand with his thumb. *You should be picking her mind with questions about Dwyre.*

"But you were with child."

His heart quickened at the injustice and he found his teeth were clenched.

"It's a terrible sin, but I didn't tell anyone for I prayed my flux would come and wash it away. Only my maid knew."

"How did you hide it from them?"

"I am small, sir, and this babe was weak. I was not yet showing."

He stood up and placed her hand in her lap.

"You'll forgive my undisciplined tongue, Lady Gwenyth, but William Feargach is dead, praise be to God. I may sound cruel but God has done you a grand favor, delivering you from him."

He clenched his hands into fists in attempt to shut his mouth. She gulped again. His lips were so tight that they had practically disappeared.

"I heard of your father's requests, Lady, saying you had been trapped as the wife of a Dwyre son but now were missing. Your beauty, he compared to heaven on a sunny day, with hair as long and pale as the River Fae. His description doesn't do you justice. But he told of a spirited girl. He told of your smiles. I see none of that. I see sadness and fear. I'm angered that you have been robbed of that by such a brute." He backed away. "Until I see you safely into your father's arms at Ballymead, trust that I'm not just a knight on an errand, but I am your loyal servant and friend. You'll be safe in my care. You may trust me."

He swung himself up into his saddle.

"One last question." He turned partway around though didn't share the full of his scowl with her eyes. "Why would you honor such an animal by gracing him with a namesake?"

She wiped the tears. "I honor my brother with the name, Sir William."

His face softened and he rode on in silence. Gwenyth hugged her legs to her chest and fell asleep.

4

"She's gone, sir," Maccus replied as he pushed through the undergrowth.

"Of course she is. It's been nearly two months," Aindreas muttered as the rain poured, matting his auburn hair. His horse, soaked, stood stagnantly beneath his weight. "Have you searched the whole of the thicket? Any sign of a body?"

"We've searched through and through, sir."

"And beyond?"

"Aye. The weather has grown bad, sir, and Collins coughs somethin' awful into 'is rag. This isn't a hunt I care t' be on when there's new ale at the tavern."

Aindreas saw the huddle of sodden men, as grey as the sky above them. If Maccus wanted to abandon the search, perhaps Lord Feargach would take it as a sign and let her go. Except Aindreas was too smart for that. The only things worth fighting for besides the lands to the east were heirs and Shea had lost his only two. Any possibility of another was worth searching to the ends of the earth. His daughters were a burden and he cursed the dowries he would have to supply to get rid of them. He had proven to make too many of those.

"D'you think she was eaten? A woman on her own in this country would not've gotten far."

I hope not. "She might have been. Are you sure this is the right place? You didn't discard her closer to the river?" *Farther away from the hut?*

"No, sir. She might've gone up in the pass. Should we search there as well?"

Maccus blew his steamy breath into his hands as the water

rolled down his hair like droplets off a goose's feathers.

"It's worth a look," Aindreas replied.

"I've got to be honest sir, I don't see why Lord Feargach wants her back. It's foul weather, an' I don't care much for our orders—"

"You'll care when Shea Feargach locks you in the pillory and has you horsewhipped!" Aindreas pointed. "You'll do well, Maccus, to remember your place. If he orders her back, we get her."

"My apologies, sir," Maccus frowned. "It's just, well, days in this drippin' slime...I only like to hunt if I know I'm going t'make the kill."

"On the morrow, we search the uplands," Aindreas said with little expression. "Let Collins warm himself before we continue."

It was as dark as pitch when Aindreas stole away from camp, leaving Maccus and the others to snore and fart beneath their tents. His horse raised his head but Aindreas knew better than to ride him and draw attention. Instead, he climbed through the brush and finally broke through to the forest path bathed in moonlight.

The moon had moved considerably by the time he came upon the little hut. It was dark. No fire smoke filled the air. He pushed open the door and looked around. Placing his hand over the hearth, the coals were still warm, though barely. The old rag, the only blanket he had been able to steal was against the wall, stiff and crusted. He smelled it. It smelled of blood.

What has passed here? he thought.

He walked out into the moonlight again, careful to keep his boots from making fresh prints. There had been a cart behind the hut. It was gone now. Wheel ruts were pressed into the soil. Fresh horse manure sat in a few scattered piles and there were large footprints, those of a man.

She's been found. Dear Christ, she's been taken!

Aindreas' heart thumped. He had been ready to abandon his search, but now felt compelled to find her, even if it meant entrapping her again. The tragedies that might befall her at the hands of a highway man were too many to count, but at least he knew what she faced at Dwyre.

A mound of fresh earth sat undisturbed across the path. He walked to it. A cross made of pebbles decorated the soil above it.

Slowly, he began to scatter the dirt until a ghastly site met his eyes. A babe, small and frail, was ridden with ants and other scavengers. He staggered away and gagged, then wiping his mouth on his sleeve, crossed himself and noticed that it was a boy.

Shea's grandson...another heir... Things look bleak, sweet Gwenyth, when your father-in-law learns that you birth sons. He'll bed you himself.

It was growing light when he arrived back to camp. Maccus was already awake, nursing a skin of watered wine. He furrowed his brow.

"Where've you been, My Lord?"

"Catching our breakfast," Aindreas replied. "Forgive me for my noble tastes, but stale bread is not my idea of a good meal."

Maccus scrutinized him as he swung three rabbits onto a rock by their hind legs, roused from their warren. He had thought well enough to return with something so that he might have an excuse for wandering.

"How about fresh meat to break our fast?"

"It sure beats wha' we've got," Collins wheezed. "I'll skin'em."

Once the sun reached the trees, they bundled their tents and broke camp. Their horses trod upon the autumn brambles as their breath puffed into the air. The air was chilled in preparation for winter. Maccus stretched his oversized gut and passed more gas as he twisted in his saddle. The men laughed.

Vile, Aindreas thought.

"Should we search upon that ridge, sir?" Maccus asked as Collins coughed and wheezed again, wiping his long nose. "There's an old peasant's hut there."

"Very well," Aindreas said.

They arrived at the hut and Aindreas noticed the mound covering Gwenyth's son. He shuddered to see beneath it again but knew that it could not be avoided. Maccus, a former animal mercenary for the monks of St. Andrews, could smell a dead mouse from a mountain away.

"I'd say someone was here just yesterday," Maccus called as he exited the hut. "Coals are cold, but fresh. There's blood, sir. Whoever was here has suffered, if they even live."

"Cart ruts, My Lord, and prints," Collins rasped as he sputtered into his rag, using it to wipe his fevered brow. "Man's and a woman's. Do you suppose it's a man and wife?"

They searched around the hut, finding all the same things Aindreas knew they would. Maccus noticed something in the soil and looked at Aindreas' feet with a furrowed brow, but didn't say anything. The piles of fresh horse manure were the obvious.

"What have we here?" Maccus had found the burial and sifted off the soil like a cur routing for a bone. "How far along was the woman again?"

"Seven months, or there about."

Maccus smiled and picked up the rotting infant by an arm like a war spoil. Aindreas swallowed hard to hold his morning meal in place.

"Put it back, man," he uttered as the breeze brought the odor to his nose.

"But it might be hers—"

"I said put it back!" Aindreas snarled. "Do you see that sign of the cross?"

Maccus the bloodhound had overlooked it. He scratched his head.

"So?"

"So it is a Christian burial! Have respect!"

"You and your Christian ways. Well it's a boy," Maccus said as he dropped the corpse back in and kicked the dirt on top.

"Should we follow those tracks? If it's her, she rides with one man only. There's only one horse. Simple enough for us to take him down should he put up a fight."

"Yes, we follow. Saddle up," Aindreas stated. "It might very well be Gwenyth." They disappeared into the trees and he offered up a silent prayer.

5

"They have fought well," Shea mumbled as he slammed through the door to his wife's chamber. "They have cause to celebrate, as do I but I…"

He was drunk and seemed to lose his mind for a moment.

"And yet, you don't seem pleased, My Lord."

The Lady Janis sent glances to her companions, two of which were Shea's older daughters. They scurried behind the screen and were all but gone to the Master of Dwyre though she knew they lingered.

"The farthest outposts of Bain, toppled, and it'll take over a sennight of riding for their messengers to reach the capital, another sennight for the deployment of knights. We'll be ready for it. We can take much more in that amount of time."

"Why then, don't you smile?"

"I want a son from that belly of yours, I need it. William's death has left me with no one, and that damned girl…"

He grabbed Janis and undid her lacing as he leaned down to bite her neck, tossing aside her needlepoint. She let her gown fall to the floor.

"I need you, woman."

Her dark hair smelled sweet like the spiced oils he had given her, the only woman he had given gifts. She never refused him, and he had only raised a hand to her once for birthing a daughter after William had been cut down, though he had been so angry at the loss, anything she did might have earned it. Janis had been a good bargain. It felt good to know he could bed a daughter of a Bainick liegeman, no matter how low ranking, and better that she seemed to like it.

Easier than the first three, he thought, who had cowered beneath his rage.

"I prayed you would come," she smiled and stepped to the bed. "You're troubled and need to relax."

She peeled off her veil and let her shift fall so that her bareness gaped at him. Her breasts were swollen like wine skins and she happened to know that he liked them.

"Come to your wife, My Lord," she took his hand and kissed it. "'Tis my duty to you."

"What a woman's for...You want me, woman, do you not?" he slurred, one hand squeezing her breasts. His eyes furrowed and his grip became tight. "Me and only me?" He grabbed her neck, pinching her skin hard so that she squeaked. "Because so help me if another man has tasted your favors I'll—"

"Only you, My Lord and never another," she choked.

He eased his hold and burrowed into her with all the grace of a mule, grabbing her breasts. How he loved her breasts, firm and engorged with milk, *the one good reason to keep her pregnant, even if it means daughters*, he thought. He squeezed them and bent down to kiss them. Again he pushed into her, rocking his body against her as she winced in pain.

Her ladies peeked around the blind. *Let them watch*, she thought. *It will do them well to learn their lot. Dwyre doesn't breed gentle men, save Aindreas.* She saw his mind wandering beneath the pool of ale that sloshed in it and slid her hands along his arms, grabbing his buttocks.

"My Lord will not lighten his burden with such gentle pats," she spoke into his ear as she pulled him against her harder. "What ails you, husband?"

He needed Aindreas back. Aindreas had masterminded the takeover of the first Bainick outpost and he feared without his return soon, his men might make a folly. No news had come from Faulk yet and the lack of it worried him. Yet Gwenyth of Ballymead was all he saw with his eyes closed.

"Gwenyth is with child," he said between grunts. "Should she carry my grandson..." He found it hard to talk and tend to his task at the same time.

"She didn't tell the women, My Lord," Janis pinched her eyes shut as he bore down harder. "She was deceptive."

32

"And I'll punish her for it," he groaned, rocking against her.

"She will deserve it, My Lord," Janis whispered, "though I shall be saddened that I must share."

That made him grin, which he seldom did. "I've been good to you, woman," he scolded and kissed her. "I try not to stray, but aye..." he breathed. "Aye, she'll deserve it, from William's father she'll deserve it but for her, it will be punishment. You'd best mind your place and be grateful I love ye."

If this is love..."I shall be saddened all the same, My Lord," she gasped beneath his weight.

She knew he strayed from the marriage bed once in a while, but tried not to care. He was about as sweet as a hungry boar. Yet Gwenyth could very well become an obsession with talk like this should she not escape all the way to Ballymead and she needed to keep in mind why she was here. It was certainly no longer for love like she had once thought.

She grabbed his face and kissed him, searching through his beard for his tongue, which was having trouble working in the way she wanted. He broke free from her kiss.

"Let me breathe, woman," he complained, his brow still furrowed.

"I'm failing to ease your mind," she panted. "My Lord always feels better when he lets burdens off his chest."

"I'm short on weapons...my metals have been cut off...the bastard's army has held the River Ruadhán...I need Aindreas back soon...and, and as soon...ahh..."

He's close, Janis, he's very close, make him finish, she told herself.

"My Lord," she quivered. "Don't slow. Keep pace, man! Keep speaking to me, I crave you so!"

"As soon as he's back...I'll, I'll, leave..."

There it is, she smiled. He collapsed on her, sweating, and she rubbed his back. It was over, *and it only took five minutes.*

Her companions were giggling but thankfully Shea didn't hear. She had a mind to giggle herself. He rolled off of her and stared at the ceiling, and she curled next to him to rub his stomach while his seed dribbled down her leg.

"Where will you go, my love?"

He let out a sigh and grabbed a rag, rubbing himself dry of her and scratching himself. "I go to the River Ruadhán to make sure we get our stronghold. I'll be leaving in a week."

"You'll take many men no doubt," she sighed and pulled up a blanket to keep from shivering. "How many, My Lord? Will there be anyone left to protect the women and children?"

"Five hundred perhaps, I've got conscriptions. The tributaries are sending warriors."

He looked at Janis who lay upon the pillow. She had let her lips droop into a pout. He couldn't be angry with her. It was nice to make pillow talk on such matters with someone who had no mind for politics.

"The guards will be here, plus another few hundred in the villages."

She pulled the blanket tight and looked away.

"What is it, woman?" he sighed.

She shook her head. "I know I sound demanding, husband, but—"

"This isn't about Gwenyth, is it?"

"My Lord," she muttered. "Please tell me what I should do to regain your favor. I wish you to honor our marriage. I wish you to tell me where I have failed so that you have no need to seek another."

He leaned over and kissed her.

"You do have my favor," he whispered. "I shouldn't talk of such things for they upset you. She has angered me, that's all, and this belly of yours refuses to give me heirs."

He chuckled and swung his legs around to the floor, still in their boots. "I've no more time for idleness. Fetch me wine and be quick about it. I've business to attend to."

Foolish Lord and Master, Janis thought as she corked the inkwell.

It was very late and Shea hadn't returned to her bed, not that it concerned her. She poured the wax on the seam of parchment and stamped it, quickly stowing the quill, ink and wax in the bottom of a trunk.

If only he knew how weak he was. It was true that the Lord of

Dwyre thought women's heads to be filled with nothing. It was his one great fault, but she would be punished badly if he found out she could read and write.

Among his men, he's fierce and secretive, but between his alcohol and his wife, he never knows what his tongue is for. It will be his demise, she thought, and slid the message between her hand and gown.

She walked out into the darkened hall. Her husband was snoring at the board and many others were passed out, snoring, or releasing odors that made her nose curl. She looked across the room at a guard leaning against the door. He rose as if she had commanded it. She floated across the rushes and as she passed him, the parchment slid from her hand into his. She squeezed his fingers for a moment and flashed her black eyes at him, then turned to leave.

Stopping, she stared at Shea.

You're not the only one who strays, My Lord, and with that, she climbed back to her chamber and latched the door.

6

Gwenyth prepared a pile of pine boughs for bedding as another night fell on their travels. Sir William sat by the fire as she tucked herself into a lump beneath her covers with her knees pulled clean to her chest. Despite it, she shivered and the knight turned to see her shaking. He was cold and his muscles twitched, but the blanket and the cloak were both with the lady as he had requested, so he scooted closer to the fire to feel the heat radiating onto his arm.

He propped up his knees and braced his sword across his legs. It would be a long night, but he was not averse to believing omens even if they were pagan. A raven had cawed above them on their journey and Titan was uneasy. He found it wise to pay heed and sit watch for the night.

She rustled on the boughs and he turned back around so as not to be caught staring at her. Still, her image stayed in front of his mind. He tried to match the solemn face with the description Loddin had given, but couldn't put the two together. She did not smile but rarely and when she did, it was not really a smile but a mere mask of her sadness.

Yet moments would punctuate her face, like when Titan routed through her hands that afternoon for berries. She talked to the horse as if a weight was lifted from her. The stallion had arched his neck over her shoulder as she stroked his face, the creases fading from her own. He gave a warning snort when William, spying, came too close.

'And a noble protector you are, Sir Titan,' she had played, believing the moment to be private.

She was nothing like any woman he had met.

She's barely a woman, he reminded himself.

She was smart, educated, versed in Latin, but he could see that behind what had once been dark, happy eyes she was always thinking, always fearing, and always watching him.

'You always watch him?' William was asking his oldest brother and their father's namesake, Andrew.

'Aye, I always do. You should always watch an enemy, little brother, whether he be your father or not...'

William shifted closer to the fire still.

"She fears me," he whispered. *You vowed, man, that you would never do this. You would never care for one. You mustn't feel for her,* he thought, *or parting with her at Ballymead will be that much harder.*

He shivered again and trembling with cold, the hilt of his blade freezing his fingertips. Gwenyth was shifting again on her bedding and he kept his eyes forward. Suddenly, his cloak draped over his shoulders and her hand rested on him for a moment.

"You're freezing, My Lord," she said.

"Am not," came his indignant reply. "I've spent colder nights than these and I cannot deliver a daughter to one of the king's vassals who isn't only sick at heart but sick with illness too, now can I? Take the cloak, Lady."

"I insist you keep it," was all she said.

His mind reached for her hand but his own hand hesitated. When it finally complied with his wishes, she was sliding hers away and his fingers met nothing but his shoulder. She wrapped the blanket around her body and knelt next to the fire.

"I should like to climb into these coals to sleep, I am so cold," she muttered.

Sir William gave a quiet grunt and smiled while Titan snorted again, shifting on his tether with his tail arched.

Easy, man, William thought. *I can sense it too.*

"There's a hamlet over that ridge. We'll reach it in a few days if we come down off the slope and stick close to the river. There, hopefully we can find you a pallet for the night and I can barter for some provisions."

"'Twill be strange," she said, "being seen traveling alone with a man."

She shivered again and clenched the blanket. He turned to

look at her.

"You still wear your wedding ring?"

"Aye, I do." She looked down at it while a wisp of rebellious hair fell into her face.

William reached out and brushed it back for her. She blushed, then smiled.

"Then it shall only be awkward for us both. We act as man and wife when we reach the village. You won't be embarrassed that way," he said decisively, turning back to his watch.

She gaped at him, not knowing what to say. "But sir..."

He turned to look at her again, shrugging at the chill to shake it off.

"They will know Sir William the Brave the moment they see the lion upon your shield," she gasped and stood up. "Everyone knows My Lord has refused to take a wife. It will never work."

William stood too, adjusting the cloak.

"The folk here don't know my face and I'm not the only knight of the Bainick kingdom, My Lady. I'll give them a false name if you like. Eh, Sir Warwick of King Bain's counsel is married to a blonde woman. We could go as them." He smiled at the dread spreading on her face. *Her weight is lifted at the moment.* "Do you fancy me that repulsive, Lady Gwenyth? Or do I simply not meet the standards of a man worthy enough of being your husband?"

Her eyes widened so big he thought they would roll out of her head.

"My Lord...you have been ever gracious to me, and I would never..." she gasped and dropped down to her knees again. "I, I pray this is one of those moments when you jest again!"

He chuckled, kneeling before her. Slowly, she smiled.

"You must get used to my sense of humor, Lady. I only tease people I like."

A twig snapped and he whipped his head around. Titan danced on his rope, breathing skittish whickers.

"What was—"

"Shh!" He threw up his hand for silence.

She flinched, flinging her arms up, taking him by surprise.

Now is not the time, man.

"Do *exactly* as I say. If I say run," he whispered, her arms lowering, "you make haste for the trees beyond your bed. There's a rock shelter just above us and I'll find you there."

He rose and paced to the edge of the trees. The horse's nostrils flared and snorted. The cursed clouds had blocked the moonlight and seeing beyond the fire was impossible. Gwenyth trembled and looked behind her at her bedding. The trees were murky there and the thought of willingly entering them scared her.

William walked the perimeter, his sword and shield at the ready and his daggers tucked in his belt and boot. When he was satisfied, he returned and resumed his smile.

"I admit I enjoy teasing you, woman. If I may be so bold, you look lovely when you're shocked—"

"William!" Gwenyth screamed.

He wheeled around and his sword met with metal. He shoved the man away with ease but two more lunged at him. He swung his sword and blocked the others, but the first recovered and stabbed at his side. Expertly, William kicked the blade, sending it reeling from the man's grip. With a jab, he struck him, slamming him with his shield. The man's nose crunched and blood gushed freely. Collins screamed.

He turned to another, a bulky fellow with a wretched stink wafting from him. He swung his sword but the man jumped aside and William fell through. He wheeled around again, blocking their blows with the Lion of Bain. He kicked his leg out and sent him reeling.

"Go, Lady!" he hollered. "Go!" She was petrified, frozen like a rooted tree as the men from Dwyre pounced upon him. "Go now!"

She found her wits and jumped up, running for the trees, watching William over her shoulder. Falling through the branches, she shoved her way through the brambles that snagged her gown. She couldn't see, but she could hear the clanks and exclamations. Titan was whinnying, rearing, and she hit something with a thud.

The wind was knocked from her and she tumbled over. Clashing filled her ears and her head spun with grunts of men battling. The hand of what she had hit reached out to her.

"Lady Gwenyth?"

She was so surprised she forgot to be frightened.

"My, My Lord Aindreas?" she whispered, coughing for air. "Is it you?"

A cry rose behind her and the unmistakable sound of slicing flesh met her ears. She held her breath as Titan whinnied again and again.

"Hurry and I'll free you from this man!"

He dragged her onward. More metal clanked together followed by the striking of a shield. William cursed and heaved the man from him. She exhaled.

"Wait!" she exclaimed.

"No waiting! I would rather know I nabbed you instead of this stranger!"

Aindreas pulled her farther but she wrangled her wrist free. He grabbed her again.

"I cannot leave him, Aindreas! He takes me home to my father!" She tugged her arm loose and turned back but he seized her yet again. "Call your men off, My Lord! This knight helps me!"

Aindreas hated what he was going to do.

"I have orders, Lady. I don't always like them, you know this, but when I have orders," he shook his head. "I must comply, despite what my heart wishes. I wanted you to be gone but Maccus found your trail and I admit, I feared for you when I saw you traveled with a man...and saw William's stillborn son." She felt her throat tighten. "Lord Shea knows of your child and bids you return, and I'll do everything in my power to assure you some comforts."

Gwenyth froze. The wood of the cart crunched and splintered. Collins screamed again as he came hurling through the trees.

"But Aindreas, *dear* Aindreas, you wouldn't deliver me back to him, to the devil himself. You wouldn't...I won't go, I beg you free me..."

He looked pained. "I cannot. The men have seen you."

"Aindreas, please," she choked, dropping down to the ground.

"Dear Gwenyth," he whispered and scooped her back up to her feet.

He hated seeing such fear. Had William Feargach been honorable, she wouldn't have been afraid.

"I'll scream," she threatened.

"Then I shall cover your mouth. I have *no other choice*. Maccus, Collins, and Keegan, they have all seen you."

"Hyaaa!" she heard Sir William exclaim.

Titan's hooves thundered away after another horse. The fighting stopped and all was still. She struggled to free herself.

"I'm begging with my whole soul. I'm frightened of him," she whimpered and dropped down again.

Tall Aindreas with his summer flowers. He must stay in Shea's good graces, he doesn't do this to harm you, he tried to free you, she tried to reason, but her fear consumed her again. Shea was just as ugly in his rage as her husband had been, and he didn't need a woman to be his wife to see that she was soundly whipped.

Aindreas wrapped an arm around her middle and pulled her up. She began to scream. Terrified screams filled the quiet trees, startling roosting birds that flapped away. He hauled her up. She kicked, she thrashed like Titan but it was no use. Aindreas held her, cradling her and clamping her legs together so she couldn't bruise him further.

"William!" she screamed again and his hand covered her mouth.

She sank her teeth into it. He winced but held her fast. They arrived through the trees to where his horse was tied. They were far from the camp now and couldn't see the firelight anymore. He set her down and began to untie his mount when she bolted.

"William! William!"

Aindreas snatched her up, this time with exasperation and yanked her forward, bracing her against the tree. She could feel his breath as he used his legs to pin her back while he fumbled with the reins.

"You go back to Shea! I don't wish to fight with you, Gwenyth!" he snapped.

"Then let her go," came a voice from behind.

Aindreas whirled around to find himself staring down the bloody tip of a sword. He froze. Sir William's eyes had practically disappeared they were so narrowed.

"I have caught a wolf," William growled. "A Dwyre wolf. It shall be a pleasure to run you through if you don't release her."

"She is the property of Lord William Feargach of Dwyre,"

Aindreas said evenly.

"And I happen to know he's dead," Sir William replied. "With no children to speak of, she may now return to her father's house, unharmed and unmolested."

"Unmolested? By a Bainick knight?" Aindreas had stared down metal before and made no sign of faltering. "Do you really trust this stranger, Gwenyth?"

His fingers began to move toward his hilt but William swung his sword and sliced the belt through so that it fell to the ground.

Gwenyth looked at Sir William, then at Aindreas, then back at the knight again. "I trust him."

William flashed Aindreas a smug smile. "My Lady," he continued, his lips barely parted. "Please retrieve that sword." Aindreas didn't let her go. "You're unarmed, sir. I suggest you release her unless more blood needs be spilt to prove my point." She pulled her wrist loose and scrambled for the sword. "He wears a dagger in his boot, Gwenyth. Pull it free."

William held his sword steady, the point now touching Aindreas' throat. Aindreas shifted.

"One more move, sir, and I'll split you open like a Christmas boar."

Aindreas stood still and Gwenyth pulled free his dagger. She moved behind William.

"How could you, Aindreas?" she whispered as her eyes watered again. "How could you?"

Crunching noises sounded behind her and she whirled around, expecting Shea in the flesh. But Sir William made no sign of moving, his eyes drilling Aindreas to his spot.

Titan moved from the trees and stuck his nose into her hair. She exhaled and closed her eyes. *Only William knows the sound of his horse.* He was sweating from hard riding but otherwise was calm. Arching his neck over her, he snorted his long mane off his face.

"You ride back to your Lord Feargach and tell him that Bainick daughters are not his for bargaining with unless he ends his rebellion and begs Our Lord King's forgiveness. You tell him, that so long as Sir William Cadogan of Bain rides with the Lady Gwenyth, she is in his charge by order of the king, and he shall kill every man who wishes her harm. Your men are dead, man. Make a wise choice. Leave."

"William Cadogan...and why, pray tell, is the famed First Knight on amateurs' errands such as rescuing damsels?"

Aindreas was a good fighter but he was no fool and his weapon was his wit.

"I assure you there are reasons our king does not share with others. I'm not too proud to trust his judgment."

"How noble, no. How *humble* of you, man. Perhaps he's growing senile."

"You forget he is ruler and your lord is not."

"Ah, touché. But things can change," Aindreas replied. *I have lost this one,* he thought. *I cannot win here tonight.*

King Bain's knights were never known for being soft on their enemy and could fight a gentle man's war or a scrapper's battle. It was their very ruthlessness that had broken Shea's uncle, the ruler of the eastern lands into concession and swearing fealty and Shea, a young boy at the time who had witnessed his uncle's execution, had never forgiven them.

Aindreas untethered his horse and mounted, turning to put distance between him and the blade.

"I'll ride back to my lord, William Cadogan, you can be sure. But I shall tell him that his son's wife disgraces him by traveling with a man impersonating her husband, and I shall tell him she bore him a grandson." Aindreas narrowed his eyes. "And you may tell *Your* Lord King that his Eastern Front has been sacked." He relished the flicker of unknowing in the knight's eyes. "Shea Feargach of Dwyre, the rightful ruler of the eastern empire will stop at nothing to push Bain back beyond these mountains to where he belongs. Dwyre is no longer under Bainick rule and you are trespassing." He looked at Gwenyth. "With stolen goods, sir."

With no expression, he rode into the night. Sir William held his ground for good measure but Aindreas' horse grew faint until it was gone. Gwenyth shivered and he turned. He dropped his implements and she flung her arms around him as he pulled her into a warm embrace.

"You're all right," he exhaled. "Have you been harmed?"

Propriety took hold of them both and they stepped apart with embarrassment.

"No, my nerves are shaken but that's all," she muttered. "You found me."

"Aye, Lady, I feared for you. You will ride. We go back to camp." He looked over his shoulder again. "We'll be all right for tonight."

He placed his hands hesitantly about her waist, which he had not touched since her childbirth, *such a small, small waist,* he thought, *as though no child was there,* and lifted her onto Titan's back. She braced herself on his shoulders and felt warm liquid.

"You bleed, sir," she said, looking at her fingers.

"'Tis but a scratch. Will you tend to it for me?"

He looked up, willing his stubborn hands to let go of her.

"Of course, My Lord. It's the very least I can do."

With the fire rekindled, Gwenyth relaxed. *He feared for me…*

William hauled Collins' body into the trees and rolled him down the hillside. Keegan was disposed of in much the same way.

"Where's Maccus?" she whispered as she gathered a skin to fetch water from the spring.

"The fat one?" William asked.

Gwenyth tried not to smile. Dwyre man or not, it was wrong to poke fun at the dead.

"He rode that way and I made chase. Killed him at a gorge and trampled his horse."

The words of a warrior, Gwenyth pondered. *He speaks them freely and yet when he looks my way…* He was looking at her that moment. *Don't be fooled, Gwenyth. That's the way of a warrior too, and the way of all men.*

She rose to fetch the water.

"Would you like an escort, Lady?"

The trees were dark and she hesitated, then shivered. "I am childish, sir. I shall be fine."

She mustered courage and marched into the woods, but only made it a few paces before she slowed. It was silent and the creaking branches sent tremors down her spine.

What if Aindreas has come back? Would he dare? She began

backing up when she heard rustling behind her and whirled around.

"Oh! My Lord, you frightened me."

"My apologies," William smiled, holding his hand to her. "But seeing as you're nervous, I would like very much to escort you."

"I am not frightened," she retorted.

"Of course not," he inclined his head. "I only offer peace of mind."

"You should rest, for you're injured, sir."

"I'm not crippled, but if you prefer to go alone, I won't argue."

He seemed disappointed, but smiled anyway and walked back toward the fire. Once more she looked at the darkness and changed her mind.

"Sir William, wait!" she blurted out and ran to grab his arm. "Perhaps I am a bit nervous."

He grinned and offered his hand once more.

With fresh water, she gathered the only clean rags they had, placing William on the ground while she knelt in front of him. His surcoat was ripped where it met his jerkin and a deep gash was gelling with blood.

"You'll need your clothing mended once more," she sighed.

"No, it's not worth the effort, Lady. I shall be thankful to get outfitted in a proper hauberk once more when I return to court," he muttered. "These jerkins are quite old-fashioned."

He smiled and she noticed a faded scar beneath his eye. *He's lucky he didn't lose it in battle,* she pondered.

She smiled and he noticed a healed welt under her chin. *It should be a sin for any man to damage such a beautiful face.*

"I shall try to keep from causing you pain, sir," she said as her finger reached out against her will and brushed his scar.

She wrenched her hand away and looked down, turning red. His smile fell and he took her hand in his.

"I've had far worse, Lady Gwenyth, and they were tended by the rough hands of men on the battlefield. If there will be pain, I would much prefer these hands to cause it."

He smiled again and slowly brought her hand to his mouth, placing a kiss upon it.

*That smile...*She turned away.

"Well it won't do with your clothing in the way. I must get to the wound."

She made a face of stern business and soaked the rag in the water. The knight undid the straps on his jerkin and pulled it off. He peeled away his surcoat and tunic to reveal two more wounds, a stab in his side where the jerkin had not protected him and a slice beneath his sword arm. She set to work cleaning each gash, wrapping them in rags she tore with her teeth. Gooseflesh sprang across his skin and he shivered.

Be quick about it before you send him to his death.

"Your cart is broken, Lady. I'm afraid it's beyond help," William winced as she cinched the bandage tight.

They stared at the heap of fragmented wood.

"No doubt Titan will be pleased," Gwenyth made a shy smile.

"Oh? My Lady jests now?" William laughed. "Aye, well my proud steed was never much for a work horse. He thinks himself royal because his mother was the daughter of a sultan's stallion. But he should like to forget his sire who was a great horse only fit for the dray."

Titan snorted.

"An odd mix." Gwenyth reached around him and retrieved his tunic, surcoat and trampled cloak. "Normally a great horse is a soldier's preference."

"His father was no warhorse, for certain. He was too brown for his breed and relegated to the farm, but Titan here got the black and the height."

"And his mother's Arab speed," she added.

"I got quite a bargain on him."

She helped him back into his tunic, her fingertips dragging gently down his skin. It sent a shiver down him. *Don't stop*, he thought, though she did.

"My father gave him to me when I left to become a Bainick page." *The one good thing he ever did.* "He wanted to castrate him. Called him an unruly giant of a colt who'd never take to training otherwise, but never a better horse I've owned."

"Surely they were much in love if Titan's mother lowered her standards for a work horse." She let amusement find its way to her mouth.

"It's a strange story, his parents' love affair," William explained as a strand of her hair tickled his face. "His mother birthed a colt before him that died. That's when his father took pity," he laughed. "Took pity enough to sire one himself."

"Ach!" Gwenyth balked at the vulgarity. "I've a mind to make that fresh wound sting again with words like those."

"I'm sorry, Gwenyth," William said with false shame. "I forget my company. I suppose we shall now have to share my mount, for a gentle man would not force his wife to walk."

She stared at him with that terrified look he was growing to relish.

"You *were* making fun and fun only when you suggested we be man and wife, were you not?"

He stood and paced to the ravaged cart, picking up a plank and sticking it into the fire.

"No, My Lady, I'm actually quite serious."

Maccus crawled all night and half the day before reaching a spring that trickled out of the rocks. His horse lay broken and dead below, and Aindreas had not come to find him.

The arrogant man, believes he's better than us because he was educated in Latin, he grumbled to himself, *probably thankful to be rid of us.*

He drank his fill as the sun leaked through the peaks and sucked in hard at the belly wound. Normally these killed a man, but after hearing Gwenyth screaming, the knight had not taken the time to fully scramble his innards before dashing away.

The upstart has made the mistake of a young warrior. He has not made certain his enemy is dead.

With fresh water in his stomach, he hauled himself up against a rock with a grunt. His beard was caked with mud and his legs were torn from the nettles he had slid through on his way down the gorge, but he was finally out of it. Survival was one thing he could manage well and at this point, it was best not to attempt dressing his wounds. The clots were keeping out infection and his flesh showed no signs of festering.

My woman'll tend it when I get back.

Staggering upward, he found his way to the road and noticed Collins' horse grazing amongst the trees. His reins were tangled in the brambles. He made his way to the beast and searched the packs, finding a crust of bread that he ate, followed by the dregs of his wine. His stomach hurt so badly it almost didn't hurt. He led the animal to a log onto which he climbed to hoist himself into the saddle, and nudged it toward Dwyre.

7

"Curse this miserable cold," Shea Feargach fumed, staring at the grey sky looming over the battlements. "Just what I need on this march."

"The men are ready and assembled, My Lord," a knight informed.

"Five hundred? All of them?"

"Aye, sir. More rain comin' in. Shall we move out?"

"In a moment. Check to make sure the ale is loaded."

The man bowed and strode away and Shea adjusted his chain mail. The horses puffed steam into the frigid air, their riders matted down beneath their coifs and heavy mail, damp like wet dogs and looking just as downtrodden. He waved his finger and his sentries at the timber brattices, wearing the brown and yellow wolf of Dwyre, heaved open the gate.

Soon, Uncle, all men in the east will swear fealty to your crest once more, and I will sit upon your throne, he thought.

A flock of ravens flew above and cawed.

"No good," he muttered, turning back to his list of supplies.

Aindreas strode across the bailey frowning. Barely an hour's rest and he was being summoned.

Shea looked up. "What news of her? And be fast—"

"Rider approaching!" a guard shouted. "It's Morgan!"

The portcullis was cranked and the men on the ground stood aside.

"Lord Shea!" the rider hollered as his horse galloped in,

spraying mud as he came to a halt.

A stable boy ran to take the reins as the messenger swung down.

"I prayed to make it here before you rode out!"

"Well, speak!" Shea demanded.

"Bain's men," he panted. "We had pushed back the eastern border as far south as the River Ruadhán and thought they had all but flown the coop. But they crept back in through the river using reeds to breathe and took our men by surprise! They've secured the port and aim to reclaim the fort at Faulk!"

Shea ripped off a gauntlet and threw it in the mud as though he meant to drive in a stake.

"Who's mistake was this!" he thundered.

"I do not know, My Lord. No one thought a soul could go in those waters and live. Many of our men believe it to be cursed. Sir Iain requests more men, if possible, sir—"

"Oh, he'll get more men to be sure...Aindreas!" *Clever, very clever. Bain's men would have been soaked to the core and unable to lift a log let alone draw their sword. Someone is helping them. I've a traitor in my midst. A true Christian indeed, with no fear of outland pagan superstitions...*

"I'm still right here, My Lord," Aindreas answered.

"Come inside," he growled.

He threw down his other glove at the board and yelled at the women who tended the hearth to disappear.

"Bring me wine!"

Lady Janis was the one to give it to him.

"Does Lord Aindreas wish for wine as well?" She flashed him a look that Shea did not see.

"Away, woman!" Shea barked, glancing at her bosom as she ducked into the shadows.

He had not had time to take her and now it would be weeks without women folk around. He'd be as crazed as a rutting stag upon his return.

"You've slept?" he turned back to Aindreas.

"Not long, but yes."

"What news, man, be quick. My troops are ready to ride."

Aindreas looked around for hazards that might get thrown and decided he was safe.

"A knight from Bain, Sir William Cadogan, has slain Maccus and the others."

"Christ's bones!" The chair was kicked in. "What in the hell is a Bainick knight doing in these parts without my knowing?"

"Working in secret, by royal order."

"For what? To know my moves?"

"To retrieve the Lady Gwenyth of Ballymead."

The firestorm continued as Aindreas knew it would. The women's spindles were scattered about and his wine was sent into the hearth, making the wood hiss.

"He travels with your Lady Gwenyth, as her protector, charged with the task by the king at the plea of Lord Loddin."

Shea steadied himself.

Gwenyth, he thought. *So Loddin cries to the king over a worthless daughter.* "What news of the girl? Please Aindreas, give me something that won't make my blood boil."

Is it not boiling? For if not, then this will surely make it. "She was in fact with child, but the birth came too early and her son now rests with God and Savior."

Her son. My grandson... "Spare me your Christian teachings, man, she bears sons. That's more than any of my wives can do. She lied to me, and to William. She damn well should have told us!" he erupted, then drifted into contemplation.

Aindreas glanced at Janis who waited with a bowed head, hand on the decanter. *At least he's sufficiently distracted to forget to ask how one knight outfights four.*

"Which way were they heading?"

"Through the Northeast Pass. They will be two weeks away by now, sir, at least, heading for Ballymead."

"What do you know of this William Cadogan?"

"Only what most know from his reputation. He was a late start as a page but earned his spurs a year younger than most, fought in the battles across the channel and delivered the slaves from King

Fernando. He's seen as a hero, the youngest son of an outland liegeman who has worked his way to the highest rank. First Knight. They say his looks favor the king. Rumor has it he's the king's bastard though it's just talk. He's young, well-trained, and brutal. Only five and twenty years and a proud fighter."

"Typical," Shea muttered. "I wonder why the king sent him instead of sending his best knights to our front line..."

"I wondered that myself, My Lord."

I bet the wretch did this on purpose, Shea fumed. *I bet she wanted to lose this babe. I'm sorry, wife, but she will be punished.*

"He does appear to be soft for the Lady Gwenyth, sir," Aindreas added. Janis gave a feeble cough and Aindreas smirked. "I should say he's struggling with his honor."

"How so?"

"He acts as her husband."

"What?" Shea blurted out.

Janis practically choked and slapped her chest to relieve it.

"Hmm...no...no," Shea continued, "This could work in my favor. He'll need to be watched. He might spell trouble for us. I've made a decision. I go to the River Ruadhán to get back what we've lost and free the river passage for trade. I have tired of Sir Iain's follies. He apparently doesn't know his arse from his stones and I believe I have a snitch to smoke out. When you've rested for a spell, a day mayhap two, you will join me there. But I need your cunning, man, so make haste in full assemblage. If I don't open that port, then Bain will starve us out. Gwenyth will give me my heir, you may count on it," he growled, "but she'll have to wait. Once the port is secure, you'll do your part to learn of this Sir William."

Shea had hardened at the thought of Gwenyth and grappled beneath his mail to adjust himself.

"Get ready, woman," he nodded at Janis.

She scurried up the steps and Shea pulled down his hood to rip loose his coif.

"Go and give that frightened messenger my words to take back to Sir Iain. Tell him his conscription is coming, along with the Lord of Dwyre to fix his pathetic mess." He pointed his finger. "He is ordered to post sentries on the river. I don't care *what* witch they think will spring from it. And men shall sleep at arms each night until I arrive with further details. And if he underestimates the black lions again, I'll slit his throat!"

He rubbed himself again, making no effort to be discrete.

"I'll be down in a moment. If I don't unload this burden soon I'm going to explode."

8

"I beg you, sir. I shall be fine to walk for a spell so you may ride," Gwenyth said from atop Titan, but her request was met with another shake of the head and a smile.

Don't look at her, man, you swore you would never do this...Christ you swore it! You should be thinking of battle, you should be questioning her for information...you should be thinking of her...no! Battle, you should be thinking of battle...

The weather continued to be foul as Sir William trudged onward with the reins. What Aindreas had told him did not sit well, and he knew that he ought to be back at court to hear what news of the Eastern Frontier, ready to pick up arms. Many times the idea of returning to court with Gwenyth, where she would be safe and where he could be briefed, had occurred to him. But he couldn't fail her or her family and admittedly he preferred her company to that of his men.

Two weeks out and you're only halfway there, he scolded himself as he looked up at her again. *Just admit it. You're whipped.* Even in the rain with her long hair pasted in a wet plait, she was lovely. The autumn chill had turned her cheeks a crisp shade of pink and as the days had worn on, her spirit had lightened more and more.

"You'll do no good fighting off the men of Dwyre when your legs have buckled from exhaustion," she said and straightened her gown over his shield tethered to the saddle.

He kept walking and smiling, enjoying her concern.

"You're as stubborn as my brother," she shook her head.

"So first I'm unfit to act your husband and now I'm stubborn," he grinned, flashing his eyes upward. *Her eyes are wide again*, he chuckled and she cuffed at his ear while he ducked out of the way.

"Tell me, what of your brother, Lady? He must be a fine boy to earn a namesake."

"Oh, you'll meet him. He's a gentle soul though stubborn as an ass, but no boy, sir. He helped raise me when my mother became ill and we're very close. He's a man of four and twenty, and one of five brothers, sir, of which he is the youngest."

That tripped his stride. *A loving father and five older brothers? Be very careful with this one, William. Not even a Bainick knight could go unscathed from their wrath should you dishonor her.*

"Did you not say once that you were Loddin's only child?"

"No," she giggled. "I'm his only *daughter.*"

"And you have...five brothers? Not one?"

She grinned the grin of pride.

"Loddin, Gavin, Hershel, George and William...and Gwenyth."

"It's no wonder that My Lady knows horses well, being raised as the cherished daughter of a male household. What are they like?"

"Well, Loddin is the first son. He's a proud knight and serves in the Western Frontier in the Highland Order of Chivalry. He's married to my dear new sister, Mary. Gavin is hopelessly a bachelor. He has loved many to Father's utter shame." She shook her head and rolled her eyes.

"I've served with many men of that description," William chuckled.

"It will be soon that he must take a bride, *finally,*" she continued. "He had his sights on the Lady Sarah from Dunstonwoodshire before I left, and Father was requesting betrothal talks for when she came of age. Hershel is stern and a scholar at heart, but he was also trained as a knight. He spends weeks sometimes at the monastery, reading ancient verses that have been transcribed. He should like to enter the cloth now that his wife died leaving us with a nephew, but Father won't hear of it," she smiled. "*Service to God is noble*, Father once told him. *But service to a wife will give me grandchildren.*"

William laughed.

"George is knighted too but stays to help run Ballymead with Father. Normally Father pays shield money for George, though he sent him to battle once before. He's also in need of a bride, but hasn't found anyone of interest yet. Both Loddin and Gavin have squires and no doubt my sweet nephew, little Hershel, will become one when he no longer needs to have his breeches changed," she giggled, looking off over the hills, her brown eyes free of fear.

"What about William?" he asked.

"Oh, William...He's a hopeless dreamer, like me. I cannot express how excited I am to see him again..."

She began to reminisce and William gazed freely at her, noticing the soft contours of her face and the pinkness of her lips. *How I should love to touch those lips,* he began, though looked away.

"Father teases him, saying there's always one leech on a family, for William would soon rather roam the hillsides and contemplate life instead of work. But he was knighted like the others and earned his spurs. He, I know would love to take a wife for he would make a gentle husband and no doubt would spoil his children rotten.

"Does he fancy a woman of interest?"

"I don't know anymore, but he used to fancy the Lady Amber of Dunstonwoodshire and used to tease her *horribly,* though no one knew it. He was too embarrassed to say."

"Why is that?"

"Well she's too young for starters, or was, anyway...and she's blind."

"I see," William nodded. "It wouldn't be a favorable match."

"No, My Lord, it wouldn't, despite how sweet she is and I cannot help but think how unfair life has been to her, for she is very pretty. I only know because William and I were always close and it was his secret I vowed to keep."

"You keep your brother's secrets?"

"Aye, of course. As he has done for me when one of Father's squires stole a kiss from me and he walked in on it."

"He didn't tell your father? I would have my squires' hides pinned to my wall if they were caught at such play."

"Of course not," Gwenyth replied. "He laughed, for we looked quite clumsy, then threw a bucket of water on him anyway." William laughed. "Though I think Father knew. It was harmless, really, and that same squire has stayed on as a loyal guard because my father was so good to him. He's a good friend of my childhood and quite happily married now too, to his Marta. Ah, my sweet brother William...It's he who rode horses with me and loved it as much as I."

She sighed and looked into the distance.

"Father and William used to take me out in the fields to ride. Father gave me a pony when I turned six and I rode that beloved animal until my feet dragged the ground at her sides. It was then that they realized I was not just in a phase. The stable boys used to let me help them. They'd tussle my hair and tease me, calling me a lad. Father's squires always took time to play when work was done. They were like my brothers too."

"Go on, woman. I'm entertained. You loved riding?"

"I *adore* riding. I hated weaving or tending the beehives with the ladies and always ended up welted from it for angering them."

"Welted from the bees or from the women?" he smiled.

The rain had subsided and the evening sun shined upon the clouds in purples and pinks.

"Oh, only the bees. I was spoiled, for Mother never raised a violent hand and Father would have sooner died before he took his strap to me..." she dropped her head as concern wrinkled her face.

William looked away.

'You'll know your place, William, by Christ you will!'

They were standing in a line at the board, quaking in their sandals.

'Rats! Setting vermin loose amongst the stables! Those cows won't be milked for days now because of your jests!'

His father swung his belt and caught young William beneath his eye. He and his brothers scattered as he swung it again and again, grabbing them one by one and welting them hard across the backs. He felt his father's hand clasp hold of his tunic and yank him back. Now he was crying, hiccupping and wailing as his father bore down upon his back. His mother beckoned him to come for comfort and his sister, Louisa, was screaming his name.

'You're going to kill'im, Da!' his brother Andrew shouted and jumped against him. 'You'll kill'im, you bastard!'

'I'm not the bastard in this house!' his father bellowed and shoved him away. 'You, William!' The strap burned. He gave up and curled at his father's feet. 'You and your brothers! The lot of you! Get out of my sight before I make you know real pain, William! You disgrace this house!'

57

His mother grabbed him from beneath the slicing belt and dragged him free. She gathered Andrew and Faegan, and his three young sisters. Together they ducked out of the room for cover.

'Bring me my wine, woman! Or so help me, I shall bloody you as well!'

He had gone to bed cold and hungry that night.

'I hate him,' Andrew whispered at the window while the others slept on the pallet. 'I hate him for beating little William and so help me, God, for I'll kill'im someday if you don't grant me the strength to resist...'

Louisa curled against William.

'It will be okay someday,' she whispered and dabbed the blood beneath his eye.

The skin had swollen so much that he couldn't see. William tried to shrug her away and curled into a tiny ball.

'He'll never change,' he whispered back.

'There's someone out there who'll love you, I know it in my—'

'You're daft! You and your stupid stories,' he snapped and blinked his tears. 'It doesn't exist, Louisa. Not for me...I don't need him or anyone else...I hate him...'

"Sir William?" Gwenyth watched him lost in thought. "My Lord? Have I done something?"

He looked up. "'Tis nothing," he smiled. "You are well indeed because your father had a gentle hand."

"And yours did not?" she whispered.

"No, Gwenyth, but I am stronger for it."

Just then the hamlet came into view, framed by the peaks around it. A small village, it consisted of a commons house and mud-daubed huts with quaint crofts and cows at pasture. Most of them were not any nicer than the one that she had abandoned. But there were happy children's voices and a roasted pig on a spit. Soon there was cheering. A party of people came dancing out of the commons house in a line. A young woman and man stood awkwardly amongst them, hands clasped and beaming at one another.

"It's a wedding!" Gwenyth smiled. "Look at them! She is fair in her flowers and he is prouder than a palfrey sire!"

"That he is," William grinned. "As I shall be," and before she had a chance to look, William had swung himself up behind her. "Are you ready now to act *my* wife, Lady Gwenyth?"

Her heart faltered and she grew bright red, reaching out to hold onto Titan who shifted and stomped.

"My Lord," she croaked, feeling his hand slide around her waist.

"It would be odd indeed for a knight to not ride with his wife, wouldn't you agree?"

She didn't turn to look but knew he was smiling.

"You'll remember that in truth you're not really my husband?" her voice wavered. "You aren't entitled any rights, sir."

Despite his closeness to her, he sat tall and held her gently.

"You have nothing to fear from me, My Lady. I do this for your honor, not my pleasure." His words were warm on her neck as he nudged Titan onward. "I may be named William, Gwenyth, but I'm not like the William you leave behind."

She was pressed to him as they rocked with Titan's lumbering and he kept his hand on her stomach, finding that he did actually find pleasure in it, as he knew he would. Reluctantly, Gwenyth allowed herself to rest upon his chest and without thinking, he sat his chin atop her head.

"Do you think we look convincing?" he jested, but she was breathing heavily. *Is it from nerves or because I'm so close?* he pondered, and suddenly it was out of his control. He became aroused and sitting between his legs, she could feel it.

"Oh please, My Lord!" she gasped and slid from the horse. "I beg you not shame me, I beg you please!"

She backed up to a tree and fell into weeping, dropping down with her head in her hands.

He looked up to heaven.

Curse you, William Cadogan! The words spun in his head. *Curse you a thousand bloody deaths!*

He dismounted and Titan tossed his head, clearly frustrated with their indecision.

"My Lady," he spoke and knelt before her. "I couldn't help it, but I would never act on it I swear it by the name of King Bain and all that's great in this world..." *Curse you again, William Cadogan!*

She looked up at him, her eyes filled with water. Titan stuck his nose in his hair and whickered.

"Away, man!" he chided, thrusting his hand up.

"Don't strike!" she flinched, shielding her face. "I beg you not harm me! I'm sorry! I'm sorry! I'll ride with you if it be your wish just please don't strike me...I will ride with you..."

She fell into a mumble of supplications. His hand lowered and his throat tightened.

"God in heaven, what has that bastard done to you?"

William reached out and took her hands. He was trembling, so angry at William Feargach he would trample his grave if he knew his resting place and knew at that moment he was falling for her. There wasn't a damn thing King Bain would be able to do about it when he returned to court and refused the next bride the king offered him. He lowered her arms and saw her eyes pinched tightly shut.

"Gwenyth, look at me." His words were scratchy and he wiped a tear with his thumb. "Please look upon me...I beg you, woman...as a man who's made a terrible folly."

She unclenched her face.

"Trust that I will never strike you. Never." He dropped his head. "I could never do it, beautiful Gwenyth. It's I who should be sorry. I shame my honor. I shame myself." The sun was setting and he rose, holding his hand for her. Gwenyth took it and stood. He was so ashamed he could hardly look at her. "You'll ride the horse and I will walk. It's best that way."

He walked her to the horse and hesitated again. Taking her waist, he placed her in the saddle quickly and grabbed Titan's reins to move on. They walked for some minutes and Gwenyth stared at his back. Not once did he turn around to look.

He cannot be faulted for his impulses, she pondered. *Only if he acts on them may he be faulted, and he has not. He has done nothing but act in your interest.*

"My Lord, wait," Gwenyth said. He stopped but he did not turn to look. "I, I trust you." She looked at twilight settling on the village. "It grows late and we're both weary. Please ride with me and save your strength." He didn't move. "It is my wish."

He swung into the saddle without a word. Titan moved on and she leaned on him again, suddenly wanting to feel his warmth. William put his arm around her tightly now as if he needed to hold her and rested his cheek against her hair. This time, she squeezed his arm. He grew hard again that instant and closed his eyes, willing it to end as he clenched the fabric of her gown.

"I'm sorry, Gwenyth, I'm sorry," he whispered.

She didn't panic, but pulled his arm tighter still.

"I trust you, William."

9

The village was still celebrating. About forty people in all, some having come from the neighboring village that had been home to the bride. Some of the men stopped as they saw Titan approaching, though with travelers coming and going all day, many didn't notice them and many more were drunk.

"Good Evening!" William called, lifting his hand from Gwenyth. She found it had warmed her stomach and wished him to put it back. "And many well wishes for your new man and wife!"

"Thank you, stranger!" an older man called back. He and his men came forth to stare at the couple. "What be your business here?"

Gwenyth moved her gown so that the crest upon the shield was visible.

"A knight of King Bain, sir?" he questioned.

"Traveling with my wife who is but a moment from collapse. May we pay the bride and groom in gold coin and rest in your stable for the night?"

"Of course, sir! Of course! Come eat, we have plenty! And you'll not be sleepin' in a stable, mind!"

All too pleased to host such ranking company, he beckoned for a boy to take the horse. The boy stopped short of the massive shadow and shook his head. William laughed and dismounted, lifting Gwenyth to the ground. He bent low and rubbed his hair.

"And who might you be, lad?"

"I'm, I'm Robert, sir, I'm eight, sir," he stammered.

"Only eight years? You look strong, I would have guessed ten." The boy grinned. "Well Robert." He pulled a coin from his purse and knelt down, clasping the boy's shoulder. "I will give you this here coin if you take my wild weasel into a sty and water him."

His little eyes lit up, but then Titan snorted and he shied back. William leaned in to tell a secret.

"I know he looks like a devil, but he's softer than a gentle maid on a spring day."

Gwenyth giggled and so did the boy.

"He seems a giant's horse but he's harmless," she added, taking the boy's hand and pulling Titan's bridle down so he could pet his nose. "And if you give him these berries, he'll consider you his bosom friend."

The boy took the berries, took the reins and then took the coin.

"A gold coin...Father! Look! A real gold coin!" he waved it proudly as he took Titan to the stall.

The celebration was merry, full of laughter and music. William acted the perfect husband, guiding Gwenyth, holding her hand and the small of her back. Food was fed them, pig and mutton, wild mushrooms, parsnips, roots and berries mixed with herbs and fresh breads that were soft and warm. Wine was put in Gwenyth's hand and all insisted William enjoy a tankard of ale that no doubt had been hard for them to come by.

Amidst the noise and dancing, a gaggle of young girls raced past them, squealing, followed by a boy who gave chase and snatched at their braids and aprons. The girls circled William and Gwenyth, giggling and dragging each other by the hands as the boy made threats.

"Stop, treacherous dog!" demanded a boy in a homespun tunic, wielding a stick for a sword and leading a clan of boys with war cries on their lips. "Sir William the Brave comes with the army of Bain!"

The men amongst them fell to laughter and swatted them as they went.

"The famed Sir William Cadogan? Run for yer life, lad!" an old man shouted. "He'll wallop ye fer sure!"

Gwenyth burst into giggles and William laughed outright as the boys ran circles around them. Much to the delight of the girls, the army staged a battle in which more than one stick was broken and the enemy was thrown upon the ground.

"Aha! You lose again and I'm the victor!"

"No fair! I don't want to be the bad'un again! It's my turn to be the champion! Da! Noah won't give me a turn!"

"It's because you keep losing!" the young William Cadogan replied, removing his bare foot from his chest. "Sir William the Brave never fails...does he, My Lord?" he turned to Sir William. "Do you know Sir William the Brave?"

"Aye, I do," William replied. "We're best of friends."

"Does he ever fail?"

"Never," William grinned.

Gwenyth giggled.

"Is it true," started the losing boy as he brushed the grass from his knees, "that he can battle three knights at a time and lay waste to them in no more than three blows?"

"Not at all!" William exclaimed and the children's' faces dropped. He motioned for them to gather round and the youngsters closed in with open ears. "With my *very—own—eyes*, I've seen him battle no less than ten at one time and knock them all from their steeds in a single swing!"

"Wow!" their faces brightened.

Gwenyth rolled her eyes. "But Sir William the Brave is a humble warrior, lads, and *never* would boast to be sure," she added.

William glanced at her and cracked a smile but before he could reply, he was dragged away to talk horses and she found herself carried off amongst a cluster of curious women.

"He's quite a handsome catch, My Lady," the women giggled, one not much older than herself. "Did you know'im before you married?"

"Oh, em, no I didn't," she blushed, and looked William's way, noticing that he was gazing back at her.

"Well, you got lucky!" they teased. "Unlike Winifred here, she got stuck with *that* one." They pointed to a man who was twice the woman's age and had a gut the size of a hay bale. "His first wife died two winters ago. It's a shame he married again...he farts somthin' awful!" they laughed.

Winifred lopped her friend on the arm and they all giggled.

"Mind your tongue! She's a lady, not a milk maid!"

"Oh, I do not mind," Gwenyth said.

"But you're fair as well. Does it take three or four maids to braid your long hair?"

"Or does it take three or four hours?"

Gwenyth did her best to ignore the sarcasm, noticing their short hair wrapped within their wimples.

"I must say I tried my mother's patience, for even today I refuse to have it coiffed."

They eyed her carefully.

"I bet he enjoyed his weddin' day when he saw his bride," they giggled some more. "Bet you didn't even need a dowry to catch'im or any other man."

Gwenyth smiled with embarrassment and looked his way again, brushing her hair back behind her ear. William was still staring at her when he was interrupted by an old man, but kept letting his eyes creep back to her.

"He's certainly got his eye on you, My Lady, as if you was still brand new to'im."

"I haven't been well as of late. I'm sure he's just concerned."

"Oh no, that's the look of a man who's smitten, that is," they all agreed as they looked back at him, then her, then him again.

She locked her gaze with his once more and he grinned a silly, boyish grin. She giggled at it and he laughed.

"Oh!" Winifred exclaimed, placing her hand over her heart. "That smile could cast the stars out of heaven, it could!"

"You must think we're awful," one of them sighed. "No doubt My Lady has finer conversations and grander parties with fresh trout and deer rather than pig and mutton."

"I'm having a nice time, I really am," Gwenyth replied. "I love dancing and music, no matter what type."

"Do ye now?"

Winifred and the others grabbed her hands and dragged her off her stool, throwing her into the fray of spinning and clapping. She allowed herself to dance despite how fatigued she was and soon could not help laughing. She hadn't danced like this in ages, nor had people welcomed her so openly since Ballymead. Not even the miserable women at Dwyre had been very kind, save the dear Lady Janis who had been her closest confident.

A smile radiated from her as she linked arms with the others, delighting in the same dancing that consumed Ballymead during Yule when her father would have to beat the young men from her while she twirled. She flashed her eyes at William and the look on his face showed he was more than pleased to watch.

"You're a lucky man, Sir Knight of Bain," the old man said. "A lovelier site a husband could not ask for."

"And I thank God for it," William returned with a smile.

"Do ye' have children yet?"

William almost choked. "Em, well, the first didn't live."

"I'm sorry, sir...was it a boy?"

William nodded, *in a strange way, my namesake,* he wanted to believe, and took a long swig of ale in hopes he could avoid further questions. The man took his silence to mean something else.

"You don't blame her, do you?"

"I could never blame her." William gazed at the stars, then back at Gwenyth. *It was God's will that all traces of William Feargach have been taken from earth, and I'll thank him every day for spotting that demon amongst his flock.*

"Good man. Men are quick to blame the woman. It's easier than acceptin' God's will."

"I'll agree with that. My, em, my *wife* has suffered from it, very much. It's good she gets to smile here tonight."

"Oh and you, *well*," the man's face lit up and he laughed a toothless laugh. "You're a strapping lad all right who knows his duty to be sure, and she's young. There is time."

The man slapped him and William coughed.

"I always say, you treat a woman with kindness and you'll end up a happy man. Like me," he grinned. "Me Mary bore me eight daughters and I thought I might go madder than a cricket in a flock of hens. Still, ne'er a prettier lass did I ever see."

William followed the man's gaze. It rested on a little woman rocking her grandson in her arms while she clapped with him to the flute. She looked up and smiled as her husband waved, her wrinkled face dimpling.

"Nary a pouch of gold I've owned and yet I still say me Mary and I are as rich as kings."

Gwenyth's tresses, spinning past her thighs, waved like the hair of the faery folk and William was thankful for his shield propped in front of him, pulling it closer, for as he watched her, he again became aroused. He feasted his eyes and made no effort to quit. Any man would be proud to know she was his, second marriage or not.

I would be proud, he began to think before reminding himself it was all pretense. *She isn't yours and you would do well to remember that. But perhaps she could be...*

A cluster of women seized William's arm and wrenched him to the circle.

"No...no, I don't know these dances!" he complained, but they giggled and pushed him in.

He fell next to Gwenyth who grabbed his hand and beamed at him. He began to stumble in a circle and gripped her, half terrified, while the faces around him laughed and the hands clapped.

"I know not what to do!"

"Simple, My Lord!" she called over the drums. "Just one foot behind, then in front!"

Clumsily at first, he managed to trip the girl on his other side and Gwenyth laughed.

"You mock me!"

"No, sir!" she smiled. "But My Lord has never danced?"

"A Bainick knight doesn't dance with idle time! We're city folk!"

"Then we country folk have wonderful lives! You've missed much, My Lord!"

Eventually he got the hang of it and grabbed Gwenyth around the waist to spin her. She laughed and he grinned, staring at her pink lips and the light from the fire sparkling in her eyes. As the dancing died down, William managed to escape and hauled Gwenyth with him, laughing. She fell with flushed cheeks against him and giggled, embracing him around the chest. He stood stunned by her show of affection, then rested a gentle arm around her shoulder. She quickly stepped away.

"I'm sorry, My Lord."

He shook his head. "It's too bad that we must stop," he whispered, making sure the proper distance was between them. "I don't believe it's possible for a woman to look more lovely than what I see right now."

Her face burned horribly and she looked at her feet.

"I act silly, sir—"

"No, Lady. Such joy on your face is worth seeing," he interrupted as the groom took his bride to their new hut.

Many bawdy boasts and vulgar gestures from the men followed them, and the bride blushed.

"Awe! Go easy on'im lassie!" they shouted.

The mothers of the couple followed her in to make sure the deed was done properly, followed by the nervous groom and a calm consumed the night. Sitting around the remains of the fire, men held their wives, rocked with their grandchildren, and stole kisses. Gwenyth began to sway with fatigue, remaining as alert as she could and William, right next to her, was careful to maintain his distance.

They heard the clumsy new couple in their wedding bed.

"The lad's only seen it done with bulls and cows," came giggles around the fire. "He's probably gotten himself lost in the linens, searchin' for directions!"

"Not to worry, man, his mother brought the cattle prod!"

William and Gwenyth giggled with the others and suddenly all eyes turned to the new novelty.

"Do the champions of Bain always neglect their fine women?" one man called across the fire.

Gwenyth froze while everyone laughed.

"Do you know your own wife, man? Or is she poison you don't want to touch?"

William grew red, though thankfully his beard shielded it.

"Aye, a woman can be pure poison," another man jested and his wife lopped him on his shoulder, making those near them hoot.

"Gettin' whipped by your mother again, I see!" they roared.

The man tossed his cup at them.

"Go on, knight," another coaxed. "Give your lady a kiss!"

"Go on, man!" they teased.

"I don't think the lady would appreciate my making a spectacle," William grinned. "I'll let you imagine it instead."

"You city men act so proper," one waved his hand. "You treat your wives like your sisters."

More laughter followed.

"Perhaps he simply cannot *rise* to the job!" someone baited with flows of laughter, and William reluctantly gave in.

"Why no, sir!" he announced, stepping forward as though addressing the council at court and pulling Gwenyth with him. "We knights are known for being champions of our marriage bed as well as of the court, am I right, wife?"

He turned to her while the group erupted with laughter again, grinning and yet dreading what he was about to do for fear she would always hate him. She was shaking, unable to look up at him.

"Well if you won't kiss her, send her my way!" another called and slapped his knee.

William grinned. "That, man, I cannot allow."

Gwenyth's mind was lightheaded from the wine, exhausted from the journey, and spinning from the moment. William leaned over her, his smile fading. His nose grazed hers softly as if a quill unsure of where to place its mark, his green eyes staring into her brown ones. He smelled her skin, and let his hand reach up to her fair face and her long, long hair.

"Well are you going to or not!" came a happy jeer.

She shivered more, clasping his hand with hers and squeezed, half terrified. He was shaking too.

"Forgive me, Gwenyth," he whispered so softly as he squeezed her hand in return. "Forgive me for wanting this...forgive me for falling in love with you..."

His kiss was inexperienced, tender, despite the growth of hair upon his face and the ale on his lips tasted sweet. She stood frozen at first but soon relented, cupping her hands through his arms and around his shoulders. She allowed her lips to guide him and he was careful not to bear down the way his blood was telling him to but held her face to his. Then his arms wrapped around her back to smooth her tangled hair.

"Now that's the look of true love," a woman sighed and Gwenyth pulled away, leaving his lips in wanting.

"I think I shall pass out from this wine, My Lord, if I don't find a place to lie down."

10

The stable they had hoped to get was refused. It was not proper indeed for a knight and a lady to sleep in a sty, they said. The wife of the old man had prepared a pallet for them beneath the window to share in the commons house with the other guests who were staying through the night. Gwenyth was too tired to be horrified.

William lay down and crossed his legs, stretching himself straight and checking to make sure she had as much room as possible. The last thing he wanted was to roll against her in the middle of the night and send her into tears for trying to molest her. But whispers and giggles rose amongst the others who stared at the strange knight with his young wife, and William extended an arm.

"Lie with me, wife," he grinned. *We must keep up appearances.*

That boyish grin, as if he always has a prank behind his back. She hesitated and glanced at the others, then back at William.

"Should we stay up and watch them?" a few snickered. "To see what the knights do with their wives in Bain?"

Gwenyth burned bright red and took a step back but William sat up.

"You'll be quite dissatisfied," William announced to the room. "For at night, the people of Bain are known for sleeping." He turned to Gwenyth and held his hand out. "It will be fine," he coaxed. "You may trust me."

She climbed in next to him and laid her head on the shoulder he offered, curling up into the protective ball she had learned to sleep in after leaving Ballymead. William pulled up the blanket and curved his arm over her shoulder, and after some more spies and giggles, the room went to sleep.

When the moon was high, the room was full of snores. Gwenyth was so fatigued and yet sleep refused to come. William's arm still hugged her to his chest, his fingers mindlessly rubbing her upper arm. Shifting for the first time, she looked up at his face. His eyes were open, gazing out the window above them. He glanced down at her.

"You don't sleep?" He seemed surprised. "Should I take my arm from you now?"

He started to drag himself free but she shook her head.

"Please leave it," she whispered.

He smiled. "Then go to sleep, Lady, for this could very well be our only...*your* only pallet until Ballymead."

She looked away again and nestled against him. He was warm and despite the blanket, she shivered. When he had told her those words before he kissed her, she had melted and had to remind herself that William Feargach had also whispered sweetnesses. But William Feargach had *never* said he loved her, and his kiss...

Never had William Feargach been so tender, so gentle. She tasted it over and over again and grew flustered to the point that she shifted to shake it. What was more, many a chance he had had to seduce her and yet, the most he had indulged in was a single kiss after stabs at his pride. Even William Feargach on his most honorable behavior had tried for much more. She looked up again.

"That scar."

She ran her fingers along the faded gash beneath his eye.

"I have many," he whispered. "The lot of being a boy."

He grinned his playful grin.

"What battle is that one from?" she asked.

"No battle. It's from childhood," he remarked and took her hand to lay it across his chest. *Please, woman, don't ask of it.*

"What games do boys play at that cause such injuries?"

He sighed. She wasn't going to leave it be. "It was no game, My Lady. It was my father's belt."

She looked away.

"I'm sorry for being so curious, but what act could have deserved such a consequence?"

He sighed again, rolling his head away. "'Twas long ago. I wish not to remember it."

"I'm too bold again, forgive me."

He didn't speak. She curled her chin down so that the full of his armpit met her face. He needed a bath and yet his smell was comforting.

"I was but eight, same as little Robert tonight," he began after some time. "Andrew and Faegan, my brothers," a smile danced across his lips and was gone, "we caught rats in the corn crib and decided to let them loose in the sty to see the cows dance..." Gwenyth giggled and William let a chuckle escape his lips. "Ahh, but my father didn't think it was amusing and had me whipped for it." He sighed. "He saw acts like these as my ideas, for surely his older sons would have known the wiser and I usually felt the better part of his strap. It never occurred to him that when the minds of three brothers converged, catastrophe always ensued."

Gwenyth wanted to wipe away his concern but was afraid to touch him again, so left her hand in his grip and brushed her thumb across his.

"How did you survive it?" she finally whispered, feeling her throat tighten.

"My Lady?"

"How did you endure? Not yet two years at Dwyre, and I thought if I could beg harder, he might relent..."

"I turned myself to stone, Gwenyth. Once I stopped fighting it, he would stop swinging his strap."

William didn't look at her but she could feel his fingers begin to squeeze hers harder.

"And yet you have a way with children," she encouraged. "With those little ones, you had such a gentle hand and with Robert, so patient."

He smiled at that. "He felt important with a knight's horse *and* his gold," he chuckled. "It's those small gifts of trust which make the man."

Gwenyth reached to his eye again and caressed the scar.

"You'll make a fine father someday when you finally choose a bride, Sir William," she smiled.

But would I...

He rolled onto his side and looked straight down at her, touching her cheek again in that way that made her excited.

"If I had a fine wife to help me sire them, I should love my children and they should have the childhood that their mother described."

Her heart popped into her mouth and she tried desperately to gulp it down.

"Is it all right with My Lady if...if I kiss her again?"

She nodded without hesitating and he smiled. This time he kissed her deeply while her hand rose to hold his neck. He didn't hold back, for no one was looking and he could feel that she had accepted him. He caressed her face and allowed his hand to slide up and down her arm. Finally he parted from her and rested his forehead against hers.

"My words were true, Gwenyth. I don't know how it happened, but I've never felt this before in my life. I feel that I love you for I don't know what else it could be." He smiled again and kissed her nose. "I know it's sudden, but would it please you if I ask your father for your hand? When the time is right?"

"Aye, William. It would please me."

Her cheeks were burning and her mouth felt dry. He couldn't help grinning, brushing his hand down her face where it lingered on the scar beneath her chin.

"I'm glad. And with me, Lady, you'll never know rough handling...never." He began to grin that playful grin. "Though you *will* be handled."

Her eyes widened like he had hoped and she pushed him. They wrestled and she squealed to get away when an old woman snorted complaints and threw a sandal over their heads, sending them into fits of giggles like children. He pulled her close and she nestled into the crook of his arm, falling into blissful sleep.

"Maccus lives," a man informed Aindreas as he lay on a pallet with his head propped on his arm. "He's as tough as iron, for that belly wound was placed with a mark to kill by someone with the experience already under his belt."

Aindreas wanted to roll his eyes. *Now Shea will send his hunter out to track.* "That's good news. I shall bring the news to Lord Shea at the front."

He rose and left the barrack. It was filling with a few bodies now and began to stink. He wanted to return to his fee, small as it was, He hadn't been home since the fighting started. His sign had still not come so he walked out beneath the night sky. If Maccus lived, he now had a score to settle and if that foul man had once been willing to slash his fellow over a lost copper on a game of dice, he would go to the end of the earth to sniff out Gwenyth, the prey that got away.

Why am I so cursed as to always play the pawn and never the bishop?

The signal was faint and he almost missed it. Water sloshed in the well three times.

"Get yer clumsy hands on that bucket, woman," a guard muttered.

Placing his hands behind his back, he strolled across the yard until he stood by the footings where he pulled himself loose to take a piss. The cloak by the well filled a bucket again and set it on the ground, accidentally knocking another into the well and walked away with the first.

"Christ," he muttered, loudly enough that the nearest guard heard him.

He shook his hand to wring off the urine. The guard looked down from the wall.

"Splattered my hand, man."

The guard began to laugh.

"Bloody pissed himself," he murmured to the next.

Aindreas walked to the well. He pulled up the bucket and sloshed his hands in, reaching into the bottom in the process. As he did so, he pulled up a coin, dropping it into his pocket as he wiped his hands on his tunic. He dumped out the water and walked away.

The coin had only been silver. *That means behind the stable.*

He waited for some time, tapping into some ale at the empty tavern that was normally crowded with low ranking knights and their squires. The ale tasted spoilt but it was all that remained. Finally, with false swagger, he made his way into the stable where he intended to pass out once this was over.

Horse manure smelled like roses compared to the barracks. The stable boys were asleep in the haylofts and the horses quiet. He moved to the back where a window was sitting open and climbed through.

The back of the stable was lined with trees from what had once been a rich forest. *Look at what is left now?* Aindreas thought. Yet the few that were able to withstand the dreary yard were all that was needed to shield him from the guards.

She was sitting so still, he almost didn't see her until she dropped her hood.

"Pissed yourself?" she smirked. "Careful word does not spread that you have become a lush."

"I'll have to tell him that Maccus lives. But you were there yesterday. He wishes me to learn of William Cadogan and this is one thing I cannot divulge, for obvious reasons. You're wise to keep yourself secret."

"Do as he asks, as he asks it, no more no less. This will give me time."

"If it means feeding her to the wolves, then I cannot. I go along with all of it, even though my blood is telling me it is wrong—"

"All of this is wrong, but we shouldn't rush it. If it means we all suffer more to gain the end, then we should be willing to suffer," she said.

"She doesn't trust me anymore and neither does he," Aindreas whispered as he looked through the trees.

The guards on the walls paced at their posts and the stable behind them was still quiet.

"That man had hatred in his eyes, hatred that only rises from primal instinct to protect the one he loves. 'Tis dangerous when that man has been trained to be a killing device! He meant to spill my innards right then and there and would have, too! I didn't want to nab her from him and yet I tried, to continue to prove my loyalty to Shea. Yet now I gain an enemy I would rather call my comrade. He was the one you asked for, was he not?"

"Aye, he was. It was wonderful to hear those words verified by your lips. Sir William will keep her safe, I know it. This knight knows what it is to come under the belt and he'll understand her, even love her for it. And to know that my messages were heard means that though I'm trapped, I'm not silent." She looked down. "Neither you nor I have a chance at life and love anymore. We're outcasts. You age to your prime yet don't take a wife..."

Except for wives of others, he frowned.

"...and I was already two and twenty when my foster family arranged this marriage. But the least we can do is help Bain keep what ought not be under the rule of a punishing man. My husband must trust us."

"His trust is painful to take," Aindreas huffed.

They sat quietly and he realized the lady cried.

"Don't speak to me of pain, Aindreas, how dare you?" she whispered. "He doesn't bed his head man. He prides you and needs you to help him be the man he's not. He uses your mind, but that is all. He doesn't use your body to dump his seed when he is drunk! And you aren't the one who must pretend you like it!"

"I was thoughtless, Lady," he muttered and brushed her cheek. "I weave a tangled web here."

She dried her tears and took hold of his hand.

"What do you know of his plans?"

"He means to take down the river port once more," Aindreas replied. "And with him there to command, I have no doubt he'll do it. His men are more scared of him than of dying under Bain's blade. He means to use catapults, from the northern side *and* from the southern bank if he can get his men to cross the river so close to Samhain. It's his hope that when fire is set within, they will run out to the east where his men will be waiting to cut them down. With the cliffs blocking escape out the back, there is no other route. If you've a messenger, Lady, that can ride faster than Shea's troops, then I suggest they make haste tonight or else I fear the worst will come."

She nodded and he squeezed her hand.

"We will be hated in life, Aindreas, but at least only God will judge us upon death."

She was really weeping now. He hated seeing her like this.

"What is it, Lady?"

"Will you do one last favor? 'Tis a large one."

A couple guards started laughing and their heads whipped up. But the laughter died away.

"Take my daughter away," she whispered.

"What? No, My Lady!"

"Take her far away. See to it that she goes to the Lady Gwenyth. I shall tell Shea that she took to fever and died, and you will see to it she never sets her beautiful eyes on this dreadful place again—"

"You cannot be serious! If Cadogan is with her, she is no doubt nearly to Ballymead. That's quite a trek and one that Shea would notice my absence, for which I would have no alibi—"

"Please, My Lord," she begged. "Should I be discovered, she would surely die alongside me."

"That's not true! Not even Shea is that heartless—"

"She would know a horrid life here and you know it! I ask this of you now. Shea will be relieved of one less daughter for whom it will seem like a lifted burden, and I shall be at peace knowing she's with Gwenyth. My Louisa will know a fine life there and then perhaps someday, if we both make it to an older age, we can go to her, for I wish her to know you—"

A guard marched by the trees. They held their breath and didn't move. When he was gone, Aindreas thought long and hard and gave her an embrace.

"Go, Lady. I'll need time to arrange it so I can get safe passage. But when a plan is in mind, I'll send a sign and you will know."

"Thank you!" she wept.

Aindreas kissed her cheek and started to rise, but she grabbed his hand.

"Please, My Lord," she breathed. "Just a moment more of your company, for I don't wish to be alone again just yet."

He sat back down and pulled her in for another embrace.

"All will be well, woman. You'll see," he said, kissing her cheek again.

She looked up at him and he slowly kissed her cheek once more, then her lips. He allowed his arm to cup her back. She returned it and reached to his neck. After some moments, his hand wandered across her shoulder and then inched downward until it reached her breast. He fondled her and she pulled open her cloak so that his fingers could wander beneath. Before he knew it, he had pulled her onto his lap.

"May I have you again, My Lady?" he whispered, holding her face in both his hands.

"Here?"

"I don't see another option. I'd like it very much…"

She nodded. "But there isn't much time," she sighed.

"It will be quick, woman, for it's been some sennights since I've bedded a woman and you make me ache for it."

He pulled her face to his again and kissed her neck and cheeks and lips as she hiked up her skirts.

"Did you do this to her as well?" she asked as her cheeks burned.

"Who do you mean?"

"Did you seduce the Lady Gwenyth?"

"Gwenyth? No. She was too proper and would have been frightened."

"You mean too good? Unlike me…" she slowed and looked away.

"I'm thankful that you share, yes," he smiled. "Lord knows your husband does his bit of sharing. But don't stop, for I enjoy this and find you beautiful."

She smiled and he rubbed her back. With quick fingers, she undid his trousers, pulled him loose, and slid down upon him. He exhaled and gripped her as she moved against him.

"Did you want to?"

"Did I want to do what?"

But he knew what she meant. He pictured Gwenyth, the few times he had seen her smile while the breeze had blown upon her hair. He remembered giving her flowers, kissing her hand as she took them, watching William punish her later, and held tightly to Janis now while she pleased him.

"Did you want to do this to her?"

He shook his head. "She would have been too scared. William made her fear intercourse."

"But did you want to?" she sighed. "Did you think her beautiful too?"

Aindreas stared at her.

"I want to be in this moment, woman, not thinking of her. Not now…"

That's not true. Of course I wanted to, Janis, I wished to seduce her and lay her in my bed in my manor, and feel that body and kiss those lips and make gentle love to her so that she would know that not all men are monsters. I want to think of her. I wish I could have shown her, been married to her, loved her...

Janis continued to move.

"You don't need to flatter me, My Lord. Were you in love with her? Like every man who sets his eyes on her? Like my husband?"

"Since you won't leave it alone, yes. Yes I wanted her..."

He trembled and peaked at the thought, just as another guard strolled by. They froze.

Slowly, his metal clinked. He stopped and stared into the trees. They did not move a muscle. Finally, he turned away.

"We are fools for this," she muttered the moment he had passed.

She parted from him and backed away while he tucked himself back into his trousers. Looking in all directions, she pulled her hood over her face and scurried back to the keep without another backward glance.

He sat a moment longer as his breathing slowed, then climbed back through the window and found a haystack. Throwing himself upon it, he felt his blood pulsing as he softened. He tried to push all images of Gwenyth and Janis from his mind. Shea would murder him if he knew and the nerves from that thought made him so uneasy, he sought sleep to knock him out. His journey the next day would be a long one and he nestled beneath his cloak, not once having noticed the other man sitting in the trees listening.

11

Dear God he's going to jostle her head off! "Hold on, Gwenyth! Hold tight! Get back here you ass of a horse!"

William ran down the slope with his cumbersome shield and sword, jerkin and gauntlets, daggers and packs, all of it bundled in his arms like a juggling jester.

"Damn that Titan! Damn him!" he swore, thrusting his sword into the ground as Titan's tail vanished from sight, Gwenyth barely holding on. "Titaaaan!" he roared, though they were gone.

He made his way down, sliding on the pebbles and brush as he leaned into the hill so he might go faster, cursing some more and cursing the rabbits that had spooked him. Finally, at long last, he was out of the mountain pass. A buzzard circled overhead in the bright sun and aside from the sound of a hawk, the valley beneath the mouth of the Northeast Pass was silent. A bird tweeted, and he began to make his way through the grasses towards the river so he could get his bearings.

"Foul, ruddy, beast of a bastard...I'll horsewhip that Titan, I swear it."

He knew he wouldn't but he said it all the same as if it might console him. Suddenly, in the distance along the winding valley, the speck of his black horse was barreling back toward him. Gwenyth was at the reins.

William's jaw dropped. She was leaning over his neck, holding the reins close to the bit, sitting astride like a man with her skirts flowing behind her in a banner of green. Her knees were pinched closely to his sides and her hair waved loose like streamers for a maypole. She galloped toward him.

"No...no," he shook his head.

The horse wasn't stopping.

"No, Gwenyth...no! Pull back! Pull back!"

He leapt aside as the horse swooshed past into the water where she spun him with a spray and charged back. Pulling up short and gentle, Titan stopped like an axe flung into wood. She was beaming, cheeks flushed, and her chest rose and fell with each breath.

"Oh, My Lord, he *is* fast!" she exclaimed. "Gloriously fast! I believe I'm in love!"

Titan pranced in place, snorting his mane from his nose with his ears pricked and ready. She patted his neck.

"There, Titan. We are truly friends now."

William stood frozen, then dropped everything in his arms like an overwhelmed squire. Finally coming to his senses, he leapt forward to offer her a hand but she swung her leg over and jumped from the stirrup like one who had done so a million times.

"I admit it's easier in trousers, but yours would never fit me," she breathed, brushing the wisps from her face and sweeping the wrinkles from her skirts.

"You...you weren't frightened?" his voice cracked.

She shook her head.

"Christ, woman! I thought you were on a runaway!" He plopped down on the earth, throwing his face in his hands and his elbows on his knees. "I thought I was going to be picking up your pieces from here to Ballymead!"

"Oh, William, I'm sorry." She dropped next to him and held his arm. "I was honest when I said I ride well. It wasn't hard to get control of him again. He just needed to trust me. Did you fear for me?"

"Of course I did!" he howled. "I was scared half to death, woman! And I saw *my* bloody head on the Lord of Ballymead's spike for letting you break your neck!"

He looked into her worried eyes.

"I'm sorry, William. Please forgive me," she murmured.

Her head was down, but she had not cringed at his shouting. Slowly the fear faded and he began to smile.

"What is it?" she fretted.

He snorted and shook his head.

"You...you are something else." Plucking a blade of grass seed, he examined it in the sunlight and then wiggled it into her face so she scrunched her nose and laughed. "You could outride the whole of King Bain's army, woman."

She smiled from ear to ear.

God, that radiant smile, that sweet, delicious smile...

"And never a finer compliment you could give, kind sir with a faint heart. Shall I help the dainty knight to his feet?" she baited, standing tall and presenting her hand like a gentle man.

"Ach! You'd better run, Lady!" he laughed, springing to his toes.

She giggled and dashed away though he easily chased her down, grabbing her from behind and spinning her as she laughed. Titan stomped forward, nipping at him.

"All right, man, all right!" he laughed as he turned her to face him. "I shall be more gentle...I believe my *stallion*," he nodded to the horse as if he would understand, "has challenged me over a fair lady and I shall have to fight him to the death to claim her hand."

"Certainly you wouldn't die for me," she smiled up at him, her arms draping around his neck.

"I would and more, for it's in the Lady Gwenyth of Ballymead's name and honor under which I now go forth." He began to grin. "However," he began, sliding his arms around her waist. "My Lady insults the pride of her champion and therefore she ought to be duly punished," he uttered, stiffening his head.

She furrowed her brow but didn't shy away, and that made him grin.

"She must pay for it with a kiss and he will expunge all wrong doing."

"Surely a kiss is too much?" she played along. "Assuming I'm guilty, that is."

"It is the only thing that will right the wrong and I'll accept no less."

He held his head high like a priest delivering the sacrament and she rolled her eyes.

"Very well then...but you'll have to come get it!" she teased and wrenched herself free.

Again he made chase under Titan's watchful eye and grabbed her hand, whipping her close as the sun shone brightly and his face looked down upon hers, carefree and so soft. He held her, letting his hands smooth her hair down her back, then slowly moved his nose and lips so they skimmed hers, his breath traveling across her cheeks until his lips fell to hers.

He devoured her, becoming aroused and pulling her close with no regard for it, for he was attracted to her like no other. Her head began to spin again and she allowed her fingers to slide across his face and around his neck so that they became lost in his hair.

"I've kissed you now," she whispered.

"No," he murmured. "You flee from authority and therefore pay double the price."

Again she giggled and continued to kiss him. He grinned and braced her to him tightly.

"Besides," he kept kissing her. "I need the practice."

"Despicable!" a voice squeaked nearby and their heads snapped up to see an old sheepherder passing, his homespun tied about him. "Have you no shame, woman?" he scolded.

"She's my wife!" William grabbed her hand and waved the wedding band. "And she'll be kissed when her husband sees fit to do so!"

"Young love never lasts!" he called over his shoulder, hobbling on his crook. "You'll end up old and fat! Despicable! Despicable…"

They fell into laughter.

They made camp near a cluster of trees as the sun went down, taking all warmth from the day with it. A miserable chill fell upon them. He set a fire while she hurried to pull loose the loaf of bread and cheese that they had bartered for along the way. A wolf howled in the distance and William grabbed the blanket.

"Come here, woman, before you freeze."

"I must prepare your meal."

"And you may do so from beneath this wool."

"You're spoiling me. I'm growing too accustomed to this treatment," she smiled, collapsing before him.

"And if I see fit to spoil you, it's my choice, for I am your man now."

She fell to his chest and divided the food while he propped his leg open to make room.

"No doubt my father would be horrified at my looseness. Whatever will I do once we reach Ballymead?"

"You'll wrap your blankets about you at night and imagine them as my arms, Gwen."

"It won't be the same."

He whipped the blanket around them as they shivered, waiting for their body heat to ease the chill. She grabbed his arm and pulled it tighter, and they huddled as close to the flame as they could without the sparks singeing them.

"I cannot seem to get close enough to you," she jittered.

"I'm not complaining," he smiled, letting his lips rest upon her head. "These arms are yours to do with as you please."

The wolves howled again.

"The creatures are out tonight," William smiled.

"I hope they mind their distance."

"I don't think we have to worry here. It *is* something to be mindful of on the royal hunting grounds though."

"Has the king let you hunt there?" she said with surprise.

"He has, on several occasions, as a boy as well. It's a great honor as it is only for royalty. The benefit of being the best squire and First Knight I suppose," he chuckled.

"And I see you're very humble," she smirked.

"It was good fun," he continued. "But there, the biggest nuisance are bears."

"Bears?"

"Not usually trouble. And in the winter they're hibernating. But they can be fierce, especially when startled. We lost a man to one once...oh, I almost forgot. A treat for us."

She furrowed her brow as he let a hand grope from beneath the blanket until he retrieved three small apples. She grinned, then he handed her two of them.

"Is there another for you?"

"No, I wish you to have them both," he replied.

"That won't do, William. You're twice my size—"

"Are you rejecting my noble gift?"

He raised his brow.

"Fine, then. If you will be stubborn, then it's mine to do with as I wish and I insist we share it."

"*Aye, Lady,*" he chuckled and bowed his head. "I would hate to get a tongue lashing."

She held the apple to his mouth and he crunched off a bite. The fire was soothing. Gwenyth gazed into the flames as she nestled against him.

"When I was little, I wandered too far from home," she began between mouthfuls. "My mother was sick with grief for the sun had gone down and I hadn't returned. She insisted on coming on the search for me. She, Father, and my brothers Loddin, Gavin and William...George was being fostered and Hershel had gone to the monks to read Latin," she clarified. "They came looking for me. Mother thought I had drowned in the pond and yelled at Father the whole time for letting me learn to swim," she giggled.

"Were you lost?" William chewed.

"Of course not. I knew Ballymead like the Greeks knew the stars, but I was seven and hardly responsible. I had found a lame fox and had vowed to stay with it and make it well, and that nothing should rip me from its side..." she said with a valiant gesture and William laughed. "William was the one who found me. He was four and ten then. He kept such a straight face the entire time he tried to convince me to leave the fox, but I knew he was laughing at me. I was far from home and it was so late that my father set camp right there. We all spent the night like travelers around the fire and I remember lying between my brothers, watching my parents like this, as we are now, huddled together by the fire like two young souls..."

"Your stories of Ballymead should be written in poems," he smiled.

Gwenyth turned red and giggled again.

"Father jested that had we children not been there, he felt certain I might have had a younger brother or sister that night."

"Did your beloved fox live?" William laughed, filling his mouth again.

"Alas, it died and I sobbed tears for its soul when Father said that foxes didn't go to heaven. To a seven year old, I took that to mean it had gone to eternal damnation instead and was angered at God for not accepting it, for the fox had committed no sin."

William tipped his head back and belted laughter.

"You make fun of me?" She made a forlorn face.

"I do, Gwenyth. You sounded sweet."

"Well I didn't understand him then, but I do now. Father took me on his knee while Mother tried to make sense of my hair and he said *'finis vitae sed non amoris. Haec olim meminisse iuvabit.' Love does not end with life. Someday we will look back on this and smile."* She shook her head. "I thought he was talking of the fox and I cried and cried that I could never see that night as anything other than tragic. But years later, I learned that he was talking of the night we all spent together beneath God's majestic heavens, for he had just learned that Mother was going to die, he just didn't know how long it would be...What about you, dark knight of Bain? What were you like before you became a legend?"

"I have no stories such as yours. I suppose I was a typical boy. Loved horses, same as you, but for boys that's expected. I revered knights, had a toy of one once, a wooden figure atop a horse whose arm swung when you pulled a lever...I would climb on the walls to watch the vassals' knights leave for the city with their mail gleaming, banners flying..."

He let his hand extend in an arch as if scanning them on the horizon.

"To a lad, they were *so* powerful. Nothing could ever harm them. I dreamt of going to court one day myself, I suppose like a damsel yearns for a protector," he chuckled and nudged Gwenyth.

She rolled her eyes and nudged him back.

"I never thought I'd get to go, for I'm a third son and not even Faegan was sent to foster anywhere. When Father told me at age ten that I was to be a page at the castle, I couldn't *believe* it, even when I stood in front of the king..."

'Young William, you look like a strong lad,' the king had said.

No child had been given a private audience with him before. William felt small beneath his throne in his sandaled feet and blue tunic bearing the Cadogan hawk. His mother had made him one with long sleeves to hide his welts and bruises, but the bruising extended up his neck beneath his shock of black hair, and the scar beneath his eye was bright despite being two years old.

'You wear your father's crest proudly,' the king noted. 'Has Andrew Cadogan come to present you today?'

He stood still and looked at his feet, knowing the knights behind him were shaking their heads. He didn't feel proud. His father certainly had not been. The moment his escort arrived, William had been placed before the manor with his colt. And his father, drunk as a rat in a wine barrel, had said 'good riddance,' as he latched the door. He knew the king was staring at him and felt ashamed.

'How did you come to have so many bruises, son?'

William knew his face was blank, but wouldn't look up.

"I play rough with me older brotha's," he mumbled, as the squire next to him leaned down to tell him to say, 'Your Majesty.'

'You'll do well here, William, I'm sure of it, but you must not lie. Have you suffered harsh treatment?' The young king had leaned forward and stared at him with his deep green eyes as if searching his mind. 'Look at me, son." William looked up for the first time. "You may tell me.'

It was then that the tears burned his cheeks, his teeth clenched shut and he tried to bolt from the hall, dodging the knights' grasps. Yet one of them caught him and held him fast as he flailed.

'His father ought to be horsewhipped,' he heard one of them explaining as he tried to wrangle himself loose. 'This boy has only known harshness. Look at him. He's been like this, like a wild fox in a snare the whole of the journey.'

'Let go of me!' he wailed and tossed in the knight's grip. 'Let me go! Let me go let me go...'

William shook his head.

"It's not important," he shrugged and loaded his mouth with the rest of his bread, dusting the crumbs in the flame.

"Of course it is," she pressed. "I must know all about you. 'Twill give me bragging rights with the maids at Ballymead," she smiled.

"My childhood, Gwenyth," he said seriously. "It wasn't like yours. My sisters learned women's work as was expected. They never would have dreamt of playing with squires or nursing foxes or my father's strap would have welted them for it. And we boys worked. When work was done we played, and when we got in trouble, we got whipped."

"I know," she said softly. "I shouldn't ask of it, My Lord, I'm sor—"

"Stop, Gwenyth. Stop apologizing as if I might get cross. I won't." He shrugged. "I just don't talk about it, never have. Up till the day we met, I had all but buried it away."

"We have something in common then," she sighed and stared ahead of her. "I'm thankful it was you who found me. You understand, William."

He sat quietly and she began to shiver again. Then he adjusted the blanket around her and without warning, started once more.

"My family fell apart, Gwen. My father drank. He cursed my mother as a whore and when I was four and ten and carrying my knight's colors for the first time to battle," he shook his head and bit his lip, mindlessly snapping blades of grass beneath his propped up knee. "My oldest brother made good on his boyhood threats and fled to Lispagne with my second sister, King Fernando's realm. My mother soon died a penniless widow on a worthless fief to another liege, my littlest sister died of cholera from a contaminated well, and the oldest of my sisters, Louisa, vanished.

"My happiest times were at court. I was a squire to the First Knight who had two older squires. They became my new brothers. I learned to set trenchers and pour wine, to polish swords until my hands went numb," he curled his lips at the memory and rubbed his knuckles. "But I also learned to fight. I learned to kill and take no mercy. At the age of four and ten, that same first battle, I killed my first soldier, a spy who sneaked into our camp. He was eavesdropping on the commanders' tent. I had left to answer nature after my knight let me drink too much ale with the men. I walked up behind him, tapped him. He turned. He jumped at me but I pulled his dagger from his belt and plunged it into him. *Over* and *over* again...such *power* I held in that dagger...and I saw my father's face the whole time.

"I was cheered for that. 'A brave deed' is what they called it." He shook his head again. "But above all, I learned to honor the king. He had rescued me from my father's hellhole by requesting my services, and to honor his generosity was to try my hardest at every challenge and prove to my father I wasn't worthless. I learned Latin, math, theology, and was proud because even the king would take special notice of me debating with the priest who I know hated me for it. And never once did the king forget the month of my birth.

"I *also* was taught," he raised his brows and smiled, "that women should be seen as vestal virgins, yet I would watch my knight take them to bed when his head was loaded with ale, those same women's bellies swollen months later when they came begging for coin after their families had disowned them. Such chivalry. Such hypocrisy. Between him and my father, I decided that I should never take a woman. That way, I would never seed babes I might end up beating, whose lives I might ruin. King Bain keeps trying to make me marry but I keep refusing."

After a long silence, he finally looked down at her.

"I've never spoken of it. I don't know why I do now." He huffed a laugh. "Mine is a tale not worth the telling, I suppose."

She hugged her knees, resting her chin atop them.

"So the songs of you are true. You live for fighting but ne'er for love."

Lifting her chin, he smiled.

"At one time, yes, but not anymore. It's only you who I have ever touched, Lady, but now that I touch I cannot seem to stop and I see that I could be happy with a woman by my side. I mean it with all my honor as a knight of Bain that I was serious about two things that I've spoken to you." She watched his lips. "I intend to ask your father to give you to me as my wife, and I now fight in the honor of Gwenyth of Ballymead. It shall be written on my banner for all to see. The kingdom will know that my heart has finally been taken."

She began to blush and he leaned down to press his lips to hers when Titan laid back his ears and started grunting, prancing, tangling his tether and rearing with stomping hooves.

"Dwyre," she said with frozen lips.

William had already jumped to his feet, his daggers stowed and arms in hand in the blink of an eye. *He has gone from gentle to warrior without a thought of it.*

"Get Titan free before he snaps his neck. Do it!" he ordered as though she were a soldier.

She hastened to the horse.

"Steady, sweet Titan," she crooned, rubbing his neck to stop the thrashing.

She fumbled for the tether to untwist him but his eyes were spooked, the reds of the blood vessels catching the firelight and there was no calming his immediate madness. A rumbling suddenly met her ears and as she turned over her shoulder, she saw gleaming eyes, four pairs of them reflecting in the trees.

She froze. They inched closer. She counted another pair, *five*, then another, then another. William was on the other side.

Please come this way, she begged.

"Undo him Gwenyth...Gwenyth?"

Do not move...one move and they will pounce you like a flopping trout.

But she shivered. It happened before she could think. The alpha lunged from the trees.

"Wolves! William, Wolves!"

Titan whinnied and reared high, snapping the tether and charging into the night. The wolf was upon her, snarling, biting, his fangs burning deeply into her arms. She blocked her face. Another leapt in, ripping on her ankle as it whipping its head side to side.

"*William!*" she screamed.

A shadow emerged above her like Lucifer himself, eyes set, sword high, a reaper about to stab her. William's sword came down from straight above and the wolf squealed and twisted. Its paws cut across her. The sword plunged again and again.

He kicked it off, drew a dagger and slashed the neck of the next. He landed atop another, noosed it with his powerful arm and stabbed its underside, jerking the knife over and over again until it lay twitching. She crawled away when she saw three more on him. He twisted and launched one off, sending it crashing into the trees, but they were taking him down.

Sweet William! No!

He grunted as fangs tore through his arm. She scrambled to grab his dagger, lodged in the blood pumping from the dying wolf's chest. It whined as she wrenched it from its ribs. Without thought, she ran to the fray. Titan thundered back to the scene and reared, landed, stamping a wolf's hindquarters with a crunch of bone. It yelped and tossed about on the ground. William rolled with one more out from under Titan's deadly hooves and Gwenyth fell atop the creature as William fought beneath it.

"Go, Gwenyth!" he choked "Please, love, run!"

Titan was crazed and chased others into the blackness.

The wolf twisted beneath her and soon had her on the ground

again, her arm locked in its jaws. She cried and plunged the knife into its face as she shied from the blood that sprayed. It retreated, yelping, but she scrambled to her knees, grabbed its hind leg, and did it again, plunging the metal into it over and over, climbing on top of the maimed beast, stabbing and stabbing, both hands clutching the dagger like it was the holy grail.

"I have seen—" she gasped for breath as she stabbed, "too—many—wolves!"

She was weeping. She was horrified by it, for all she could see was the yellow and brown wolf of Dwyre and the face of William Feargach as he raped her, beat her, humiliated her.

"Lady! Lady!"

William's hands were around her wrists as she continued to stab the animal she straddled. He tried to slow her hands, soaked in blood and growing sticky.

"Gwenyth! Stop now, stop...he's dead, dead, Gwenyth, you killed him..."

He struggled with her but her swinging finally slowed, then ceased and he peeled the knife from her clasp. Casting it aside, he pulled her hair out of her face as she bent over, retched, and then cried some more.

"Wolves...Dwyre wolves will haunt me... William Feargach will haunt me forever...he'll haunt me..."

She fell forward on the animal and wept and Sir William, the ruthless knight, dragged her into his arms and held her tightly while the piles of fur finished draining on the ground around them.

"I have you," he whispered and kissed her head. "I have you, I have you..."

"Please hold me. Pease don't ever let go," she whimpered.

"Never, Gwen. I kill ghosts that haunt me too," he whispered as he rocked her on his lap. "We weep together."

12

Gwenyth had made William think of Dwyre. She had reminded him of his job. He had managed to push what had happened to her from his mind, for their month of sweetnesses had been much easier to endure. But as the days passed, the closer they got to Ballymead, and soon he would have to return to his role as commander.

The real world doesn't wait. This tryst will soon be over. The whole of this journey, and not once have I pried her for questions like I should have. He sighed. *I don't want it to end. For once, the affairs of men are of no interest at all.* His brow was furrowed and his teeth clenched, though he was so lost in thought he didn't notice.

Gwenyth glanced up at him.

"William? You have been most lost for quite a while."

Still he stared on ahead.

"What has crossed your mind?" she asked.

He broke his focus and cracked a quick smile.

"I'll have work awaiting my return to the capital. I'm planning."

"I see. What sort of work?"

"Mmm, it's not important."

She raised her brows and smiled. "Not important? You're quite intent on wearing your concern in your eyes."

"Am I that obvious?"

She giggled at him. He huffed and shook his head, then resigned himself to finally bring up the subject.

"I've just been thinking...about difficult things."

"Leaving me at Ballymead?"

Again, he cracked a smile. "Yes, that, and of course my work."

"Like what?"

"Well," he took a deep breath. "You will know, I wish not to talk of things that might cause you pain."

She lost her smile and turned forward again. "You wish to ask about Dwyre."

He bowed his head and thought for a moment.

"I've let it go for these sennights, Gwen, but I cannot ignore it anymore. That man, Aindreas?" She sat perfectly still. "If there's truth to his words, that Lord Feargach has toppled Faulk, it means I will be at best, held up in countless councils upon my return, at worst, deployed with at least part of my army, if not all."

Her voice wavered. "I had never known Aindreas to be cruel before that night."

Her whole body had tensed and she looked down at the wounds from the wolf bites on her hands.

"I'm sensitive to what happened to you. You being the woman I wish to marry, I don't want to speak of this at all, yet my position as King Bain's First forces me to do so. I should have done so already, except your company has been a sweet distraction."

Her hand found his fingers resting upon her thigh and she clenched them. He tightened his grip.

"You will know that if the uprisings require the army of Bain, I will lead it to battle?"

She nodded, though kept looking forward.

"You will know that if I am to lead it, I need to know all there is about Lord Feargach's motives?"

Again she nodded. "I wondered how long you would wait to ask about it. I was beginning to think forever."

He remained silent, then wrapped his arm about her and leaned in to rest his cheek against her head. She began to breathe more easily.

"Will you tell me what you know of Lord Feargach's army?"

He continued to hold her, speaking the words gently as if to pass confidence to her.

She took a deep breath. "I'm afraid I don't know much," she replied. "I once overheard him holding council in the great hall."

"Of what did he speak?"

"That with the new conscriptions he had levied, his numbers were swelling to over two thousand."

"Did he say if those were foot soldiers or knights?"

Gwenyth's stomach was rumbling. Their food had run out yet again and there had been no villagers for bartering with in the passing days.

"I don't know. But there were always many knights coming and going in the last months I was there. There might be more conscripts now."

"But he said they were levied?"

She nodded.

"Then they're likely foot soldiers," William deduced.

"I don't think all came willingly. My husband was at this council. I was with Lord Shea's wife."

She pictured it clearly and as she spoke it, found herself reliving it anyway. Lady Janis's behavior had been strange that night...

'Come, Gwenyth, let us hear what the men have to boast about tonight.'

Janis was laughing, as if spying on them was a pleasant pastime. She cast aside her needlepoint and pulled Gwenyth out of her chair. Gwenyth trembled. The very thought of willingly going near William made her cringe and the bruise on her cheek was a reminder that he only preferred her company in bed and nothing more. Her hands shook so badly, Janis squeezed them.

'Why? Would this not be eavesdropping?'

Janis laughed but didn't answer her question. 'There's nothing to be frightened of, my dear. I wish not to be cooped up in this chamber tonight. That is all.'

'You may go, Lady,' Gwenyth squeaked. 'Lord Shea doesn't punish you like he has me. I wish not to be caught. I'll surely feel the wrath of it.'

She tried to sit again but Janis took her needlepoint and tossed it in the chair. She pulled Gwenyth close.

'I must teach you to play this game. You've been trapped in this marriage for a while now, same as me, and ought to learn how to manipulate it.'

'Game, My Lady?'

'Aye, a game. The men play it, and so must we. We won't be seen. I have oiled the hinges here and they won't even know we have opened this door. Besides, they are growing drunk and the feasting is getting loud.'

'It's when William is drunk that I trust him the least,' Gwenyth replied.

Janis pulled her even closer still and spoke into her ear. 'Knowing what they're plotting gives you power. Here, come change into your sleeping gown. If there's trouble, you may pretend that you were preparing for sleep and were fetching water from the maids. I know how to handle my husband, especially when he's drunk.'

Janis stripped off Gwenyth's gown and laid it across the chair. She shivered in the chill and clenched her arms tightly until Janis brought her night shift.

Slipping into the corridor, they crept into the gallery behind the half wall that overlooked the great hall. Gwenyth was so petrified she gripped Janis to the point that Janis winced.

'Relax,' Janis mouthed.

They squatted low so that their eyes barely peeked over the top. The lack of torchlight gave them a cover of shadows. Shea was standing at the head of the board with many of his vassals swigging their ale. Many more were crammed along the walls. William was laughing and Shea was passing him ale. Aindreas sat at the other end. He glanced up. Gwenyth turned stark white and dropped down quickly.

'Lord Aindreas has seen me!' she whispered. 'I must return—'

'Aindreas won't say a word if he did, my dear.' Janis peeked back over. 'Aye, he's seen us, and our presence will remain secret. Surely you've noticed he isn't like the others.'

She dragged Gwenyth back up so that she peeked over once more.

'We've grown in numbers!" Shea was announcing as he rolled out a large map. "Three hundred more conscriptions signed up today at a village meeting. That puts my army over two thousand now!'

'Hey!' came the cheers. 'Enough to rival the king?'

'Not yet, though enough to cause quite a problem,' he smiled. 'The villagers only needed a little persuasion,' he chuckled. 'But it did not take long for them to see my way.'

William chuckled too, along with Shea's top lords who had been there.

'Aye, he only had to whore one of their wives,' William snorted and tipped back a swallow. 'The rest plunked their marks upon our contract in a blink!' This was met with laughter, though Gwenyth noticed not all of the men seemed at ease with it including Aindreas. Once more, he looked up and spotted Gwenyth as if to see her reaction. 'You should have seen her, screamin' and carryin' on like a floundering sow...'

Gwenyth gasped so loudly some of the men heard and the room fell quiet. Janis abandoned her and fled to her chamber so quickly Gwenyth scarcely saw her leave. William was looking up and his eyes locked with hers. She felt sickened and fell to the floor holding her stomach.

"We've an eavesdropper, Father. You'll never guess who it is."

The hall fell quiet. She heard William's feet storm away and backed up to the wall. He ascended the stairs and was now coming around the corner. She gripped the wall. William walked up to her and looked her over. She scooted off to one side and attempted to run, tripping over instead. He grabbed her wrist and pulled her upward.

'What do you think you're doing? Spying?' he growled.

She shook her head, unable to speak. He slapped her.

'You've got explaining to do. Look at you,' he rebuked. 'In your night clothes, no less.'

'No...' she whimpered. 'No...I beg you...'

He dragged her down the stairs and thrust her into the center of the hall, bright with torchlight. She could feel the men staring at her shift. She trembled. Shea was glaring at her. Slowly, Aindreas rose to his feet.

'She's been caught spying,' William stated. 'My own wife.'

Some murmurs surged through the room. She shook her head, quaking so badly she could not form any words.

'No, my...I was...'

'Spit it out!' he shouted and wrenched her tightly to him.

She collapsed at his feet and clasped her hands at her mouth. 'I wasn't I promise I wasn't! Please believe me, My Lord! The Lady Janis...she asked me...'

Her eyes bubbled and she clenched them shut. He bent down and yanked her back to her feet, grabbing her face so hard she could feel his fingers making bruises.

'Awe, leave'er be,' one of the vassals waved his hand. 'She's just a woman.'

'I'm not offended. There's no need for this fuss,' another man interjected.

Just then, Janis hastened into the hall in her nightshift and robe with her hair let down.

'Gwenyth, my dear,' she approached her and then bowed to Lord Shea. 'Husband, what has passed?'

'We hold a private council, woman, and she was caught just now in the gallery. Eavesdropping.'

'Oh no,' Janis sighed and looked at her feet. 'Husband, I am afraid there's a terrible confusion for which I'm the one at fault.'

Shea folded his arms and huffed. 'Well?'

'The ladies prepare for sleep. I asked sweet Gwenyth here to fetch more water just moments ago.' Shea furrowed his brow. William had still not relented his grip. 'She begged me not send her, for fear of being caught in the halls. She tries so hard to be obedient. But I scolded her and told her surely she would not be punished for fetching water.'

A few chuckles escaped the vassals.

'This wasn't her fault, My Lord. I beg you hold me responsible for I would never have sent her had I known this council was so private. She was only trying to be dutiful.'

The room was quiet and the men watched.

'Come, sir, this seems to be purely a woman's lack of sense,' a man called.

Gwenyth saw Aindreas watching her as if he wished to speak in her defense. William looked to his father. Shea, brow tight, nodded once.

William turned back to her. 'You get lucky this night,' he whispered.

'I meant nothing I swear it, husband,' she mouthed. 'Please believe me. I'm sorry, I wish to make it up to you. Please let me make it *up to you. I'll wait up for you...in, in bed, My Lord.'*

William seemed to soften for a moment and kissed her head.

'Thank you, husband...thank you...'

He released her and she threw her arms about him while he patted her back. 'Go to bed, wife. I shall come later.'

She grabbed his hand and kissed it over and over again. 'Thank you,' she whispered.

Janis wrapped an arm around her while she cried.

'Come, my dear, this was all my fault.' They began to walk back to the stairs. Gwenyth clenched her and leaned her head onto her shoulder.

'Lady Janis!' Shea boomed. She turned. 'You will use better judgment next time!'

'Most certainly, My Lord. I thank thee.'

They rose to her chamber and Janis shut the door loudly so that the men would hear.

'I thought you had abandoned me!' Gwenyth sobbed.

They embraced each other, Janis clenching her to her breast.

'Never, Gwenyth. I'm sorry. I thought you would be used to this place now! I thought you could begin to help me!'

'He raped a man's wife!' Gwenyth whimpered.

Janis's face fell. 'That he did.'

'And you're not horrified? He has dishonored a lady, and, and he is your husband!'

Tears began to stream down Janis' cheeks and she gripped Gwenyth. 'There's nothing I can do about it, nothing...'

She shivered. It had been one of the few occasions that her husband had shown a bit of compassion though her gut had told her he only did so to save face in front of the vassals.

"He said his father only had to...em...he used a very vulgar word to describe it..."

"You may tell me," William encouraged. "They are his words, not yours."

She gulped. "It seems Lord Shea only had to..." she barely spoke the word and shuddered, "*whore* one of their wives to prove his point. The rest of his vassals then agreed to sign a contract for conscription."

William nodded. "Did you hear his councils often?"

This time she shook her head. "I did my best to avoid him and Will—my husband. They considered me bold and I knew if I was caught nearby, there might be punishment."

William squeezed her.

"You are not bold, Gwenyth. You have courage. Keep going."

Gwenyth searched her mind.

"I cannot think of anything else," she muttered. "Other than I knew my father-in-law was interested in metals."

"How so?"

"I cannot say for sure. 'Twas just something he always talked about. He used to curse our king at board for denying him trade metals. Is he not allowed to trade for metals?"

William shook his head. "No, he has been barred from trade."

"Then that would explain why he wants to occupy the fort on the River Ruadhán..."

"He said this? What would he say?"

"Not much, just that he needed to control the port so he could buy them. He and my husband complained of it many times. He sent out an order for his vassals' goods, iron hinges, those types of things to be melted down and reworked. He even sent a group of his men to rummage through the women's quarters and collect our things, if we had any. I once overheard my husband when I took him his wine in the armory. He was counting up what had been stolen from a Bainick outpost near the River Ruadhán."

Even this brought back pain. The wine she had delivered had tasted sour and he had thrown it aside, demanding she return with a new decanter. Much of what he had thrown had splattered upon her.

She hesitated.

"Don't stop explaining, Gwenyth."

"I knew not why they hadn't any metals but it clearly angered them to rely on weaponry stolen from Bainick guards." She paused and then gulped. "William? I beg you not ask me more about that place. The thought of it does nothing but resurrect terrible pain. Please."

Neither of them spoke for a moment. A gentle mist had settled in. William sighed with disappointment.

"Then I won't ask you more," he murmured next to her ear. "Thank you, Gwen. You have done well to tell me this. But will you look at me?" She did so. He smiled and brushed her chin with his thumb. "You are strong. You can overcome this. Have you not noticed that you've done this already? For you are here and your nightmare is over." She smiled and he kissed her head. "You may tell me more if you wish, but I won't mention it again."

She leaned against him and returned his kiss.

"Good, then let us talk of glad tidings instead. Let's talk of you and me, and how we shall be married, and our wedding. 'Twill be at Ballymead of course, in our little chapel with summer flowers and rich mead and pretty ribbons and rosemary."

William smiled. "It sounds perfect."

"We will have real sugar and berries, fine wines, our friends will give us gifts, and I shall adopt Titan as my own and the famed knight will be reduced to walking," she giggled.

"Adopt him? Am I to think you marry me only for my horse?" he smiled. "I've been had by a woman."

"Aye, you have. You underestimate a gentle maid, sir."

He chuckled. "And yet I'm gladly being led along."

Her stomach rumbled once more. She tried to ignore it instead of complain, for there was nothing to be done, but it caused her to shift nonetheless.

"If I must feel your stomach protest again, Gwen, I shall die, for I have failed to keep you well."

"It cannot be helped," she replied. "Though I'll admit, I could eat a horse right now." Titan grunted and tossed his mane. They both laughed. "I'm sorry, dear Titan," she reached out and stroked his neck. "I didn't mean I *would* do it."

Droplets of water began to sprinkle their faces and hair.

"If you care to hunt and do the skinning, I shall cook it for us," she continued.

"I've a mind to try, though aside from a bow and some arrows, I fear I have little to hunt with and the deer don't seem to be out in these parts. Besides, we would be trespassing on someone's lands and stealing their game."

"Then we will endure it."

She patted his arm and smiled. William chuckled.

"I'm pathetic. Truly a man of the city, for I have an entire purse of gold and silver against my hip and yet I have nothing to show for it."

"You have the beard of a countryman, so no one needs to know," she giggled. "Perhaps we should stop by the river and refill the skins?" she continued.

William nodded. "I could use a rest and so could Titan, for he's looking worn."

Gwenyth slipped from his grip like a piece of silk and stretched as Titan grunted again.

William dismounted. *It will not be long before we reach Ballymead,* he thought with a frown. *She's mine, and I will have to relinquish her...*

"William?" she questioned. "Are you all right? Do you still think of, of—"

He quickly smiled. "It's out of my mind completely. Let's rest for the remainder of the day. We only have a few hours of light left anyway if the rain continues. Those rocks would make a decent shelter for one night."

"They shall be cold though, with naught but one blanket betwixt us."

William grinned and bowed dramatically.

"*My Lady.* That's what your protector is for."

She knocked his arm. "To keep me from freezing?"

"Aye, not the most desirable job, but I can try my best."

"Ah!" she exclaimed. "Am I so hideous, like a warted witch that you should be so repulsed?"

"Well I've not seen any warts as of yet," he teased, drawing her close by the top of her bodice with a peeking finger. "But if I must make a closer inspection, I'll do so."

"You are *bold,* My Lord!" she exclaimed, though she grinned all the same and tilted back her chin so his view would be clearer.

"I'm sorry, Gwenyth," he muttered, dropping his hand and stepping back. "I *am* bold. Forgive me."

Turning away, he raked his hands through his hair and

grabbed the skins. She stood in contemplation. It was a sin, and yet the very thought of him made heat swell through her stomach. Never had she felt it for William Feargach. She slid one hand around her neck and the other around her belly, watching him as he unbuckled Titan's bridle and saddle, relieving him of his burdens.

Staring up and down the length of him as he inspected Titan's hooves, her eyes settled upon his waist with his sheath hanging upon his narrow hip. They traveled up to his powerful shoulders, to what had once been a cropped mullet of hair now grown shaggy over his ears. He strode to the stream, dropped his belt and ripped his tunic over his head so that he was bare. Hunching over the water, he began splashing it upon his face and neck until he glistened. With scrubbing hands that made his muscles twitch, she inhaled, exhaled. His scars rippled and she felt goose bumps rise across her skin.

William shook the water with a flip of the head and sat back with one knee propped up.

You take too many liberties, man, he scolded while rubbing his face again, as though the act of rubbing would scour away his desire to rip her gown from her and lay her down beneath him. *You begin to believe your lies about that wedding ring.* His own stomach began to rumble now. *Hunger will make me crazed if she does not.*

She came hesitantly to his side and knelt down to take water. He glanced sidelong at her, her eyes focused on the water in front of her as her hair fell forward into the stream. He watched her hands, now marred with unsightly punctures from the wolves. She felt his gaze and turned to him, smiling coyly and then flipped a handful of water at him.

He jumped, losing his balance, and she giggled.

"Do you still underestimate a gentle maid, sir?" she baited.

"Aye, woman, I do...though I'll not do so again!"

He returned the splash. She started, her eyes blinking and splashed him back.

"You make a mistake, My Lord! For I always win at water fights!" She sprang into the water.

"Do you now?" he taunted. "I should like to see a little lady beat me at a challenge, for I too always win, no matter what battle!"

He flung more water and leapt into the river after her.

"Perhaps My Lord must lose from time to time to retain his humility!"

"Careful, woman! Or I shall make you pay me with another kiss!"

"And I shall freely give them if it means your favor rests on me!"

"Then you will die of breathlessness, for you'll be kissing me from now until eternity!"

She laughed without reserve as he ducked away from her tosses, saturated in so much water that her gown hung heavily. Neither of them relented, sending sprays of water through the air. Suddenly she tripped on the weighty fabric, stumbled backward, and fell into a quiet pool in the riverbed. Her blonde hair disappeared from view and she sank.

"Gwenyth!" he hollered, splashing to the edge. "Christ!"

His joy vanished like a puff of smoke. Searching into the depths, he could not see her. Bubbles were rising, but then they stopped.

13

"Christ!" he cursed again.

He stripped off his coin purse and tossed his boots aside, panicking. He thought of the superstitions of the water, knowing they were preposterous yet fearing them all the same, the way he feared a raven cawing. With a deep breath for courage, he sat down and scooted off the edge into the water, clinging to the side.

He crossed himself, then filled his lungs and dunked under, feeling his way down as he descended the natural spring. Opening his eyes, he tried not to think about what Pagan creatures might dwell there waiting to capture his feet, scolding himself all the same for being daft. The water was dark beneath him and he groped outward in hopes of feeling her hair.

His heart was thumping. He pulled himself up for another breath. *Please don't drown! Please God, let me find her!* He dropped back in and shimmied down again, feeling outward, unable to see a thing.

Gwenyth shot like a catapult to the surface. She sucked in, gasping for air. Clenching her skirts together, she crawled out of the depths and staggered to her feet beneath the weight of the gown. She looked around and realized she was farther downstream from whence she had fallen. William was not there. She let her skirts fall. Like a punctured bladder, water splashed and three fish flopped into the grass.

"William?"

She saw Titan rummaging through the grasses and watched a bird flit across the sky.

"William?"

The fish bounced and flipped their tails, their gills flattened together. Looking back at the pool, she saw bubbles rolling up to the surface.

"William!" She splashed back into the water. *What if he cannot swim!*

She reached her hand down and felt for him. He was not there. Her gown was so heavy it felt as though she dragged rocks at her feet and quickly, she reached to her laces and pulled the bodice loose. The dress slackened and she stripped it off, kicking it into a soggy pile. Gathering her shift over her knees, she jumped in once more, plunging past him, eyes open in search. A foot kicked outward and caught her shoulder as he flailed.

He is! He's drowning! "William!" she bubbled.

She grabbed his legs and he began to kick to get free. Her hands groped up his side to find his arms clinging to the rock wall. Kicking expertly, she caught him beneath the shoulders and pulled him up. He flailed in her grip.

Finally her head broke the surface and she gasped for air, dragging him and snapping her legs to propel forward. Reaching out, she gripped the edge of the spring. Both his arms clung to hers now, clutching her so tightly while his hair floated at the surface she almost sank back under. She contorted herself so that she twisted her legs onto the shelf of rock and maneuvered onto her knees.

"Quit struggling!" she complained, straining with his bulk until he managed to grab the wall and heave himself up.

He sucked in a deep breath and climbed out, falling forward, flattening her beneath him in the streambed.

"You're alive!" she exclaimed, throwing her arms about his neck and scattering kisses on his face. "You didn't drown!"

"Of course I'm alive, woman!" he complained.

"Why did you fight me so?"

"I had no idea what was gripping me!" he fussed. "Who knows what lives in those depths! I'm not a skilled swimmer! I thought I was getting pulled under!"

"But why did you go in if you cannot swim?" she scolded.

"I was searching for *you*, and you're not drowning, you are...you are..." He suddenly realized he was on top of her and she was clinging to him, offering her kisses freely. His breathing slowed as droplets dripped from his nose and hair onto her. "You are beautiful."

He allowed his hands to travel along her arm, and then he noticed her gown flung into the grass next to a pile of dead fish. His eyes darted back at her, her long hair flowing down the shallow trickle *like the River Fae...*The contours of what lay beneath her shift were clearly defined, the small points of her breasts protruding upward toward him, water running around her body making her slick.

"Your gown, Gwen," he whispered.

"I needed to swim more freely," she breathed, feeling him between her legs as he braced himself upon her. "I feared I had not much time to find you."

"You don't make it easy for me to resist you," he mumbled.

He didn't move, but studied her cheeks as they turned pink, her lips as they swelled with blood. The thought of those lips intoxicated him and he felt himself begin to desire her, this time not against her buttocks as they rode, but between her legs.

"I don't want to resist you anymore," he whispered and wiped her hair from her forehead.

She sucked in labored breaths, her arms trembling around his neck, and lay still for him, allowing her legs to part, unable to remove her eyes from his.

"'Tis a sin, My Lord, what I'm feeling right now," she whispered and brushed her finger across the scar beneath his eye. "It's a terrible sin, Will, and yet—"

He kissed her. He kissed her deeply, his hips pushing against her as if they willed themselves and he had no control of them. She accepted his kiss and held his neck, letting a hand travel the length of his back until it rolled onto his buttocks, which was tightening and loosening as he pressed against her. His wandering fingers stroked down her side, his thumb grazing over her breast as it slid down upon her thigh rising beside him.

She sighed, enjoying the excitement within her that his roving hands provoked as he released whispered moans. His touch was gentle, as if he might break what he handled if it was not done with utter care. His fingers strayed beneath her shift, pushing it upward as they traveled to the inside of her leg. She caressed him again, indulging in the lips that he was freely giving. His fingers came upon the waist of her leggings. They slid around to the arch of her back and down beneath them onto the skin of her buttocks.

"Please let me make love to you," William whispered.

She gasped and every muscle tensed. He released her. Scrambling backward onto his knees in the water, she wriggled out from beneath him.

"What? What have I done?" he begged.

The searing pain of William Feargach flooded her mind. She threw her hands over her face but could not speak.

"Christ," he muttered, breathing strongly.

His bare chest rose and fell and he ran both hands into his hair and rested them on the back of his head while he clenched his eyes shut and willed himself to soften.

"I'm sorry," she whimpered, hugging her knees as she sat along the bank. "I behave loosely like a prostitute. I'm shamed."

"No, Gwen, you aren't to blame for this." His words were sharp. He sighed and crawled beside her while she buried her face in her knees. "I begin to think you really are mine. I take liberties I should not. I'm a fool. I just…"

He shook his head but didn't say anything else and she waited. No sun hoped to shine through the clouds and the steady mist floated down upon them. She shivered, and he took her hand and turned to face her.

"I just want you. In that way," he confessed. "My judgment is as foggy as the sky is now." He pressed her hand to his mouth. "I don't think with my mind and I forget how you have suffered…I forget, for I'm selfish enough that I might dishonor you for my wants. But *God*, woman, the more I'm with you, I feel completely powerless." He gulped. "I'm sorry I try to dishonor you."

They didn't move. He was afraid to. He was certain she would reject him.

"William? You don't dishonor me."

He gazed deeply into her eyes, her face serious and for once, experienced and not so youthful anymore.

"You have done nothing *but* honor me. Many men don't care enough to stop, but you respect me. I can trust you."

She thought of the Yule celebrations at Ballymead. She had danced and danced to the flutes and drums, adorned with her berry crowns and festive holly while the manor celebrated despite being good Christians. Father had always said that the birth of Christus needed more excitement, for it was a joyous day of which all should be proud. And so each year they danced and feasted and she got to be the winter maiden and her poor father, never able to let his attention wander, had hauled many a flirting boy from the party, sending them home with a foot to the backside.

Then she thought of William Feargach and how the first day she had known him, the day of their formal betrothal, he had tried for much more. She let the thought go for it made her shudder.

"You have more trust in me than I have, Gwen, for I don't trust myself anymore. I look upon your fair face and I wish only to—" he hesitated, holding her hand to his forehead.

"I wish to bring the honor of Ballymead into marriage with me," she said in his absence of words.

Each word was marked with clarity that he heard well.

"I have not virginity to give you, Will. I gave that to a horrible man and for that, I'm sorry for I wish now more than anything it could have been my gift to you...but I at least have my honor."

He began to shake his head.

"Gwenyth, hear me when I say that I despise the name William Feargach of Dwyre, but I must thank him." She furrowed her brow. "For if it hadn't been for him, I would never have been sent to find you, and I would still be alone with my battles and bloodshed and high ego of a knight champion. If you were still a virgin, I wouldn't know you. 'Tis that very beast who has given me the charge of protecting you and you are honorable for being a dutiful wife—"

"And I wish to bring that honor to *you*, before God and church."

Her eyes remained serious, though she took her hand from his grip and looped it through his arm. He took a deep breath and nodded with conviction, kissing the top of her head.

"You shall, woman. I'll not spoil what I'm going to have someday." He caressed her face. "I love you, Gwen, *you*. Not just this lovely body."

He leaned over and kissed her in the way that she adored, slow, gentle, as if he was discovering her taste and she welcomed it, squeezing his arm with hers. She shifted in front of him and he pulled her against his chest where she nestled.

"So, you, the knight of all Bainick knights fear creatures in the water?"

She allowed a smile to crease her lips and he turned red.

"Of course not."

She nudged him again and leaned in to see his face.

"All right, I admit the thought is not out of my mind completely. But you're not to tell a soul, Lady," he warned while she giggled. "My men consider me fearless."

His stomach began to grumble again and she placed her hand upon it.

"You sound like the lion upon your shield."

"Aye, I have hunger, as do you."

"Well, it would be a shame to let those succulent fish, which just *happened* to get caught in my skirts, go to waste."

"That's a skill, woman. Fishing with no net or line..." he shook his head. "I'm impressed."

"I just couldn't let them get away once I felt them swimming against me. I knew not when we would eat again."

"You provide my meals *and* try to rescue me on top of it? Are you sure it is not you who was sent to save me?"

"It isn't my fault I was taught well to fish *and* swim, and you were not!" she teased, bumping his chest deliberately with her shoulder.

He scoffed and grabbed a fish. It hung limply in his grip.

"Well, since I'm *clearly* not as skilled, I shall submit to your superiority, Lady, and push my pride aside...for I'm completely famished!" He jiggled it in her face and she scrunched her nose. "Go gather kindling whilst I skin these scales."

Darkness settled in as rain dripped down beyond the rock shelter. They lazed by the fire, she in her shift and his surcoat, he in his undergarments, and together, beneath his cloak and blanket. She curled against his chest like so many nights before and he wrapped his arm around her, running his fingers along her shoulder. His other sat atop her stomach. She laced her fingers through it and squeezed.

"Gwen?" he began, gazing into the flame.

She looked up.

"When we're married, do you wish for boys or girls?"

She sighed.

"I suppose it's best for men to have boys," she replied. "You will need a namesake and if he should not survive, you would need others. You would have no need for girls, *and* the cost of dowries."

"I would be proud to have a namesake," he smiled, looking down at her. "But I asked *you* what *you* want."

She thought for a moment. She had never actually considered what she wanted. William Feargach had never bothered to ask her. He wanted sons.

"Well, all men wish for sons, do they not?"

"Of course we wish for sons. They're an honor to any man. But I think I should like to have both. 'Twould be sweet to have girls amongst our brood and it's not as though I'm too poor to pay a dowry. Mostly I just hope they're complete and healthy whether they be a boy or a girl."

She looked down.

"I fear I might disappoint you then."

William's arm tightened around her.

"That's not what I meant, Gwenyth," he lifted her chin. "What happened was God's will and nothing more." They stared at one another. "And if having children should risk your life, then I choose naught to have any. The thought of losing you...it's too dreadful to..."

Unable to complete his words, he shook his head.

*He cares what you want, woman, he cares how you feel, cares that you not suffer, he's like the men of Ballymead...*and before she could change her mind, she reached a hand around his neck and kissed him. She strained to reach his lips and climbed onto her knees to face him.

He sat still at first, unsure of how to receive the affection, then both of his hands slid around her waist. His kisses grew stronger until he was sitting forward, bending toward her and bearing down as hard as his impulses wanted. She accepted it, kissing him back with all the passion that he felt for her and more. Her fingers wove into his hair and slid around his shoulders hard enough that he could feel her nails gouging his skin. He welted her lips and lifted her onto his lap so that she faced him.

With his strong caresses sliding up and down her back, his hands became lost in her tresses, bracing the nape of her neck. She ran her fingers over his chest, around his neck, over his shoulders, unable to choose a place to stop. He was stiff between her legs. A sigh escaped her as she began to move instinctively against him, her legs parted around him, and he cinched an arm about her waist to pull her down to meet him.

Cheeks pink with excitement, her lips were so full he thought them berries that might burst and kissed her harder. Harder still, he pulled her down upon him, his other hand now roving across the surcoat slipping off her shoulder to reveal her shift. He moaned and pulled her again, making more friction.

She thought of William Feargach again and tensed mid kiss.

"What is it, Gwen?" he whispered, sweating despite the chill, breathing labored.

She held his face and stared into his eyes. He was grasping her so tightly she would not be able to break free even if she wanted to and yet, she wasn't afraid of him and felt confusion. This had always been a violent act before, though right now she desired it more than she had desired anything else.

"If you choose to stop, I'll do my best to leave you be..." His forehead was pressed to hers as their chests rose and fell and he kissed her cheeks. "I'll never force you to do this, trust in that...you needn't do this to please me...but you *do* please me, very much..."

Her mind made up, she kissed him again. A groan worked its way out of his throat as she rocked against him despite the layers of clothing between them. As she tossed her head back, he grazed his lips across her neck.

"This is a sin, Will," she whispered. "I'm shamed for this and yet I don't wish to stop...my honor..."

"You will have your honor. I won't take it, woman."

"This feeling...I'm shamed..."

"I'll not tell a soul, I swear it."

His fingers took her breasts in his hands, despite his surcoat in the way, which only aroused him more.

She wears my colors, her favor is mine...

He pulled free the surcoat over her head and tossed it aside so that he could hold her breasts more firmly. They were the perfect fit to his palm and it was all he could do to keep from ripping away her shift and leggings as her movements grew faster upon him.

She felt heat within her and it was good. No pain. He pushed and pulled her over his trousers, faster still as he grabbed her buttocks, feeling the muscles of her slender form tensing and releasing. He held her breasts and tugged her hips, guiding her faster and faster.

"God, woman, I'm at your mercy," he breathed.

"I need you. I shall be miserable without you, I shall..."

Her breathing was rapid and she sighed. He grappled to hold her, feeling a surge rising within him like it did when he sinned and pleased himself, yet never had it felt so sweet.

"Don't slow, woman, keep pace—"

"I am, I—" she whispered back.

"You what?"

"I love you."

With a final pull against him, he released his burden and she quivered as she felt her own warmth. She draped her arms around his neck and he fell back against the wall of the shelter, clutching her to his chest as his seed soaked through his tunic and seeped onto her belly.

He was squeezing her so hard she could scarcely breathe. They were damp with sweat, and the blanket was kicked down to his feet.

"You said you love me, Gwen," he panted. "For the first time. Did you mean it?"

She nodded and burrowed against him. He was grinning, and swallowed in efforts to master his breathing.

"You have no idea how that pleases me," he murmured and kissed her head as she clung to him. *No one has ever said they love me.* "You make my pride swell to hear it."

She rolled off into the crook of his arm. He groped for the blanket and pulled it back up as he laid her down and nestled beside her. Their breathing slowed.

"It's never been so..." she began.

"Never been what?"

Why must I think of William Feargach now? she struggled.

She nestled closer and looked up at him, pulling his arm to her belly as her eyes welled with water.

"No, Lady," he panicked and sat up. "Gwenyth, tell me you're all right. I'll never do that again if it makes you weep—"

She placed her finger over his mouth and smiled up at him.

"Now I know a man's love, for the first time," she sniffled. "Loddin's wife spoke of pleasure with a man, but I could never understand until now."

He exhaled and smiled, nestling against her once more.

"I give it freely to you." His eyes began to twinkle. "And since *loving* you is so easy, I'll make sure you're never neglected."

She scoffed and nudged him as he grinned and dried her eyes.

"Careful, kind sir, or you'll get that tongue lashing you fear."

"If it's your tongue doing it," he began. "It might be quite enjoyable."

Her eyes widened like platters and he chuckled, kissing the side of her face and allowing his hand to settle upon her breast. He cupped his palm around it and let his thumb caress it through the linen as he watched her. The fire crackled and cast dancing shadows on her face and neck. They gazed at one another and she rested her hand upon his.

"You're quite lovely, Gwen. I'll be proud to boast you as my wife. Do you...do you think we could do that again?" he murmured.

"You're bad," she giggled. "Not yet even five minutes and—"

"You've given me an appetite, woman, and now I have hunger," he interrupted.

She giggled again and rolled over to face him while he pressed himself against her and moved on top. She reached her long cord of hair around his neck and pulled him close.

"Then you must be satisfied, My Lord," she played. "So long as our clothes stay betwixt us."

"Aye. No matter how much I want to bed you," he whispered. "I promise our garments won't come off until we are married before God and church."

14

Maccus's belly still ached.

"The bastard," he fumed as he lay on his pallet. "The bloody bastard."

He wasn't sure who was more of a bastard. Both Aindreas and William Cadogan were on his list.

"Lord Shea has been had, by His *Christian Grace*, Lord Aindreas de Boscoe... helping that bleedin' knight... beddin' his woman... that *whore*... sending off his seed without his permission... those bastards—"

"What is it now?" grumbled his wife.

"None a'yer business, woman. Tend my supper."

Though he was bitter, he wasn't foolish enough to make an attempt on William Cadogan's life.

I'd have to go to the capital. He will have gotten his sweet Gwenyth back to her father by now and will be back in the protection of Bain's castle...the bastard...had no trouble cutting me down...

He knew well when he was out matched. Sir William would be too difficult. Getting rid of Aindreas and capturing Gwenyth for Shea would be the next best thing.

He roused himself. Grunting, he walked to the chamber pot and squatted. His wife moaned and made a face.

"What?" he complained. "Can't a man shit in peace?"

He took a rag and proceeded to wipe himself, then dropped it in the pot and stood.

"You *shat* louder than a sick mule," she sighed, shaking her head.

"Shut it, woman—"

"You can shut it!" she complained, slopping his stew into a bowl. "All these years...takin' care of an ass an' I don't even get me a child from the deal."

Maccus rolled his eyes.

"You'll make me silence you!"

"I'm not scared of ya's. Been kissin' that fist of yers for years and you still 'aven't silenced me!"

He made a move for her but she lifted the ladle up.

"Keep your distance, man! One finger and I'll poison this 'ere stew!" He frowned at her. "Right after's I club ye silly! An' I would too! Ye knows it good'n well!"

"Nothin' but talk you are...get me my drink, y'old hag," he muttered and waved his hand. "And tend to that chamber pot while yer at it."

"I knew ya's didn't 'ave the bullocks," she grumbled. "Wouldn't have no one to take care of ye and heal y'when ye come home battered..."

It was true. The wound had been well tended since he had arrived home, his wife doctoring him with doses of calendula and insisting he bathe with soap. He had actually listened to a woman's advice and to his surprise it was working.

It had been pure luck that he had crawled away to steal his drink so that his wife wouldn't yell at him for it. Having passed out behind the stable where he had soaked his stomach in an entire skin of whiskeybae to escape the pain, it had been like discovering a treasure to wake to such a conversation as that of the Lady Janis and Aindreas.

Such treachery. It is beneath even me.

He had relished heaving himself into the saddle despite the tenderness to chase after Janis' messenger as he disappeared into the woods that lay beyond the gate. The poor soul had not seen Maccus' bludgeon coming.

'A traitor, you are,' he had said, as the messenger quivered beneath him in his blood.

'Please, Maccus!' he had sputtered. 'You're mistaken! I simply deliver a message from the Lady of Dwyre!'

'You have been relieved of your duty,' Maccus smiled.

The man had not been difficult to finish. Maccus had ended him with a simple slice across the throat.

In the messenger's tunic was her letter. It had been specific about the catapults Aindreas had explained, as well as Shea's technique. She had outlined the number of men so that the Bainick soldiers at the port would know what they were up against. Then there had been another letter, this one roughly the same but more of a report, and he concluded this one was meant for Bain.

This is what happens when women are taught to read and write, he thought. *Turncoats, the lot of'em.*

"Give me that mugwort, woman!" he barked.

"I'll take me time, old man!" she replied, but poured the hot liquid anyway and scurried forth.

For a moment, he spared a thought for his wife and felt shame. The pallet he slept upon was separate. He could not make use of a woman and had always cursed that his equipment had never worked. Now almost forty, she rested as a virgin and there was not a thing he could do about it.

"'Ere," she said, and thrust the foul tea into his hand.

He took a sip.

"Ah! It's bloody boilin'!" he howled and spit it out.

"Of course it is! Just took it out o' the pot! Ye *thick* mule...married me a bloody scholar I did, a brilliant scholar..." she mumbled and tottered off.

"Shut it, or you'll feel the back of me hand!" he fussed, but she ignored him.

He curled beneath the blanket and farted while she tended the fire, and went back to his glorious contemplating.

He had to tell this plan to Lord Shea and inform him that his woman had betrayed him in the worst way. And when Aindreas returned from battle with the rest of the army, he would have the satisfaction of humiliating him, before the Lord of Dwyre slashed his throat.

The coward, raised on Dwyre generosity.

He would prove to Shea that his house was corrupt, and he would have the glory from it.

"Awake..." William was rousing her as her head lolled upon his shoulder. "Awake, love. This is not a sight you'll want to miss."

The days had grown tiresome. She was dust covered, her hair as knotted as a fishing net beneath her veil that despite its sheerness bore a film. William was an equal match. His tunic, ripped from his fray with Dwyre's men and the wolves in the pass, was stained with rings of sweat and dirt. What had been a stubbly beard was now a dense forest of blackness encircling his face.

She opened her eyes and there it was.

"Ballymead..."

Beautiful, glowing Ballymead sprawled over the sun-drenched hills now fallow for the winter. The beehives dotted the slopes and the little hamlet just within the outer walls was bustling. Beyond the clusters of serfs' homes where Mrs. McIntosh lived with her gaggle of grandchildren, all of whom she had delivered before their mother died, the hillsides rose to the proud bastions of the keep beyond the inner battlements. Her father's green banners waved high above, kissing the sky and displaying the golden sun upon the family crest.

She imagined the meadery, its boiled water and honey cooling with her father's blends of spices and berries that wafted out across the entire manor, the storeroom stacked with casks of succulent great mead, racked for at least two years' time for which vassals across the land would travel. She envisioned the pond beyond the keep sprinkled in its floral edges in the summertime, and the woods even farther where she had ridden with her brothers and the squires who had come to be fostered by her father.

It was all there and it took a moment for her to comprehend that it was not a vision. She sat up.

"Oh, sweet Mary, Mother of Iesus...blessed Mary I'm home... oh, Will, I'm home!"

She twisted around and kissed him, throwing her arms about him. He let it come and drank it in, running his hands up and down her sides, for this would be it.

We won't be lovers once we come out of the trees, not anymore. The time has come to give her back.

She lifted his hand to her cheek and curled against the warmth of his chest.

"And it's thanks to you that I'm here in one piece, My Lord."

My Lord...we will be back to formalities soon enough, Gwen, no need to rush it. "It's a fine home and one to be proud of," he smiled. "Like your stories of it."

She twirled back again with happy urgency. He didn't want to take it from her, for it was the radiance in her that he adored, but at that moment, he had to be selfish.

"Gwenyth."

She turned.

"Gwenyth I..." *Don't sputter like a dying man, speak your piece!* "I must dismount and walk you in a proper lady."

She sat still and so did he, unable to remove himself from the saddle.

"I ask...as a favor...I ask for one more of your kisses," he said stiffly, forcing each word out, "so I might be tided over until I'm able to have your hand in an honorable way." He had grown so close to her that he feared being without her would be like living without his right arm. "I don't want to envision the months of betrothal when I might very well be at battle again...I dont want to pine for you yet." *You pine already, man, and neither God nor the stars are fooled.*

"William," she sighed. "I am selfish. I was so excited to see my home and for you to know them—"

He placed his fingers over her lips.

"This look upon your face has been worth seeing. You're not selfish. One more. It's all I ask."

She nodded. Reaching her hands to the sides of his face, he wrapped his arms around her so that they laced through her helpless hair. He pulled her body tightly to him in sadness he was already feeling. A tear trickled down her cheek to her lips.

"You cry. Why?" he asked.

"I am so happy to be home and yet, I shall feel so alone without you," she whispered. He brushed her tear away as her eyes replaced it with another. "I wish to lie beside you in my bed tonight, and wake on the morrow next to you and every day thereafter." She strained to put her lips to his once more. "I feel as if you are already my husband."

He dragged her down from the saddle in his arms, into the grasses where they collapsed together, stomach to stomach.

"I will think of you *every day*, My Lady," he whispered.

Her tears ran down her cheeks and he consumed her, his tongue mingling with hers as he pulled her against him, one last time.

"It's the Lady Gwenyth!" the guards called. "She has returned!"

"Lady! Welcome home!" the foot soldiers exclaimed as they opened the gates.

"You are well!" a young one called down from the wall above.

"I am, Mathew!" she answered. "And how goes your fair bride?"

He beamed and clutched his spear as they passed. "Marta graces me with a babe, My Lady! Due in a moon's time!"

Gwenyth smiled. "Blessed news!"

"Your father just returned from court less than a fortnight ago! And your brother Loddin has just ridden in this morn! He was granted leave of duty to come home! The Ballymead men are all together! They will be overjoyed!"

William was surprised at the display of companionship between guards and mistress.

"Thank you, Knight of Bain, for returning the sun to Ballymead's banners!"

"'Twas my honor to do so!" William waved back.

The guard smiled a sly grin.

"And My Lady! He is indeed a fine looking one even if he is in need of a bath! I saw you swooning in his arms on the hillside and I've a mind to tell your father! What other swooning have you done?"

There now, that's the talk of soldiers, William grinned.

"Mathew Whitcroft!" she exclaimed as the guards chuckled. "My father knows better than to believe a fox in a hen's clothing! Do not think he was blinded to your wiles, *laddie!* You're still the silly lad whose pony threw you in the trough and I've a mind to chase you down as I did when I was a girl!" she lobbed back. "And you know that I did!"

The guards belted laughter beneath their green and gold surcoats.

"Whipped by the mistress he was, time and again!"

"Eh, he liked it," another chuckled.

William laughed as he watched her beam a superior smile, the greetings continuing. They made their way through the outer pastures and Mrs. McIntosh, all a flutter, ran up to the knight and planted a kiss square on his lips.

"You've returned her, dark knight! Oh, you're home, My Lady!" she clasped her thick hands together and smiled. "Praise be to God you are safe!"

They rode further up the slope, past crofts and thatched huts, past the guards' cottages. Breads were baking and children could be heard.

"Listen," Gwenyth smiled.

A song was rising as they neared a hut.

"...Sir William the Brave, to knighthood from knave, champion of kings and savior of slaves. His honor is pure, his sword is true, but ne'er a husband will he be to you..."

William shook his head and scuffed his boot into the dirt, pleasantly embarrassed.

"...with aim like the elfin, his spears were slung, emeralds for eyes, and battles he won. But shed all your tears on the cloth of your dowry, a lone knight of Bain, he always will be. Sir William the Brave to knighthood from knave..."

"You're a handsome legend in these far off parts, My Lord," she smiled shrewdly as they came around the hut. "I was but one and ten when I learned that song around the spindle."

"One and ten," he thought. "That was when I was just one less than twenty. That's the year I earned my rank in the battle against King Fernando. You're young, Gwen."

The song continued as they came into view.

"And they're younger still, with images of you that are no doubt as grand as mine were."

"Then they shall be sorely disappointed when they see that I'm a filthy beast with the beard of a magus."

A group of older girls, sitting in a circle around a basket of raw wool that they combed and cleaned, looked up. Their song stopped and they fell into fits of giggles.

"My Ladies," he bowed deeply, his lions about his neck twinkling sunlight. "You sing my praises too kindly!"

The girls noticed the Bainick shield and all but died of embarrassment.

"Lady Gwenyth! You're back!" one of them called, motioning to her.

With a scandalous display of chivalry, William let a smile dance on his lips. He reached up to Gwenyth and lifted her like a feather from the saddle. Then he bowed a courtly bow and knelt, kissing her hand.

"My *Lovely* Lady."

She snorted with laughter. "You're *terrible*, My Lord."

"Terrible? That is not. I'll show you terrible!" he whispered with a wink.

She shook her head and politely curtsied to him, then walked to the girl who cupped her hand to Gwenyth's ear.

"Is that really Sir William the Brave?"

"Indeed it is," Gwenyth laughed.

The girl turned red and threw her hand over her mouth.

"It's him!" she whispered to the others. "It really is him!"

The girls fell into giggles again.

"May I have your acquaintance?" William stepped forth and took the girl's hand.

She trembled and her face turned so red, Gwenyth thought she was going to cry. "Beth."

"The fair *Lady* Bethany," William bowed. "What a radiant and pure beauty you are. I am honored to have a hand such as this delicate rose to kiss." He bowed deeply and planted a kiss on her fingers.

Gwenyth fell into a fit of laughter. The girls were in hysterics and Beth wrenched her hand away as she blushed, smiled, giggled, and teared up all at the same time. Her friends rescued her and dragged her away, and they scrambled off to their homes.

"Oh *humble* knight!" Gwenyth teased. "Don't you know that the only thing that spreads faster than a forest fire is girls' gossip around the spinning?"

"Was that terrible enough, My Lady?"

"Aye," she smirked.

The word was spreading as she had predicted. People

scampered through the fields talking and gesturing as others ran on to continue the telling. The main portcullis was already being raised for their arrival and the scrambling in the bailey was that of people who had heard glad tidings.

"Sister!" a deep voice boomed.

Loddin, her oldest brother who was washing his own traveling grime at the well, dropped his rag. His chest was broad and bare and he wore nothing save his undergarments, yet she leapt from the horse before William could offer her a hand. Her brother ran to her and swept her into the air. In a whirlwind of dust, three more grown men, all the spitting image of one another with deep, brown eyes and dusty blonde hair swarmed her, nearly toppling her to the ground while the ladies of the home gathered round and the blacksmith quit pumping his fire.

"I've missed you so!" she cried. "I thought I would never see my beloved family again!"

"You're safe, wee sister!" George wept into her hair. "But these scars, what happened?"

"Wolves attacked us!"

"Wolves?"

"Aye, but we fought them off!"

"Butterfly."

The door to the great hall opened. An older man, grey and crippled yet broad and lean stood in it. Beside him was her oldest brother's wife holding her brother Hershel's son.

The child squirmed free from her grip and bumbled down the stairs.

"Father..." She looked up and her brothers parted from her. "*Oh,* Father," she wept and ran up the stairs to fall at his feet.

She grasped his hand and kissed it over and over again. He knelt down, placing a gentle palm on her head.

"My daughter," he whispered, then scooped her into his arms and cried. "My sweet daughter! Praise be to God, he blesses this house today!"

He held her for some moments and William remained dutifully quiet.

"Sir? Lions...lions..."

"Who might you be, lad?" William looked down to see little Hershel tugging on his surcoat.

He knelt and the toddler reached his stubby fingers for William's chain.

"Wawr!"

William laughed, scooping him into his arm.

"That's quite a roar."

"You're a lion knight," the boy said and took hold of the chain.

"That I am," William smiled. "Do you fancy lions?"

The boy nodded.

"Here then, will you wear these for me? They're heavy and I'm tired."

The boy's cheeks dimpled. William lifted it from his neck and draped it around little Hershel's, ruffling his hair and patting him on the rear to send him scampering.

"Look, Papa! Look!" the child exclaimed, tripping upon the chain.

Finally the brothers turned.

"Hershel, give those back," his father scolded as he swung his offspring into his arm.

"'Tis of little consequence, man. I'm fond of children," William interrupted. "He may play with them."

A young squire raced to him and took Titan's reins.

"Don't worry, sir knight," the adolescent assured in his most adult voice. "We have sweet oats and hay for your steed, and he will get the finest grooming for his reward."

"I thank you, man." William inclined his head and presented the boy with a coin who did his best not to become giddy.

Young Loddin laughed.

"That's Michael, my squire. He's determined to show his worth to a Bainick knight. I would recognize you anywhere. You grace our house, Sir Cadogan," he said as he clasped wrists, knight to knight. "I fought amongst your conscripts in the war against King Fernando, and I know you do all your orders proud."

"I'm honored that one of Ballymead's bravest was amongst my men."

"You'll get your chain back," Hershel added, also clasping wrists. "As soon as my son falls asleep I shall retrieve it. It's the only time to reclaim what he has stolen."

"Father," Gwenyth began. "Come meet Sir William Cadogan, my rescuer and sworn protector," she beamed with swollen eyes as she led her limping father down the steps.

"Sworn protector?"

Loddin looked down at his daughter who watched the knight with stars in her eyes, and then at the knight who returned the gaze as he clasped wrists.

"You're the welcome guest of honor in the House of Loddin. Young Michael, my son's squire, will assist you for your stay. He's only two and ten but a hard worker and I'm certain you'll be happy with his service. Please. Come and unload your weight from your feet," he grinned. "For he must be tired, Butterfly, would you not agree? Surely he walked the entire way."

"Father!"

Her brothers began laughing at her. It was now William's turn to refrain from jesting. He fell down on his knee and bowed his head.

"I esteem your daughter, sir. I swear on the bible of King Bain that she has been handled with care—"

"Rise up, man," Loddin cuffed his head playfully. William raised his head to see all of his children humored and Gwenyth giggling. "You must lighten your heart if you're to fare well here during your rest. If the lovesick poetry that spills forth from the lips of Ballymead's maidens has any truth, I trust the fabled knight has acted with utmost honor."

"Where's William?" she asked.

"He's inside. Come, all of you!" He turned to the yard. "We celebrate tonight! Tap a cask of ale! All of you with me and the sons of Ballymead!"

The serfs and servants cheered, and the women scrambled away with the new burden of preparing food. They entered the great hall, the green shield with the sun hanging over the hearth flanked by the Ballymead banner and the banner of King Bain's black lion. William was resting at the board when she entered.

"Sister," he rose. "Come, so that I might see you."

"William!" she ran to him and he held her, then patted her face and arms.

"You feel scrawny, Sister, like a bare bone on a winter's night. What have you fed her, sir knight?" he jested. "Twigs?"

He held her face and smiled.

"William?" she asked. His eyes weren't focusing. "Dear brother?" She tipped her head but his eyes didn't follow. Her face dropped. "Oh no...no, William, it cannot be..."

"Aye, I'm blind, Gwenyth, and as crippled as a legless dog, but I can see your sunshine hair despite it all."

He kicked out a leg fastened to a wooden peg beneath the knee. Her hands covered her mouth.

"How? What happened to you?"

"Dwyre men, Sister. As you know, Father and I came for you and they turned us away. But we came back for you again, with soldiers, only to find they'd thrown you out like a scrap. But I would gladly have given the other leg and the whole of me if it had meant my baby sister would be delivered."

She stood petrified, knowing her eyes leaked again. The joy of her homecoming vanished like a water droplet on a hot coal. She looked at her father and brothers, all silent and suddenly grave, then at Sir William who's fists were clenched so tightly his knuckles were white.

"Don't weep for me, Sister. Shea Feargach isn't worthy of your sweet tears, and you know me, I am as mulish as an ass and would rather die than let him claim my dignity."

"But Brother—"

"No!"

He grasped her and shook her, and the fear she had all but forgotten returned with a dreaded flinch. No one spoke.

"You won't weep for me, Gwen! Say you won't!"

"I won't, Brother, please, I won't," she whispered, trembling, her eyes pinched tight. "Forgive me for disobeying, please forgive—"

"Unhand her!" Sir William growled.

He stormed forward and wrenched Gwenyth from her brother's grip. She fell against him, cinching her arms around him as he returned her embrace.

"You're well, Gwen," he murmured and kissed the side of her head. "Calm yourself, woman, this is your family. No one will harm you here."

"Sister," William croaked, groping outward. "Gwenyth, I didn't mean to frighten you."

She recoiled more firmly against Sir William who gripped her and smoothed her hair back from her face.

"Sir William?" Loddin began, eyeing him with suspicion. "You seem very free with my daughter."

William suddenly realized where he was and tried to let her go.

"I'm sorry, Lord Lodd—"

"No, Will!" she exclaimed. "Please don't let go of me!"

They all stared and he felt helpless.

"'Tis all right, woman. You're safe." He tried once more to pry loose her grip but she refused to let go.

"Butterfly, go with Mary, wash and rest. Your chamber awaits your return," Loddin intervened and pulled her away.

She fled ahead of her brother's wife, up the stairs in stark silence.

"Sir William, you will do the same. And then if you would be so kind as to indulge an old man, will you join me at the stable to talk horses?"

His eyes were serious and conveyed that 'horses' was not what he had in mind.

William bowed his courtly bow. "Of course, My Lord."

15

He shaved his face smooth and washed the grime from his body as the women of Ballymead huddled in the shadows to catch a glimpse of the famed young knight standing shirtless before a bucket. After heavenly sleep on a soft pallet, warm, fresh bread and fish, he walked in a crisp, new tunic to the stables where he found Titan, clean, watered, rubbed down and nuzzling a chestnut mare with a star in the shape of a crescent between her eyes. He grunted contently as his master patted him, but remained still.

"Your stallion has found Gwenyth's beloved Luna," Loddin said as he approached.

William fell upon his knee.

"My Lord, I must apologize to you. I meant nothing by...it was bold of me to interfere...what I mean to say is that I wasn't taking liberties...*damn*," he muttered. "I promise Gwen was respected in my charge—"

"Gwen?"

William's face burned. "'Tis just my way of, well, it's just an affectionate name, sir, and not in that way..."

Loddin grinned.

"Rise up, lad," he chuckled, offering his wrist. "I've spoken to her and know you meant well. She thinks the world of you."

Titan grunted again and William stood, giving him another pat, inspecting him to make sure the squire hadn't missed any care.

"Michael has done a fine job, sir. Titan is in great condition."

"And you've a fine beast here. It's good that there is a stall betwixt these two, for she is still in season," Loddin remarked.

"She is safe, sir. My warhorse is likely too tired to act a man," William added, earning a laugh from Loddin.

"He's an interesting mix of breeds. Certainly my daughter informed you all about his parentage?"

William laughed.

"Good lass, I taught her well. You know, she brought Luna into the world, stayed with her mother and helped turn her as a foal when she wouldn't come out. She was only one year past ten. My, how she *does* love horses. I trust she has all but stolen yours from you?"

"That she has," William grinned. "And he would gladly follow her, I believe."

Loddin ran his hand through his silvery hair and grew serious.

"Will you ride with me, lad?" he asked.

They mounted two palfreys and rode out of the bailey to the pasturelands behind the keep.

"My father was the vassal of this land, William, all that you see, and his father before him under Dwyre rule. He taught that to make it wholesome, all those who worked it had to know they were important whether they be my sons or my servants and more importantly, that they were protected. My children knew all the serfs, played with their children, tended their dying and if you're from court, you will know that's unheard of.

"I give them hunting rights twice a season, allow them to fish the river on Sundays when mass is through. Gwenyth's job was to take a loaf of bread each morn to those huts with children or mothers with child. When food is plenty for me, it's plenty for all those who live and work here, and when it is scarce, we all go hungry together. But this land is generous, and that hasn't happened often. They pay their fealty and in return, I make sure they live plentifully. It's not huge in the way of fiefs, but I'm proud that I'm only liege to the High King and not another lord."

They rode on.

"It gave me the clout I needed to take my plea before him after Dwyre's men took my son's leg and his sight. We had come for her once before, my lad William and I, with no luck, so we returned once again and demanded Gwenyth back at their main gates but she had already disappeared...quicklime." He clenched his reins and gritted his teeth. "They threw quicklime in his face and lacerated his leg with their sword, forty of them chasing us and our ten soldiers away. There were too many and by the time we reached a safe distance, the damage had been done and his eyes couldn't be helped. That boy loves his sister. He cared not for his leg and instead of crying for his eyes that night, he cried for her. *What have they done to my sister?* That's what he said. *What have they done to my Gwen?*"

The afternoon light was fading and golden warmth was cast low across the slopes.

"Alis volat propriis..." Loddin sighed to himself. "You are versed?"

"I have been schooled, Lord Loddin."

"Her mother used to scold her with that phrase. '*She soars with her own wings.*' Up until her marriage, my Gwenyth ran free, without a veil and sometimes in my squires' trousers, chasing animals or riding her pony." He laughed and William smiled at that. "*Pure scandal*, my wife always said. The only thing to tell you she was a girl was that long hair. Oh, man, she was a beautiful child. I admit my wife was right and I was too soft for she was my only lass. I should have been strict. For now, she has tasted the bitterest side of mankind and she will forever be changed. Watching her cower beneath her brother saddens me. Two years ago she would have told him to eat worms or stomped his foot in. Though two years ago he *never* would have done that. His pride is ruined. I'm ashamed I fed her to Dwyre's wolves."

"You couldn't have known, sir—"

"I damn well should have. I was blind, lad. Blind as my William is now. The Feargachs are proud warriors, former rulers, and it made sense as a good match and alliance. William Feargach yearned for her and all she saw was a handsome man of strength who claimed to want her, when all he wanted was a fair woman to warm his bed. I gave into that look of excitement in her eyes and arranged the betrothal but I should have refused, and so now," he breathed long and hard, "I *must* know everything that has passed. Spare the courtly civility of your training and tell me plainly, all you know of her suffering."

William took a deep breath and did so. He told of her abandonment, of the bruises and her tears and the crying on the highroad when she thought he would strike her down. He told of the ill-fated pregnancy and of the attack by Aindreas and his men who sought to retrieve her because she had birthed a son. He told of the wolves and all that she had cried out when it was done. By the time he had finished, Loddin had dismounted and was leaning on a fence, silent as the grave and mouthing the Pater Noster as tears streamed down his cheeks.

"...et ne nos inducas in tentationem, sed libera nos a malo...Pater Noster, qui es in caelis, sanctificetur nomen tuum...she bore me a grandson...*blessed* lass..."

William bowed his head, his own throat tight. He then fell to his knees in the spirit of honesty and confessed to how he had comforted her and how he had rejoiced in acting her husband though wisely he spared the details of their trysts.

"I don't live up to the praises sung of me, sir," he croaked, "for I kissed her sweetly at that hamlet and many times thereafter. I allowed myself to tell her of how I should be proud to be her man if she be my wife. And I did so without the consent of her father."

He shook his head.

"I always vowed never to take a woman. But she...I don't know how she did it. Your daughter has laid claim on me, sir, and I allowed it to happen, not only that, but I yearned for it and I have fallen so deeply in love I'm drowning in it. Therefore I'm duty bound by what little honor I retain to be punished, sir, and will withstand any sanction you declare."

He waited for a lashing, a punch, something, but it never came. Loddin turned to look down at him. He didn't ask him to rise. After a time, William looked up to see Loddin staring at him.

"You retrieved her from hell, William. To know that she was braving it alone...I'll always be grateful you were there to lift her to her feet. Perhaps you took some *bold* liberties," he flashed his eyes with a sternness to say he should feel ashamed, "but I don't believe you did so with the intentions of most men."

Loddin stared into the distance, over the beehives that produced the honey for his trade.

"As for your love for her," he gestured at him. "Rise up, man. Many have claimed to love her. She was cursed with the beauty of her mother, the spirit of a hawk and the intellect of a scholar. I turned away many men, William, many men, all of them claiming to be in love with her. But she never regarded any of them with as much trust as she regards you. You protected her well."

Loddin looked more closely. William knew he was about to be told to let her go and the pain on his face showed it.

"You grieve for my Gwenyth?"

He turned his face to stone and leaned onto the fencing, shaking his head. "I must be weak. She began to smile, spoke in such a way as if a candle had begun to burn in her and melt away her fear. To see that fear return today is painful...I overreacted with your son, sir, for I've sworn myself her protector and I take that declaration seriously."

Loddin nodded. "Let us talk business, lad. Is it your wish to marry her, even though she's no longer a virgin?"

William practically swallowed his tongue. "Em, I, I had not intended on asking you like this, but yes, I would."

"And you, the First Knight in our king's army wishes your first woman to be a widow with not even a virgin womb?"

"I would be a liar, sir, if I said that I didn't find her body beautiful. But I've come to know her on a level of companionship, fought alongside her, lived alongside her. It's true you learn of a man's character when you serve in battle with them, same with her. She's stronger than she knows. And forgive me, Lord Loddin, for I risk sounding vulgar, but that's more important to me than a maidenhead. I should like my woman to be my companion and more, not just a broodmare to birth my children. She gave her virginity with wifely honor. It's not as though I seek a beautiful whore."

Loddin nodded, his eyes furrowed in concentration on every word William spoke. William exhaled and propped a foot up on the fence.

"I feel old sometimes, hardened from battle, scarred as though my body is a quintain. I've known violence my entire life, sir. The security of our king and his kingdom rests upon my judgment and I don't take the task lightly. But she reminds me I am only a man of five and twenty and that I haven't lived a long life yet. The talks we had at campfire, the jesting, the rides on my warhorse..." he laughed. "If I didn't know better, my Titan mistook himself as her protector for I had to fight him back several times." Now Loddin laughed. "And there were times, sir, when I felt certain God sent her to *me* instead, as if he knew I needed her. I didn't want to relinquish her today, I'll be honest, and held her close to me for some time outside your gates before resigning myself to continue. If it cannot be her that I wed, it shall not be any woman."

Loddin nodded, then smiled, then thought some more.

"Come, fabled Knight of Bain." He reached out and patted his shoulder like a son. "You're the guest of honor. I'm in a difficult spot, for I can see that your feelings are very true. Understand, lad, that I cannot let her marry again—"

"Please, My Lord." William's eyes flashed desperately at him. "I beg you reconsider, for I'm quite wealthy and have private quarters in the castle and she would have a fine and rich life with me and if you refuse, Gwen and I will both be miserable—"

"*At least*, not so soon," Loddin finished as his mouth twisted into a smile. "Give her time to heal, not *just* her spirit, but her body too. She has only just birthed my grandson and has not even been churched yet. Right now, it's all rainbows, for you have lived up to the poets' verses by rescuing her. Be patient, lad, and if this is still what you both want in a year's time, I shall invite your betrothal contract and she can begin embroidering her dowry linens for you, for I believe I would enjoy having you as a son and she will be eight and ten soon with need of having her future secured. Is that agreeable to you? But that must be my sanction," he grinned. "If you can bear it."

"You're as gracious a father as she has expressed, sir," William mumbled as they walked back to the horses. *A whole entire year before I can even be betrothed...*

"Be advised, William, she loathes needlework. Your dowry linens will be little better than a peasant's table cloth."

This invited laughter from both.

"If she gave Luna to Titan, I believe I could overlook it."

"Know this, lad." Loddin paused as his voice quieted. "I will always be grateful you were there. Always."

He nodded and patted William's shoulder and William bowed his head. They mounted and rode back in the dusk. Torches had lit the keep and even from afar they could hear the preparations for dinner.

"Tell me, Sir William, for we've all been curious. The king didn't say who he would send to find my daughter, so it's rather a surprise to see you here today. Why did he choose you? Would it not make sense to have you, his prized knight, ready to quell the rebellion to the east?"

'Rise and approach me, Sir William. I'm charging you with a special task, and only you can accomplish it.' He stood and walked across the council chamber to the carved throne of King Bain beneath his banners. 'You are aware of our problems with the east?'

'Aye, My Lord King, and I'm ready to carry arms and lead men to quell the sedition.'

'I know you are, but this isn't that kind of task.'

The king himself poured the wine and handed him a goblet.

'You may leave,' he waved at his guards and pages. They hesitated. 'Yes, yes, exit this room.'

They gathered robes, parchments and regalia, and then moved into the hall while the door was sealed. Charles Murron Bain, the High King, stood.

'Ballymead is in the farthest reaches of the highlands.'

'Yes, My King, I know it.'

''Tis remote, and should the easterners take the mountains, it will be cut off from Bain. What do you know of the Loddin Family?'

'I regret I know only of mead, sir.'

The king chuckled. 'As does every man. Never a fighter was Loddin. He's too soft, always wanted to run his father's farms. When we were boys, he was fostered here in the city and we learned Latin together, did you know?'

William shook his head. 'Where is this leading, Your Majesty?'

'Loddin has but one daughter. She was married into Dwyre. Loddin complains that the Dwyre family has treated her unfairly and that now she has disappeared. Loddin swears her husband is dead and that she should be returned home as a widow, or in the event she is dead, for burial.'

The king paced away, his fur-trimmed robe clasped with gold lions trailing behind him.

'I'm not certain if any of this is true, but rumors I've been getting, rumors of a most unusual nature. So far, they've helped Bain greatly. I need Loddin's fief and I value his fealty, both in taxes and in friendship. Therefore, I'm sending you to find this girl and return her to her father.'

'Am I to understand, My King, that you wish me, in a time of impending war, to take leave of my post and hunt down a woman? Have you no mercenaries to do the job?'

'Look, man, I know your thoughts on women. Christ knows you've turned down many a bride and I'm tired of supplying betrothal contracts that disappoint the maidens when you refuse. When you came here as a squire, I could see you were a fighter. You've worked your way up the ranks to become the highest leading man of my military, my First Knight, and only aged five and twenty. Perhaps it's because you're afraid of women. Perhaps it's because of Andrew Cadogan for bloodying you *enough that you feel no pain now. Do you know why a third son of a low-ranking vassal was sent here as a page boy?'*

William didn't like where this was going, but the king looked as though he was walking to a confessional to unburden a taxed mind.

'Your mother pleaded for it. I might be blonde, and you dark—' He cut himself short, and William wasn't certain he had heard him. *'I'm willing to trust an instinct on this, William. You not only have the keenness to find her, but the stealth to retrieve her, and the duty to protect her."*

"And if she is dead? Or missing? Then it has been nothing but a waste of time."

"I think you'll find her. Alive. After that, you must return to Bain and by that time, I should have news of the Eastern Front. If this is something our border troops cannot handle, you may count that I'll send my most cunning knight with all his power to stamp out the fire before it becomes a blaze.'

'But, My Lord King—'

'You won't challenge me, Sir William. I have given you an order. You leave in the morning. Alone.'

"I cannot answer that, sir," William stated. "In private council, which isn't common, he informed me of the quest. There were few clues to go from, but he told me to scour well the Northeast Pass and do my best not to be seen by easterners. I was surprised by the order, but he said his word was my command and not to argue it."

"That *is* interesting," Loddin said, and that was all.

16

Aindreas sat atop his mount. Shea had twisted his mouth into a smile and though the sky was as dark as weathered stones, he could see the pleasure in his lord's eyes. Blood had stained his hauberk, his cloak hung ripped and cached with the excrements of battle and yet Shea loved it.

"Infinitus est numerus stultorum," Shea remarked. "The number of fools is infinite. That, men, is what you do to pussycats that wish to conquer werewolves!"

Not quite the scholar My atheist Lord, In inceptum finis est. The way you begin is how you end, Aindreas thought while Shea's men laughed.

They sat on the ridge overlooking the Bainick fortress on the river, a magnificent bonfire that lapped at the starless sky. Hundreds of commoners as well as Bainick lions lay scattered across the plain below while his men scavenged for what spoils they desired. Men, soldiers, women, children. None were spared.

Shea nodded.

"Onward, men! We've *soiled* the meadow and must tidy up! For we haven't any womenfolk left to do it!"

They descended to the river plain.

Her message didn't get through in time, Aindreas thought. *There will be no stopping now the floodgates Shea has opened.*

"When news reaches the capital, My Lord, and we know it will for they are certain to have dispatched riders at the onset of the siege, there's no telling what might occur," Aindreas remarked. *And if Sir William Cadogan has pulled his head out of his heart, the consequences will surely descend upon us like Moses releasing the sea.*

"Don't spoil the fun. We've had a great victory. Perhaps now that king will realize we're not in this for amusement," Shea said as his horse trod around a corpse.

He shuddered.

"Weak stomach, man? You fought so well. Not even my older son had a mind as cunning as yours," Shea laughed.

They dismounted. The wooden lintels supporting the fort's gates crashed in with a spray of sparks. Shea walked to a dying Bainick soldier and with a smile, bent down and slashed his throat, then spat on him. He took his daggers and retrieved the sword, handing them to a foot soldier who added them to a cart of plundered goods being wheeled behind them as the stench of blood rose around them.

"The port is ours and so is Faulk to the north of us. The entire eastern border to the river has been taken again," Shea continued, having rampaged in and overthrown it all while slitting Sir Iain's throat just as he had threatened.

"The river is now in Dwyre control. My metals trade is freed. Weapons'll no longer be a scarcity. We keep these spoils and barter the next shipment to come through. I must put the smiths back to work soon." Shea slapped his back. "Now. What news from Dwyre?" he asked, grinning.

He reached down and stripped off the red and black surcoat of a Bainick body, letting its head thump back to the earth while folding the garment as a war spoil.

"None new, My Lord, except that Maccus lives after all."

Shea plunked another dagger into the wagon and turned.

"Does he now? How did you overlook this, Aindreas?"

This could not be avoided, man, you knew that. He had prepared for the question.

"When I found him, he neither moved nor could I feel his heart. 'Twould be safe to assume that the knight, who made such a mess of Collins and Keegan had made sure to slay Maccus as well." He looked down at the intestines of another strewn like links of sausages and curled his nose. "And since I know how you and Maccus both value my Christian faith, I saw it excusable to leave him where he lay."

Shea caught the sarcasm and snorted. They came upon a young girl sprawled upon the grass and looked down.

"I cannot help but think it a pity," Aindreas murmured.

"A pity she was on the wrong side," Shea remarked. "Pretty face. Too bad she's dead. Much sweeter when their lips work. Collect the remaining weapons, men!" he turned to the train of soldiers in processional behind him like ladies in waiting. "Away, and get them all! I've brought wine and ale as your reward!"

Shea's men cheered and got to work and the two of them continued on together.

"I have a spy, Aindreas," Shea muttered. "I have a spy and I cannot find him, but he's here...he's here." He pulled a sword from one of his own and wiped the blood with his cloak.

"A spy? I didn't know there was a single man at Dwyre with enough faith in his bollocks to dissent you."

"Sir Iain failed one too many times for it to be bad luck and these dead lions you see before us took back this port too easily. The reason I see for our victory tonight is that *this* time, my plans did not get here before I did." He turned to look at Aindreas. "You can count that I will rout him out, then quarter him and send the pieces to the king. But I need your eyes and ears open. I'm changing my plans. I am sending you out, Aindreas."

"My Lord?" Aindreas looked confused.

"You are to be a sleuth for me. You have the manners of a Bainick gentleman, seeing you're kin to my inland ties. You fight a good fight, but your brain is your weapon. I have conscripts coming in from the north, other vassals who were turned into Bainick whores along with my uncle. They're sick of paying fealty that contradicts their senses. Bain's capital is far from here. They've spread outward like the Romans and we've let them treat us as the Gauls. My father's king was his brother, not this fair maid of a man, nor was it Bain's father. He was seated in the east at Dwyre when it was our capital..."

Aindreas stifled a yawn and let his mind wander. Whenever Shea needed affirmation for his quest to reclaim the eastern empire, he recited the history lesson like a soliloquy.

"...and therefore I'm going to take control of the Northeast Pass, on my own with my men, and cut Bain off from the highlands. That man over there," he pointed, "is being promoted to Sir Iain's place and he will hold this port with five hundred men to ensure my trade stays open. You will go to court and learn how this spy is getting through, and you would do well to learn all there is about William Cadogan," he shook his finger and laughed. "I haven't forgotten about that upstart. And Maccus, when he is healed, will go retrieve the fair

Lady Gwenyth from her marble towers." Now he grinned. "Since I'm not a Christian, I shall be granted the rights of a husband and if Cadogan is lovesick for her like you say, he won't be able to fight both his battle of duty and battle of the heart at the same time. *And* if he's Bainick, he won't want her if she's spoiled."

"What about the Lady Janis?"

"What about her?" Shea shrugged.

"Do you not care for her?"

"My women are none of your concern, man. Maccus will go to Ballymead and get Gwenyth. It will be you who gives him his instructions."

"But do you think this necessary? Why not just take another wife? Or a mistress? Perhaps she'll be able to birth you sons."

Shea turned to look at him.

"Just how soft on Gwenyth were you, man?"

"She's only a woman, sir," Aindreas shrugged. "I don't see the point in all this effort for one when there are many others."

"Only a woman?"

Why must he press on? Aindreas huffed. "I will admit, as far as women go, My Lord, she was a fine one but she did not fit at Dwyre. Her father encouraged her disobedience her whole life, something your son struggled with for he couldn't get her under control. It might be best to let her go."

"Let her go? I didn't ask for your advice," Shea fumed.

Aindreas bowed his head in concession.

"She killed my grandson and for that she'll be punished. So she will give me something better than a grandson. A son." Looking down, he cracked in the jaw of a quivering Bainick soldier with his boot.

17

"In nomine Patris, et Filii, et Spiritus Sancti. Amen."

William let the body of Iesus Christus soak on his tongue, mingling with his blood as he knelt beneath the crucifix in St. Andrew's Chapel. The priest delivered the Eucharist and moved on, and the chapel emptied. Yet he remained. His head hung over his clasped hands. The votives wavered along the walls of icons of the blessed virgin and the silence consumed him.

"Mary Mother, harden my armor so I might endure without her..."

Only two weeks without her and it felt like a lifetime of exile. In his chamber at night, he had throbbed for her like a young squire at the slightest thought without control enough to stop it. He imagined her nestled against him, fitting into the bend of his lap like a hand within a gauntlet, stroking that silky hair as she slept.

He could feel her fingers interlocking with his while she dreamed, a silent plea to never let go. He could feel her legs around him as he pleased her while her hands gripped his shoulders, back, rear. He could hear her whispering that she loved him.

He imagined her caressing the scar beneath his eye. Of all his many scars, some which had been near fatal, she chose that one, as if she understood the pain from that one wound and wished to take it from him, as if she wished for no one to feel what she had suffered. For the first time in his life, he had gotten so drunk he considered taking one of the tavern wenches to bed just to ease the burden but had wisely been dissuaded by what little intellect had not been poisoned by the ale.

You are a clever man, Loddin, for this is sanction indeed.

The look on her face had been gut-wrenching as she stood

alone outside of Ballymead, hands behind her back like a stoic priestess. She, in a green gown with gold embellishments to match her river of hair, had flowed in the breeze like the banner of her home behind her.

She had begged her father to let her come, so she could remain at his side and become his wife but of course, Loddin had been too wise to give in to her whims. Seeing what had happened with the first William he had sent her with, he was in no hurry to try it again.

And of course, he would not have dared kiss her again. He had not even touched her skin since they arrived at Ballymead. And it had been by far the most difficult thing he had ever done, bowing to her beneath the eyes of Ballymead's men before mounting Titan and turning the reins to return to the capital. The moment he left the bailey she took to flight, running down the hillside as he quickened his pace to try and bounce out the burning in his heart. Now the uprising. He hadn't even had time to rest from his travels, but left in just one more day to rouse the sleeping lion of Bain's fury and lead it to the east.

That man Aindreas was right. I should not have let him live. I should have skewered him as well.

The king had not forced a meeting on him when he arrived, but now that he had slept and washed, he was on his way to the High Council Hall to be briefed, or to brief the king, which one he was not sure.

"Blessed Mary...virgin mother of Iesus Christus give me strength to push her from my mind so I may focus on the task at hand...so I may root out the evil that led me to her arms...I beg you harden my heart like it once was and calm my mind..."

"I've never seen you pray so hard," the soft words of Father Kearney met him.

He looked up, eyes weary and broad shoulders hunched. His childhood tutor and the only other soul who knew of Andrew Cadogan's strap approached him. He was now the priest of the castle and stood before Sir William in his bleached alb and proper vestments.

"You used to laugh at prayer."

"I need it now, Father, like a fish needs water," he croaked.

"I would argue that you always needed prayer, William, and God has finally found a way to make you see that."

He walked around the altar and strolled into the sanctuary.

"Will you walk with me in the garden and take a moment of peace before your leave?"

William obliged and lifted himself from the kneeling pad. He followed him through the screen into the narthex and out the side doors. The sun was not out, but the foliage rising along the walls was orange and red, and birds were flitting merrily about their business. He could smell the herbs in the patch and noticed the monks in their humble cassocks against the farthest wall, weeding. Neither of them spoke.

The little priest was aging now and had always been of short stature compared to William who had sprouted taller than him by the age of three and ten. Father Kearney had always teased that he would become a giant like King Bain himself. It turned out, he was right.

"So tell, me," he finally began. "What adventure have you come back from? Was evil slain as is your gift?"

William didn't answer right away and averted his gaze as they walked.

"I would say wounds have reopened, Father, that never really healed."

"A way with words. Speaks little serious, but when he speaks..." Father Kearney smiled as he shook his finger at him. "You've always had the brain of a scholar, William, and had it not been for your physical strength and desire to wield it, I believe I could have pulled you in. What kind of battle has returned Bain's champion bruised of heart?"

William laughed for the first time, a wry huff with a smile.

"A woman."

"Ahhh!" the priest knocked William's shoulder and sat on a bench. "A maiden has finally warmed the heart of our celibate knight."

"She's no longer a maiden."

"Have you dishonored a woman, lad?" Father Kearney was suddenly severe.

"No," he laughed again, scuffing his foot like a boy fessing up to a crime. "No, that was her husband's doing."

"So you cuckold another man and make his wife your whore?"

"Father!" William chastised. "You're blunt."

"I don't wish to play your guessing games, that's all. So you

141

have done this?"

"No, Father, I have abstained."

Again silence fell between them until finally it bubbled out.

"He beat her, raped her like a whore, turned her into a scared doe who falls to her knees at the slightest word for fear she shall feel the wrath from it. I delivered that brute's seed after his family dumped her full of child in the wilderness and I, *hardly* a priest," he snorted, "gave the infant its last rites, begged God to accept its soul even though it had not been baptized and buried it for her, the babe which she had named William."

He shook his head and turned, sitting on the ground at the priest's feet like he had done so many times as a boy in their lessons in that very garden.

"I swore I would never claim a woman, I *swore* it! But her husband was killed by Bainick soldiers, praise be to God and Savior..." He flashed his eyes at the little priest. "I'm sorry, for using the Lord's name..."

"A few Hail Marys and I believe you are forgiven," the priest grinned.

"She's almost eight and ten and is so fair and so smart that I believe you would enjoy sparring with her over words. Her father is unorthodox and let her grow as her spirit dictated, and when I was there, I saw a family of generosity who wanted her back no matter how broken she had become. It is from that, Father, that I fear she has forced me to face demons."

"Of your own father?" the priest asked carefully.

William looked into the distance but avoided the question.

"'Tis her dead husband's father that I ride to face on the morrow and I fear that this desire to rip his heart out will lead to all out slaughter of him and his and I won't be able to stop—"

Father Kearney laid a hand on the warrior's head. They sat like that for minutes as the birds sang and the calm of the garden slowly stopped his raging pulse.

"You have always handled the innocent with mercy and will do right by God, William, I know you'll do right. You hold all of our soldiers' souls in your hand, thousands of men who will follow your lead. One word and you seal their fate, whatever that is."

"I will see my father's face on Shea Feargach. I do already. But the whipping isn't happening to me any longer. It happened to her and I cannot allow him to get away with that. I will see his face on every one of them—"

"Look at me."

William shook his head. "I'm weak."

"Look at me, lad." The knight raised his head. "Do you wish to marry this young woman?"

"I need her like no other, and her father has told me to wait a year for which it feels as though I've been all but damned to limbo."

Normally his poetics would have made the priest smile, or scowl, but he didn't now.

"Then you must be well at heart first. Your father taught you to hate, but a woman needs you to love. She must not be given to a man who is in many ways also a brute. God called her husband home, perhaps because he knew you would need her, perhaps because she needed freedom from him, but perhaps not. The reasons will always be a mystery. But your anger at your father makes you a risk. It has made you a champion, yes. You're a *liberator* of souls that are, shall we say, *burdened* by their mortal bodies."

William smirked. "You mean I'm a sanctified murderer."

"William, lad, you must be absolved, truly absolved of all hate for those who have trespassed against you, not before me or the citizens of Bain, but before your own mortality or else your warrior talent will corrupt you." He smiled and the priest tussled his hair. "Go forth, Sir William, and slay dragons," he lowered his voice. "*All* of them, son, but do so for the right reasons."

18

His talks with Father Kearney had always been good ones, even when they both disputed. The man beneath the alb was no proclaimed saint nor was he corrupt. William questioned whether or not he even believed half the things that he preached, save his faith in God was fierce. After a cup of watered wine and a meal, his squires accompanied him to the room of the High Council through the castle's roving corridors.

The king stood by William's commanders over a table, a long map rolled out with tokens like chess pieces upon it.

"My Lord King! May I announce Sir William Cadogan!" said the guard, slamming the floor with his staff.

"Ah, Sir William." King Bain's voice was deep and jovial.

"My Lord King."

He dropped to his knee, his chain of lions jingling across his shoulders.

"You may rise." Charles Murron looked at him. "So, come, Sir William, come. Sir Cavanaugh and Sir Thomas have been waiting for you so that we can discuss your tactics."

"Before we begin, My Lord King, I must know all facts and all, *rumors*. I've been without news for over a moon's full cycle."

"Did you believe other rumors, Sir William?" the king was careful.

"Did those rumors lead me to my latest charge, Your Grace?" he returned with as much tact.

King Bain studied him, then smiled while the two other knights watched their cryptic exchange.

"Indeed. This is fact, Sir William. Dwyre brings men from all across the east. We have no standing there right now as all of those vassals have been coerced into swearing fealty to Shea Feargach—"

"He raped a man's wife to scare them," William muttered. "Or at least, that's what my latest charge has said."

They all stood silently, unsure of whether or not to be shocked.

"Well, those men he scared have taken the Eastern Front," the king continued. "Sacked Faulk, and now have toppled the port on the River Ruadhán with fire. This is dangerous because now, long awaited shipments of metals, which we were staving off have—"

"Found their way through open trade to Dwyre. My latest charge has also expressed that this was important," William interrupted again. "Shea Feargach has been planning this for months. This leads the way to weapons production, which leads the way to better fighting and makes Dwyre more than just the slight nuisance that it was."

The king cleared his throat. "Well, Sir William. You seem to have much of this figured out. Perhaps you have had some news, hmm? Now this is *rumor*. With the river secure, Shea Feargach means to march on the Northeast Pass and secure the mountains, thus cutting the highlands from us."

Ballymead...Gwenyth...

"If this is true, we cannot allow it, William, and men," he turned to the others who nodded. "The highlands are enticing, for, em, *many* reasons I'm sure," King Bain flashed his eyes at William once more. "But their taxes and fealty are no doubt needed by Dwyre who controlled that land just less than fifty years ago. Even with metals, they will be in need of coin and many fiefs in the east are but poor substitutes for places like Dunstonwoodshire, Brynmor Braith, and Ballymead.

"Shea is but one imbecile amongst a sea of scared vassals who have all enjoyed prosperity more so under *our* law. He's bitter about three things. He's bitter that his family isn't ruling the east, he's bitter that my father made his uncle yield, and he's bitter that he has no heirs, for both of his sons are now pronounced dead with certainty, leaving him with no one to carry on his name..." *Gwenyth's son would have been his heir*, William thought. "... and of a less impending rumor now, Sir William, call it a hunch or not, for it's from a trusted source. But he means to produce heirs with the only one who has proven to bear Feargach men sons—"

"No! You'll not speak such words!" William pounded his fist upon the table and all the pieces toppled upon the map. "I should have gutted that Aindreas!"

Guards clattered to flank the king with spears crossing his chest in protection, two more aimed at William.

"You'll maintain your respect for your king, sir!" one shouted at him.

William seized a spear and tossed it to the floor and Bain grabbed another.

"Get these out of my way!" Bain complained, shoving through the rest of the weapons. "Go back to your posts, men...now! William does not yell at me! For *Christ's sake...*"

William fell to his knee, knowing he could have taken all four of them easily.

"Forgive me, Your Majesty. My incivility is my shame, but there's only one woman he seeks and I know this young lady well. I have sworn myself her protector and cannot allow my honor as a knight to fail her if she's been put at risk."

Stunned, the chamber fell silent. His officers stood immobile by the table, wine in hand, capes completely still.

"Certainly during a tryst, man," Sir Cavanaugh chuckled, "we've all made promises that can be discarded—"

"With all due respect, Frances, I would rather die under Dwyre's own sword than break my vow to her."

The mood grew quiet again.

"This is out of character for you, Sir William," Bain smiled. "Am I to gather that you, my chaste knight, have proclaimed your honor to a woman? That the Lady Gwenyth, daughter of Loddin of Ballymead in the highlands, widow to William Feargach of Dwyre, is the woman you now fight for?"

William looked partway up and nodded his response, then back down.

"Praise God in heaven, I never thought the day would come...but she was right again..." the king was muttering to himself and shaking his head as he walked away.

William sat on bended knee, not having been told to rise. "My

King?"

Bain strode back and plunked his finger on the map.

"The highlands must not be cut off. 'Tis the richest land and the taxes from my vassals there that I need to keep, yet that is a *rumor*. But the river needs to be shut down for it is there that they draw their immediate strength and that, men, is *fact*. Where do we begin, William? For the sake of the *whole* kingdom, man, at which end do you suggest we start?"

Think with your head, man. Military moves have no eyes for love... "I've been told that months ago Dwyre already had more than two thousand conscripts."

"Was this also spoken by your *latest charge, Sir William?*" the king raised a brow.

"Yes, My Lord King. She said they were levied. This would likely be in addition to his army. I believe we can trust that since she overheard this months ago, there are many more men now. I must assume that I face at least four thousand, and with his trade open, I must assume he has access to the same weaponry as we have. Therefore, I mustn't take any chances but must plan to employ the whole of my army. I cannot base this campaign on your rumors unless they are valid and because of that, we must start at the river and reclaim the port."

"But what if the rumors are true? Like they were before?" King Bain added after some moments.

William huffed. Word games were only amusing with Father Kearney and that was if it was a good day, which today was not.

"Your Majesty. If you have more to tell me, I'd be *honored* if you would grace me with that knowledge, sooner rather than later."

King Bain stood quietly and looked down at him.

"I irritate you," he smirked. William did his best not to roll his eyes. "If my council and staff would be so kind as to give Sir William and myself a moment of privacy?" The guards, after William's outburst, remained planted to the walls. "I order you all out now! Or I shall remove you myself and don't think for a moment that these hands which have slain King Fernando have lost their strength!"

The room began to drain of people, banners above wafting in the breeze they created. Soon it was William and Bain. Once the door was sealed, the king laid a bar across it and beckoned him to follow.

"Come. They'll be pressing their ears to the keyhole."

William traipsed after him as he walked to a staircase beyond the throne. They reached a balcony with sheer curtains that grazed his face, *like Gwenyth's veil*, blowing in the crisp autumn air. He stepped outside, well above the inner yard and beyond any window with eavesdroppers.

"You're a son of Bain and a proud one. I did well to answer your mother's plea all those years ago...Oh how I've prepared for this speech and yet I don't think it shall come out right." He leaned on the rail while William waited.

"Speak plainly to me, my king. There is nothing anyone could say that would shock me after the battles I have fought."

"Is there not?" Charles Murron turned to him. "I advise you to be ready anyway, for I have wronged you, William."

"My Lord?"

"I've been receiving messages from a source within Dwyre for some months now and I'm glad I trusted my instinct with them. As you know, I'm aware of the tragedy that befell your family. I'm sorry for the murder of your father—"

"I'm not," William muttered, but the king let it go.

"The rumors," Bain paused. "They come from your half-sister, Louisa."

"My, my...what?" William shook his head. "I haven't heard you—"

"Yes, you have, and I believe if you're shocked by that, your shock shall not dissipate now." Bain turned to look at him square in the eyes. "Your brothers, Andrew and Faegan are your half-brothers, and your little sisters in truth, your half-sisters."

"How is..." William leaned onto the railing himself. "How is that possible?"

"Your father, mother, and brothers came to my coronation years ago." Bain took a deep breath. "Your mother was beautiful. I saw her black hair and black eyes like her Moorish ancestors in the crowd, and thought I should have her. I didn't know her. There was no cause for it, and the act was random. I simply wished to take her and knew that as King I could. It didn't matter to me at the time that she was married." He shook his head. "I was new to power, cocksure, and abused my privilege for I arranged for her to be brought to me in secret and I took her to bed."

William's head began spinning and his chest began to pump.

"I've debated telling you over the years but feared that your anger would turn to me—"

"And why should it not?" William growled.

"I assure you, the king you see before you now has learned that taking liberties with his liege lords' women is not how you sue for peace. But we all make mistakes and this was one of mine, though I cannot say I'm completely sorry."

"Go on, man," William croaked, gripping the railing while he clenched his teeth.

"I didn't think I would see her again, her being a low liege's wife, and at the time didn't even care. I cared not of the damage I might have done. But when I received her letter ten years later, I was no longer so vain. I knew generosity had to be bountiful, honesty had to be sacred, and authority had to be swift, which is how I have run my kingdom. She told me I had fathered her child and begged I see fit to remove the lad from her home before her husband bloodied him to death. The child was sent for... Immediately and without question." The king placed a gentle hand on his back. "This young, scared, *angry* boy was you, William..."

"Is there more?" the knight asked, his face having gone cold. *You shame my house with your presence, William! You disgrace it! I'm not the bastard in this house!* The words had stung when his father spoke them, but now they rang true. He shook the king's hand away and fell against the wall.

"One look at those eyes of yours and I knew you were mine, and I spent many nights dreaming up ways to punish the man who would *dare* beat my child and prince. Your father would not have dared accused his king of cuckolding him, but he knew you were my bastard, lad, and your mother knew that that was why he took his anger out on your hide. I just wish I had known when you were a babe. I could have spared you much suffering. I could be the reason your family became what it did and with that I struggle. But you wouldn't be here if it were not for me. For that, I'm grateful for all of heaven and earth that I seeded you. God works mysteriously."

"*Spare* me! I don't want your justifications!" William spat. "You're grateful that I slaughter men and keep your throne secure! If you were grateful for a son, you would have made it known."

He peeled himself off the wall like a soggy washrag and looked out over the inner ward of the castle.

"Do you have any idea how my mother suffered?" he choked. "Any idea? My father was a tyrant. Her lot was as awful as mine, though he raped her as well. We all heard it late at night..."

The silence was intrusive. Normally it put William at ease but now it rang like church bells in his brain. All he wanted was Gwenyth's soft hands draped around his neck, her comforting smell, her need for him. No one had ever wanted him except her.

"There was no good time to tell you, but there was no way to not tell you either. Business being business, Dwyre has grown unruly. Shea has massacred our soldiers on the river and taken control of the whole Eastern Front in the amount of time it took you to find, fall in love with, and return Loddin's daughter. Before that, I had been getting the messages from Louisa and we were able to keep Dwyre at bay. Those messages have now ceased and the tides have shifted to Dwyre's favor. I'm afraid the good of the kingdom is at stake."

The king gripped his shoulder and William let him, though would not look his way.

"Look upon me as you will for now. I won't argue your anger. But this *does* make you my successor, and my three young daughters are your kin as well. When the time is right, I will admit my fault to this kingdom. I won't patronize you, William, but you are my blood, truly a Bainick lion and it's given me pride to watch you grow and honor my crest by carrying it, for it's yours. And when I die, you will be King.

"You should know that Louisa befriended the Lady Gwenyth when no one else would," he continued. "She has a fellow spy that knew where Loddin's daughter was hidden, which is how I knew to send you to the pass. It was at her request, knowing how you suffered as a boy, that I send *you* to get Loddin's daughter. She said she believed you needed one another and through your hardships, you might find strength together. Was she right?"

William watched a servant carrying a tray across the ward below but did not speak. *'There is someone out there who'll love you, I can feel it...'* Louisa had played the matchmaker.

"I couldn't act on Louisa's request alone, but when Loddin pleaded for the same girl, I was able to claim a high liege of mine had been offended. It was the legitimate claim I needed to send you in. I decided to take a chance on Louisa's request for I knew I needed you to marry if you were to be King, and you have been so jack-ass stubborn about it, that I thought perhaps your sister would know better than I."

"It could have been a ploy to get me out of the way for these attacks."

"Yes, I suppose it could have been, but I decided to take a risk and it seems to have been the right choice."

The look on William's face was telling. *I, the lead commander have been a pawn.*

"You can quit killing Andrew Cadogan every time you go to battle, William, for you are my son, and not his."

"With all due respect, killing my father's ghost is what gives me the power to kill your enemies."

"Then perhaps the ghost of William Feargach is the ghost you need to chase now," the king replied. "'Twould seem your lady needs him to be dead."

They descended back into the council hall and the king unbarred the door.

"You may enter."

Sir Thomas and Sir Cavanaugh reentered, followed by the perplexed scribes, pages, squires, and guards.

William was numb. His sister. He had not heard from her since he was four and ten. What had caused her to end up at Dwyre, risking it all as a spy?

How have I become so entangled with Dwyre? War has never been personal before. This is my profession and I excel at it. Get your head out of your heart, man, he told himself. *I cannot go after Gwenyth and my sister at the same time. I have forces, yes, but I cannot split my front. If I march on the Northeast Pass first or Dwyre first, I leave trade open on the river. Both options let Shea and his army grow strong enough to put up a challenging fight.*

He could not take back the port, 'liberate' Shea Feargach from his body, and save his sister, Gwenyth, and the highlands, all at the same time, and felt as though he was betraying Gwenyth already. His heart began to ache.

I should never have done it. I should never have touched that beautiful lady, should never have let my heart feel.

"Are you well, William?" Sir Cavanaugh asked. "You look as though you've seen a ghost."

"I'm fine, man," he commented, though his voice sounded raw.

King Bain looked at him directly.

"So, Sir William, after what has been discussed, what say you now?"

"You know I'm duty bound," he mumbled.

"Yes, to king and country, and now to a woman," the king replied.

William slowly reached for the tokens on the map and rolled them in his fingers.

"I have not been put in a fair place, My Lord King," he rasped.

"Fair or not, it's the place in which you stand."

Cavanaugh and Thomas watched him, itching for the meeting to end so they could ask about what had passed. He took a deep breath, mastered himself, and slammed the tokens into order on the map.

"We must put all our force on the port first, march our way to Faulk, then Dwyre. After that, we work our way through the Northeast Pass to the highlands. We can spare five hundred horses, double that in archers and foot soldiers, and those should be sent around from the west to converge on the highlands with us at Dunstonwoodshire as we come through the pass to flank Shea Feargach from behind. They'll secure the entrance to the highlands until we meet up with them there. I would advise you to send word to the Lord of Dunstonwoodshire immediately so he isn't worried by their arrival. That's the best plan I can make."

"Is that what you really want—"

"I cannot use my men to fight my own wars," William interrupted. "I must do what is right for the kingdom first and you know it." His words were icy as he looked at the man who had given him life. "I must protect my kingdom and honor My Lord King despite the words he shares with me." He bended down on one knee again. "If that's all, *my king*, I should like to take my leave."

Bain nodded. "Yes, that's all. God Speed, Sir William..." but William had already risen and was striding to the door.

Cavanaugh began to smile in hopes of lightening the mood.

"I should like to congratulate you with a tankard of ale, man," Sir Cavanaugh teased as they went, slapping him on the back. "Shall we go to a tavern and talk of sweetness now that you've tasted it?"

"I could use ale, man, and a lot of it," William answered. "I should like to drown in it tonight."

19

Gwenyth shook her hair as she sat upon Luna, bareback with no bridle and only her brown mane for reins. The air was frozen and her lungs felt icy every time she breathed. Snow flurries had drifted in amongst the grasses and the days were growing shorter by each sunset. She had ridden past the pastures and the dormant beehives, and now stood alone in the quietude.

She looked down at her trousers, stolen from Loddin's squire, and watched Luna nibble grass. It was growing late and dusk would fall soon. She turned back the horse with her loose hair waving to return to the keep, noticing a rider approaching through the outer walls.

It had been over three sennights now. She ached, but could not speak a word to her father. Her family was no comfort for the emptiness she felt. She had sat next to her mother's grave many times despite the cold, hoping for some solace, sometimes crying, sometimes remembering happier times. Alone each night, she imagined William's silly smiles and jests. She could feel him near her as though her memories were teasing her, but then would open her eyes to find herself alone.

Her dreams had been cruel. She could feel herself curled against him in the bend of his lap. She could feel his lips graze her cheek in his sleep as if checking to make sure she was still there, his unshaved face tickling her skin, as if to feel close to a soul who understood his own torments, which he had refused to speak of further.

She imagined William riding back out of the trees beyond the gates, Titan rearing, his green eyes professing his longing for her. So much longing, and pain, and respect had been held in that head beneath that sable hair, so much darker than William Feargach's.

Luna walked on and she closed her eyes, imagining his hands sliding around her waist, his body pressed behind her as he begged her forgiveness for his sinful want. She grew warm in her belly at the thought of their trysts despite the snow lapping her cheeks. But when she opened her eyes, the fields were barren for the winter and things were as they were before. Cold.

Her time at Dwyre seemed so far in the past, like a surreal nightmare. William Feargach had arrived with his father and entourage through those very gates that the rider was well beyond now. They had received Lord Loddin's answer stating his willingness to discuss a betrothal. She had been nervous as they gathered in the bailey. Mother had fussed over her hair and gown, having woven ribbons the color of Ballymead's banner into her plaits as her daughter readied to meet her suitor, despite the illness that forced her to do so from her bed, and the soreness in her fingers that made the task take twice as long.

The Feargachs were powerful with many vassals. They were proud fighters, carrying that now cursed crest of the wolf upon their banners and William had been handsome with his auburn hair hanging to his shoulders. The first thing he had done when she stepped out of the keep was peruse the length of her with his grey eyes, then he turned to his father and muttered something that no one else could hear.

They had eaten dinner as Loddin's squire, only a page then, poured the tankards and filled the goblets, eating the delicious frumenty and the peppered trout upon the fine wooden trenchers. Aindreas had been there too. He had smiled but always looked away from her.

He knew what would happen.

William had watched her the whole time. He didn't speak to her and she took it as a sign of respect. He stared at her body and she thought it meant he would love her in bed. He spoke to his father as they gazed at her brothers, and she was certain he was impressed with her family. But now she realized it was because her family was good at producing sons.

When she had escaped the excitement to sit with Luna, he had found her alone, wrapped his arms around her without invitation and said thank the Lord he could be alone with her to taste her lips. His kiss had been strong, marked, and practiced. It had been when his hands traveled with purpose to her breasts that she shied away but he held her to the spot as he felt her through the beadwork of her bodice.

'Do you feel that, woman?' he had grinned, grabbing her hand and pressing it to the front of his trousers. She tried to wrench herself loose. 'That's what looking at you does to me.'

He had forced her hand to rub him even though she begged him to stop. Of all the kisses she had shared with Matthew Whitcroft, not once had he ever done such a thing.

'You'll be mine soon, woman. 'Tis agreed. Your father signed the contract just now. We're practically married already. I shall enjoy our wedding night...'

'My Lord, it's a sin to speak of this,' she whispered.

William smiled. 'And with words like those, I know you're a virgin. No doubt with sweetnesses like highland roses—'

'Please let go,' she murmured and shied away.

He chuckled. 'So you've been teasing me these days with your coy smiles? I thought the innocence was just an act. Do you find me ugly?'

'No, My Lord, but...but I thought you gentle.'

'Aye, I'm gentle, to be sure. Come here, Lady, and you shall feel how gentle I am,' he grinned.

She shook her head but he lifted up his tunic and pushed her hand down the front. She did not know what to do and turned her head as her face flushed with color.

'No need to be a puritan about it,' he said as he grasped her breasts once more and kissed her.

'I beg you stop!' she whimpered as his hand moved from her breasts around to her buttocks, and began to hike up her skirt.

Finally, she managed to wrench herself free, pushing him away as she backed up. She wiped her mouth and curved her arm around her stomach.

William grinned.

'You'll make a good wife, Lady. You'll give me sons. You should be proud.'

He forced another kiss upon her and left.

Those were the first words he ever spoke to her.

I should have listened to my heart. I was too naïve. Father would have revoked the contract had I just said something. But the past always looked clearer when one was beyond it looking back. *And our wedding night...*

Gwenyth shivered at the thought instead of the snow.

'William, are you satisfied with you wife?' her mother had asked him, for William's mother was dead.

'Aye, My Lady. Most satisfied,' he replied humbly.

'And Daughter? Are you satisfied with your husband?'

She looked over his nude body. It had been so muscular and despite the awkwardness of the moment, he was growing ready. She looked at his face and he stared back, willing her to say 'yes.'

'Daughter?' her mother said again.

She looked at her mother whose eyebrows were raised, then back at William who furrowed his brow in question. Then she dropped her head.

'Aye, Mother.'

Her mother smiled and embraced her despite her nakedness.

'You're a fine lady, Gwenyth,' she had whispered. 'Don't ever let anyone make you feel otherwise, for you go to another man's house now and no longer belong to your father.'

Gwenyth trembled. 'I'm frightened, Mother,' she whispered.

'Don't be afraid, Gwen. You can manage this. You truly become a woman this night and my job is now complete. I am proud.'

With a kiss on the cheek, Lady Amaranth took a seat outside the door. Once they were alone, William smiled at her and picked her up like a prize. He laid her on the bed and didn't spend time romanticizing, but got to business straight away.

'Please move slowly, My Lord. I'm nervous,' she whispered so that her mother wouldn't hear.

He grinned and whispered back. 'I've rights as a husband, Gwenyth, and I intend to claim them. You'd best be dutiful.'

He felt at her body, already knowing the proper places to match himself to her and braced his powerful arms next to her head while he pushed into her. She had clutched the linens for it hurt so badly, begging him to slow in choked whispers as tears streamed forth. He ignored her pleas.

'You'll get used to it, wife. You'll learn to like it,' he breathed, and

continued until he had peaked within her.

When it was done, he helped her from the bed. 'Lady Amaranth,' he called. 'You may come in now.'

Her mother hobbled back through the door and came to examine the sheet. Her eyes widened, then she looked at Gwenyth who was shaking so badly her knees were knocking. Tears had swollen her eyes and she would not look up.

'Sweet daughter, are you all right?'

She nodded, wrapping her arms about her middle as she tried to hide her crying. Lady Amaranth's eyes traveled over her body, to the fluids that had stained her thighs.

William saw the lady's concern and embraced Gwenyth.

'Are you cold, wife? Should I get you a cover?'

Her mother peeled back the linen and carried it to the door. Gwenyth could hear the muffled talking.

'Are you satisfied, My Lord?'

"Tis good indeed,' Shea Feargach had replied. 'I'm most satisfied, My Lady. She was, without a doubt, a virgin.'

Her father had remained while her brothers escorted Shea back to the great hall.

'And Gwenyth is well?' Loddin asked.

'Husband, I fear it was painful. She cries.'

She had felt like crying all over again when she saw the wedding linens hanging in the hall the next morn. Yet the men were impressed and the ladies wanted to know the details, so she pasted a smile on her face while William was slapped on the back as though he had just won points at a joust.

It was as if she stood naked in front of them all, her most private treasure displayed like a crest for everyone to inspect. She knew right then that he had been the wrong choice but what was done was done, her chastity was proven intact, and she convinced herself that they would grow together over time.

Yet when she thought of William Cadogan, her heart melted. In just a month's time, they had shared more together than her husband had ever wanted to share. They had frolicked and laughed like children. They had talked about heaven and earth and everything in between, in both Latin and in modern tongue. They had teased each other and cried together and above all, he had not judged her. He had been honest, he had trusted her enough to confide his deepest memories in her, and he had saved her life.

*And those kisses...*had been slow to come as his nose brushed her cheeks and neck, as if he explored her whole essence for the perfect spot before he dared press his lips to her, as if every time was the first. So brutal a warrior was he and yet so soft, quiet, and withdrawn was the man when he was not teasing her. She could trust him after not being able to trust a soul for so long. He had promised her she could trust him and each day he had proven it.

Now he was gone. Father had sent the right William away and he had not looked back, but ran Titan faster and faster as he left her running behind him crying his name. It felt just like abandonment. A year of waiting just to be betrothed made her blood sting as it coursed through her.

What if William loses his love for me?

Luna walked up to the curtain wall and made her way to the gate. A guard bowed his head, noticing the tears streaming down her cheeks.

"Lady Gwenyth, do you need assistance?"

"No, I'm well, I suppose. I thank thee," she sniveled as the guards announced the rider at the front.

"State your name, man!" one hollered over the wall. Loddin the brother turned away from his squire who fought against the quintain and ordered him to halt. "State your name if you want entrance!"

Their father came onto the steps now, followed by Gavin, Hershel and George. There was a pause as Gwenyth made her way around from the side of the wall.

"I bear an urgent message for the Lady Gwenyth!" came a muffled reply.

"What business is it, man?"

"I must see this package into the hands of the Lady Gwenyth!" came the reply.

"You will tell us your name or you shall be turned away!"

Loddin limped to the footings.

"He will not declare himself, My Lord!" the guard called down. "He is alone and bearing a package for the Lady Gwenyth!"

"Let him enter!" Loddin called. "Men?"

He turned to the bailey and every man available took formation. The gates were pulled open and Gwenyth came around to the front of the keep to find herself staring at the back of Lord Aindreas de Boscoe. She froze as he walked his horse into the yard under at least forty swords all pointing at him in an arc like sunrays.

"No..." she shook her head.

Fear swept over her. She paled and clung to Luna's hair.

"What is your name, man? Who sends my daughter packages?" Loddin asked.

Aindreas dismounted and turned to see her, his eyes falling wide open.

"No..." Gwenyth said, her heart banging like hooves in full gallop. "No, Father! Make him leave! Make him leave!" She leapt from Luna's back, squeezing between the nearest sword and the footings. "Make him leave! Oh *God* make him leave..." She tripped up the steps in her haste.

"Lady Gwenyth!" Aindreas called as he stepped forward, but Loddin's hand clamped around his throat before he could land his stride.

"Your name!" her father boomed.

Loddin the son whipped his sword to his chest. Gwenyth whirled around to see.

"Aindreas de Boscoe," he rasped.

"Why does my daughter fear you!"

"I," he coughed. Loddin eased his grip. "I come from Dwyre."

Loddin's hand was around his throat again in that instant. He pushed Aindreas all the way to the footing of the wall and put a dagger to his neck.

"You're not welcome here!" he growled. "You had better spill your message," he jerked his throat as Aindreas winced, "and hope that I don't make you swallow this for so help me, nothing would give me greater pleasure."

"Lord...Lord Shea Feargach..." he wheezed, but Loddin held his grip and narrowed his eyes so that they had become slits. "He does not know I come..."

"He lies, Father!" Gwenyth cried, braced against the door. "He tried to nab me and take me back! It was Sir William who fought him off!"

William thumped to the door and reached a hand out. "Sister, come," he said quietly. She fell against him and hugged her arms around him. "Father will kill him if he tries a thing, you need not fear."

Aindreas gagged and made a retching sound as his face began to grow purple. "Ple...please, I bring...a babe..."

For the first time, everyone looked down at the bundle to see that it squirmed. Loddin removed his hand and Aindreas buckled over, coughing as he filled his lungs.

"The Lady Janis," he breathed, "bids that your daughter guard little Louisa."

20

Gwenyth sat by her father and brothers at the board, holding the infant who now, after fresh milk, was fast asleep. Aindreas sopped up stew with his bread beneath the watchful eyes of guards.

"I thank thee for the meal."

"I don't want your thanks," Loddin frowned. "Nor do I want your company. This babe comes from Dwyre?"

"'Tis the daughter of Lady Gwenyth's friend, the Lady Janis, fourth wife to Lord Shea."

"And what am I to do with his seed besides spit on it? I have good lands and a prosperous trade, and surely his seed would poison them, as his other seed poisoned my daughter—"

"Father," Gwenyth started at his harsh words.

"Don't interrupt, Gwenyth."

"She bids the Lady Gwenyth foster her and keep her secret so that all may believe her dead."

Gwenyth's eyes flitted back and forth between them, then at her brothers. Her father had never been so angry in his life.

"I don't want this child in my home, on my land, or—"

"Father, may I interrupt? I have some questions if I may."

Loddin the son leaned forward as his father nodded and threw down his bread in disgust.

"Why does she send her babe to Gwenyth?"

"There's much that cannot be told," Aindreas began.

"Of course. It's called deception, lads," Loddin fumed.

Aindreas ignored him. "The Lady Janis is in a terrible spot, for William learned his ways from his father. She fears for her daughter's safety. Your sister is the only other soul she trusts."

"Is Lady Janis in danger?" Gwenyth interrupted.

"Gwenyth," her father began.

"Please let me speak, My Lord," Gwenyth lowered her head. "I'll be acting as this child's mother. Do I not have a right to know such things?"

Loddin smiled at her and patted her hand.

"Of course, lass. I'm sorry."

"My Lady, she is indeed, very much so. You would be doing your friendship to her well to honor her like this."

"Why else do you come?" Gavin began. "What do you learn by coming here? Do you stake out our fief?"

"If you mean, what will Lord Shea learn, then nothing. I have no motive to do so and I don't return to him. He believes me to be in the capital."

No one knew what to say.

"I don't know that I believe you," Loddin replied.

But Gwenyth felt she could see some truth.

Shea would never let Aindreas out of his sight for this long unless he had sent him on a task, she thought. *And daughter or not, he would never send Louisa away, for if his demon soul knows an inkling of love, it's Lady Janis he feels for.*

"This child...how is she to be raised?" Gwenyth began. "Who should she be told is her mother?"

"Call her a peasant's child perhaps. All that matters is that she's well. I'm on thin ice here," Aindreas began.

"Then at least God has graced you with a working mind," Loddin stared at him.

"Lord Loddin," Aindreas huffed. "I don't wish to take your daughter back. It was never my wish. It was only my orders. I hated seeing what happened to her and tried to give her comforts that—"

"What?" Loddin threw his fist on the table and the baby started.

"No...sir...not like that I would never...a kind word, or a flower, never that."

"It's true, Father." Gwenyth turned red with humiliation and dropped her head, "No one except William ever did that with me."

Loddin eased himself back into his seat again.

"Because Lord Shea knows not of my whereabouts, he will know not of my coming here, and Lady Janis has begged this. I swear it as truth, on her friendship with Gwenyth—"

"*Lady*, Gwenyth," Hershel corrected.

"Of course," Aindreas bowed his head. "But regardless of any more questions, I cannot answer them, and everyone here including your guards will be better off if you pretend I never came." He looked straight at Loddin with his hazel eyes. "Perhaps running your dagger into my throat, Lord Loddin, would not have been bad after all, for I bear too many secrets now. I know it's a lot to ask, but I must have a private word with your daughter."

He had finished his meal and sat still while Gwenyth looked down at Louisa.

"You think too much of our generosity, man," George began.

"What I must say must be spoken to her alone or to no one."

Loddin looked at Gwenyth, then at his sons.

"Daughter, a word with you."

He rose and she followed, passing the child off to a maid.

"Gwenyth," Loddin breathed as they entered the corridor above to the solar. "One word is all it takes to send this man away."

Gwenyth shifted, but didn't know what to say.

"Butterfly, *please*. You haven't uttered a word to us about that dreadful place. I have no idea what has been in your mind."

His hands were shaking.

"Father," she sighed. "I believe he speaks truth, and I feel we should protect the babe." She dropped her head. "I couldn't give a rat to Lord Shea, let alone see a babe returned to him. The Lady Janis was kind to me. She was my only friend and this babe cannot help her father. 'Twould be unchristian to punish her for it."

He nodded and planted a kiss on her forehead.

"Then the babe stays and we honor the fruit of your lady's womb, rather than harbor the seed of a demon." She smiled. "But I don't want you to share the same air with a Dwyre man, let alone give him private audience, if you choose naught but to walk away."

Gwenyth took a deep breath and threw her arms around him.

"Oh, Father, I don't know what to do with my sadness!" Loddin wrapped his arms around her as she buried her face in his chest. "I shall talk to him. It will be okay."

"Is this what you want?"

"I will do so, Father. His message must be important for he has been so insistent."

Aindreas and Gwenyth stood outside the keep.

"I'm at a loss for words at your attire, My Lady," Aindreas whispered, bowing his head and stealing glances at her legs. *My, she is fair. William Feargach was a fool.* "Does Lord Loddin not see fit to have you disciplined? I don't mean to be vulgar, but—"

"My father doesn't believe the clothes define the person, sir," she remarked. "I ride horses. A gown will never do for that."

"You ride well, I never knew..."

"There is much no one at Dwyre ever knew. A frightened rabbit hides in its warren."

"And yet a pearl can come out of its shell," he added.

She didn't know how to take that, but softened anyway.

"I must be brief, Lady. I can see you're loved here, and I'm glad that my heart has been reassured about your knight." His eyes traveled up and down her form again, then he looked away with shame.

"What reassurance? You tried to take me from him—"

"I did so only because I had to! And I lied about why because I had to."

"I don't understand."

"Lady," Aindreas breathed so low that even she could hardly hear. He looked about and took her hands. "I'm not who you think I am, nor is your Sir Wi—"

"Maintain your distance, man!" the guards shouted.

Bows and arrows were drawn taut. Spears and swords were at

the ready. Loddin swept down the steps from the great hall followed by her brothers before she could even breathe.

"It's all right, Father!" she begged.

Loddin's fingers stretched for Aindreas' throat again.

"Trust that I shall let the world hear my lungs if things have gone sour! I beg you, My Lord!" she dropped to her knees and clasped him.

His outstretched hand turned into a pointed finger that jabbed the air in front of his face.

"One wrong move, whoreson! Just one! And I'll gut you on a pike and swing your limbs from my brattices for all my people to see what happens to those who harm my children!"

"Your daughter is safe with me, I vow it."

Loddin stomped back inside with his sons, all of who rested just beyond the door like floodwaters pressing on a cracking dam.

"I fear that I might never return to Shea," he continued softly.

"What do you mean?"

"Swear, Gwenyth, swear you won't tell a soul, swear that you will not,"

"I...but to swear?"

"I cannot tell you if you don't."

She swallowed. "I promise, Aindreas, whatever weight you must lift, I shall keep it locked at heart."

"I'm a spy," his words were more quiet then a windless night. "But...*Christ*," he huffed.

She was shocked. Aindreas was a pious man.

"But not for Lord Shea. He knows he has a spy. There's a reason Sir Iain lost so many attempts to topple Faulk, and a reason Bain's men took back the River Ruadhán before Shea came in and slaughtered."

"Oh, Aindreas," she said, putting her hands over her mouth.

"I'm not the only one. We're the ones who sent letters to the king, warnings about Shea's tactics...and warnings about your condition. It was at the request of, of, my comrade that Sir William be sent for you."

She felt dizzy. "Aindreas, my father is the one who pled to the king."

"Yes, Gwenyth, but we told him that you lived, and where to find you."

"Then you were helping me all along," she murmured. "Oh I have been foolish to doubt you!"

"Shhh! Tell the Lord of Ballymead that Shea wishes to cut the highlands from Bain so he can claim his fealty. He marches now through the Northeast Pass with his army. Already the River Ruadhán has been felled. And promise me that you'll not stray far unattended on horseback, for Shea is going mad to punish you." Her hands remained at her mouth and she took a step back. "He sends Maccus to capture you. I delivered his orders myself."

"But Maccus is dead, my William slayed him—"

"No. He misjudged his mark and Maccus crawled back to Dwyre. He now has scores to settle and returning you to Lord Shea is only one of them."

She paused, then threw her arms about him while the guards looked at each other.

"What's she doing?" a guard muttered. "Daft woman... ready at arms, men."

"I have but few chances to get word back to Lady Janis about her Louisa. What say you, Gwenyth?" he whispered in her ear.

"Make it known that I love her as my sister and that her daughter shall prosper in the care of myself and the Lord of Ballymead as her surrogate grandfather. We accept her, please make it known. Tell my sweet Janis that I hold her hands now and forever!"

"I will, dear lady."

Aindreas pulled himself from her, though she clenched his hands. Dusk had fully fallen and it was difficult to see.

"If I'm figured out, I will be hunted down, Gwenyth. But I will have died for my king..." He paused, and brushed a strand of hair out of her face. "You must know how I favored you, how I wished to tell you..." *How I would have cherished you.*

She blushed, but let him tuck it behind her ear.

"I hope you can forgive me someday. I should have done more to help you, Lady."

She shook her head and caressed his face. "You're already

forgiven, My Lord."

He inhaled deeply.

"Your William leads the Bainick army to the Eastern Front. He has blood in his sights and the fury to spill it. Once Shea meets him face to face, I have faith he will realize too late his folly." He had the look of wanting to kiss her on his brow. "You soften your knight's armor, Gwenyth, as he strengthens you. You're a perfect match and for that, I will always be envious. I pray he gets to Shea before Shea gets to you."

He bowed to kiss her hand, but she lifted his face and pressed her lips to his in a chaste but meaningful kiss.

"Lady Gwenyth?" Mathew Whitcroft stepped forward but she ignored him.

He didn't dare embrace her, yet allowed his lips to kiss her back.

"You're a kind soul and I thank thee for it, dear Aindreas. I shall pray every night for your safety," she whispered.

"And I shall hold that gentle kiss next to my heart forever." He caressed her face once more.

"Lady Gwenyth," Mathew said more firmly.

"No need for alarm, man," Aindreas said, then turned back to her and spoke loudly. "May God continue to keep you well, My Lady. Don't forget my words to you. Any of them."

He backed away, bowed, and then strode across the bailey where he mounted his horse. Climbing into the saddle, he turned the reins and trotted through the gates.

"Aindreas, wait!" she yelled.

Once again, Loddin and her brothers streamed through the door. She ran forth and took his hand, her father pausing before them.

"Yes, My Lady?"

She glanced around the bailey, then at her father, then back at him.

"I have this terrible feeling that I'll never see you again. I won't, will I?"

He sighed and looked at Loddin again, then squeezed her fingers. "'Tis of humor that I now finally have the courage to tell you what I wish, yet I'm not afforded the privacy to do so. No, Lady. This is most likely our last meeting."

She glanced at her father once more. Mathew was gesturing and talking to him and Loddin's face was growing red.

"Em, then god speed, Sir Aindreas." she said. He brushed his fingers across her cheek.

"Yes, Lady."

Without looking back, he released her hand and cantered down the slope. Loddin was marching forth.

"Daughter! What is this I hear of loose behavior—"

"We shall be cut from Bain, Father," she interrupted.

"What?"

She watched Aindreas grow smaller in the distance until the dusk had consumed him.

"Lord Feargach marches on us. All of the highlands. He has toppled the Eastern Front and ousted Bainick rule. Sir William Cadogan and the army of Bain have been deployed to cut him down. You might wish to devise a plan. I was a fool. Aindreas was on my side all along."

"Or so he'd wish you to believe," Loddin retorted. "To extort affection from you."

"No," she shook her head. "He truly was. Discipline me how you will, Father, but I would gladly give the favor of my kiss all over again with you and the rest of the world watching."

Loddin and her brothers stared at her, but she turned back to the great hall and drifted up the steps.

Almost a week out and the trees were thinning as Aindreas neared the Northeast Pass where it branched to the west toward the capital

A couple days' ride before I reach it, he thought.

Aindreas had pushed his horse through the night, stopping only in the early morning to give his mount a rest by a stream where there was still plenty of grass peaking above the snow. The sun was coming up but the clouds in the sky that sprinkled flurries made everything look grey. A raven cawed as it flew overhead and landed on a stone support that had once held a bridge, watching as he pulled out a loaf of bread and meat tidbits. He tore off a piece. The bird cawed again, flapping its feathers and then cawed again.

"Away with you, bird," Aindreas waved his hand and it lifted into flight.

Devouring his piece in only a few bites, he pulled out a skin of wine and gulped it down. He didn't see the men hiding in the thick of the trees and his horse, too hungry and tired, didn't offer much of a warning. A bow was drawn and an arrow released. Aindreas's eyes widened and burned. Another came, then another, silently through the air, only whirling when they got too close for him to duck.

His back became a dartboard. Blood trickled out of him and the snow in front of him faded into light. A mirage rose before him, and took his head in her lap as she knelt, petting his face and hair with icy hands. Her pale hair fluttered around him, engulfing him.

"Gwenyth…is that you?" he sputtered.

Her dark eyes mourned above him. Her fingers caressed him again and again, they were so cold, so cold…

"Gwenyth, is that you?" Maccus mocked as he took the reins of Aindreas's mount and dug through his bags for food. "Won't Lord Shea be pleased when I tell'im I killed his spy?"

"Should you not rest, Maccus?"

"Nah. This wound is healing fine. A bit sore, but satisfaction is a good cure for pain." He grinned and stared at Aindreas whose body gave a shudder.

"How d'ye know he was the one?"

"I heard the bastard plottin' his conspiracy," Maccus replied. "I was going to expose him in front of Lord Shea and the whole army, except Lord Shea did not come back with'im. He sent this here traitor with my orders instead."

"You don't think Lord Shea will be cross that you didn't tell'im first? Lord de Boscoe is very close to Lord Shea—"

"Patrick, man! He was gettin' away! And he wasn't coming back to Dwyre either! He'd have been a fool to do so. It was either now or never. I thought now. Otherwise, he'd live on to help King Bain wipe out the Dwyre Army."

"Well I hope he hasn't spilled anything important. He was not a stupid one, for sure. And he did just come from Ballymead," his companion said.

Maccus nodded. "Aye. Gwenyth. Well we'll have to pay her a

visit, will we not?" he grinned.

"There are but three of us and hundreds of guards no doubt," his companion replied. "I don't wish to kill myself, Maccus."

"Well, this is why you let me do the hunting, man. I am an expert."

Maccus started a fire with his flint over a pile of kindling. His bare legs beneath his plaid and jerkin seemed unaware that frozen water sat beneath them.

"We will observe, men. No need to make a hasty charge. Nabbing her would be the best, if we can get into the walls without being seen. If the snow keeps up, then our tracks'll be covered. It would be some time before they discover her missing and if we do not leave straight to Dwyre, even better, for surely that is the first place her father'll look."

They ate Aindreas' food and rested by his body as it quivered. Then up the three of them rose, mounted, and headed for the trees upon the ridge with the spare horse.

Aindreas lay in the snow as the wind lapped over him. His blood had stained it deep red. His eyes lay open, dull, and lifeless. Slowly, a drift formed and by early dawn, he was covered.

21

"Am I ever going to get my trousers back, Lady Gwenyth?" Michael interrupted Gwenyth's thoughts.

She sat on a wall outside of the stable in the early morning snow, her knees drawn to her chest, lost in thought.

Please fight bravely, William. Please, God, watch over him and see he returns from battle in one piece. He is a hero, but not immortal.

"Lady Gwenyth? Are you well?"

"What? Oh, dear Michael, I'm sorry." She rested her head sideways so she could smile at him.

"You're not as happy as you used to be."

The youth with red hair and freckled cheeks climbed next to her on the wall, setting down some training equipment. She decided to divert the topic.

"What does my brother have you doing today? More jousting with the quintain?"

"No, My Lady. He had too much ale last night and has given me the morning to play while he sleeps in with Lady Mary, but the boys in the village have chores so I'm bored."

"You could take your pony for a ride."

He shook his head. "That's boring."

"You could help the ladies with the bread I need to take to the village. They're slower than usual this morn."

Michael scrunched his nose.

"My Lady, I don't bake. I'm a squire...a *man*?"

"I'm sorry, and a fine one. You look lovely serving me bread at board, page *boy*," she teased as he rolled his eyes. "Perhaps then you could show me your moves, for I shall be easily impressed."

He huffed. "I suppose that's better than doing nothing."

The boy jumped from the wall and took up his wooden shield and waster, taking his stance, then swinging, then withdrawing, then plunging.

"I'm pleased to see you becoming so valiant. But what good is all that when you've no one to strike at?"

"Well," he stopped to think. He looked at her and screwed his mouth sideways as if weighing options. "You like *man* things, do you not?"

She furrowed her brow and tossed a pebble at him as one of the guards chuckled.

"Why would you say that?"

"Well, you know just as much about horses as a man and you hate spinning and you fought wolves, did you not?"

"So that makes me like a man?"

"No, but mayhap if you hold a shield, then I could have a target."

"I don't want you to run me through!" she retorted.

Again the guards chuckled, now turning to steal glances below.

"My Lady, you just hold the shield and I take my strike, and you block it. The sword is made of *wood*."

"Wood still leaves a terrible bruise!"

"*Never mind*, My Lady. You would never do."

He walked away, sulking, and Gwenyth thought for a moment.

"I'll make an accord with you."

Michael turned.

"I'll be your *target* if I get to keep these trousers."

He rolled his eyes again.

"I may as well, for I'm used to being without them now." He took her hand and led her to where he wanted her. "Right. I'll come at you and you throw the shield up to catch my swing so that it doesn't hit you."

"And if you then go for my legs?" she fretted as the guards

chuckled some more.

"Well then you *lower* the shield," he huffed as if it were obvious. "I'm ready, My Lady." He positioned himself a distance away.

"Wait! Can I at least prepare?"

"Lady Gwenyth." The boy grew perturbed. "I can see that you lack training. As your enemy at battle, I would not make sure you were comfortable first, now would I?"

"Are we at battle?"

"Go on, lad!" a guard teased. "She's easy pickings, a levy, maybe foot soldier at best!" Gwenyth scowled at them.

"All right, Michael, I'm ready," she sighed, feeling nervous for no known reason.

He charged at her and took aim at her midsection.

"Oh, my sweet Lord!" She fell to her knees and cowered behind the shield as the sword whacked the wood.

Hoots of laughter rose from the walls and the few guards who were not already on duty and awake had come out of their barrack to watch. Her face grew red but she could not help but giggle.

"I must look a fool, young Michael," she admitted.

He was grinning and offered her his hand. "Aye, My Lady. Let's try again."

She brushed her hair back and took up the shield once more, quaking from the rush of it. He came at her again and she cringed, pinching her eyes shut. No blow came. Laughter ensued again as the smith came out of his shop to watch. She unscrewed her face to see Michael staring at her with his hand on his hip, pointing at her with his sword.

"I could have taken your legs, side, or neck right now. You have to *watch*, My Lady."

"Shall we try again?" she said, both humiliated and amused for the first time since her return.

"Okay. Another go then."

Michael sprinted forth once more and this time she watched as he went for her legs. She pulled her legs back as though dodging a running dog, but dropped the shield and the sword bounced away. The men in the bailey cheered.

"Hurray, Lady Gwenyth!" they laughed.

George and Hershel came to the door from the great hall, then Gavin. Again she blocked the blows, even if she looked frightened in doing so.

"Michael's taken a squire," Hershel snorted. "How *does* Gwen always end up acting a lad?"

"Five brothers probably didn't help her become a lady," George answered.

"Go and wake Loddin," Gavin said.

The more she blocked the sword, the easier it got to anticipate his blows and the less afraid she grew, preparing for each attack. Loddin the brother came into the hall, sick at head from his ale but nonetheless alive.

"What is all the thunder?" their father asked, emerging downstairs from his chamber as more cheers rose outside.

"Father, watch!" they called him over.

He limped to the window as Michael delivered another blow aimed at her neck. She not only blocked it, but biting her lip, she leaned into the thrust and poor Michael spilled over backwards.

"Oh! Dear Michael!" she exclaimed, throwing her hands over her mouth, dropping the shield with a clatter.

The men of the yard were beyond hysterics, holding their bellies and shouting insults.

"Go on, lad! You let a fair maid take you down?"

"Aye, man, he will in a year or two!"

"And it's much more fun when ya's not fighten'em, lad!"

"Go on, Lady! Don't pity the enemy!"

She knelt to pull the boy back to his feet who too was laughing in full, fast rolls, shaking his head.

"Lady Gwenyth, you have much to learn!"

The Loddin boys laughed.

"This might just have been what your sister needed, lads," their father chuckled, then grew serious. "Aye...this is exactly what she needs. Self-defense will bring back her strength and take her mind from Sir William. Gavin!" he pointed. "You have a new squire. Go show her how it's really done."

"Let a man show you how it's really done, Sister," Gavin smiled as he came out of the keep.

To her surprise, he tossed her a practice sword and took up one of his own.

"You must watch your opponent's moves, anticipate where they are going. Once their swing is in motion it's hard to change directions but be careful not to fall for a feint. If I bring my sword like so, you must bring yours like..." He grabbed the sword held limply in her hand and raised it to position. "Like so. Take a high guard. There. Now my blade cannot cut yours. The closer to the hilt, the better force you have to push me away. At the tip, I can easily push yours in."

He did it and she fell backwards under the pressure. Her sword clattered to the ground.

"Mind your sister, son!" Loddin warned.

"A squire will earn their bruises, Father! I intend to make her tough!" Gavin replied.

"It's all right, Father!" she called, rubbing her backside, ignoring the guards' laughter. "A *squire*, Brother?"

"Father wants you to train. You're stuck with me," he grinned. "Hold it with purpose, Gwenyth, not as though it is a limp fish. Right, here I come now."

Gavin swung a practice waster, making it look more forceful than it really was. Gwenyth felt her stomach fall and dropped her sword to run. The bailey roared with laughter.

"Get back here, Sister!" Gavin teased.

Slowly she returned, hanging her head.

"The jests will be plentiful tonight, Gwenyth!" Mathew shouted from his post.

"Oh go on with your fun!" she hollered back. "And I shall make you my first victim! Then all will laugh at you!"

"We shall see, Lady!" Mathew replied.

Gavin did it again after she calmed down and once she began to work at it, she had gotten fairly good for a beginner. Loddin joined in, then George, all three taking turns while she grew accustomed to using her shield and her sword to block the swings, and Michael took a seat on the wall to dangle his legs and watch.

Loddin came at her again and she caught his sword with hers. It slid down to her hilt as she had planned and they stood locked.

"Hurray, Lady!" the guards cheered.

"Spin yours like this, Sister, and you send mine under."

She braced herself against the pressure as he bore down harder, and twisted his sword beneath hers. Then without warning, she rammed the shield into his chest while his waster lay locked beneath hers. He staggered back a step and smiled.

"Oh, you play rough now?" came the sarcasm. "Careful, Sister. You toy with a man's task!"

She smiled as sweat beaded her brow in spite of the freezing air. Even though the sword was wooden, she felt empowered. If only she could have felt this way with her husband.

"I shall—*practice—every day!*" she huffed as the sparring continued.

"And you shall become the champion of Ballymead, Gwen!"

They worked throughout the morning and slowly, the fears of Maccus, of the threat of war heading their way, and of Dwyre were buried in the back of her troubled mind.

I will never be just a victim again, I will never, she thought, then threw the training sword up high to block her brother.

22

William shivered. Snow fell all around them and the chain mail hauberk and chausses froze him through his gambeson. He crouched behind the jagged peak with Sir Cavanaugh and Sir Thomas at his side. A fire rose from the field before the fort and smoke floated upward, drifting over them with a foul odor.

"The one problem with burning down a wooden fort, men, is that you have nothing to stand upon when you're done."

His commanders chuckled.

"As usual, William makes me pity the enemy for being the brunt of his jests," Cavanaugh remarked.

Making laughs had not been William's intent, not this time. Battle was as serious a dance to him as were the taxes owed by a serf on a bad harvest and this time he was not finding much humor.

"Five, maybe six-hundred men at most...no women or children, only soldiers by the look of it," he muttered.

"What is that awful stench?" Sir Thomas muttered.

"Our lions."

"What?"

"Corpses, man. They dispose of our soldiers and their families from the sennight earlier."

The smell made him wish to spill Dwyre blood right then and he was frightened of the lust he felt for it. He prayed Father Kearney's words would seep back into his soul, but as he watched the fort below him, he knew it was unlikely.

"See that ridge?" He pointed along the peak. It wrapped down and around the north of the fort, the river cutting past it on the south.

"It has a good slope for a charge. We will begin with the archers, then foot soldiers, then we will send in the horses to cut down those that flee. We've got five hundred crossbows which can take aim up here."

"Do you think the crossbows are necessary?" Sir Cavanaugh asked. He looked down at the valley behind them where their army had pitched its camp. A massive beast of wine and black surcoats, plus the smaller chivalric orders that had sworn loyalty to the king, were sprawled across the basin. "Those *were* just banned by the church as being sinful. We have thousands more men to easily overpower them."

"I don't intend to take these wolves to the fair on a leash, men." William's words were terse. "I intend to kill them swiftly, like floodwaters."

Shea's men were working their fastest to get scaffolds built, but with the peak behind them, nothing took the place of the tower that had once stood.

It has been ill-fated from the beginning Shea, why could you not see?

"I agree, we cut them down, no mercy," Sir Cavanaugh replied. "I didn't come to the second highest rank by being soft on my enemy, William, I just don't want to go to hell for it, or have the bishops slap my wrists."

"The way the nuns did when you snuck into the convent to see the converts bathing?" Sir Thomas chuckled and sipped from a wine skin.

Cavanaugh knocked him on the shoulder. "You're not to tell my wife I was such an awful lad."

William grinned. "I don't feel like tangling in the many bible verses that the church has contradicted, men, nor the many verses within it that contradict each other. Should I thank you, Frances, for protecting me from slaughtering innocents when you suggest we do not use crossbows? Because I don't see them as innocents and the Church has sanctified this mission to kill."

"I too don't see them as innocent," Frances defended.

William snorted. "Well don't be fooled, for we are not innocent either," he continued, pausing to note the shipment of ores being pushed up river on a barge. "I didn't reach my rank by being soft on the enemy either, man, but it is because I make blood spill. It doesn't matter how it spills, it only matters that it does."

"And yet if we do so honorably without the crossbows, we'll be praised for it and the church would have no cause to complain," Sir Thomas added.

Now William huffed. Sir Edmund Thomas would not have made a scholar. "The way I see it, men, no killing is honorable. We all are wicked for the lives we take, not just them, and we do not answer to the bishops and the pope, but to God himself when the day comes that we fall from our horse under the blade of our enemy." He didn't remove his watch on the Dwyre men below. "And they won't care that they have used a mace, a lance, a poleaxe, a sword *or* a crossbow. They'll only care that they have made *our* blood spill.

"If you believe priests to be in touch with God, so be it, but I believe them to also be of the flesh and men can say the damnedest things to preserve their power no matter what type of robe they wear. Besides," he cracked another smile and turned around to face them, leaning on the rock. "Many of these wolves are pagans, so why should the church care?" Cavanaugh chuckled. "But if you still feel a crossbow is any less gallant than a sword, then I say you're a fool. It does not leave our soldier bloodstained and reduces the laundry."

They chuckled again and shared the wine skin. William wiped his sleeve across his mouth.

"Let the crossbows sit up here. King Bain wants the job done. If it's more Christian for you to use your holy water sprinkler, my good man, then so be it."

His officers met this with a hearty laugh.

"I'm convinced," Sir Thomas smiled.

"Father Kearney was right to have been irritated with you," Cavanaugh reminisced as they started back toward camp. "You could rationalize the burning of our only food supply and we would all go along with it."

He slapped him on the shoulder and William chuckled.

"Right, until your stomachs begin to rumble," William retorted.

"How *does* the fair Lady Gwenyth tolerate his dark side?" Cavanaugh added.

William thought of her again. He had pushed her from his mind so that he would not feel weakened. Now, he saw her holding her knees and staring into the flame.

'So the songs of you are true. You live for fighting but ne'er for love...' Your songs are true, Gwen. I get pleasure from this...

It seemed so long ago that he sat with her by that fire while he shared his most personal thoughts. Many of those words had not even been spoken to Father Kearney. He, the leader of the king's army, had been but a toy in a scheme matching him with a woman and yet he wanted her so badly and cared not that he had fallen for it.

"I pray to God she sees the man and not the murderer. We get in formation tonight, men, after the soldiers have rested through today," he continued, before his men could make further light of his love. "We made haste to get here and have arrived early. I don't think they will have expected us so soon."

"And when the sun comes up, we'll be their morning star," Sir Cavanaugh finished, throwing back the last of the wine.

"It's a white flag, man," Sir Thomas noted. "Shall we ride to talk of the rules of engagement?"

William raised his brow. "Do you think the rules have changed, man?"

"Presumably not," Thomas huffed.

"Behind that white flag, those wolves are scrambling for arms, gauging us as we do to them, only right now they are frantic and we are not. And don't think for one second that if we give them an advantage, they won't say to hell with the rules and pounce."

He let his eyes dart to the peaks. A sharp flash met his eye.

The mirror signal...my cross bows are in place. Thanks be for a bit of sunlight.

Behind him sat a meager cavalry two hundred strong. Out of the corner of his eye, William saw a lone rider along the trees beyond the delta, running his horse. He motioned quickly to three knights.

"A messenger. Cut him down. Now."

He pointed and the knights galloped away.

"Well now, a flag of truce? From Dwyre? We certainly caught them by surprise. Let's make this quick. I want time to break my fast afterwards."

He turned to a ranking knight who sat before the others.

"If they so much as sling one arrow, you are ordered to release the archers and send in the levies."

William handed his banners to his squire, the blue Cadogan

crest of the hawk upon which the name Gwenyth was stitched in bright letters. Above it waved the lion of Bain. They trotted down the slope to the field and came face to face with three men from Dwyre in brown and yellow surcoats, filthy from weeks in the field.

"Good day, men," William greeted as he came to a halt. "I thank thee for holding down our port. What say you and your *ladies* move along now?"

He snatched their white flag with his sword, using it to wipe his face. Sir Thomas rolled his eyes.

"Never one for pleasantries," he sighed, adjusting his reins.

"Especially when they never work," Cavanaugh added.

The fighting always starts, they had heard William say once. *It's just a matter of timing and I have learned never to let the enemy have the advantage of control.*

"You've got some nerve, lion," the Dwyre wolf growled. "A flag of truce and you disgrace it?"

"Was there a flag of truce when Shea Feargach took this port under siege? Was there a flag of truce when these wives and daughters that fuel your pyre now were raped and murdered? If so, I would like to see it!" William snarled, Titan dancing with excitement beneath him. "Or perhaps this is the flag *Lord* Shea carried, and it is so clean because it was never used—"

"This land was Dwyre dominion and we reclaim it. King Bain's father had no right to it!"

"And yet it prospers beneath Bain, whereas the Dwyre *roi* had so much fealty and his people so little tribute to give that they starved! Or they came under his wrath and were kicked off their lands, roaming into Bain for handouts because their own lords were just as corrupt as their king!" William narrowed his eyes. "It made sense to make them part of our kingdom and replace your lords!"

"Those lords have sworn their loyalty and provided conscriptions!"

"Those lords have been forced into it, man, and you know it!"

"You have no proof of that!"

"I need no proof. I have witness testimony," William growled. "Lord Shea's house has ears."

They fumed and soon Dwyre gave up.

"This gets us nowhere. What are your terms, lion?"

"My name is Sir William Cadogan."

They stiffened but tried not to show it and William raised his eyebrow.

"Oh, so you have heard of me? Good. Because if you don't fear me now and you manage to live today, my face will haunt you, man, like a reaper, until I cut you down. My term is but one. You leave, and we do not kill you. Yet."

"You're as cocksure as they say, Cadogan. An upstart with muscle but no mind to go with it. You have only two hundred horse. Hardly worth it."

"Have we only two hundred, Sir Cavanaugh?" William asked.

Cavanaugh snorted. "Last I checked it was more like two thousand."

"Did not Our Lord King tell you? He ordered a thousand more," Sir Thomas added and the three of them chuckled together.

"Your bluff is weak! We have already sent messengers to warn Lord Shea! You won't get away with this!"

"Was he riding that way?" William pointed with his sword. The Dwyre men looked angry enough to spit. "Don't be worried, it was only *one* messenger and we have saved him of his labor."

"Our terms, lion!" he yelled. "You return to your ridge with your pathetic mules and *we* do not kill *you*!"

"Then it has been a pleasure, men."

William bowed his head and turned the reins as Titan responded to the blood coursing through his master, breaking out into a full gallop of excitement.

"Done with all the proper Cadogan antics! Never let them have the first word!" Thomas said.

"Or the first move. Cavanaugh, release the archers...*now!*" William ordered.

He stabbed the white flag back on his sword as they galloped ahead, waving it high in the air. The cries from the port behind them assured him that the crossbows had seen it.

23

"Archers!"

"Archers!"

"Archers!" the call went down the line.

Cavanaugh raised his flag. A string of archers stepped forward, extending all the way down the ridge. They dipped their arrows in the fires that had been lit. Turmoil had consumed the fort. The crossbows were lobbing a splendor of metal arrows, raining like elf bolts from the clouds. Screams and shouting rose from the port.

"Readyyy!"

Sir Cavanaugh swung his flag down and a rainbow of flames arched through the sky.

"Readyyy!"

He swung it again. The arrows blazed forward. Soldiers toppled from the scaffolds. The crossbows continued to hail the fort. Dwyre soldiers began to flood out onto the field, three hundred strong.

"The foot soldiers! Cadogan, they send them!" Thomas skidded to a halt.

"I see it, man!" William shouted. "Raise the flag! Foot soldiers!" William hollered.

"Foot soldiers!" Thomas raised his flag.

"Foot soldiers!"

"Foot soldiers!"

Four long ribbons of men stepped up from behind the ridge with their shields put forth.

William charged forward.

"Thomas! End this! Order the charge now!"

"Yes sir!" Thomas nodded and held his flag high as he ran down the line.

Let us squash them, William thought, and trotted through the men to the crest of the ridge.

"Soldiers!" Thomas hollered as he galloped the length of them and dropped his flag. "Chaaarge!"

They swooped down the hill in a magnificent arc, swords and bludgeons ready, roaring on their lips.

"Cavalry!" William hollered.

A column of knights rose upon the ridge and joined the two hundred already there. Squires began running forth with shields and extra weapons.

"Cavanaugh!" he shouted. "We stage a charge!"

"But look...our men on foot overpower them—"

"It's an order!" William pointed. "We take no chances!"

"But William! Our foot soldiers out number them, at least five to one—"

"And we will catch the stragglers!" he fumed, *if there are any.* "Your flag, man!"

They snatched their flags from their squires and turned in opposite directions.

"Cavalry! Ready!"

Cavanaugh was watching him. William threw down the flag and so did Cavanaugh.

"Chaaarge!"

Their horses lumbered into a gallop and the spears came forward. Bainick foot soldiers before them clashed with the men from Dwyre and engulfed them. William set them in his eyes and drew his sword.

The Dwyre men who had not been felled saw the horses and turned to flee. Clattering echoed out of the basin. William panted as he drew closer, searching for yellow and brown and seeing Thomas waving frantically.

Cadogan! William! We've conquered them! Frances! Stop!"

came Thomas's call.

He waved his sword back and forth. The Bainick soldiers were crying out victory.

"William! Stop! Stop now!" Thomas yelled.

William pulled back on the reins and Titan tossed his head. He sheathed his sword and threw his hand up.

"Haaaalt!" he hollered. "Halt, men!"

Slowly, Titan relaxed into a trot. Cavanaugh was repeating the command. The army slowed until they had all stopped. William scanned the field and dismounted, handing the reins to a soldier. Dwyre's men lay strewn across the slush, twitching, or dead.

"Our men made a mess of it," Thomas said as he too jumped from the saddle. "We have won. But I can't help but think that—"

"We've not killed them all," William interrupted.

He strode forward into the corpses. He climbed over the limbs and the groans. A yellow and brown surcoat was limping away, holding his stomach. He glanced back and saw William.

"No, no..." he mumbled as he tried to run.

But William reached out and grabbed his surcoat.

"No! Show mercy!" the man begged.

William spun him around and thrust him back. The man cried out and toppled backward, revealing a gash across his belly. It was the commander he had met with on the field. He tried to sit up.

"I warned you," William seethed and sent him back into the snow beneath his boot. "I said I would haunt you like a reaper!"

"I beg you! I..." he fell into coughing.

"I said I would haunt you and I meant every word."

He pulled his sword and placed it at the man's throat.

"Be merciful!" he cried, shaking.

"This is mercy. You're dead."

He lifted his sword high.

"No! No!" the man thrashed on the ground. "Noaaaaah!"

The sword sliced into his gut. He screamed. William jerked it hard.

This is for being on the wrong side, he thought and clenched his jaw. *This is for siding with a lunatic.*

The screaming turned to coughs and a couple twitches, then stopped all together.

Pulling it free, he reached down to wipe the blade on the dead man's surcoat and resheathed it. He turned around to renewed cheering and laughter from his men.

Thomas and Cavanaugh walked to his side and looked at the damage as his squire came galloping forward.

"Anything you require, My Lord?"

"No, Jonathan. Will you see to it the shovels are brought forth and order in the priest? We've graves to prepare, and see that one cart of casks are tapped. Our foot soldiers drink first today! You shall be boasted to His Majesty for such a glorious victory! Congratulations, men!" he hollered.

His call was met with cheers and his men slowly turned back up the field. Cavanaugh clasped his wrist and chuckled.

"Your strategies are golden, William. You had them so frightened they couldn't think to fight. Should the rest of our venture be as simple, I might forget I am at battle and imagine myself on a holiday."

William summoned a smile. "Aye, a simple quest would be nice. But I don't anticipate such ease as this. Shea travels with the most numbers and we lost a handful today. It will get harder. Frances, order forth our surgeons to tend our wounded."

"Yes, William. Then you must indulge in a tankard with me."

"I would not complain," William replied.

Frances strode back to his horse and cantered to the ridge.

"We did not even *need* the horses," Thomas remarked, shaking his head. "That was not a fair fight."

"Is there such a thing as fair in this profession, Edmund?"

"I suppose not. Our men fought well and should be pleased, and of course I'm proud to have led them in."

"And you are not pleased yourself?"

"There was no challenge at all. I cannot help but feel that there was no honor..."

William slapped his shoulder.

"And that, my friend, is why King Bain named me commander."

"Do you not show mercy at all? William, you're like a hunter. *That* man was as good as dead and yet, because you hadn't yet suffered a bloodstain, you descended upon him as if killing is a lust. That was more like pure slaughter."

"That was necessary, man, and that is all." William set his face and ripped off a gauntlet to wipe his brow. "Which side do you prefer?" He replaced the glove. "The side that finishes their enemy and buries their dead with Christian rights despite their wickedness? Or would you prefer the side that rapes maidens, butchers children, and burns their bodies in a heap?"

Thomas shifted and nodded. "You make your point, man."

"You may not like my tactics, but my tactics keep you alive *and* employed. Had that man not died, he might have *lived*, if not forever, long enough to talk. I'm not a chivalrous warrior. I don't fluff the enemy's pillow for him. This discussion is over. We move on to Faulk. I intend to get to Shea Feargach before he gets to the highlands." William paced away before turning back around. "And I'll not hear of these complaints again, Edmund. That's my order and you will obey it. Don't make me wield authority in front of our men." He threw his hands outward and began to grin. "Besides, Father Kearney blessed us all. Your soul is safe."

Thomas succumbed to a chuckle. William slapped him on the back and they walked up the field together.

"We didn't know! I swear it! Have mercy! We didn't know!"

Dwyre soldiers thrashed down the crofts and hacked through the cattle enclosure.

"I beg you, not the cattle!" pleaded the old man.

Shea sat atop his horse at the edge of the hamlet with his army lounging behind him in the trees. He watched as one hundred of his men ravaged it.

"Burn it. All of it," he muttered.

"No, My Lord! I beg you…no…no wait! Not the women!" He fell at the horse's feet and clasped his hands. "Please don't harm the women! He said they were man and wife! He said he was a Bainick knight! That they were very much in love, she had lost her son—"

"His whore was *my* son's wife! And her son was *my* grandson!" Shea boomed. "Get out of my way!"

He trotted into the village in the Northeast Pass and watched as his men tore it down. Screaming rose as the huts were set to fire.

"Run! Run!" the old man urged his wife who dragged her grandson behind her.

The women fled desperately and the children were wailing, bouncing upon their mothers' hips.

"Not my wife!" the new husband cried. "Not my Bruin!"

Three soldiers caught the new bride as she tried to flee and dragged her back into her hut. He chased after them.

"Leave her be!"

"Away, peasant!"

They thrust him backwards. Instead, he picked up his thresher from the wall and swung it into the soldier's back. The soldier stumbled forward. He beat him over and over again until his back was spilt open and he was screaming.

"Away with you!" another soldier shouted, wrenching free the thresher and drawing his battle axe.

"Husband!" Bruin cried. "Malcom! Please run away!"

"No! You'll not rape her!"

They ripped loose her clothes while the other prepared to swing his axe.

"No, man," Dwyre's men chuckled. "Let the lad watch how a real man beds a woman!"

They laughed and he watched as his wife, sobbing, was thrown on the pallet.

"Damn you all!" Malcom screamed, kicking the soldier's stomach.

But as he scrambled forward, the knight tripped him and pinned him face down in the dirt. He wrenched back his head and twisted it sideways. "Now be a good farmer, lad, and watch!"

The soldiers laughed while she cried. He managed to wrench himself free once more, punching the soldier's face as he struggled to get to her. No sooner had he gotten to his feet, he was tripped again, fell, and the axe landed across his fingers.

"Ahhhhh! God! Ahhhhhhh!"

"God won't save you, beggar!" the soldier growled.

"Husband!" she wailed as she was flattened onto her stomach and the soldier flipped aside his surcoat.

Outside, the grain store was taken. The livestock was slaughtered and the village glowed while the townsfolk huddled together in the snow, too afraid to move.

"Let it be known!" Shea bellowed. "If you harbor my enemies, *you* are my enemies! Bainick knights and their whores are not welcome here! This is Dwyre land once more! I am your rightful ruler! You and the Lord of this fee swear allegiance to me!"

Shea's men let up a holler.

"Onward, men! To Dunstonwoodshire!" Shea called. "We've got bigger things to pillage then a couple farmers and their fat wives."

24

"How does the Lady Gwenyth do?" Maccus remarked. He pointed out of the trees. "Look at that."

From afar, they could see a tiny figure making her way down the field, long blonde hair giving away the person.

"A sennight, lads, and now we know her routine. Visits the serfs each morning, how *kind* they are to their slaves," he mocked. "Rides her horse in the pastures almost every afternoon."

"How do we get her out here? Beyond the guards?"

Maccus scooted back through the snowy leaves until he was well hidden, then stood.

"She'll not come out to these parts alone, Ballymead or not. Her father would be a fool t'let her. I've got to go in."

"But how will you know where to go?" the other asked.

"Now, this is what makes me the expert, man." Maccus rubbed his belly and pushed back his greasy hair, ripping off a bite of the remaining bread and dusting his beard with crumbs. "I came here during her betrothal to William. Even then, Lord Shea told me to look around for all the weaknesses of the fee. I know the layout of the walls. Tonight I go in t'look around. If it works well, then I'll trap her on the inside."

"I don't think it wise, man. If we get caught, then it's all of Ballymead's guards and soldiers against us."

"See those walls? No fee can have guards around the entire wall. The weakness is beyond the southern wall, where the tree line comes close. In the dark, I will not be seen and I have brought rope for a reason. Besides, snow moves in."

Maccus gazed at Gwenyth from afar as if stalking prey. She

turned down the road to the cottages of the guards and came to Mathew Whitcroft's cottage. The chickens clucked in their roosts, too afraid to brave the snow. She pushed open the gate made of willow branches woven through posts.

"How goes it, Marta?" she called at the door and pushed it in.

Marta stood over her hearth, sweating, holding her back and trying to stir the oats potage though her massive belly was too swollen for her to see beyond it.

"Oh, Lady Gwenyth," she attempted to bow.

"Silly lass," Gwenyth sighed as she set her basket down on the part of the table not covered in turnips. "I expect no such formality from you. You'll topple over for sure."

She grabbed the young woman's hands and pulled her up.

"You should see about having one of the girls come and assist you. In fact, I will see to it myself." Gwenyth turned back to her basket. "Will you sit a moment and share some bread and cheese?"

Marta looked at her pot on the fire then smiled.

"I could use a moment. This burden grows too big. Mrs. McIntosh tells me I should have parted with it a sennight ago." She shuffled across the rushes and plopped down on a stool. "I feel myself tighten during the days, not often, but they are not comfortable."

"Then it will be very soon, for Mother Nature will see to his eviction," Gwenyth smiled.

"*His*, My Lady?"

"Oh, well your husband was always late to help with harvest, Marta," she jested. "Surely, this is a lad like him, for he is late to meet the world."

They laughed together.

"It's nice to see you smile. I see you on the hills sometimes and I know you are sad at heart."

Gwenyth's smile faded. "Aye, well, I had an ordeal but I shall come through it. May I feel?" she changed the topic.

"Of course, Lady."

Gwenyth knelt and placed her hands on Marta's belly.

"He kicks! He will be as strong as a horse," she smiled as tiny feet pushed her belly out of shape.

"I believe he will be a jester, for I'm certain he is turning cartwheels in my womb."

Again, they laughed.

"His feet are in the right place and you have dropped. You will meet your child soon."

She cut the bread and cheese, handing Marta a piece.

"You will still assist the birth, will you not? Mrs. McIntosh said you're quite able as a midwife."

"Of course, Marta. I'll be ready."

Marta smiled and rested her hand atop her belly.

"The women are sewing a blanket for the babe and I would be honored if you would add a stitch or two, gossip with us or share our company. We are all dying to know of your Sir William."

Gwenyth looked down and withdrew, and Marta knew something had struck a chord.

"I'm sorry, Lady Gwenyth, I should mind my tongue. You are the daughter of Lord Loddin and we are not of equal birth—"

"We are daughters of the same earth, Marta. You must know by now that Ballymead is different from Brynmor Braith."

"Well, if you need to gossip, I'll listen. It grows quiet here when the women are working, except for our visits."

"I will do well to remember your friendship," Gwenyth smiled.

She noticed Marta's belly again, for who could miss it, and thought of baby William. She realized she had wanted him. She pondered Louisa, the quiet baby girl who gurgled happily at night in the cradle that had once been her own. How could she be evil? Shea was a monster and yet wee Louisa was her own soul, separate from him and sweet.

Perhaps wee William would have been the same. Perhaps William was meant to die so Louisa could take his place, she thought.

They ate their slices of bread and Gwenyth rose to leave.

"You are blessed, Marta," she said as she opened the door to let the sunlight cast a glow about her. "Your husband is a gentle soul and you have a healthy babe. These are things I didn't have, despite my rank."

"Then perhaps Sir William the Brave will give you both, should you be betrothed, hmm? You mustn't lose heart."

Gwenyth hesitated.

"It's hard not to lose heart. If I never love again, Marta, then I will cherish the days we spent together...though I will tell you," she let a smile curl her lips, "he kisses sweetly, but I can promise no babe is coming from it." Marta threw her hand over her mouth and giggled wide-eyed while Gwenyth pulled closed the door. *There will be gossip in the hamlet tonight, that is certain*, she thought.

That night, Gwenyth lay wrapped in her blankets by the window, still wearing her trousers. Gavin had drilled her all day again on swordsmanship and dagger draws, not to mention he had begun to make her exercise and lift a bar with sacks of grain tied to each end. She had grown so sore from the practice, her arms ached to lift them and her thighs twitched, but each day had strengthened her and she felt good. The guards cheered her now and instead of making fun they paid compliments. She could even hold her own on basic defense against her brother from time to time, who despite being stronger, acknowledged that her small size made her quick...

'It's not all about strength, Gwen, it's about agility and knowing your enemy's move before he does it,' Gavin had encouraged as he shifted a dummy, making her avoid its arms with bags of rocks swinging from them.

One of them had hit her and she flinched backwards.

'Don't show fear, Sister. Fear is what feeds your enemy's strength,' he continued, then let go of the dummy and pulled her beside him.

'If there's one thing you learn from all of this, Sister, this is the most important thing. Do not ever give your enemy your fear. Power is intimidating. A battle, a fight...a beating...'

He let those words hang, knowing she heard him clearly.

'Whoever has the power of fear is in control. You must never let your enemy have the power of fear over you, do you understand me? You must turn yourself to stone. 'Tis not enjoyable to beat someone who is not afraid.'

Stone...like William did. That's how one endures pain and fear...

She wondered how much Gavin had let her win on some of their spars. Perhaps he was being soft so he could build her up.

"My Lady…" she was being shaken. "My Lady! Marta Whitcroft asks for you! Her babe is coming and she begs for you! Mathew waits in the main hall for you…My Lady…My Lady…"

"What? Oh! Her babe!"

Gwenyth jumped up and grabbed the deerskin boots she used for the snow. Grabbing an old gown from her chest, she stepped into it, pulling it up over her tunic and trousers as her maid cinched the laces and banded her hair together.

"Hurry, Lady. She's in much pain," Mathew begged as they left the great hall.

"Relax, Mathew. We can only move so fast in the snow."

"Please hurry all the same," he fretted.

It was late. She and Mathew raced to the stable where she readied Luna herself rather than wake a stable boy.

"Move quickly, please," he continued as they descended the slope, though Luna trudged slowly in the burgeoning blizzard.

The hamlet was practically invisible through the snow and the wind was howling. It was not until they arrived that the lights could be seen. The cottages were mostly sleeping, except for the one next to his where women boiled water for clean linens.

She jumped down and hustled through the drifts, juggling more fresh linens and a lamp. Thick flakes were freezing her hair into a stiff chord. She could hear Marta groaning. Mathew turned to her, frightened, his hair greasy from raking his hands through it.

"Help her, Gwenyth, she's hurting."

He held her hand, his trembling.

"Dear Mathew. Your baby is ready. Don't fear, despite the cries she makes."

"But will she be well? For I need my Marta—"

Gwenyth smiled. "There's nothing to say otherwise. She has carried this child perfectly. Have faith, Mathew. She is in good hands."

A couple men came out of the next cottage and slapped him on the back.

"Come have ale, man. You could use it."

Marta began to cry out and Mathew looked at the cottage again, but Gwenyth took his arm and steered him away.

"Have your ale and relax, Mathew. There's nothing you can do, save wait," she smiled, and ducked into the cottage.

"Lady Gwenyth!" Marta cried as Mrs. McIntosh scuttled around her like a field mouse.

The cottage was dark, save the fire in the hearth and the candle flickering across the rushes. She lay on the pallet, her legs parted and her belly round and tightened. Her fluids had stained the linen and she had soaked her flaxen shift with sweat.

That horrible night, she suddenly thought. *The blood and the groaning, and the babe...*

"I'm here, and your babe will be soon as well," Gwenyth clasped her hand and wiped her hair from her skin. "You must be strong now, for the hurt will get worse. But there is not a woman nearby who doesn't know your pain. You'll be fine, you'll see."

"Thank you...thank you," she panted, as nature tightened her belly again.

She moaned, then cried out and squeezed Gwenyth's fingers.

"Breathe through it. Breathe, Marta," Gwenyth whispered. The tightening died down and she lolled her head on the pillow. Mrs. McIntosh came to sit by her and reached her hand between her legs to feel.

"Okay, dear. When you're ready to push we will bring your baby out."

She smiled. Marta began to moan again, then she cried out once more. Over and over again her belly tightened then subsided. She began to weep.

"You are well, Marta lass. Does your back feel pressure?" the old woman asked.

Marta nodded as a wave of pain came again. She didn't cease wailing this time. Mrs. McIntosh nodded at Gwenyth and pushed her sleeves back up.

"Get the water out of the hearth, My Lady," she ordered. "Mix in some cold so it doesn't scald. This babe will be soon and it's freezing out tonight."

She did so, wrenching her hand from Marta's clasp and heaving the pot of boiling water out.

"Lady!" Marta cried. "Lady, I need you!" she begged as her hand waved outward.

"I'm here!" Gwenyth replied, pouring the water and gathering the needed rags.

"Lady, please!"

"All right, Marta! Grab hold now!"

She offered her hand again and Marta clamped it as though hers was an iron vice. The tightening happened again and Marta wailed.

"Marta. You must push. Bear down," Gwenyth crooned as Marta squeezed her hand again.

"I can't!" she sobbed.

"Yes, Marta, you can!"

She pushed and cried, and then the tightening was over.

"Give this to her!" Mrs. McIntosh fussed.

Gwenyth pulled the stick from her grip.

"Here. Open. Now rest your teeth upon this."

She placed the stick between her teeth and Marta clenched it as her pain started again. She screamed a grunting scream as the old woman reached between her legs and smiled.

"You make *fast* progress, dear!"

The tightening came again. She screamed again, clamping her teeth so tightly on the stick Gwenyth thought she might crack her teeth.

"Keep breathing, Marta!" Gwenyth encouraged.

Yet she felt saddened despite the excitement. There had been no soft hand to caress her and tell her she was fine when her babe had come. She had been alone. Sir William had been a strange man at the time.

"Please God!" Marta screamed as the stick fell from her teeth.

"Push, woman! Push!" Mrs. McIntosh ordered.

She bore down with all her might, sobbing.

"Push, I say!"

Mrs. McIntosh reached around the neck and shoulders of the baby and eased it out onto the pallet.

"Marta you have done it!" Gwenyth cried and kissed her soaking forehead.

The old woman flopped the child across her arm and scooped out the fluid from its mouth with her robust finger. The telltale crying began.

"Dear woman, you have a son! You have a healthy son!" She cinched a string around his cord. "Listen to those lungs!"

She took a knife and cut through it.

"Here, Lady. Bathe this babe!"

Gwenyth scooped the baby toward the warmed water that sat upon the table and the blankets heating by the hearth. The baby cried and cried, short, punctuated wails as his chin quivered. After he had been duly scrubbed, she swaddled him into a bundle.

"There now, child. Shall we meet your mother?"

Gwenyth took the babe in her arms like she had done dozens of times before, and gazed at him, healthy and round.

"He is perfect, Marta," Gwenyth whispered as she rubbed his little cheek, setting him into his mother's waiting arms.

Marta's face glowed.

"You must let him suckle," beamed Mrs. McIntosh.

She helped the child latch to Marta's breast. The baby wiggled his head back and forth like a routing piglet and took to it.

Marta giggled. "He's like his father," she remarked.

"Aye, men have a way of knowin' these things! Even as babes!" the old woman grunted as she scooped the soiled linens into a basket.

"Will you call him, My Lady?" Marta sighed. "If I know my Mathew, he's slumped over drunk with worry."

"Of course," Gwenyth smiled, and ducked out into the snow.

Mathew was drunk, just as Marta had thought, murmuring to himself at a table with his head in his arms. Several men stood around him while he doused his stomach with another swig.

"She stopped crying. Please, Lord, let her be well, let my Marta be well."

"Have faith, man," one of the guards said, patting his shoulder.

"She's not crying, and the babe stopped crying..."

"Be strong," another reassured. "You'll know soon enough."

"My Marta...oh God," he mumbled. "I promise to be more pious. I'll, I'll go to mass every Wednesday if you just see fit not to take her yet—"

"Mathew Whitcroft! You have a beautiful son!" Gwenyth burst through the door.

The men erupted with cheers and pounded him on the back, sending him flopping. A guard swept Gwenyth off her feet and spun her around.

"A son?" he croaked. "I have a son? And Marta? She is well?"

Gwenyth nodded. "She's tired and will need your help, but very well in spirit. She has made you and all of Ballymead proud!"

The pounding continued as the men cheered and scooped him to his feet.

"Praise be," he murmured.

"Who would have thought a scruffy lad like you would have ever done something so wonderful!" she teased.

The room filled with laughter as Mathew grabbed her face and planted his lips to hers. The laughter burst into a ruckus of jests.

"Aye, I turned out all right after all then," he grinned as she swatted him.

"Come! Your woman begs your company!" She grabbed his hand and dragged him away.

It was the depths of night when Gwenyth left for home. The snow had picked up more and climbing through it was going to prove daunting.

"You ought to stay here tonight and return when the snow stops, Gwenyth," Mathew said.

"Of course I will not. Marta and you need to be alone with little Mathew. I shall go on my way and spread the news."

"Then I'll ride with you to the keep, My Lady," Mathew began.

"Don't be silly. Your wife needs you here."

"But the snow is fierce—"

"I grew up on this land and I'll be well to go alone, Mathew."

"But My Lady, I would be a lousy man indeed to let a woman

brave this storm by herself."

"I won't argue it," she said with a stubborn smile. "Stay. Enjoy your new babe. I insist upon it. And I'm your mistress so you must obey."

"Mistress or not, Gwenyth..." He pulled her aside and lowered his voice. "I still consider you someone I care for deeply. I would worry for you out there."

"Then don't worry," she admonished and grabbed her cloak. "I will tell the family the good news. As I said, I won't argue it further."

She began up through the snow again, having left the lamp at the cottage. It was so thick and windy, she let instinct direct her and Luna where to go. The lights from the cottage disappeared and she thought of Marta's soft smile. And Mathew, completely drunk, was so proud he could hardly keep himself from crying as he kissed her and cradled the babe in his arms. It had been perfect. Perhaps the day would come when it was her again, with the right William this time, William Cadogan. The wind whistled and she clutched her cloak.

Suddenly she felt a thud. The blow struck her head so hard it almost didn't sting. She grew dizzy, then collapsed to the snow below.

25

Her head was pounding like hooves galloping to battle. She woke on horseback in the clutches of a man. All was still dark. It took a moment for her to realize that it was because her eyes were still closed.

Wincing, the light made her feel green with illness as they emerged from the trees, yet her eyes would not focus. The horse was cantering through the snow. She reached up to her head and felt it. The pounding was enough to knock her out again and each bounce of the horse made blood bang her skull like a mallet. She moaned, then heard laughter.

"She's wakin' up."

The voices sounded garbled.

"Guess what, Lady Gwenyth. You've been naughty. Lord Shea wishes to console you for the loss of his grandson." More laughter and a stinking breath near her face made her stomach turn. "Unless the handsome Bainick knight has already eased your pain."

"My William is honorable..." she slurred.

The laughter continued, though it sounded jumbled. She could see blood on her fingers and her hair was gelled with it on the back of her head.

What is happening? Where am I? Lord Shea...they take me to Lord Shea...Lord Shea...Maccus...Aindreas was right...no...no... "No!"

She wrenched herself from Maccus's grip and fell out of the saddle onto the ground. The impact sent her head spinning and she toppled over. Maccus turned back his horse and dismounted, grabbing her around her waist.

"You'll do well not to fight me, woman," he grunted as he

heaved her back onto her feet. "Or you can feel Lord Shea's strap for it."

Don't show fear. Gavin said not to give the enemy fear, don't give Maccus your fear, or he wins... "I'll feel his strap anyway. What does it matter?"

Maccus grabbed her face.

"Insolent wench. I'm warnin' you. Don't try my patience or I'll bloody your backside."

His fingers were pinching her cheeks but she made no sign of being frightened. With a thrust, he let his grip go and tried to heave her back into the saddle though she wriggled down.

"And if you bring me in all bloodied and bruised, what will your lord think then when he is expecting a pretty face to warm his bed?" *Think Gwenyth, think.* She begged her mind to become clear. *What has happened? How long have I been gone?*

The snow was still falling, her surroundings were unfamiliar and the coldness on her skin was rousing her into full consciousness. Maccus let loose the back of his hand and her face reeled against the horse's neck.

"I don't take kindly to bold women! Quiet!"

She twisted free yet again as he struggled to lift her.

"Do it again!" she yelled in his face. He lifted his hand. "I was William's wife! There's nothing you can do save take my life that I haven't already endured!"

Maccus stared at her, his hand ready to strike.

"Do it!" she hissed, her eyes narrowing. "For I will die before I give you the pleasure of my fear. *You* are not worth it!"

He glared long and hard, then lowered his hand. "I don't have time for this. Patrick! Come'ere and hold her."

A stocky man climbed down from his horse with a greedy smile on his face. He grabbed her wrists and slowly slid a hand up her arm as Maccus climbed back into the saddle and got ready to haul her up. She tried to shrug it off.

"You're a fair little thing, whore or not."

His teeth were grey as he smiled and she furrowed her brow.

"I'm no man's whore."

"You're a Bainick knight's whore," he chuckled and let his hand slide across her shoulder while Maccus laughed and waited for Patrick to have his fun.

Gwenyth's chest heaved. His fingers traveled across her breast. She tensed.

"I've never been a man's whore, save William Feargach's!"

Without thought, she spat in his face and thrust her knee into his groin. He buckled forward with a moan and she bolted to his horse.

"Damn!" Maccus cursed.

She leapt into the saddle and wheeled the horse around in one move. The horse was already in motion as she swung her leg over in her cumbersome dress.

"She's a *God-damned* woman for Christ's sake!" she heard him shouting.

Gwenyth looked over her shoulder. Maccus was in hot pursuit. She charged back over their tracks, breathing rapidly. Searching the landscape, she saw nothing familiar. There were foothills, but none that she recognized.

Think, Gwenyth!

She begged her mind to summon a plan. Maccus was gaining on her. She leaned forward, practically hugging the horse's neck as she willed it to move faster. A wood was coming up. She entered the trees. Branches whipped her arms. Dodging the pillars of bark, she descended a slope and soon lost the tracks that the horses had left. Maccus was crashing through the brambles behind her. She looked forward again and her heart sank. The trees were only growing thicker and she would never lose him in it.

She slowed her mount and splashed through a stream, the horse's hooves cracking the ice. They bounded up the bank through more branches that scraped her legs, her horse barely squeezing through. The branches thinned again and she nudged the horse to move faster.

"Please, horse! Please!" she whispered to it, "Please deliver me from them!"

Again she kicked the creature. It veered back and forth to dodge the forest growth. She looked back again. Maccus was on her tail. The horse swerved sharply and she whipped her head around, ducking and barely avoiding a crack to the skull. But as she turned over her shoulder again, her cloak snagged on a limb. She was wrenched from the saddle. The force crushed her neck. She gasped, slamming against a tree with a thud and all went black.

When she woke again, she was flopped belly down across Maccus' lap. Her head dangled over his calf and the ends of her hair were wrapped around his wrist. Whether this was meant to keep her in place, or keep her hair from dragging, she could not decide. Every breath hurt. Her neck felt raw. She tried to swallow but it was pure agony to do so, so she refrained.

As she came to her senses again, she squinted her eyes open and could see that it was getting dark. Maccus rested his fist holding the reins on her buttocks and she decided that pretending to be unconscious was the wisest choice at the moment. He shifted and farted, hacking phlegm into his throat that he spat to the side.

Revolting, she thought. *The foulest person I have ever known.*

"I'd say about another hour or so, then we'd better stop for the night," Patrick commented.

"We'll do well to stop," Maccus agreed. "A day's ride tomorrow and we'll be to Dunstonwoodshire."

"Is she still knocked out?" Patrick asked.

Maccus leaned over her and peered at her face. "Aye, sleepin' like a li'le foal," he chuckled. "Puts up a strong fight, I'll give her that. She never would have done that before. Lord William would have killed her. Can't say I blame her for wantin' to flee. I'd not want to be a woman in the House of Dwyre."

"I'm not one for puttin' up with a mouthy whore," Patrick fussed with resentment.

"Shut up, man," Maccus huffed, "Yer only sore because she got the better of you."

"And she'll not do it again!" Patrick replied. "She ought to know her place. Once a whore, always a whore. That Bainick knight probably had his way with her," he chuckled. "Lord Shea wouldn't know if we tasted her sweetness too. She's no virgin."

"Careful, man," Maccus warned. "All she has to do is say it, and Lord Shea would have your stones ripped off and shoved down your throat. He might intend on beddin' her himself, but he'll not take to others spoiling what's been kept in the family."

"You don't think that knight took her? You think he rode with her for sennights and not once took her to bed? He's from Bain, man, those men conquer whatever they choose and I've seen plenty of those honor-bound knights with their hands beneath a woman's skirts. You said yourself he acted as her husband."

Not my William, she thought.

"No, not this one," Maccus said as if he was agreeing with her. "He's got a reputation of *untarnished honor*," he exaggerated in a voice from court. "No, he fancied her for sure, we could see it at the camp before the bastard tried to gut me, but I don't think he had the nerve to rape her. Besides, she had just given birth, probably was still bleedin'. Nothin' more disgusting than a bleedin' woman, fair or not."

Patrick laughed. "Never a problem for me before."

Gwenyth's stomach turned and she wished her ears could silence them.

"You risk your health, man," Maccus muttered with disgust. "A woman's full o' poison when she fluxes."

Squinting again, she made out the shape of a dagger stowed in the laces of Maccus's boot, right below her head. Her heart quickened. Her hand was dangling just past it.

All of a sudden she felt her gown being lifted.

Let them be distracted, she told herself. *The last thing I want is them paying attention to me.*

"I'm warnin' you!" growled Maccus. "Leave her. I let you grab her bosom but you'll not get much else."

"But...she's wearing trousers!" Patrick exclaimed. Maccus looked as well, then flipped down her skirts.

"Hmm," Maccus pondered. "She rides horses like an expert too...put up a damn good fight...wonder what else she's capable of," he murmured.

They came upon a shelter, falling over from abandonment and half buried in the snow. Gwenyth was heaved off the horse as Maccus's jerkin creaked. She groaned and rubbed her eyes.

"Wakin' up are we?" Maccus whispered. "I'll not have any more mischief woman, you hear me? One wrong move and I'll kill you myself and tell Lord Shea you were dead on the high road."

His teeth looked like stained nubs of wood and his breath was so repellent she couldn't mask her disgust.

Act, Gwenyth...act...

"You'll not kill me, Maccus," she croaked, her throat stinging to do so.

She curled her mouth into a knowing smile and swayed on her feet.

"You mind yourself that I don't have to prove it to you. You just stay as quiet as old Jasper over there."

He jerked her head around to see the third man who had remained silent the whole of the journey.

"Jasper!" he called. "Show our fine lady your tongue!"

Jasper turned his horse and parted his lips to reveal a mangled mouth. Maccus laughed as Gwenyth's face dropped with both horror and amazement.

"Had his cut clean out in the Land of Spices, woman, for mouthin' off to the tax collectors." He jerked her head back to face him. "I'd hate to cut out your pretty one. No doubt it has its uses."

"From the rumors I heard at Dwyre," she smiled, "'twould have no use for you."

He pursed his lips and thrust her towards the hut as Patrick stifled a laugh. She tripped forward, her whole body aching as though she carried the burden of a pack animal. Patrick was sent to gather wood along the tree line and soon a fire was lit, smoke rising through the holes in the remains of the thatching.

The warmth was a small blessing and so was the chunk of bread tossed to her. She considered throwing it back, but wasn't sure when she might eat again and realized she was ravenous. When it was finished, she grabbed scoopfuls of powdery snow that had blown in against the wall and ate them, satisfying her thirst. Maccus threw a blanket at her and stinking though it was, she huddled beneath it with her cloak, thankful for the extra tunic and trousers she still wore beneath her gown.

26

Janis huddled next to the fire in her chamber. No word had come from Aindreas about Louisa. She moved to her chests and pulled out the inkbottle and quill, finding a scrap of parchment. Her supply had run low and she had not been able to barter for more. She had learned no more news of Shea's plan since he had left for the siege on the river. Aindreas had come swiftly for her daughter upon his return from battle and had been gone the next day when she went in search.

Staring at the blank parchment before her, she simply wrote: *Is there news of my package's safe passage?*

She moved into the corridor, down the stairs and into the great hall where she spotted the guard at the door. She moved to pass him but he stepped away from her. She stopped, her little paper about to slip from her hands when she looked at his eyes. His grim face made her heart jump. He kept his hand firmly on his spear, the other behind his back, and barely shook his head.

"Do you wish to exit, My Lady?" His words were barbed.

"Em...no, I'm fine...I mean yes. Yes I do."

He pulled open the door for her. The air was freezing and she had no cloak.

"On second thought, I think I'll stay in," she whispered, turning white. *Something is amiss...* "May I ask you a favor?" she began.

"I don't wish to make idol chat with the Lady of Dwyre. I have guard to keep. Good day, Lady."

He shut the door, this time stepping through it to make sure he was on the opposite side.

Anxiety swept through her. But when she returned to her chamber, three men were inside. Her quill and ink were still out and her pulse began to rage. Slipping the parchment into her sleeve, she cowered beneath them as they turned to look at her.

"What're you doin' with all this?" one of them asked.

"I should like for you to leave my chamber at once, or I shall report this to my husband upon his return!"

They chuckled. "Your husband is the one who ordered us to do this." Her face was ghostly. "Who're you writin' to, *Lady*," they mocked.

"No one, My Lords, I only wished to draw a new embroidery design. Do you see my needlepoint beside it?"

They noted it and nodded, though none looked convinced.

"Do you need sealing wax to draw designs as well, My Lady?" another said as he picked up the wax and her stamp. "Perhaps it depends on the type of, *design.*"

She chose to ignore it. "Lord Shea asked you to pilfer my possessions?"

"No, he asked us to rout out a spy. We found someone here who *knows* something, shall we say, and so far you're the only one they've pointed at. Now, who're you writin' to?"

"A spy?" she gasped indignantly. "Are you accusing me of spying on my husband? That's preposterous! Get out!"

"You shouldn't talk like, woman. It's unbecoming."

"And you will suffer punishment for this!" she hissed. "Get out!"

They took her writing tools and left her in her chamber. She leaned against the door and began to whimper.

He'll kill me! Is that what has happened to Aindreas?

Just then, a bar shifted into place outside of her door. She froze.

"They know," she mouthed, turning pale. "My Louisa...you didn't make it. What have I done?" Heart thumping, she slid down the door and collapsed as her chest heaved. "My dear girl, have I signed your death warrant, and your father's too? And now mine?"

After what had been hours, she peeled herself up and moved to the hearth where she pulled the note from her sleeve and thrust it into the flames, watching as the edges of it curled.

He'll kill me. It is over.

She began to search her trunks for any sort of paper, ink, anything. She pulled loose her garments and linens, digging through the chests until she had made more of a mess than the men had. Then she came across a pile of embroidery.

"I shall stitch a letter," she decided.

With trembling fingers, she pulled loose a strand of yarn.

Titan trampled through the trees until William reached his tent.

"Are you ready, man?" Cavanaugh said. "Shall we go to strategize?"

"Aye, up the hill. We'll have a clearer shot...Thomas!" William called.

Thomas handed his reins to his squire and came forth.

"See to it none of our men have lit fires. Last we need to do is send Faulk a warning."

"Yes, sir."

William and Cavanaugh climbed through the trees until they could see the fortress beyond, a massive palisade of wooden spikes and brattices that protected a stone tower. The one road that passed through, forking towards Bain in one direction and the Northeast Pass in the other, was well-barricaded and swarming with Dwyre soldiers.

"'Tis a shame I have had to leave so many on the River Ruadhán. I pray our messengers make haste back to Bain for reinforcements. This will be a tougher battle to win."

"But we outnumber them still," Cavanaugh added.

"Yes, but unlike the port, this one is well-fortified."

They had already toppled this fort when I came upon Gwenyth, William thought. *God how I should have been thinking battle...*

He felt himself drifting away to that terrifying night as Cavanaugh talked on. Gwenyth's wailing became intense in his mind, so much so he didn't notice the snowflakes drifting through the trees against his dirty face. It had been so horrifying he had shut it out with much success.

He had never heard crying like it and had kicked in the door, thinking a beast must be attacking her. He had never seen anything like it and had felt helpless as he stood before her, not knowing the first thing to do as she writhed on the pallet.

Boil water. That's what he did. *The women always say boil water...why?*

He tried to talk to the young woman though she didn't hear him through her anguish. Eventually she had passed out. He hesitantly rolled her on her back, her small belly tight. He saw blood. He saw lots and lots of blood, all over the bed cloth and all over the bottom of her gown.

'She's with child,' he had said. *'Her belly is far too small to give birth.'*

Breathing heavily, he pushed up his sleeves...and felt fear. He never felt fear.

She was limp and he was afraid she had died. Gulping, he placed his fingers to the heartbeat in her neck. She thumped, but her skin was cold, pale, like white marble yet wet with fever.

Pulling off her slippers, he tossed them aside and crossed himself, lifted her skirts, pulled off her stockings and parted her legs. He saw the top of a small head from her private space. He crossed himself again and again. He felt like he was raping her, fearing she might awaken.

God, dear God what do I do? Tell me what to do! I pray you!

He had begged for divine advice and when no answer graced him, he washed the dirt from his hands, said a short prayer, crossed himself once more, then reached to the infant's head and placed his fingers around its tiny crown. Her belly was tightening again and it was pushing forward. He let nature urge the child out.

Its ears and forehead finally came through. Despite the pushes, nature was not moving quickly. The anxiety was making him mad and he felt sweat collecting on his upper lip, trickling down his face and pooling around his neck. He waited for yet another tightening and when it came, the head finally came through and he could see no life lay upon the face of the babe. It was blue. It was then that he grabbed it and began to pull, only to realize that its cord had it trapped.

The lady moaned an unconscious cry of pain and he froze, but she didn't wake and soon he had the child in his hands, not much bigger than a rat with its life cord cinched around its neck. It had suffocated the baby boy, though he was so small and undeveloped he would not have lived anyway. There was not the telltale crying, no joyous smile on the mother's face and he felt his heart drop for the poor girl before him.

With no capacity of mind, he trembled from top to toe and had to sit. He unwound the cord with shaking hands now covered in blood and waited. It was still connected into her private space and he had not the first clue how to extract it. He tried not to look back but she was blood soaked, all over her slender legs. Of all the battles he had fought, not once had he felt pity, but here, pity was all he felt. If she lived, he would have to tell her the news.

Nature finally solved his problem and he took the babe with its afterbirth away, severed the cord from its tiny belly and laid it by the door. She was bloodied up and down her legs. He couldn't leave her like that.

Summoning more courage, he untied the laces of her gown and dragged it over her head, then removed her shift and she lay naked before him, fading bruises exposed and still unconscious. Despite it all, he had noticed she was beautiful if not extremely thin, with soft, rounded breasts. Her ribs expanded and contracted beneath her skin already stretched flat across her hips.

He had never been in the same room with an undressed woman before, though he had seen many through cracks in the doors as a squire when he spied on his knight and many more when his men seduced the wenches at the inns. Yet she was by far the loveliest woman he had cared to lay eyes on. He was ashamed for admiring her and busied himself with a rag dipped in warm water, which he used to clean her.

Lifting her into his arms, she was so slight and her breasts had pressed against him while he held her. He had, of course, never touched an undressed woman either and found himself reacting to it in the most inappropriate way for the situation. And yet, though he had felt the natural urge time and again, he had never felt it for any particular woman, until now.

Placing her upon a new bed cloth, he dug through her basket and found an extra shift, a delicate linen garment made for a lady, not a peasant. He then uncovered her veils and her circlet and a soft pair of beaded slippers. '*A lady?*' He was thoroughly confused and found himself staring at her yet again, then set to dressing her with prayers that she stayed asleep a little longer.

'*What stories do you know, woman?*' he whispered as he sat beside her, holding the bronze circlet, now knowing she was a ranking woman of a high liege.

He took a lifeless hand in his, hoping her touch might answer his queries.

'Who are you, fair one? Are you the one I search for?'

He allowed himself one caress of her cheek, clammy from fever, icy to the touch, which she responded to by tilting her head on the pillow so that her neck opened up in case the caress continued. He obliged, running his fingers along her skin. But when she sighed a soft sigh, he could no longer resist. He leaned down and pressed his lips to her neck, kissing her and cupping her cheek in his hand to hold her there. She sighed again and shifted.

It was the first kiss he had ever offered a woman and even though she was not returning it, it was wonderful. He moved his lips slowly up her neck to her jaw line and rested them there as his blood pulsed, urging him to go further and taste her lips. But instead he parted from her and covered her beneath his cloak and blanket.

Brushing her hair from her face, he noticed her wedding ring for the first time and was mortified. He stood abruptly, severed his emotion, and strode outside where he fell to his knees and begged forgiveness for coveting another man's wife.

Falling in love with this creature had never been his intention, but as she spilled her story days later, he was already feeling it, wishing to touch her, comfort the scared mouse of a person that sat before him for he knew what it felt like to be the mouse beneath the fist of an angry giant. And now, the closer they got to Dwyre, the more his pulse raced and the more he wanted to be the one to gut Shea Feargach and spit on the graves of his sons. The more he wanted to find his sister wherever she was, the more he wanted to hold Gwenyth and tell her how he had been there for her, how he had cared for her, how he needed her and how he loved her more than life itself...

"William? William, man, where is your mind?" Sir Cavanaugh huffed and knocked his shoulder. "Are you in there somewhere? I've been talking now for minutes."

William shook his head. "I'm sorry, man. I'm not myself."

"I should say not. You've never been one to drift. You ought to focus now. Faulk? You *are* aware that we must stage a battle here on the morrow?"

William nodded, cursing his restless mind.

"What has burdened you? Ever since the king spoke to you, you've been miles from here."

William chuckled. "'Tis nothing of concern."

But Cavanaugh would not be put off this time.

"I'm your friend, man, and at risk of sounding soft, I care what has ailed your spirit. Don't try to shut me up. 'Tis insulting."

Cavanaugh did not budge or make any move to relent and William sighed.

"The king shared information with me that has helped us know Dwyre's moves," he said.

"That would normally be a good thing. Why are you not pleased?"

"Because it's my sister who has sent him messages. She is trapped in Dwyre somewhere."

"Your sister? I had no idea you had any kin, save your brother Faegan, one of our prison guards."

"Aye, I had two brothers and three sisters, one of which is dead."

Cavanaugh looked surprised. "I thought I knew you better."

"She's in Dwyre's clutches somewhere, man, and—" He didn't finish, but went back to staring at Faulk, then upward at the clouds. "Not the most ideal conditions for staging a battle. I'd rather it be less wet."

"Don't stray from the subject, Will. What else?"

William huffed and swallowed hard, folding his arms and kicking cached mud off his boot.

"I keep seeing her, Frances, the Lady Gwenyth. How she feared. I keep thinking of how Shea and his seed are the ones who did it to her." He shook his head again and leaned his shoulder on a tree. "The closer we get to Dwyre, the more my blood boils. It's not good for battle because I'll become unleashed and I am afraid of what I might do."

"You cut them down, same as always," Cavanaugh patted his arm.

"That's not good enough. I'm tasting blood revenge."

"You really love this woman?"

William looked down with embarrassment, for most men his age were well experienced with women.

"I'm not capable of just a tryst. I thought I wasn't capable of love. 'Tis of humor too, because it's *this* love which makes me hate so much it's clouding my judgment." He waved his hand. "Thomas was right, back at the port. That man was as good as dead and I could have sent a soldier to finish him, but no. *I* needed to kill him, tasted it."

William sighed once more.

"If Ballymead is cut off from Bain, I fear she'll be captured and she will suffer for leaving Dwyre, and she will suffer for having been with me and if she's dishonored, how can I take her to wife when she has been made another's whore?"

"She must be incredible to have won your heart. But don't rule out that even if she has been dishonored, it doesn't mean she would make a poor wife. Even my wife had a lover before we married."

"Did she?"

"Well, at least one that I know of," he chuckled. "I've resigned myself to never ask how many. 'Tis better that way."

William stood stunned.

"What did you do on your wedding night?"

Cavanaugh shrugged. "I cut myself."

"What?" William exclaimed.

"I made myself bleed and we stained our wedding linens together, our homemade maidenhead. We laughed the whole time. Our mothers outside of our chamber must of thought us mad."

"You're devoted," William shook his head.

"And quite a bit drunk, the both of us," he laughed. "Which meant the blood ran loosely. Everyone thought she was the bloody Virgin Mary. Those customs of virginity matter to most men but not me. I've enjoyed women and surely an experienced wife makes a better lover to her man. But Shea Feargach seems a beast. We mustn't allow him to whore your lady," Cavanaugh said plainly.

William's glare gave Cavanaugh his opinion of his words.

"Don't talk of her in such a way."

"Hear me, William." Cavanaugh grew serious as they watched the fort. "There are few beautiful things in this world. We kill and our kingdom praises us for it, but that's not beautiful. I have my wife and two young sons, Sir Thomas has his hunting, our army has its wine, women, what have you...but not even those things are beautiful in the way you describe, they are comforts that we love. But you, William...you've had nothing ever since you came to the capital. I'm two years your senior, man, and I remember it well. You were angry, like a little banshee. Then, as you realized the ladies weren't going to have you whipped every time you spilled a trencher, you became the jester. People liked you for it but no one could ever really know you *or* your secrets...you seemed empty."

"I learned to fight, and that glory of winning filled me and made me strong. It was good for me."

"Fighting and winning are *your* comforts, man, but those aren't beautiful. But now, you have the Lady Gwenyth and she completes you. The way you talk about this girl...she must be incredible to have gotten your attention. What ever happened to you as a boy?"

William shifted. Cavanaugh had always been his closest friend, or at least, William had let him be closer than the others.

"What does it matter? That was five and ten years ago, and longer."

"You weren't treated well by your family, that much was clear to all of us—"

"It doesn't concern you, how I was treated," William said. "Leave it be."

"How were you treated? Certainly every man felt his father's strap once in a while," Frances pressed. "'Twas odd indeed for the king to interfere with how a liege lord ran his family and then take his son away."

"Frances, use your imagination and it probably happened."

"*What*, happened?"

"He beat me, Frances!" William grabbed his surcoat and shook him. "He whipped and beat and kicked and cursed...once," he laughed at the preposterousness of it, "he even spat on my dinner before he let me eat, but I was so hungry I ate it anyway. Imagine your father doing that to you. Of all of my memories, not once was he proud of me. But I overcame. It's my mother who couldn't, and I hold the bastard responsible for ruining her. I've only just learned the reasons why, but I've a battle to stage on the morrow so we must get back to the matter at—"

"Like?" Cavanaugh was not going to relent.

"It's not my place to tell you, man. Besides, I just learned of them myself."

"What did the king say to you? I know you're hiding something from your private meeting. Don't offend me by talking in circles around me *as is your talent*."

William released his grip and Frances shrugged out his surcoat.

"It's a private matter. I wish he'd never told me." He paused, but Cavanaugh was pressing him with his stare. "You must keep it under your coif, man. It's for the king to share."

"Sir William sharing secrets now?" Cavanaugh teased. "William, I consider you my closest friend. I'll not spoil the news by spreading it."

William took a deep breath. "I'm a bastard."

Cavanaugh cracked a smile. "Yes, I've had a mind to call you that once or twice myself."

"No, man, I am really one."

Cavanaugh thought for a moment. "Well certainly half the men who exist are bastards. Men sow seeds and we would be fools to think that our women wouldn't want in on the fun too—"

"I'm the king's bastard."

Cavanaugh's mouth hung parted and he said no more. William looked at him, eyes serious. He smiled, raising his brow.

"Not quite what you expected?"

"Well, I mean, there have always been rumors, but we assumed that they were just rumors, you know, not really true..."

"Imagine now, Frances, that you've just returned from leaving the one woman you want, for her father has said no to marriage, to find that you go to war against the family that wronged her, that your sister is spy to the king, and by the way," he waved his finger as though he was having a premonition, "she is but your *half*-sister because the king whored your mother and made your father raise his *bastard*. It's no wonder my father bloodied me so badly. He wished me dead for I disgraced his house by living. That's why the king sent for me, when he found out."

"Then you would be his only son," Cavanaugh said quietly. "You are a prince, heir to the throne..."

"And Gwenyth might be my queen someday." He shook his

head and furrowed his eyes. "I'd rather die than let Shea rape her and if he's already done so, there isn't a strand of his entrails I won't rip from his gut to strangle him with."

Cavanaugh got his wits back.

"Your mind is in the highlands and we must get your body there as well. The king wouldn't have shared all of that with you if he didn't want you to do something about it. He doesn't want you marrying a whore either, it seems."

"I must strategize to serve the kingdom first—"

"To hell with strategy, man! Let us lay waste to this fort and move on to the highlands, toward Ballymead. We've got the men to do it too. Our men fight for king and country, but above all, at your command and they would be proud to know they've gotten you one step closer to bedding down," Frances smirked, earning William's first smile of the day. "They're trained well to trust your bidding."

"They mustn't know."

"That isn't my point, *Your Highness*," he cracked as William threatened to lay him flat with his glare. "They fight under William Cadogan's command. They know not a William Murron of Bain."

William pondered a moment longer and watched the fort.

"I don't want to get cocksure."

"Damn it, William, call it *my* strategy, but when you rage, we win battles. Shea doesn't know that *we* know he moves toward Dunstonwoodshire. Let us make our move swiftly while you've the anger to do it, and get you to your woman whose name graces your banner. We'll come back for Dwyre when it is through, for Shea is not there."

"All right." William nodded and peeled himself off the tree. "All right. Let's make our move. We get into formation tonight so that they are surrounded when the sun rises. On the morrow, our crossbows sit here, in the trees. We divide our men and I'll create a feint to lure their officers out onto the field. If I come down from those hillocks to the north with Sir Thomas and half our troops, you lead our other knights from the south once they're engaged with our feint...I pray to move onward afterwards as swiftly as possible."

"We'll help you get to the Lady Gwenyth. It's my promise that you're not alone, man." Cavanaugh clasped wrists with him. "And do not think me as soft, for I find it much easier to give the maidens compliments," he jested before growing serious again. He gave

William's shoulder a firm pat. "But you're a fine man and a good friend. You deserve to be happy for once."

27

William approached the fort. His Bainick surcoat had roused immediate suspicion. Yet with his white flag upon his sword and Sir Thomas at his side, Dwyre's men sent out their commander and his entourage.

"What is a lion doing on this side of the divide?" Dwyre's man demanded. "How did you get through?"

"We have been separated from our party and only wish passage through these gates to arrive back to Bain," William replied.

"That is the worst lie I've ever heard," the wolf replied. "Bainick knights are of considerable rank. You'll become our prisoners, or if you flee now, you'll be shot down like the other pussy cats who held this fort before."

"Before a traitor in the ranks made them sitting ducks, you mean," William remarked.

"Mind yourself, man. You're in no position to be arrogant. Dismount now and disarm yourselves, or we will dismount you."

"We won't be your prisoners today. We only wish passage through. There's nothing to be gained from it."

The Dwyre knight turned to his fellows and chuckled.

"I believe that if they try to bargain, they might really be telling the truth. What can we gain from letting you through? Nothing. What can we gain from taking you prisoner? Ransom money, perhaps?"

"Money would be good," another chuckled.

William waved his flag again while their guard was down. Three hundred mounted knights clattered to the top of the hillock and William smiled at their surprise.

"Oh yes, you've been suckered out here and you know not how many more we have, but if you've ever tried counting the stars at night you might have come close. Let me guess. All of Shea's ranking men are standing before me?" Their agitation told him he was right. He nodded. "Good then. I am Sir William Cadogan and the army of King Bain has arrived. We shall take back Faulk now, with no problems, man. And what was it you said, sir? Oh yes. And if you try to flee, you'll be cut down like the other wolf pups we sent into the afterlife on the river port."

A Dwyre soldier whirled his horse around toward the fort, barely having gotten to a gallop when one of William's crossbows let loose and lodged between his shoulder blades.

"They attack! They attack!" the leader shouted. "They *bloody* feinted us!"

The men scrambled to return to the fort. William and Thomas bolted back up the hill as archers from the fort began to rain arrows upon them. Three hundred Bainick archers were already responding with fire and arrows. William kicked Titan harder as the Bainick crossbows picked the entourage off until all of them lay dying.

"All the archers! Get all our men on that ridge!" William shouted.

He hid beneath his shield, an arrow stabbing clean through it next to his face.

"Damn it! Use them all!"

All of the archers rose from behind the hillock. A splendor of retaliation was unleashed. Yellow and brown surcoats toppled off the walls. Those patrolling the outside now lay dead. But the lucky ones retreated inside the battlements and the soldiers dropped the portcullis.

"Damn!" William cursed as he maneuvered Titan back and forth. "We attack on the fort! Before they have a chance to ready for it!"

"But the initial damage has been done!" Thomas called. "They might listen to reason now!"

"No!" William snapped. "It's not enough. We finish them!"

He hailed his squire forth.

"William!" Thomas hollered and skidded his horse to a halt. "There's no sense in wiping out men who might now surrender—"

William grabbed his surcoat, practically ripping him from the saddle.

"Do you argue with me? Do you?"

Thomas sat stunned and gripped the reins.

"We've been through this before! *I* lead this army! I shall discipline those who are disobedient! I won't return to His Majesty the king and report that we let his enemies live! I have clear instructions to see them dead and if you've grown soft, then I shall see to your replacement!" he growled. "Well? What say you?"

The crossbows stopped. There was nothing left to shoot. William glanced at the fort preparing for battle and fumed.

We've lost our moment. They are prepared now... "Well? We waste valuable time!"

"I'm sorry, sir," Thomas mumbled.

William released his grip and looked around, his men pretending to ignore them.

"We don't negotiate with them, as you have ordered. My humblest apologies, Sir Cadogan."

William looked back at Thomas. *What has come over you, man? You would never threaten your commanders.*

"It's I who am sorry," William replied. "I embarrass you in front of my men...change of plans," he continued. "For despite our discord, we must win this now. They prepare for us. The battering ram. We'll plow through that fort if they're going to run."

Sir Thomas hastened to order it to the front. A huge log, shaved to a spike and doused in oil was pushed through the waiting army, up and over the hillock by at least twenty men holding cross-joints beneath it.

"Keep up, archers!" William hollered and cantered to the edge of the hill. "Thomas!" he called back. "Get Cavanaugh on that ridge! Full frontal attack when the portal is breeched!"

Thomas fled on horse down the slope close to the tree line to be out of the archers' range.

"Archers! Keep lobbing your flames!"

His officer galloped down the front line with his flag of attack once more.

"Readeeeey!"

The flag swung down and the firing continued.

"Readeeeey!"

More arrows soared.

The battering ram was moving across the field. Dwyre archers fired at the soldiers. One by one, his men were hit.

"Replacements!" William ordered. "Our men fall! Levies!"

Soldiers ran to the field and took up the empty places.

"This will take an entire bloody year," William grumbled. "I'm going in!"

He grabbed a flagon of oil, galloped down the field where he jumped down and dodged an arrow. With a crack, he smacked Titan's rump and sent him fleeing to his squire. He took hold of a cross joint in the front.

"Light this damn thing on fire!" he barked.

A soldier ran behind them, cracking his flint until a spark ignited the oil. They rolled past the fallen, heaving and sweating from the flame. Their feet slipped on the snow. The volley of arrows was ceaseless. It was hard to tell whose arrows were whose now. The man behind him screamed. He fell and the massive wheels rolled upon him, crunching him as he pierced the chaos with his cry.

"Keep pushing! *C'mon* men!" William demanded.

They neared the portcullis and gained momentum.

"Onward! Run, men!"

They rammed the point into the grate. The whole battlement shivered.

"Pull back!" he ordered.

Boiling water cascaded down through a murder hole from above. A scream rose from the man opposite him.

"Again! Readeeey! Heave!"

They wheeled the ram forward again and it smacked the portcullis. The tremor vibrated through his bones, yet the portal remained intact.

"Again!" he shouted.

Stones fell through the murder holes and a large cobble knocked him on his shield shoulder.

"Damn!" he cursed and buckled beneath it.

But the battering ram wasn't stopping for him. He jumped back to his feet and winced. Grabbing the cross joint, searing pain ripped through his shoulder. He gritted his teeth and pushed it from his mind.

They heaved forth once more and cracked into the portcullis. The wooden grate crackled, yet still didn't break. He spied the inner compound catching fire. Well-placed arrows were igniting bales of hay.

"Again, men! Again!"

Exhausted, they back wheeled once more and pushed forward again. The portcullis splintered and part of the gatehouse buckled with it. The wood crashed down. Men inside began to flee.

"Onward!"

Their war cries lifted their spirits and his foot soldiers right behind charged through the broken gate. Grabbing his flagon, he doused the walls and gates with oil. They sprang into flames and he lobbed the empty flagon into the fire. Dwyre men retreated farther to the inner gates sealing the passage through to Bain.

William ran back down the field again, jingling beneath the weight of the mail and raised his sword.

"Jonathan!" he shouted.

His squire was running in full gallop down the slope with Titan's reins and William's shield. His knights poured in behind him, Cavanaugh's command flooding in from the south.

Sliding to a halt, his squire's horse sprayed snow.

"Your shield, sir! Your mace!"

William grabbed the reins and sprang into the saddle, jammed his gauntlet through the straps of the shield his squire held for him and secured his mace to his back. His men stampeded around him. The weight of the shield made his shoulder throb.

"Get back to the tents, lad!" he shouted. "God speed now!"

His squire jumped into his saddle, whipping the ends of the leather against his horse's rump.

Titan, cavorting and puffing steam, charged ahead of the foot soldiers and wove in and out of the horses. Cavanaugh's force had merged with them. They reached the portcullis, spilling through the burning beams. The horses leapt over the embers and bodies.

His men had already breached the inner gates. Roaring, thousands of voices strong, was ringing through the madness. William let loose his sword, slashing it downward at a man with a lance. The wood snapped and his sword struck through to his neck.

More soldiers took aim at Titan's legs. William pulled back and plunged his sword like a dagger. It broke clean through the mail and into his chest, but another stabbed at his side. He yanked free his flail mace from his back, swinging it over his head. The man reeled backward into a burning hay bale, screaming. A sword slashed through his boot beneath his chausses and he wheeled Titan, swinging his mace again and splattering the soldier's face.

A Dwyre man raised a white flag but William cantered forth.

"No..." he shook his head. "No! I surrender! I surren—"

William twirled his mace as he breezed past, the spikes landing against his head. He set his jaw and pummeled him again and again as the wolf collapsed to the ground.

28

Soon, within the burning walls, it was only Bainick Knights who stood. They looked around and let up fatigued cheers, swords, shields, and bludgeons thrust upward.

William took an inventory of the mess. His lungs puffed and he tried to shake the rage that was coursing through him.

"Well done, men!" he hollered, "We claim the victory!"

His shoulder burned and he dropped the shield, glancing at Thomas who walked amongst the slain. From within the inner gatehouse, a timid stream of soldiers came out, weapons raised above their heads in surrender. His knights began to lunge forth. The Dwyre men turned to run. Thomas looked up at him and a glimmer of compassion caught William off guard.

"Hold!" William shouted, riding Titan out in front.

His knights stopped and the Dwyre soldiers slowed. William dismounted as blood oozed from his boot.

"Hold, men!" He held up his hands and his knights backed up. "Men of Dwyre, come forth!" The yellow and brown surcoats made their way back into the yard. "Your weapons! Disarm yourselves!"

They did so, throwing their swords and daggers into a pile as the walls lapped upward in flames. He waved his finger at some foot soldiers who began searching them, then collected the pile.

"Who here is from the Dwyre fee?" he demanded.

No one answered.

"Who here is a Dwyre conscription?" All of them raised an arm. "You there! From where do you hail?"

"I'm the son of a low liege near the coast, sir! Cromlech

Manor!" he replied.

He could not have been much older than twenty, with a thin beard that had not grown into full.

"Did you volunteer your services, man?"

"Lord Shea Feargach ordered me liege lord, who sent all his knights and their sons to his aid. I wished only to run me plot of land, but Lord Shea threatened me crops burned and me new wife raped if I didn't comply!"

William thought. *It's just as Gwenyth said. The sick bastard. Dear God don't let him reach Gwenyth.* "That sounds like a Feargach move. Have you similar stories, men?" he called.

All heads nodded. William remounted Titan.

"Did any men here today come from Dwyre?"

"You killed them on the field, My Lord," the same one answered. "The rest of us were levied."

William thought of how to answer. No doubt many an innocent man died today, *and for what?* he thought. *Fear that their women would be abused.*

He looked wistfully away at the grey sky and burning battlements, and thought of how scared he was for Gwenyth, the same fear that all these men before him had felt.

I have become unleashed, just as I knew I would and now, how many women will never see their man again? How many children will grow without their father?

"William?" Cavanaugh came forth. "What say you? Do we finish them?"

'You have always handled the innocent with mercy, and will do right by God, William, I know you will do right,' said Father Kearney in his mind. After a moment longer, William shook his head.

"No. No, we do not."

"We do not?" Cavanaugh raised his brow.

"We send them home."

"What?" Cavanaugh exclaimed. "Since when do you soften?"

"Since I now understand these men's fears."

His knights stood waiting, watching for the signal to end the enemy and Cavanaugh smiled.

"All right, man. All right. No doubt Sir Thomas will appreciate this new chivalrous side," he jested, then turned his horse away.

"You shall go home to your wives and children!" William announced as he adjusted himself in the saddle.

A murmur swept through his men.

"I am Sir William Cadogan and I speak on behalf of Our Lord King Charles Murron of Bain! He is merciful to those who comport themselves with honor!"

He waved at Cavanaugh.

"Sir Cavanaugh! Take a convoy and see that these men receive one ration apiece, and then release them in defeat to their families. See to it that our men show no abuse toward them, for they have surrendered and the battle is won."

He rotated his shoulder around and winced, reaching up to rub it. Cavanaugh came forth again.

"Are you well, man? You favor your arm," he muttered.

"Just some discomfort. It'll no doubt mend with rest. Pick your men to escort these soldiers."

Cavanaugh turned his mount.

"Frances?" he stopped him once more. "Should they feel so inclined to relieve themselves of those Dwyre crests upon their surcoats, allow them to stoke these flames with them. If they have truly been wronged, it might give them satisfaction."

Cavanaugh smiled and rode away as Thomas approached.

"We're too late, Cadogan. Messengers were already released to warn Lord Shea. We'll never catch them."

"Damn..." William shook his head. "There's nothing to be done. Order forth our squires and surgeons. We have wounded needing tending. We move on the morrow."

"Toward your Ballymead, sir," Thomas smiled. "'Twas noble, what you did here," he stated and turned his horse away.

"Has your sister come down yet?" Loddin asked while his sons broke their fast. "Normally she's early to rise."

A servant brought in firewood and the wind blew powder across the rushes.

"No. Mathew Whitcroft came for her last night well after she retired," Hershel said as he tore his bread. "His wife began birthing pains and begged her to assist."

"You were not asleep?"

"No, sir, but I was on my way, after having read the monks' Aramaic testament."

Loddin scoffed. "Aramaic...you and your bible study. I sometimes wonder that my seed were too well-educated. The cloth will never cultivate the rich lands I intend to allot you someday."

"The bible is pure poetry from the lips of God, Father, and I intend to cultivate my soul with it."

Again Loddin scoffed. "What is it your grandfather always said?"

Gavin chimed in. "I believe he said, 'only eunuchs should be priests. For if God blessed you with a workin' willy, you should we workin' yer woman day and night so that his blessing is not in vain,'" he recited to the laughter of all the brothers.

"As Mathew Whitcroft has apparently done, hence Gwenyth's absence," Hershel smirked.

"She might need her sleep then." Loddin resigned himself and sat down, taking the cheese and meat that young Michael placed before him.

Just then, muffled crying filled the solar.

"Louisa begs to break her fast too," George chuckled.

"The demands of women start at a young age," Lord Loddin jested.

For some minutes the crying persisted. Gwenyth's maid finally scurried up the stairs. Soon she scuttled back down with the squirming bundle and headed to the buttery.

"Did Lady Gwenyth sleep through that commotion?" William called after her, though she had hurried too quickly and didn't hear.

The men chuckled.

"She must be *very* tired then," Hershel deduced, sipping his watered wine while he stood and adjusted his belt about his tunic.

"I couldn't sleep through it," young Loddin complained, tearing pieces of bread and forcing himself to swallow them. "Mary still wishes to conceive after losing our first, but I'm not sure I could handle a babe's demands."

"That's why the womenfolk handle it," laughed Gavin.

"Then you should keep out from beneath the women's skirts, Gavin, if you don't want any," his older brother retorted. "One of these days, a woman will knock upon our door and hand you a great responsibility."

"A babe is a joyous blessing, as are the women who bear them. It's your habit with ale that hinders you, Loddin, not a crying babe," their father stated shrewdly. "Too much time serving on the borders with naught but a hoard of men for your company."

"You're probably right," his son conceded to his brothers' laughter. "But I have at least been doing my duty since my return," he grinned. Their father gave a humored humph. "Notice Mary hasn't woken yet? Very tired, that one is."

Again, they laughed.

"Mary has done well to tolerate you," their father replied.

The crying finally stopped and the maid brought Louisa back into the great hall with a skin of milk plugging her mouth.

"Hand her here, Beatrice," Loddin gestured.

The maid relinquished the nursing child to his arms. He gazed down at her while she kicked her feet inside of her swaddling, then up at the maid and all of his sons.

"It's like holding all of you again, though no child of mine would ever have such raven hair." He shook his head. "You're busy with work, Beatrice, and need not compensate for the Lady Gwenyth. How sleeps she?"

"My Lord," Beatrice curtsied. "She hasn't yet returned from Marta Whitcroft's birth. I sat with the babe through the night after Mathew came for her."

"Not returned?" Loddin furrowed his brow.

"These things can take time, Father," George reasoned. "Perhaps Marta is having a difficult labor?"

"That could be true, but on second thought, Beatrice, will you tend the child a moment longer?"

She bowed again and took the baby back, making her way to the women already sorting the spindles and yarn to take a seat and rock.

"Gavin, you ride with me. Let's check on how Marta fairs. Gwenyth might need to rest for a spell."

By the time the stable boys had readied the palfreys, the sun was well up despite the quilt of grey clouds that smothered out the light. Passing under the portcullis, they wound around the slopes and finally arrived at the hamlet where the cluster of guards' cottages sat above the huts of the peasants.

Serfs and off-duty guards were coming and going from the Whitcroft cottage. Loddin dismounted. The guests bowed as their lord approached them, going on their ways, chattering and smiling.

"Something isn't right," Loddin murmured.

They tethered their horses to the fencing outside the croft, buried completely in white and made their way up the path. Mathew stood at the door.

"My Lord," he bowed, a huge grin upon his face. "Your daughter is a blessing. She helped deliver my son."

"You've a son, man?" Loddin smiled and clasped his wrist. "My congratulations. We shall send a package upon our return."

"You didn't know?" Mathew looked confused.

He ushered them inside. Warm stew was simmering. The neighboring women and their daughters were cooking for them and Marta, wearily propped up in bed, waved.

"Thank you, My Lord, for coming to visit," she sighed, holding her bundle.

"I wish to stay longer, but I come in search of my daughter. Did she just leave?"

"Why, no, My Lord," Mathew sputtered, and the women by the hearth looked up from their preparations. "Marta's birth was quick, she left long ago, well before dawn broke."

Gavin turned back.

"I'll go rouse the night guards, Father, and question them. Perhaps they let her back in and she is roaming somewhere."

Loddin nodded and rubbed his chin.

"The Lady Gwenyth insisted I not escort her," Mathew bowed his head and fell upon his knee. "I tried to convince her to stay on until the snow relented, sir, but she was adamant to leave and bid me stay with Marta and the babe. She threatened her authority. I'm sorry, My

Lord. What shall I do to right this?"

Loddin smiled and clasped his wrist again, urging him up. "God has blessed your house and your babe graces Ballymead. Stay with your family. We'll be back to give a formal visit as soon as Lady Gwenyth is accounted for."

He too went to the door.

"Shall I come to assist?" Mathew asked. "I'm pained, sir."

"No, I'm sure all is well. We will keep you informed should we need anything further."

By the time Loddin arrived back to the keep, Gavin was sounding an alarm.

"Father! She didn't return! And Luna's not in her stall! We're preparing search parties!" Gavin strode forward with purpose. "The women pack food and blankets! And Loddin has ordered Hershel to ride to the hamlet for help!"

The men of Ballymead scrambled to gather supplies, putting on full winter dress. Michael ran forth with Loddin and Gavin's horses and then ran back for the others.

Loddin swung down from his saddle and hobbled with all the speed he could summon from his crippled leg. "I shall be ready! Leave a party for me to lead! Scour these hills! Turn up every flake of snow!" he shouted to the bailey. "Every step of your horses, not one hoof better land on my daughter! Not one! William! What're you doing, lad?"

"I come with, Father!"

"Don't talk nonsense!" Loddin said. "Go back inside and wait!"

"Then I must be disobedient, Father! This makes twice that we've lost her and I intend to find her!"

Loddin conceded. Hershel led a party down to the hamlet and guard's cottages, and soon had gathered every able man to assist. The search began. Men and women called and dug through the snow in the hillsides.

"Gwenyth!" her brothers yelled.

"Lady Gwenyth!"

The calls continued throughout the morning. Slowly, they churned up the hillsides, through the fallow fields of wintertime and into the pasturelands.

"The pond is frozen through, My Lord! There's no sign of her!" a man hollered, riding up to Loddin. "Your eldest son bids me tell you that the northern pastures show no sign of her either!"

Loddin trembled. *Where are you, lass?*

After hours of work, Loddin called a rest. All parties converged again.

"What news?" he drilled his men.

"There's no trace of her, My Lord." Mathew Whitcroft sighed and fell on bended knee. "This is all my fault, for I was too overjoyed to refuse the Lady Gwenyth's insistence. I beg you sanction me." His head remained low and he would not look up.

"Gwenyth was raised on these lands, man. She knows how to brave the snow," Loddin muttered. "Rise up, Mathew. You shall not be sanctioned."

He walked to the outskirts of the huddle of men and stood alone, hands on his hips.

"I have a terrible feeling that I cannot shake, for if she is not here and no guard saw her leave, then I fear we have a crime on our hands and I would be willing to blame Shea Feargach..."

"Don't jump to conclusions, Father," Loddin intervened. "We haven't finished our search yet. There are still the southern pastures."

The men ate and quenched their hunger and thirst. Loddin forced a swig of wine and readied to resume. William, crouched on his heel, picked a long strand of grass through the snow and broke off pieces, then finally stood and huffed.

"I'll not stand idle and feed my stomach when our sister might be dead," he grumbled.

He hobbled onward on his wooden peg, reaching his horse.

"We don't stand idle. We must talk of a plan," George replied, grabbing his arm.

"It's easy for you," William breathed and shoved his arm away. The others all looked up and watched. "Father and I had a plan to get her back the first time while *you* stayed to run Ballymead."

"Stop and listen, Brother. We're all worried sick. You're not the only one. But you make a scene—" Hershel began.

"No, man, you listen!" William whirled around. "This is what a plan got me! Worthless eyes and a worthless leg, and no hope for a wife and family of my own! I won't stand here when she is missing! I rocked her as a babe, kept her as a child while you were all being fostered and going off to battle, or reading your ancient texts! *I* stayed home, *I* learned how to coif her hair even though I was a lad, for some days the maids were busy and Mother was so ill she couldn't make her hands work!"

He gripped Hershel's coat and lowered his voice barely above a whisper.

"I've shared secrets with her that no one else knows, ridden these hills with her time and again while you were all busy with your lives. Whatever has happened to her, she must be scared to death and knowing that makes my heart ache for her. I go to find her without sparing another moment. To hell with plans. They don't work."

He bumbled onward, determining south by the slope of the land and mounted his horse. His brothers watched silently, then joined him with their father and several others in their party. They made their way through the southern pastures and as they came over the crest of the hill, one of the guards spied Luna in the distance.

"Sir William!" he shouted. "Her horse! Down there at the wall! By the woods! This way, sir!"

They made their way through the snow and found Luna, cold, nervous and well hidden along a section far from any bastions. William groped for her reins and found them.

"Father!" he shouted, and blew a horn hanging at his belt.

Loddin and the others came galloping.

"That horse would follow Gwenyth anywhere!" Loddin exclaimed.

"Do you think she followed her here? To the wall?" Gavin asked.

"Gwen couldn't have climbed it, in a blizzard in the middle of the night, no less!" Loddin the son remarked.

"She wouldn't!" their father erupted. "We check the trees for any tracks protected from the storm! She's been taken! God, she's been taken!"

29

In full gallop, Loddin sprinted along the walls to get to the main gates followed by the others in hot pursuit. They bolted through the outer gates and trailed up to the tree line.

"Tracks, My Lord!" a man motioned.

"Search these trees!" Loddin ordered as rage overtook him.

The trees had blocked the snow from forming drifts. But the tracks didn't go far before they disappeared. Loddin cursed and searched, all his men tracking into the trees. Every passing minute compounded his anxiety.

"Poor Gwenyth. She must be terrified." George dismounted and traced his hand across the depressions in the ground. "Father, what if they've—"

"Don't think on such horrors," young Loddin interrupted. "Gwenyth is well and in one piece, we must believe that."

"There were at least two horses, perhaps a third, but the tracks are unclear," Hershel deduced. "Father. The way is unclear—"

Lord Loddin didn't wait, but threw himself into his saddle again and charged back down the slopes to the outer gates, spraying powder behind him as his sons and soldiers followed.

"Damn it!" he cursed, bursting through the door to the hall. *"God—Damn It!"*

He swung his gloves upon the board with all the force in his arm and slammed his fist upon it over and over again, cursing as he trembled. The women scurried from the hearth and cowered.

"I'll bloody kill'im! God damn it all, I'll kill'im!"

234

The board cracked. Louisa and little Hershel began to cry. Ballymead's men flooded into the hall behind him.

Mary crept forth and bowed at his feet. "My Lord, we are terrified. This is most unlike you. Whatever is wrong?"

"Oh, daughter of marriage...I'm unruly, forgive me!" he gripped her arms and pulled her up as his voice quivered. "My Gwenyth has been nabbed!" Mary threw her hands over her mouth. "God grant me strength...parchment and ink...now," he breathed.

A maid flitted away to retrieve it. Scribbling upon the parchment in panicked words, he folded it, poured a sloppy splotch of wax upon the seam and slammed his seal into it.

"Mathew! See to it this leaves for King Bain immediately! Find a messenger!"

He thrust the letter into Mathew Whitcroft's hands who dashed from the hall.

"We leave as soon as we're assembled! Provisions now!"

Mary gathered the women and tasked them each with packing the essentials.

Michael dashed to each son's chamber to unpack the trunks of chain mail and equipment. Loddin pulled out a map and unrolled it upon the board.

"We ride toward the mountain pass, here, along the tree cover in case Shea and his army are already on their way. We aim to pass Dunstonwoodshire. We shall seek the Bainick army and, *deo volente*, we will find William Cadogan."

"Why seek him out? Gwenyth might be anywhere right now. We cannot afford to spare the time," Gavin asked.

"He leads the Bainick army and there is none better to have on our side. If it's just us, and we run into a skirmish, we risk death ourselves—"

"I would rather die!" George fumed, "knowing I had gone straight after her!"

"And then what good would you be to her? She would be left both trapped *and* grieving! What a stupid thing to utter, man," his oldest brother began.

"I care not to waste time, as Gavin has expressed! What if she's been raped? Lord Shea is mad enough to do it!"

"I said, quit thinking of it! 'Twill do us no good to dwell on such things!"

"Gwenyth suffers and all you do is argue!" William interjected.

"Enough!" their father exclaimed. "Do not think these fears are not on my mind! They are *eating* at me! Listen, Sir William has declared himself her sworn protector. I believe he holds much honor in those words. Under his command, his army will help us I know it. William, son, you must stay here and run Ballymead—"

"Why!" he demanded, throwing his fist down on the board.

"Because someone must, and I wish it to be you."

"Why, Father?" William said.

"Because you are most capable—"

"Say it!"

"Because you are blinded, son!" Loddin exclaimed, grabbing him by the sides of his head. "Because you are blind and crippled! If we encountered Dwyre, I would lose you and so help me, I cannot bear for Shea Feargach to damage my seed again! Not ever again!" He rested his forehead to William's. "Shea tears our family apart. I won't risk his taking your life! I love my daughter, but I love you too, for despite your being fully a man, you are still my youngest son and I cannot ever replace you!"

With the surcoats of Ballymead belted over their mail, Loddin and his four sons gathered full arms. Hershel lifted his little son into his arms and embraced him while Mary cried and grabbed young Loddin for one last kiss.

"Please, husband, come back in one piece, I beg you come back to me in one piece."

Loddin kissed her deeply. "I love you. I shall not be taken from you, Mary. Trust that all will be well, and pray. Pray for us all and pray for Gwenyth." Swinging into the saddle, he trotted after his father and brothers and departed through the portcullis.

It was the early hours of another morning when Gwenyth woke to the stench that typified her traveling companions. Jasper the mute slept and Patrick snored like a pig routing for truffles. But Maccus was awake, sitting against the door. He stared at her, his leg propped up beneath his plaid to reveal that he wore nothing else. She cringed and looked away.

Dear God, if Lord Shea must rape me, please let him not be as abominable beneath his trousers...I have to get away from them...I have to, I have to...

Her mind was clearer today but the ache in her neck and head more sensitive. One swallow and she rocked with pain. Her whole neck felt swollen to the touch.

"Sleep well, woman?" he whispered.

"I must answer nature," she forced the words out.

"By all means."

Maccus rose and moved out of the way. Tenderly, she got to her feet and emerged into the pale light eking over the horizon. Snow was falling again.

If I could only get away while it snows, my tracks would be covered. If only... But Maccus followed her out.

She turned to look at him.

"That's right. You get an audience. I'm no fool, woman."

She could feel the cold metal of Maccus's dagger in her sleeve, pressing against her skin, reminding her. The horses, tethered beneath a dilapidated sty, perked as they came nearer.

"Right here is fine," Maccus stopped her.

She looked at the trees, then back at the hut.

"Please, Maccus," she strained on each word. "I should not like for Patrick to wake and see me squatting."

Maccus looked at her and squinted, then seemed to agree that he wouldn't want to be a woman around Patrick either, and nodded. Walking her toward the trees, they descended behind the edge of the sleeping woods where under his watchful eye she hesitated.

The bare branches creaked above. Maccus folded his arms and set his sights on her. She tried to move behind a tree trunk but he stepped forward and grabbed her arm, wrenching her back as his fingertips bruised her skin. She winced.

"I said no more mischief," he growled. "You hike up your skirts and piss right here, where I can see you, or you'll feel my wrath I swear it." Slowly he let go of her arm and stepped back.

She would have to outsmart him. *He hasn't brought any weapons with him,* she noted. *This might be my only chance*, for they were far enough away that the others might not wake if they struggled, and the snow was falling to cover her tracks if she could get enough of a head start.

She turned around and pulled up her gown to reveal her trousers. Turning over her shoulder, Maccus was eyeing her curiously. In an awkward act of balancing, she pulled them down and out of the way while her gown fell to the earth behind her, shielding her buttocks from him. Against her belly, she pulled loose the dagger from her sleeve as discreetly as possible while she let her water flow, slid it into her grip, then hiked up her trousers again. It was then that she realized Maccus was walking to look over her shoulder.

His face began to drop. "What have we here?" He reached for the dagger.

She jumped out of the way.

"Give me that!" he exclaimed.

"I'll not go back!"

She jumped aside again as he tried to grab her.

"I'll bloody kill you!" he rumbled.

He swung an arm down to his boot to grab his dagger when he realized nothing was there. His face dropped with shock. Throwing caution to the wind, she kicked his jaw while he was bent over. He reeled backward and stared at her like he really might kill her. As he charged at her again, she swung her other arm up. He twisted it backward and she cried out, clutching the dagger away from him in the other hand. Maccus pulled her close and reached over her.

"Give it here, bitch!"

"No!"

Her arm twisted more and she grimaced, doubling forward. She fought with all her strength to resist his pull. He almost had her other wrist and grappled for it, kneeing her in the stomach. She lost her lungs, gasping, but swung the dagger down across his leg as she coughed excruciating hacks.

He grunted, his grip relented, and she staggered up. She closed her eyes and swung the dagger wildly, caring not where it landed. Her eyes watered and her throat raked with each cough.

For a moment, nothing happened. He froze and slowly his eyes widened. Then red blood began to ooze from the ragged gash that appeared across his neck. She stepped backward, still clutching the metal, and covered her mouth in horror.

"Oh, God I...I didn't mean it..."

"How could you?" he gurgled as blood dribbled from his lips, his eyes bulging.

He fell forward and grabbed her skirt in a final attempt to bring her down. She kicked him free as tears flowed from her eyes.

"I said I'll not go back," she croaked.

"You...you've killed me...a woman..."

His voice trailed away in chokes as his blood rolled down his jerkin. He rocked on his knees, still staring at her as the heartbeat in his neck began to drip with steady surges.

"Not even the knight killed me."

She stifled a sob, horrified at what she had committed, yet knew it wasn't over until he breathed no more.

"I'll not make his mistake," she whispered.

She made one final swipe and shied away, cutting his throat once more. He fell forward in a heap. She shuddered and closed her eyes.

I will burn in Hell, Oh Iesus Christus! Father, forgive me!

She fell to her knees and crossed herself over and over again as she rocked and sobbed, forgetting her aches, still clutching the knife. Finally she looked back at him. He didn't move. She rolled him over so he was face up and realized he was cold and blue. The snow around him looked like rich velvet. His eyes were wide. She turned away at the sight of them. Shaking, she laid his arms upon his chest and crossed him.

It only took her a moment to regain her wits. The sky was brightening and the snow fell in heavy blankets. She scrambled through the trees and crept to the sty. Patrick and Jasper had not woken yet.

She untied Maccus's horse and removed his halter, pulling the bridle from the corner. Working the bit into the stallion's mouth, the horse fought it and whickered. She threw a glance back at the hut, then heaved the saddle onto its back and cinched it.

The wood creaked and she whirled around.

"The wind," she sighed.

Checking the other saddlebags, she found a half a loaf of bread and some cheese, which she took. She adjusted the stirrups and swung into the saddle, urging the horse out, and crept into the trees where she made her escape.

30

Gwenyth cracked the flints from the saddlebag though the sparks didn't ignite right away. Her arms were tiring. She blew on the thread of smoke rising. Finally, the dead kindling began to burn and she piled on a stack of twigs, then broken branches. She had wandered for two days and still had no clue as to where she was.

The bread was finally gone and her stomach protested as she filled it with more snow. There had been no sign of Patrick and Jasper following her. Her stomach unsatisfied, she nestled into the stream embankment, huddling in her cloak, and pulled her knees up. Closing her eyes, she thought of her fires with Sir William.

Keep me warm, William, she thought.

'You'll wrap your blankets around you at night and imagine them as my arms, Gwen...'

Night turned to miserable day though she hadn't slept for fear she might be captured, and took to fleeing once more. Her horse, hungry, was waning. It was midday when she came out of the trees again. The creek flowed beneath the timbers of the outer walls of a manor. Her heart pounded. The guards wore the red and yellow horse rampant on their surcoats.

"Dunstonwoodshire," she smiled. "They know me here."

She remembered well the childhood visits, long before Gavin became betrothed to the Lady Sarah. William had always spent the days teasing them, especially Amber, or taking them riding.

Lord Edward will summon Father if he isn't already looking for me!

Nudging her horse into a canter, the guards spotted her and called out. She waved joyously and kicked the horse into a gallop as she began to run the length of the wall. Finally, the main gates came into view and she trotted to a halt.

"How goes it, woman?" a guard called down from the brattice.

"I seek protection from the Lord of Dunstonwoodshire, sir!" she answered back.

They looked confused. She was unescorted with the long hair of a ranking lady, yet her dress was plain and worn from travel.

"What be your business?"

"I'm the Lady Gwenyth of Ballymead! My brother Gavin, son of Lord Loddin, is betrothed to the Lady Sarah! I've been abducted, sir, by men of Shea Feargach of Dwyre and have escaped my captors! Dunstonwoodshire is a beautiful sight for my sore eyes!"

He turned to discuss with his fellow guards and waved his finger at one of them.

"All right! We shall give you an escort to the manor, Lady of Ballymead!" he answered back as the gates were pried open. "Messengers ride to the great house to announce your arrival as we speak!"

She rode into a swarm of red and yellow-coifed men who stared at her. Several guards smiled and nodded, and one moved forward, nodding to the sentries on the wall.

"The Lady Gwenyth, men. I would know that hair a mile away! Since you was a young lass! How goes you, Lady?" he bowed and squeezed her hand, kissing it.

"I am weary, but strong in spirit."

"Ride with me to the manor," he smiled, mounting his steed.

They wound through a hamlet and up the snow-covered road until they arrived at the inner walls. The portcullis had already been raised. Lord Edward of the manor, a broad man with a paunch over his belt and his daughters, Sarah and Amber, were already on the steps. The guard dismounted to offer her assistance but Gwenyth had already jumped down.

"My Lord," she bowed.

"Rise up, Gwenyth," he offered his hand, and then pulled her into an embrace. "My dear, what is this news I hear of your suffering?"

"Oh, Lord Edward. I thank thee from the depths of my heart."

He walked her in, Sarah wrapping a blanket over her

shoulders. Amber felt her way over to them, gripping the table as she went. Gwenyth began to spill her story by the fire as Sarah's maids fussed over her. Lord Edward's pageboy served her watered wine as she told of Marta's birth.

"It was snowing badly, My Lord. I never saw anyone coming at all. I must admit, my head is still very sore from the blow and I know that I bled a lot."

"Will you allow me?" he asked.

She nodded. He sifted through her hair and found a scab, crusted together with clumps of tresses.

"Heaven have mercy. That blow would have been enough to knock out a soldier. And your neck is badly bruised."

"Father?" Sarah whimpered. "What sort of animal does this to a lady?"

Edward's teeth were clenched and his voice began to rumble.

"What else have they done to you? This man, Maccus, has he dishonored the name of Ballymead? Has he abused you—"

"Father! What a thing to ask in front of our staff!"

"*Dear lass*, tell me he has not," Lord Edward begged.

Gwenyth reddened but shook her head. "Thank Iesus he did not, My Lord. I tried to escape them once but it was only the second time I managed to succeed, and have been without food for more than a day." She dropped her head. "I was lucky to stumble upon you, for I was so very lost!"

"You must be starving," Edward fumed. "Bring food, warm and fresh for the lady!" he ordered.

"There now," Sarah patted her. "Father, whatever will you do? They have stolen her from her father's own land! They tried to dishonor her and made her course through these hills to survive!"

"You're brave, Lady," Amber whispered as she reached a hand out to find Gwenyth's.

"I am so thankful for your generosity, My Lord," Gwenyth bowed her head. "But I must ask more of your kindness. Will you see fit to send word to Ballymead that I'm safe here? My family will be ill with worry by now."

"Of course, Lady Gwenyth, of course! It's already to be done. And Our Lord King shall hear of this crime as well for I send messengers to both. Let your sister-to-be give you comfort. Daughter," he turned to Sarah. "See to it these rags she wears are dumped in the rubbish heap and have her cleaned and dressed in something respectable for board."

He stormed up the stairs and the door to his chamber slammed.

"He is angered, Sister, for you've been violated," Sarah said with satisfaction. "He'll protect you until your father comes. Do you think Sir Gavin will come with him?" she added.

Gwenyth smiled and took Sarah's hand.

"Gavin and all my other brothers would come to the end of the earth for me. However, I'm sure he will be pleased I arrived at Dunstonwoodshire." She flashed Sarah a grin and they put their heads together to giggle. "Once he knows I am well, I doubt I will be the first lady of concern to him any longer."

Sarah led her and Amber to her chamber off the solar after warm bread, meat and berries had filled her stomach.

"You must tell me all the news," Sarah began as the maids pulled down Gwenyth's gown. "Oh!" she exclaimed. "You're wearing trousers! Whatever for?"

"You wear trousers, Lady?" Amber asked, finding a seat on a cushion.

"We must get to know each other better. I ride horses at home."

"So do I, Gwenyth, but I don't need to wear such things to sit aside my palfrey," Sarah replied.

Gwenyth giggled.

"I prefer to ride astride. Have done so since I was a child."

"And your father lets you? How vulgar!"

"Of course. Amber knows, don't you? For we have been riding with William many times." Amber nodded. "My father gave me my first pony as a wee lass," she replied.

Her trousers too were stripped from her.

"I should like to keep these," she turned to the maid who held them by her thumb and pointer.

"My Lady?" she questioned.

"Aye," Gwenyth said. "I'll keep these. I had to fight my brother's squire for them."

"What?" Sarah exclaimed.

She drifted to her bedding and sat down with her head propped in her elbows.

"You spar as well?" Amber asked, her eyes wandering in their direction.

"Of course she doesn't, bonny sister," Sarah replied.

"Well," Gwenyth began. "'Twas my brother Gavin, Lady Sarah, who has trained me thus far." Now Sarah smiled. "My father insisted he take me as a squire and teach me to fight after they saw me sparring with Loddin's boy. Or losing miserably I should say."

"Your father must be most unconventional," Sarah said. "Whatever have I gotten myself into with my betrothal?"

Gwenyth laughed.

"You'll be happy at Ballymead, Sarah. I promise that."

The maids washed her down. She stood in the center of the floor as they dropped a clean shift over her head and then a gown.

"It's full of sunshine in the summer, the smell of boiled honey, the pasturelands and crops of barley that our serfs do well to tend...the Yule and Christmas celebrations in the winter are good fun and we lasses always get to bind the ashen twigs for the fire. If you will at least sit aside a palfrey, Gavin will be most pleased for we all love to ride and are known for taking to the hillsides. But do not fear my father. He is so gentle, he makes a spring breeze seem harsh. And Gavin will give you freedoms of almost any kind."

By the time she had finished, Sarah looked lost in a dreamy trance.

"But fighting? Why did he make you act a squire?"

Now Gwenyth frowned and Sarah could sense something great for gossip might slip out. Amber too leaned forward. Gwenyth sat down in a chair and Sarah came to sit by her.

"I'm sure you know of my marriage by now?"

"Aye," Sarah replied. "Most tragic. How did you manage?"

"It was because of my heartache that my father told me to train, so I might find strength again. Sir William Cadogan of Bain rescued me and brought me home—"

"Sir William the Brave?" she interrupted.

"*The* Sir William?" her younger sister squeaked.

Gwenyth nodded. "He's most honorable, and..." she smiled.

"And?" Sarah begged.

"He's perfect." Gwenyth looked down at her hands. "He swore himself my protector and should like to marry me. Father has said I can't be betrothed again for another year."

"What's he like? What's he like?" Sarah pressed.

"Do tell," urged Amber.

"He's tall, slender, but heavy with muscle," Gwenyth began as Sarah smiled. "Strong and only five and twenty. Terribly scarred yet very gallant. His hair is as black as a raven, his eyes, green, just like the poems. Oh, he's so handsome, I couldn't stop looking at him despite the awful beard that grew upon him!" They giggled together. "And he killed men for me."

Sarah had stars in her eyes.

"And did he kiss you?"

Gwenyth blushed but could not wipe the smile from her face. "I admit he did—"

"He didn't!" she exclaimed.

Amber threw her hands over her mouth and giggled.

"Aye, he did, such sweet kisses. He is so tender, and quiet, contrary to many outspoken knights. By the time we arrived at Ballymead, he swore he needed to marry me and me only." She became lost in her own words.

"But the legends say he refuses marriage."

Gwenyth's lips contorted into a wry smile.

"Aye, and he confirmed *the legend* to me, right before he touched my face and said, 'It's only you who I have ever touched, Lady, but now that I touch I cannot seem to stop and I see that I could be happy with a woman by my side. I mean it with all my honor as a knight of Bain that I was serious about two things that I've spoken to you. I intend to ask your father to give you to me as my wife, and I now fight in the honor of Gwenyth of Ballymead. It shall be written on my banner for all to see. The kingdom will know that my heart has finally been taken'"

Gwenyth had memorized those words, the sweetest words she had ever heard spoken.

"How romantic indeed, Lady," Sarah sighed, placing her hand over her heart and falling backward on a pillow. "And he kissed you." She bolted upright. "He didn't try for liberties, did he?"

"Lord no!" Gwenyth scolded, imagining their trysts when his hands held her breasts, his lips nibbling her neck as he all but committed the ultimate sin. "He's bound by his honor like no other, but those kisses melted like sweet sugar on the tongue...and he said he's in love with me."

"It sounds too good to be true, like a dream," Sarah smiled, flopping back in her chair again as a brave maid came forth with a comb for Gwenyth's hair. "But you are so fair despite your wild ways. Any man would fall at your feet, widow or not...Sir William the Brave..."

Gwenyth did her best to ignore the comment for Sarah did not mean anything by it. But she was not a virgin and William was, and it wasn't supposed to be that way.

"Well, my brother Gavin insisted on a beautiful bride. Did you know?" Now Sarah blushed. "Father asked if he would consider the oldest daughter of the Lord of Brynmor Braith, but Gavin insisted that she had the snout of a pig and that the Lady Sarah of Dunstonwoodshire was like soft rose petals and the one he pined for."

"Oh, he didn't say that," Sarah waved her hand, face burning pink beneath her auburn hair.

"I'm not a liar, Lady. He most certainly did, and you *are* fair. The Lady Mary is fair as well, Loddin's wife. So was Hershel's sweet bride before she died. I don't think my brothers would accept anything less... It feels like so much time has passed there, since I left for Dwyre. My nephew has grown like healthy crops and not only walks but runs. Many of the young lasses from the hamlet will be ready for marriage soon, like Amber here," she smiled.

Amber looked down. "No one will marry me."

"Why not, Sister?" Sarah chastised. "You don't see it with your crippled eyes, but Father does not call you bonny because you look of a toad!"

The three of them giggled together.

"My brother William always said you were quite lovely," Gwenyth smiled. Amber began to burn and looked down. "He always wished you just a little older."

"Did he?" Sarah seemed happily scandalized.

Gwenyth nodded.

"It is a shame what happened to him. I missed them all so much and when Dwyre's men took me, I feared I might never see them again for Lord Shea Feargach—" She took a breath and looked at her hands.

"What is it, sister-to-be?" Sarah reached out a gentle hand as the maid banded Gwenyth's hair into three practical rings that cinched into a cord down her back and exited.

Having not spoken of any of it, Gwenyth trembled, for it might bubble out and she didn't want to seem weak. But just the thought sent her over the edge.

"Oh Sarah! It is too awful to put into words the reasons he has in mind for capturing me! Your father received my father's warning about Dwyre's army, did he not?"

"Yes, Lady, and he has sent away to the king for aid, but that was only a few days ago." Sarah rested her hands around Gwenyth's in her lap.

"I pray that Bain's army reaches them before they reach the highlands, for they mean to cut us all from Bain and take us over. Sir William Cadogan leads the army. I know he'll try to get here, but I'm afraid of Shea Feargach, for my husband learned from his father. He wants me now, because I bore him a grandson that didn't live, but a son no less and now with both his sons dead...he wishes to make more!"

"My sweet heaven..." Sarah was so mortified she trembled. "And to think he almost got you...no wonder you fought so hard to get away. I would rather wander lost in the highlands as well than accept that fate."

"Sarah," Gwenyth whispered. "I should like to pray in your chapel, for I have killed one of Shea's men in order to escape and must talk to God for peace of heart, for I am surely going to hell."

"Of course you may. And God doesn't condemn his daughters to hell for killing barbaric animals! You shouldn't worry."

"If Shea Feargach finds out I killed him...Sarah, I'm afraid. Until William has squashed this army, I won't have peace of mind—"

A fierce banging on the door interrupted them.

"What do you suppose that's about?" Sarah fussed. "Enter!"

"Daughters, Lady Gwenyth," Lord Edward said.

Servants were racing through the halls.

"You must stay well hidden here come morning. Don't come down, do you understand?"

"What is it, Father?" Sarah inquired.

"The army of Dwyre is but a half a day's ride from the mouth of the mountains. If they continue this way as they must, they will be at our gates by morning."

Gwenyth turned chalk white. Her mouth was suddenly parched and she paced to the window as nerves coursed through her.

"And who's leading Lord Feargach's army?" she croaked.

"The lord himself, Lady Gwenyth. You of all people will appreciate why you must stay in this chamber. I don't want to frighten you, but we haven't nearly the men to put up a fight against invasion. We will have to let them occupy us until the Bainick lions arrive for I cannot ensure the deaths of my soldiers by sending them to slaughter against such odds. We will offer them food and play host...and the Lady Gwenyth will stay hidden while we mock that she isn't here," he added.

The door closed.

"I must leave!" Gwenyth whispered, beginning to strip off the gown.

"What are you doing? Gwenyth, stop!" Sarah scolded.

"I must leave, I must leave. Oh, God, I cannot be here..." All of the horrors of her life at Dwyre began to rush over her.

"You speak nonsense! You cannot leave!"

"I shall find my way, Sarah," she rambled, the tears beginning to flow again. "I must try to get home!"

"Gwenyth, I must tell my father! You cannot brave the wild alone again—"

"Shea will rape me!" Gwenyth whirled around. "He will rape me and my life will be over! For if ever I was miserable with William Feargach, I knew that my chastity had been honorable until marriage! But Shea has a wife and would not even think twice before he forced me to bed! He aims to punish me for his grandson! For not telling them that I was with child! He is mad, Sarah, madder than a sick cow!"

"Please, you frighten me..." Sarah quivered as Gwenyth grabbed the tunic and trousers that the maid had reluctantly left behind.

She pinned the brooch of her cloak and dashed out of the door.

"Gwenyth!" Sarah called after her.

But Gwenyth was already down the stairs and bolting through the hall.

"Lady Gwenyth!" Lord Edward yelled.

She streamed out into the bailey and made a run for the stable.

"Father!" Sarah cried as she ran down the stairs. "She's frightened! She aims to flee!"

Edward grabbed Sarah's arms. "Don't worry, Daughter. The guards have been ordered to refuse leave to anyone, save my messengers. I will go talk to her."

He walked out to the bailey. Gwenyth was already mounted and cantering to the portcullis.

"Lady! You must remain here!" a guard called to her.

"No!" she panted. "I must leave!"

"We have orders, Lady. You'll be safer here!"

"You're mistaken, sir!" she called back. Anxiety consumed her stomach like dry wood in a fire. "I am former wife to Shea Feargach's son and I cannot be here when they arrive! You must let me pass!"

"I'm sorry, Lady, but I must insist you go inside!" he held his ground.

"Lady Gwenyth," Lord Edward approached her. "Please dismount and come inside. We will keep you well hidden."

"You don't understand!" she cried. "He's like the devil himself and will surely sense my presence like a hunting hound. I'm safer in the hills."

"I don't agree. We have time to prepare. His army does not arrive until the morrow."

Her lips quivered and she clenched the reins, looking back to the unyielding guard.

"I *do* understand, lass. Your father's letter was most detailed. Come inside, child." He held his hands up to her and with a sigh, she resigned herself to being lifted from the saddle.

Sleep that night was impossible. The clattering of soldiers stashing weapons and foodstuffs rang out into the early hours. She tossed and turned in the bed she shared with her sister-to-be who also couldn't sleep. Finally, she gave up and paced to a table where she found a rosary. She sat at the window and curled her knees to her chest, rubbing the wooden beads.

They will be coming over those hills on the morrow. Please, William, please be following...

31

She was still sitting in the chair when morning came. The ladies went to break their fast but she refused. As she stared out the window, the ridge of the hill well beyond the gates of Dunstonwoodshire appeared to rise. She sat forward. Brown and gold banners were lining the ridge. The rosary slipped from her fingers and clanked upon the floor as the door to the chamber flew open.

"They have arrived," Sarah said.

"My life is over, Sarah. It's over."

"Don't speak such rubbish! Come with me now so we may hide you."

Sarah grabbed her hand as Gwenyth, still in her ugly trousers and tunic allowed herself to be whisked away like a mindless waif. Sarah and a maid pried up the floorboards in her room and crammed her into a crawlspace, sealing the planks over her. It was completely dark, like an oubliette, save the thin streams of light seeping through the cracks, and she felt forgotten.

Hours passed like minutes and soon she could hear men's boots clattering into the hall, the jingling of chain mail, loud voices, the many horses in the bailey as the occupation took hold.

Mary, mother of Blessed Iesus, please deliver me, please give me strength...

Panic pounded her chest and she clutched her knees like she had trained herself to do at Dwyre.

'Whoever has the power of fear is in control. You must never let your enemy have the power of fear...' 'I turned myself to stone, Gwenyth. Once I stopped fighting it, he would stop swinging his strap...you must become stone...' She took a deep, calming breath. *You killed Maccus and*

escaped. You are strong, Gwenyth. You can escape again.

But before she could do anything else, shouting was coming up to the solar and boots were clopping hard and fast. A door was thrust open next to Sarah's chamber and she held her breath. Shuffling and searching traveled in muffled sounds through the floorboards. Sarah's door was then thrown open, banging the wall. Her heart leapt into her throat and she crawled as far against the wall of the crawlspace as she could, burying her face in her knees. Boots stormed over her head and the wardrobes and chests were thrown open.

"Where is she!" boomed that horrid voice.

She sucked in a lungful of air and began mouthing the Pater Noster, trembling so badly she thought her bones might rattle apart.

"Who do you seek, Lord Shea?" Edward asked. "I have offered hospitality to you and your men, what more do you require?"

"You're a highlander," Shea replied, stopping directly over her so the streams of light were blocked. "And you are only biding your time in hopes that aid will arrive," he laughed. "Traitors to our eastern Empire. Don't think for a minute, man, that I'm not aware of your true intentions. There's no hospitality here, only a scheme and I can sense it. Even though you once belonged to my uncle's domain."

"We have prospered beneath Bain, and we have chosen our alliances. But there is no reason we cannot get on together, friend—"

"Spare me!" Shea spat. "You're a bloody liar! Where is she?"

"I don't know who you seek, Lord Shea," Lord Edward replied.

"Gwenyth of Ballymead, since you have chosen to play the idiot. Hand her over and we shall have peace as we restore you to our kingdom."

"Gwenyth of Ballymead?" Edward snorted. "Loddin's lass? You come with an army more than two thousand strong, all in search of a lady? Why would she be here?"

A dagger was drawn from its sheath and Sarah screamed, falling to her knees. "Please, Lord Shea, be merciful to us!"

"Not until I find her." Shea's words were marked and even.

"I have no information for you—"

"Don't play me for a dimwit, Edward. My scouts followed her tracks here, after she killed one of my men." There was a pause. "Oh that's right, you didn't know? She's a murderess and I have the right to prosecute her."

Lord Edward's words were choked.

"I offered her protection until the arrival of her father." She looked up with horror. "I had to keep her from trying to escape several times when we heard news of you beyond the ridge. I locked her in a chamber downstairs, but we haven't seen her all day and it's likely that she has found a way out, for we have been too busy to pay her mind until now and she was quite determined."

Gwenyth furrowed her brow. Lord Edward spoke falsehoods. Slowly, the dagger made its way back into its sheath.

"We shall have the grounds swept for tracks then."

Shea stormed from the room, followed by Edward. Sarah gripped the wood above her as if she offered a sisterly embrace, then scrambled to her feet and followed them out.

"I cannot stay here," Gwenyth whispered. "I must get out, I must..."

She began to crawl beneath the flooring as her hair tangled under her knees, slowly feeling her way so as not to make the ceiling squeak below her. The crawl space, she discovered, was really a passageway. Finally she came to steps. She crouched and turned sideways, feeling her way down. The stone leveled off into floor again. It smelled of stagnant moisture and she felt liquid at her feet. She tried not to think about what it might be or the rats that were sure to forage through it.

She found herself at another door and could hear the sounds of men in the distance. The unpleasant smell of rubbish wafted through the wooden slats with the wind.

I've reached the back. Oh, just a wee bit farther beyond the wall and I might get free...

She pressed her fingers to the cracks and listened. No one appeared to be close by. She pushed the door but it didn't move. With several jerks, it gave way with a loud crack and she wrenched it closed again. The sound of Dwyre soldiers passing made her stiffen. But they didn't seem to notice and the talking died away.

Slowly she eased it open again and peered out, looking to where the voices had come from. No one was there. She crept out into the snow behind the rubbish heap. Once satisfied they would not return, she jumped to her feet and whirled around the other way, smacking right into the chest of Lord Shea Feargach. He smiled and folded his arms.

"*My Lady*. You look well."

He looked her up and down. She stepped away, tripping backwards over the heap.

"No…"

Her voice was nonexistent as she scrambled to get to her feet. He was on top of her in an instant.

"Help me! Help me!" she wailed beneath him while he chuckled.

"Oh, I like it when they try to flee!"

He grappled to get her under control but she squirmed onto her back, kneeing him hard between the legs.

"I hate you!" she screamed.

He winced and held his stones. Yet no sooner had she gotten free, he reached out and grabbed her ankle and she fell forward again. He stood up and this time sent a foot to her stomach. She lost her lungs, seeing spots in her vision and expelled coughs.

He reached down to her waist, wrapping his hand around her cord of hair and yanked her to her feet. Turning her to face him, he grabbed her cheeks.

"'Twould be a shame to bloody this lovely face but I'll do it if you don't come with me without a fight."

"You won't get away with this, Shea—"

"*Lord* Shea to you, woman, and I'm warning you—"

"You are not *my* lord! You're a dog who will burn in hell with your two sons!"

"Woman!" he roared and squeezed her face in his grip.

"Discedere ad inferos!" she spat, wishing him to hell.

He released the back of his hand, her hair still in his grip. She could feel her lip split open. The taste of blood flowed over her tongue and rolled down her chin, filling the cracks in her teeth.

"You had better fear me, woman," he growled as a gathering formed around them.

"I fear God only, but I don't fear pain." He thrust her onward, her hair tugging at her scalp. "Your son has numbed me to it."

I won't be raped, I won't be raped, she told herself, yet she was so afraid she could hardly breathe.

He pushed her through the soldiers and dragged her around to the front, barging into the great hall. With a shove, he released her into the middle of the floor. Lord Edward was so surprised he choked on his watered wine.

"My Lady," he sputtered, wiping his mouth. "Wherever have you been?"

Dunstonwoodshire's men and sons watched her bleeding though at that moment, they made no moves.

"Dear sister-to-be!" Sarah cried but Shea blocked the way.

"She deserves no pity, woman. Away with you."

Sarah inched away to her father's side but Gwenyth bolted. She raced out to the bailey and darted to the stables, praying for an escape route to grace her.

Shea was right behind her and as she struggled to free a horse, he had her in his grip. He struck her face again, this time knocking her nose so hard it didn't hurt. It was only moments later that she realized it poured blood. Grabbing her again, he didn't speak, but she could tell he was getting frustrated. She kicked and began to scream again when his hand clamped over her mouth. She bit it with all her might, but though he winced, he held it there.

"This is enough, Shea!" Lord Edward stormed out after them. "Release her! I promised her my protection!"

"So protect her! And then we can go to war and I can wipe out your pathetic army!"

Gwenyth struggled, her body taut as she flailed in his grip, tears streaming down her cheeks.

"I think it's best to wait for her father and investigate this murder, for a number of things could have happened—"

"She will be punished according to my standards!"

He tightened his grip, her face dripping blood and tried to push her onward. Edward stepped in the way.

"It's my understanding that they captured her against her will, by the sore on her head," Edward continued.

"If you do not stand aside, you will know much pain."

"Loddin is a friend. His children and mine have been close since childhood. I cannot let you molest his daughter."

Gwenyth thrashed and he grabbed her hair again. Yet no

sooner had Edward reached a hand to her, Shea pulled his dagger and stabbed him, slicing clean into Edward's stomach. Edward recoiled and Sarah screamed. His sons ran forth as he buckled over. With that, Shea hauled her inside again and up to the solar where he thrust her into Sarah's room.

"Not a soul comes in no matter what you hear!" he yelled, then slammed shut the door and barred it.

"Come here!" he demanded.

"Never!" Gwenyth cried.

He made a dash for her and she picked up a candlestick, throwing it at him with all her might. He knocked it away and she backed up around the perimeter.

"Curse you, woman. I said come here," he muttered as he stalked her.

"And I said no, Shea Feargach! I'm no longer the weakling your son trained—"

"You killed Maccus!"

"He was a disgusting pig!"

"You'll pay me for his life, and for my grandson's death!"

"Then you'll have to steal your payment for I will *never* submit to you!"

"With pleasure, woman."

He charged at her but she flipped the table over in his path. Hate boiled in her dark eyes and it made him angrier, for she was not giving in but fighting back.

"Bitch! I'll kill you if you don't relent!"

"Do it then! Then what good will I be?"

He charged forth once more and grabbed her by the cloak, pulling her backside to his front and held her like a vice. Arms flailing, she reached her hand back and pulled free his dagger from his waistband. She swung it backwards so quickly it grazed through his tunic. He let go of her and she clenched the knife with white knuckles, trying not to tremble.

"I choose death over being your whore, Shea Feargach!"

He charged at her. She slung the knife again and it caught him across his face before he grabbed her wrist and twisted her arm back.

She cried out and the knife fell to the floor. Twisting her over, he punched her stomach.

She buckled. Tears blurred her vision as she coughed. He dragged her to the bed and tossed her down, wrestling her into his grip. She kicked and flailed and screamed for her father, screamed for her brothers and Lord Edward, and screamed William's name. Shea laughed and held her down, yanking loose her trousers.

"Please, William," she cried tossing her head to the side to avoid his lips. "Please..."

"He's Bainick, woman. You'll be no good to him. You're mine from now on..."

She kept kicking and broke one arm free, pounding him with it. He didn't flinch and loosened his pants.

"I'll have you now," he grunted as he pinned down both her arms.

"No!" she cried, "No! William! My William...*please!*" she begged.

He grinned as he shoved himself into her. She screamed and tried to kick him off but he was too heavy. She writhed beneath him, everything becoming surreal as though her mind was not in her body. She tried to pin her legs closed but he pried them apart again. Every thrust felt crushing. She sobbed distant sobs that seemed a mile away and called to William.

She begged the guards in the corridor to open up. He released an arm and ripped up her tunic so her bare chest gaped at him and squeezed her breasts. She beat his face closed-fisted, so hard that her hand ached before he pinned her arm down again. She squirmed, every muscle stiff, and twisted her face out from beneath his as he groped with his lips to welt hers.

And then with a final shove and an ecstatic grunt, it was done. He was panting and she was no longer fighting, but sobbing. He released her arms.

"There now, it wasn't that bad, was it?" he breathed with a triumphant smirk. "You'll learn to like it and I...well, a bit more work than I'm used to, but *well* worth the reward." He played with a lock of her hair and whispered. "You're by far my favorite."

'You will get used to it, wife. You'll learn to like it...' She felt raw and broken all over.

He stood from her and pulled up his trousers. She curled into a ball on the bed with nothing save her tunic scrunched around her neck and sobbed into the linens for William, sobbed for her father's honor, *her* honor, and begged William to forgive her for being disgraced.

"You put up a *damn* good fight, woman," he muttered, dabbing his fingers into the slash on his cheek. "Wash your face. You look like hell."

When she didn't move, he laid a blanket across her, lingered a moment longer, and walked out.

32

It was the early hours of morning when she finally moved again. It seemed so unreal. She blinked her eyes into focus, unsure of whether she had slept or not. It was still dark. The moon was going down and all was silent except for the occasional guards out the window making their rounds.

Her face was crusted over and her nose throbbed from the blow he had dealt her. Her throat was raw from screaming and she ached, but finally decided to move in spite of it.

It was freezing cold. No fire lit the hearth. She pattered to the washbasin, taking a rag and pouring water from Sarah's pitcher onto it. Dabbing her face, she winced. Her lip was fat. She looked down at her bruised legs and arms, and felt the moistness of his seed seeping from her.

She doused the rag and began washing between her legs, then scrubbed, then silent, angry tears began streaming down her face as she took more water and splashed it on herself, scrubbing madly to scour his poison from her. There was not enough water in the world let alone in the pitcher and she used it all.

The pitcher slipped from her shaking hands and shattered upon the floor, punctuating the quietude of the manor.

"Please God, take this pain from me..."

She collapsed down to her knees, landing in the broken shards and doubled over, sobbing silently and breathing deep, unsteady breaths.

The door opened, then closed. Shea came in, saw what had happened and walked up to her.

"Gwenyth, get up."

She didn't move and after some time, he reached down to lift her.

"No...no..." she cowered beneath him, but all he did was scoop her up.

"I'll not hurt you now," he said.

She hung limply in his grip as he took her to the bed, then picked up the pieces of the pitcher and came back to sit beside her.

"You should not've fought me, woman. I didn't want any trouble."

She stared out the window in the way he had laid her.

"You fought like a warrior." She didn't move. "I've never known a woman with so much spirit and I have been thinking."

She couldn't hear him. He was like noise in the distance as she saw everything that had been good in her life slowly spiral away.

My life is over...how can I stop feeling? How can I go numb?

"When you come back to Dwyre, I won't beat you again and you'll have all the privileges of the Lady of Dw—"

"I wish you to kill me," she whispered.

"What?"

"If you know mercy at all, I beg you take my life for I do not want it," she whispered.

Once more the water flowed from her eyes and she finally looked up. She sat up and slowly reached to his dagger on his hip. He let her. She pulled it out. The point was freshly cleaned and shone in the moonlight that filled the room. She studied it and ran her finger along the edge, pressing it against the tip so that a small droplet of blood oozed out.

He watched her.

Reaching for his hand, she took it and placed the handle in his fingers, then guided it to her throat. He studied her. Her fingers were clenching his and she closed her eyes as she forced his hand to press the knife against her skin.

"Please take this life from me so I feel no more."

He pulled the knife back and resheathed it.

"No."

"I beg you," she sobbed and pinched her eyes closed.

He leaned forth and kissed her gently. She didn't return it, but sat still anyway. He had used mint and his beard had been trimmed. She could smell that he had washed. He wasn't stopping so she gave in and finally returned the kiss, crying all the same. Her affection seemed to strike a chord.

"I'm sorry, Gwenyth," he whispered and laid her down once more upon Sarah's pillows.

His hands began to travel over her and pushed up the tunic past her waist. She didn't move, flinch, or shy away, but lay limply and cried. His hands found her breasts and then his lips did the same. Still she didn't move as he kissed them, but shivered and cried while his hand roved over and between her bare legs.

I'm his whore now. There's nothing more for me, she thought.

He removed his belt and dagger and moved on top of her, holding her face and kissing her some more. Suddenly a loud clank sounded up from the bailey. Shea looked up. A few men made exclamations and a plume of fire flashed. Then there was laughter. Shea stopped and paced to the window.

"Those fools," he muttered as he readjusted his belt.

He came back, pulled up the blanket over her naked legs, and left the chamber.

She lay still until the sun had risen, then got up to slip her trousers back on though the act of dressing didn't seem to hold any meaning. She thought of Lord Edward.

I ruined it all, I should have stayed hidden in the floorboards. 'Tis my fault Shea stabbed him.

Picking up the rosary, she began to pray for him, mouthing words that she was too afraid to say out loud for fear of her own voice. Without realizing it, she found she was praying for William.

He will understand this pain. He will love me, he will, he will...

She prayed for her father and brothers who were no doubt searching for her and she prayed for her soul to find calm, but the more she prayed, the more the tears flowed down her face.

It was at that moment she felt more liquid seeping out of her and went for the rag again. Pulling down her trousers, she wiped it and soon realized it was her flux.

"Praise heaven!" she breathed. *Oh, Lord God you've heard*

me...it is a miracle...

The next few days passed like a distant mirage. She sat in a stupor too afraid to come out and curled into the chair by the window to watch Dwyre's men mill about the battlements. Shea was quick to refuse her once he realized she bled, holding to the superstition that it was poison. A small blessing.

He brought her wine, bread, and cheese to break her fast. She didn't divulge that her flux had been light and was already ending, and remained curled in the chair as he left her meal on the table. She shivered. He brought her blanket from the bed. Without moving, she let him tuck it around her.

"You will eat now," he mumbled.

She sat still and stared out the window.

"Gwenyth, I said eat. Don't make me force you."

"I'm not hungry," she whispered.

"It's been two days since last you ate anything," he began, reaching out to brush her hair. "It's not my wish to starve you—"

"My Lord, you must come!" A guard barged though the door.

A commotion was rising in the bailey below.

"Speak man!" Shea jumped to his feet.

"Bainick soldiers, My Lord!" Gwenyth perked with a spark of life and whirled around to look. Shea glared at her. "Beyond the ridge, thousands of them, sir! The whole army! We've not but a couple thousand total!"

"Damn!" Shea slammed his fist on the table and the wine splattered on the floor. "Damn it all to hell! How did they know to come here?"

"Patrick and Jasper have been questioned thoroughly about Maccus's death, My Lord! Patrick said that Maccus killed one of your spies! Perhaps the spy sent word to the king about this plan?"

"Who did they kill, man? Who do they claim was a spy?"

"Sir Aindreas de Boscoe."

Shea actually looked dumbfounded. "Aindreas? Not him..."

"Aindreas is dead?" Gwenyth gasped. "But he was just—"

"Just what, woman?" Shea rumbled.

Aindreas knew this would happen, Gwenyth, he said so. He died for his king, sweet Aindreas...

She stared back at him, then smiled and stood, walking to face him.

"He was just at Ballymead," she hissed. "He didn't go to the capital as you ordered. He delivered me an important bundle, and you'll soon regret all you have done, for Bain has sent his army to take the life from your eyes."

"What did you say?" Shea whispered as his temper began to rise. "Why did Aindreas come to you? You had better explain, for I believe a harsher punishment will be in order if you do not."

Gwenyth drilled his eyes with hers and stood tall.

"He was a spy, Shea Feargach," she spoke, reaching up to brush his cheek with her fingertip. "For King Bain. You have struggled as much as you have because he was against you all along and died for his true king."

"Ma...Maccus found him talking to the Lady Janis, sir," the soldier hesitated, watching Shea as he glared at her. "He heard them plotting to thwart your takeover of the port—"

The words caught him off guard and he turned back to the soldier. Gwenyth furrowed her brow and her mouth dropped.

"Not my Lady Janis...I haven't heard you correctly," he stuttered.

"The Lady Janis? But she, she worships you...no wonder she and I listened to..." Gwenyth uttered, and then comprehension dawned on her brown. "No wonder she sent..."

"She begged Aindreas to...em..." the soldier looked nervous, "deliver your daughter to...em..."

"Speak your mind you stuttering fool!"

"To deliver your daughter to this woman here," the soldier finished and pointed.

"An important bundle...my infant daughter died recently."

"No," Gwenyth said. "She's alive and well and knows Ballymead as her home now. A daughter for a daughter, it would seem, for you have stolen my father's."

"I'm sorry to be the one to impart this news," the soldier continued. "But Maccus heard your wife beg this of Lord Aindreas, to take your daughter Louisa away from your guardianship and place her with Gwenyth of Ballymead as her new mother."

Shea was so struck with anger he could do nothing but shake. Suddenly, he exploded and struck Gwenyth.

"What else do you know of this, woman!" he erupted.

She reeled backwards. He gripped her and shoved her to the wall. She ached and had to summon strength to kick him.

"Nothing!" she choked, shaking her face for air as it turned red.

"I will squeeze every last drop of life from this throat if you don't tell me!"

"Noth..." her eyes began watering and spots appeared on her vision as she suffocated.

Thankfully, Shea fell into a tantrum and released her. Her morning meal was first to go, then the table upon which it had sat. Gwenyth remained against the wall as he kicked his foot hard into the bedpost until his fit fizzled out.

"We must handle this army first, My Lord," the guard said, once he deemed it was safe.

Gwenyth sprang from the wall and raced to the window, praying to see the Bainick colors flying.

"Bar this door!" Shea shouted. "She goes nowhere!"

"They're led by a young knight, brutal as demon as if he's seeing blood!" she heard him say as Shea strode out.

"Sir William Cadogan?" Gwenyth exclaimed.

The guard turned to look at her.

"Aye, woman," he replied.

Shea's brow furrowed.

She whirled back to the window and pressed her fingers to it. *William, my William...*

Shea chuckled. "You're not worth a damn to him now, you wait and see."

"He laid waste to both the port and Faulk, took no mercy! Our men are all slaughtered!"

"And the Dwyre land?" Shea was boiling.

"We don't know the reason, sir. Riders have just arrived with the messages, but surely these spies gave him wind of your plans and he chose to route this way instead, towards the highlands."

The door closed and she heard the bar go across it.

"He's coming for me," she whispered.

She grabbed her cloak and pinned the brooch, then raced to the door but it was well sealed. She rushed to the window again and saw the colors come onto the horizon. Black and wine were streaming like standards of perfection. The bailey ran with soldiers. Dwyre knights bullied the men of Dunstonwoodshire to take part.

"We hold the estate! We've got a fighting chance!" Shea shouted from below as he jammed his hands into his gauntlets. "They've only a couple thousand on that ridge!"

Looking up, she saw a tiny black horse skirted in Bainick colors kicking up snow. The king's banner was flying above a blue one, and she would know that horse anywhere.

"William!" she cried, banging the window, though she knew there was no way he could hear.

Not even the men beneath her window could hear with the din of battle preparation. She ran back to the door, her head clouded with excitement. She slammed it hard with her fists to no avail and dashed to the window again. Titan was charging back the other way and up the hill as he returned to his army.

"No!" she cried. "Don't leave! Don't leave!"

She pounded the window so hard the glass rattled. Then, acting before she could think, she picked up the washbasin and thrust it at the window. It shattered down on the men below.

"William!" she screamed. "William!"

He was much too far away. Shea looked up at her window and clenched his fists.

"You'll stay in there, woman!" he hollered.

"No! I'll get out!" she yelled, the hate back in her eyes.

He turned to storm back inside.

"Lord Shea!" one of his men called. "We must send men to talk of engagement!"

Shea whirled around.

"Christ's bones, man! I'll not talk of rules with Bainick shite! We fight them!"

"He tries to bluff! He hasn't put nearly all his knights on the ridge! He counts on us to come forth to rattle us! 'Tis his tactic!"

Gwenyth looked out at the horizon, already a thousand horse strong, and swelled with pride. *That is only a little?*

"Then we don't fall for it, man! Get our archers on the outer battlements!"

"We must do something faster than that! Scouts tell us this instant that there are archers thousands strong preparing to assault without notice!"

"Archers on the wall, now! Boiled water at the murder holes should they get this far! Our conscriptions and knights go out to defend! I'm busy!"

He turned back to Gwenyth.

"Lord Shea!" his man persisted, seizing his arm. "She's a damn woman! As fine as she is, this isn't the time!"

Shea turned back and jabbed his finger in the man's chest.

"I'll not have one of my men ordering me—"

"With all due respect, My Lord!" the soldier shoved his hand away. "You sentence us to fighting! You owe it to your men to be our leader! Punish me as you will later, *if—we—live*, but right now, quit thinking with your cock, man!"

"I control this woman and she aims to flee!"

"Who will care when we're all slain!"

Shea punched him hard in the face and sent him tumbling backward, but knew the man was right. Gwenyth was still in the window shouting William's name. He scowled at her and stormed passed his felled soldier to the portcullis.

Gwenyth looked around the room. Her head was spinning.

The crawlspace! she thought. *Sweet heaven, I have a way out!*

33

Without sparing another thought, she hid her hair beneath her cloak and threw on her boots. Ripping up the flooring again, she jumped beneath it, crawling as fast as she could and cursing like a foot soldier as her hair fell under her knees. She reached the stairs. It was black, yet it was as though her feet found the way. Reaching the bottom, she splashed through the water to the back. She threw the hood of her cloak over her head and kicked her way out, springing to freedom again and certain this time that Shea was preoccupied.

She ran through the snow, the freezing air biting at her body. Dwyre knights were mounted and receiving instruction. Shea was hollering his commands, throwing looks at Sarah's quiet window. But with her hair completely hidden, she looked more like a squire. No one noticed as she darted into the stable.

It was deserted except for some horses and a few squires in hasty preparation. The horse stolen from Maccus was still there and she grabbed the bridle off its pin, working the bit into its mouth. She threw a blanket over its back and grabbed the saddle, tossing it up. Cinching the strap, two Dwyre knights slammed through the doors. She dove behind a pile of hay.

"I'd desert if I could. I never signed up for suicide when he called for conscriptions," one of the soldiers was saying as he threw a glare at his young squire. "Hurry up, lad! I needed my mount moments ago!" He turned back around. "He's mad, he is. No honor in a man who rapes the wife of his son."

"He's not as mad as that Bainick commander! Shea has sentenced us to death and that knight will be pleased to cut us down! Did you see how he mangled our man who ran out to inquire?"

Gwenyth smiled at the thought of William and held perfectly still so as not to rustle the hay.

"Did you see his banners?" the first one said. "Says 'Gwenyth' on it. Which lady do you suppose it is?"

Gwenyth sprang from the hay, startling them both.

"Me."

She was bursting with pride. He stayed true to his word.

"Woman." They stared at her. "You shouldn't be here."

One of the knights came for her but she fell at his feet.

"Please help me escape this place!" she beseeched.

"You'll feel Lord Shea Feargach's rage again if you don't go inside," he continued, reaching down to take her arm.

She quaked in his grip as he pulled her to her feet, and folded her hands at her mouth. The knight examined the bruising on her face and her scabbed lip.

"I'm the Lady Gwenyth of Ballymead! I beg you not hand me back to Lord Shea! I must get to William Cadogan, the knight you speak of! He's my sworn protector!"

The men looked at each other.

"I'm desperate!" she cried.

The squires had readied the horses.

"Formations, men!" came the calls from the bailey.

But the knights took pause and let go, moving away to have a council.

"I wouldn't give a cur I hated to Shea," one of them mumbled, "let alone hand this woman back to him, after hearing her screams. He's turned this lady into his whore."

The other one nodded. "But she'll not last for a moment on the battlefield, and her Sir William will not see her in the fray...he is in for a surprise once he realizes Shea has spoiled her—"

"But look at her! She would rather die trying to escape to him than live, which is honorable. Do you honestly believe she is better off here?"

The other finally nodded.

"Then we must outfit her as best as possible. She'll need a jerkin, for she's too slight to wear mail."

"Can you carry a sword, woman?" they called from their

huddle.

"So long as it's not a broadsword, I will try," she answered, her voice rising with hope.

They were in agreement.

"All right, we'll help you. Come here." They hustled her away. "We'll make you look a man. You ride out with us to the main gates but beyond that, you'll have to fend for yourself."

Her hands went to her mouth, nodding, unable to find words. They threw her into a jerkin and pulled a Dwyre surcoat upon it, all the while throwing wary glances over their shoulders. A belt was wrapped around her waist with sword and sheath. Then a coif of leather was placed over her head and yoked around her shoulders, making her look broader.

"Can you use a dagger, woman?"

"Have you seen Lord Shea's face?" she replied.

"That was you?"

She smiled, hearing noises from the battlefield far away. Fighting between foot soldiers had commenced.

"Then place this dagger in your boot, for you'll need all help possible."

The surcoat was like a long dress, flaps hanging upon her legs and hiding her curving hips. She was as complete as they could make her. She took both their hands.

"There are not words in existence that can tell of my gratitude. I shall pray for you both to be well."

"Shea is a brute, woman, I shall pray that you escape him," the man replied.

"I've done so once and I shall do so again," she smiled.

"Perhaps you're mad, but you have more guts than a Bainick lion, woman. Godspeed."

The bailey swelled with men on horseback. Dwyre knights were already marching to the outer battlements with Shea in the lead. Gwenyth fell in behind the two knights at the end and lowered her head, passing the guards at the portcullis without issue.

Down the sloping path to the outer walls they rode, a long procession of brown and yellow, and her heart faltered every time a knight turned her way. She rode through the little hamlet nearer to the main gates and looked down, unable to glance at the serfs' huts for fear of what Shea's foot soldiers might have done to the peasant women. The ringing of battle was growing louder in her ears.

As they continued, the battlefield came into view as they rose to the crest of a hillock, strewn with men fighting. Bainick archers were lobbing an onslaught of arrows. Weapons clashed and the sea of violence they formed made her stomach drop.

The knights saw her apprehension but made no move to show concern. William's army stood in a long stretch across the ridge, but William was not there. She rode closer to the main gates, scanning the horizon, from the north where the trees ended, to the south where the foothills to the Northeast Pass became more dramatic. Still, there was no sign of William.

Blood was running more freely than wine at a Roman banquet over the snow, and as they passed through the main gate of Dunstonwoodshire, she paled. Swords, bludgeons, axes clattering and the cries of slain men were wrenching to her stomach. She searched for William again as the horses fell into rows. He was nowhere.

"There is an upstart knight named William Cadogan who leads this rabble!" Shea hollered as he ran his horse the length of them. "Carries the hawk! Cut him down! If I don't finish him first!"

Just then, she saw a sight that made her heart pause. Sir William was rising along the ridge from the foothills, Titan's beautiful body skirted in black and wine, blowing like wings outward from his side.

"That's the man!" Shea bellowed and pointed.

The horse bounded in the long leaps of an Arab stallion. Emerging from behind him came five men in mighty green surcoats with bright yellow crests of the sun upon their banners. They were bedecked in full costume.

"Father," she whispered. *My father, my family, my William...they have all come for me.*

The battle between them melted from her view as they glowed in her sights. Without a thought, she backed her horse out of line as Shea made another run.

"Get back in line, man!" he shouted, but she ignored him.

The other knights watched her as she turned her horse and charged down the row. Shea didn't spare the time to make chase. Coming to the end, she turned toward the field and saw William upon a prancing Titan, desperately searching the land within the manor walls as her father and brothers gathered around him. They were yelling and gesturing. William turned and made another sweep of the field as Titan streaked away, only to stop short and come back the other way.

He knows I'm here! Her heart leapt, but an arrow soared just past her head, and she snapped back to reality.

"Christ! Why?" William fumed.

"You aren't speaking clearly, man!" Cavanaugh exclaimed. "Where in the hell is your sanity? The battle is now!"

"My daughter is in that manor!" Loddin interrupted. "We fight with you, Loddin of Ballymead and his four sons!"

"Your Lady Gwenyth is in there?" Thomas said with disbelief.

"Yes! She's there!" William shouted back. "Loddin just received word on the roadside from Dunstonwoodshire's messenger. She escaped to here from her captors! Shea Feargach had her nabbed from Ballymead! *Christ*! Why was she out in the middle of the night?"

"She did midwifery in the village and was returning home!" Loddin the brother replied. "They trespassed and struck her down from her horse!"

"Lord Edward was offering her protection until we arrived!" Gavin exclaimed.

"But Shea is right there!" Cavanaugh realized. "She escaped only to fall into his lap!"

"Damn it, man! Do you think I don't know this?" William fretted. "Gwenyth is at his mercy! If Shea has ruined her for me...let us send in the Cavalry and end this! We will find her afterward!"

William sprinted away and Cavanaugh galloped in the other direction. He raised a flag. The men of Ballymead fell into line.

"Cavalry!" he bellowed.

A second wave of knights broke onto the ridge in an expanse as broad as the heavens. Suddenly, another wave came upon the hill. Gwenyth grinned. What the soldier had told Shea was true. He had bluffed his numbers. The sight was so splendid it made her cry, until the severity of it all set in.

They will cut me down as well! He won't recognize me! Nor

would her family. She knew nothing of battle or the commands, having only practiced with her brothers.

An arrow stabbed the ground beside her and she jumped. Her horse tossed his head. She looked back at Shea. He was matching William's threat of attack. His knights readied their lances and swords. Her head twisted back to William atop Titan with his sword drawn high. He was about to attack. She turned back to Shea. Again, he was meeting the threat, two long fronts of men and horses like the teeth of a clamp about to snap together.

"William!" she cried. *He'll never see me!*

Her horse started.

"William!"

Untying the laces, she yanked the coif free. She pulled her hair from her cloak like a rope. The wind caught it.

"William!" she screamed. "William!"

She charged forth into the bloodshed. Another arrow sliced into her thigh. She screamed. Her horse twisted in circles as she dragged on the reins.

"William!"

William held his sword high.

"Cavalry!" he exclaimed.

Cavanaugh ran one way. Thomas ran the other. Their swords were ready to throw down the command as soon as William released it.

"Readyyy!"

His sights sat upon Shea. He thought of Gwenyth. His eyes narrowed.

"Readyyy!"

The Bainick knights behind him were brimming with anticipation. But Shea was suddenly sidetracked and maneuvered to one side, staring out into the battle.

Now's my chance! William thought. *While he forgets himself!*

His eyes followed Shea's to a flow of blonde hair. He was bringing his sword down. The knights behind him were ready to kick their mounts.

"Holy God..."

His heart stopped. There she was, a tiny speck in the sea of men. She was turning and sidestepping, arrows raining around her. Men in battle had surrounded her. He could see her struggling. She raised her sword and knocked away a foot soldier.

He looked back at Shea. Shea had seen her too.

34

His sword lowered. Cavanaugh and Thomas looked to him for a sign.

"What is it, man!" Cavanaugh shouted.

He galloped back. The horses behind him jerked forward with anticipation.

"Shea sends his men! We go now, William—"

"Gwenyth...Holy God, Frances, it is her! Gwenyth!" he bellowed.

Titan stomped in a circle.

"*Iesus*, Frances! It's her! She'll be trampled! Gwenyth!" He charged away to the edge of the battle, leaving Cavanaugh without any explanation.

"William!" she screamed.

She grabbed the arrow and snapped it off at the neck with a grunt. A Bainick soldier charged at her.

"No! I'm on your side!" she yelled.

He pierced her horse's chest. The horse reared up. She was thrown.

"Don't harm me!" she shrieked.

The horse was coming down now. She rolled out from beneath it, forcing the arrow farther into her leg. She screamed again. The Bainick soldier was above her. She rolled away again as his sword landed by her head.

"You die, Dwyre woman!" he seethed. "You're mad to fight a man's battle!"

"I'm Gwenyth!" she cried and scrambled to her feet. He swung his sword again. She jumped back and grabbed hers. "William Cadogan is my protector!" Her tears were streaming. "I'm the Gwenyth on his banner! I'm Dwyre's prisoner! I try to get to Sir William!"

His sword was already swinging when she said it. He could not stop, but his face dropped. She matched his sword, buckling under his trained force. His sword grazed her shoulder. Her leg stung as her muscle tensed around the arrow point.

"Is that true, woman?"

She nodded and wiped a tear with the back of her hand.

"On your feet then!"

He grabbed her wrist and pulled her up, dragging her as he ran back up the field. Another Dwyre soldier ran at him and he let go of her, engaging in battle. Soon it seemed she was forgotten as he fought his opponent.

She whirled around as though disoriented and pulled free the brooch on her cape. Then she yanked loose the belt and pulled the Dwyre surcoat off, tossing it in the mud. Two men fighting pounded into her and she fell beneath their feet. She scrambled out of the way. A Bainick soldier lay dead next to her. She pulled free her dagger and slashed through his belt. It fell away and she stripped off his surcoat with the Bainick lions. Throwing it over her head, she ducked as an arrow flew passed. Dodging the soldiers, she limped across the muddy snow.

"William!" she cried again as she saw him running the edge.

He was looking at her.

"Gwenyth!" he hollered, and she smiled.

He sees me!

"Gwenyth! Gwenyth! Woman!"

"William! William!" she ran, sword in hand.

He charged into the melee. But the ground started rumbling. She turned over her shoulder and saw Dwyre cavalry heading into battle, lances and swords aimed forward.

"Oh God!" she whimpered.

William suddenly turned and charged back up the hill.

"No! Come back! Come back!"

A Dwyre man rushed at her, clumsy from fatigue. She swung her sword, knocking his away. She started running again but was attacked once more. She jumped back as his sword swung in front of her, nearly slicing her stomach through her jerkin. She set her face with determination and gave a mighty swing, slicing him across the face and sending him to the ground screaming.

"That's my woman down there!" William barked as he ran the length of his knights. "That is *my* woman! Gwenyth of Ballymead! Your swords had better not harm her! So help me God, they had better not harm her!" His knights began murmuring. "Cut down those wolves! No mercy! They shall burn in hell for what they've done! Cavalry!" His voice was deep. "Readyyy!" He lifted his sword high. Titan started beneath him. "Chaaaarge!"

Bain's army was released. Thousands of knights began to thunder down the ridge, a storm of war cries rising from them. Gwenyth's stomach dropped to her feet.

"Mary Mother..." she clenched her sword and crossed herself.

Dwyre men were coming from behind, Bainick men were waving down from the front.

I'm going to die...

She stood frozen like a fence post until her senses reclaimed her. Jumping over bodies, she took to running up the field once more. William put her in his sights and headed her way.

"Williaaam!"

Her voice was almost gone. She tripped upon the surcoat. A soldier came at her and knocked her with his sword.

"Gwenyth!" he wailed as she fell.

She swung her sword around her feet and caught his ankles. The soldier spilled to the ground. She sprang back to her toes just as Dwyre horses converged around her, nearly trampling her beneath their hooves. William leapt forward but was intercepted. He sliced the man down, then another. Powerful swings, his mouth set firmly, loud grunts, hate-filled eyes.

Gwenyth forgot for a moment where she was as she stared at the demons spilling out of him. Suddenly, a hand wrapped around her arm and she was jerked upward.

"Damn you, woman! Damn you!"

"No!" she sobbed. "No! William!"

"Gwenyth!" William yelled, though could not free himself from the assault of knights.

Twisting and flailing, Shea lost his hold and she tumbled back to the ground as his horse's hoof landed upon her leg. She screamed again but luckily the horse skipped aside and nothing was broken.

"Run, Sister!" she heard the words and saw Hershel engaged with Shea. "*Go, Sister!*" he begged.

Shea knocked him hard.

"So the men of Ballymead have come!" Shea shouted.

"And we will gladly lay down our lives!"

"And I'll gladly take them! You know you fight for a whore!"

Hershel narrowed his eyes in an angry look that Gwenyth had never seen on her brother's face.

"What have you done to her?"

Their swords met again and Shea chuckled.

"She put up a damn good fight, dear brother, which made victory all the more sweet!" He struck Hershel, sending him reeling and lifted his sword once more to finish him.

"Hershel!" Gwenyth screamed. "You'll not slay my brother, you bastard!"

They were both so surprised she had cursed that they stopped to look at her. Sword still in hand, she slashed at Shea's legs, puncturing his leggings. He faltered. George appeared though the madness as Hershel recovered and lunged forth. He bludgeoned him. Shea retreated and Hershel and George chased after him.

"Gwenyyyth!" William bellowed again.

He charged at her once more but was confronted yet again. The knight knocked his sword away. William reached back and grabbed his ball mace. He swung it and ended the man in one blow.

"Lady Gwenyth!" a Bainick knight with blue eyes reached to her. He was decorated and ranking. "Grab hold of me, woman!"

She didn't hesitate, but held her hand high as he yanked her up behind him.

"Hold on tightly, Lady! I'll take you to William!"

He began to charge back out of the battle, only to run into more Dwyre knights. He raised his sword and let loose upon them.

Another came at his left. Gwenyth twisted her sword arm over and struck him hard. He flailed, but held his reins and attacked again. His blade sliced across her thigh where the arrow had struck. Screaming, she clenched the knight who carried her as tightly as her fingers could manage. The Dwyre knight recovered and attacked once more. She jabbed at him, knocking him off his beast.

But another horse rammed into the one she sat upon and pinched her leg between them. She cried out and lost her grip, falling once more.

"Frances! Get her out of there!" William bellowed, yet Cavanaugh couldn't free himself of his attacker.

A loose horse came dancing by. She grabbed the reins. It skittered around in a frightened circle, tossing its head as she jumped into the saddle despite her injury.

"William!" she cried again, her voice raw and hoarse.

William made another go for her, shouting her name. Again he was confronted.

"Daughter!" Loddin's voice boomed as her horse was cut from beneath her once again.

He galloped to help William with his onslaught. Shea was also galloping at full speed.

"William! Look!" Gwenyth screamed from the mud.

William wheeled around and his sword met with Shea's. Every swing Shea made, William blocked and countered, shoving him backwards so that Shea almost teetered off.

"I'll kill you, bastard! I'll kill you and gut you if you've caused her harm!"

Shea grunted and held himself on, grinning all the same. William swung again and grazed his arm. But a surge of cries began to rise. Dwyre men were retreating. William swung again and Shea held up his shield. Shea's men were yelling. He glanced back.

"William! Our replacements! They arrive from the west!" Thomas's voice rose from somewhere nearby.

William wheeled around. Swelling out of the foothills, the army that William had sent to secure Dunstonwoodshire had arrived late and was charging down the ridge. Shea circled his horse back and rumbled for retreat. Gwenyth looked around, then back at William who was making chase.

"Come back here! You coward!" he called, running Titan.

Shea ran harder and William flew past her.

"William!" she croaked. He ignored her and continued to make chase. He was gaining on Shea. "Will," she sobbed one more time, and he skidded to a stop.

She was alone amongst the bodies and tripping after him. He glanced back at Shea, then her, then Shea again.

Please don't leave me again, she thought.

He glanced once more at Shea who was disappearing while Titan pranced.

"Gwenyth!" he shouted, and turned back towards her.

She stumbled forth and he sprang from the saddle, running to her in all his chain mail and bloodstained surcoat. Shea was gone from view.

"Gwenyth!"

"William!"

She tripped over the dead bodies, scrambling to stay afoot as her leg throbbed. Dropping the sword, she lifted the surcoat like a skirt to run.

"William!" she cried and crashed into his arms, wrapping her legs about his waist.

She planted her lips to his. He spun her around, her hair crusted in blood and streaming about them in a fan. Dropping to the ground, he kissed her desperately, holding her head to his as he braced an arm around the small of her back.

"Thank the Lord!" he cried, his stubble grating against her face. "Thank the Lord you're alive!"

"My William! You came for me!"

"Aye, I feared for you! I *bloody* feared for you!"

She kissed him back, clenching the chain mail on his head as he rocked her on his lap. She latched tightly to him and sobbed, hungrily searching his lips as he clutched her so hard she couldn't breathe.

"Christ, Gwen, what were you thinking!" he admonished, still kissing her. "What in the hell were you thinking! What happened to you?"

He gripped the sides of her head, having ripped off his gauntlets. His thumbs felt her scabbed lips and bruised face from Shea's lashes, and he kissed them all one at a time.

"Your lovely face...who did this?"

"Shea did but I escaped! I wanted to get to you! He nabbed me, William! I would rather have died than stay there!"

"Did he hurt you, woman?" He kept kissing her. "Please tell me you're well!"

"I'll be fine now that I'm with you."

"You're safe now. Thank Iesus you are safe..."

She nestled her face into his shoulder and he clutched her, his face buried against her. Bainick soldiers were shouting the up cry of victory. Neither of them looked up. It wasn't until they heard whistles and bawdy jests that they noticed Sir Cavanaugh and Sir Thomas with a large gathering of soldiers and knights watching them, grins lighting their faces. Gwenyth didn't care. William grinned, finding her lips again as he kissed her deeply.

"God how I love thee, woman," he murmured.

"Marry me now, William. Elope with me. Don't make me wait," she begged.

"But your father said a year, he said I cannot have you yet," he replied, his lips still tasting hers.

"Eh-hum."

A throat cleared. They looked up to see Loddin of Ballymead standing in front of them.

"Perhaps one year was a misjudgment," he said sternly.

Gwenyth scrambled away and William pushed her from his lap, both jumping to their feet. The soldiers laughed.

"Father, forgive me for my disgraceful behavior," she begged as she bowed her head. William stood a good foot from her and dropped down to his knee.

"Lord Loddin, I'm sorry I take such liberty," he stammered. "But please don't make me wait longer than a year. I beg you be generous, for I'm so happy she's well."

Her brothers were laughing and her father's mouth curled into a smile.

"Sir William, First Knight of Bain, bowing down to a liege lord," one of his soldiers snickered.

Gwenyth looked up and her mouth fell open. She pretended to cuff at her brothers. Loddin held his arms open and she ran to him, clenching him as he lifted her face to see the damage.

"Sweet Daughter what happened to your beautiful face?"

"Father, I'll be fine, I will."

"Gwen, you bleed," William noticed as Hershel rode up on his horse, his face grave.

The arrow and slash were gelling over with blood.

"Lord in heaven," Loddin bent to look. "Daughter, that must be treated immediately or it will fester. Sir William, have you surgeons in tow?"

"Aye, but I'll not have their hands groping her," William insisted.

"Right indeed," Loddin agreed. "We shall treat her. My sons, we ride to their camp to tend Gwenyth's wounds—"

"Father," Hershel interrupted. "I must speak with you and my brothers."

"What's the matter?"

"Father, it must be private, the five of us."

Loddin studied his son's grim face, then looked at Gwenyth.

"Go with William, Butterfly. We will join you when we can."

William bowed, then cradled Gwenyth in his arms and carried her to Titan.

"Look who it is, man?" he spoke as Titan stuck his nose in her belly and nuzzled. "He hasn't been the same without you, woman."

"Oh, Titan, you're magnificent," she whispered, stroking his sweaty neck.

35

The camp was loud with celebration. Soldiers who had not gone to secure Dunstonwoodshire remained in camp, drunk and jovial. Singing rose and died and fires burned brightly.

Gwenyth lay on William's pallet. With the surcoat still draped around her, William peeled away the trousers to examine her leg, washing it with boiled water despite her cries.

"It's an ugly one," he muttered. "It's starting to fester. No good."

He managed to dig out the arrow. She cried and gripped the side of the pallet. It had worked open a hole that showed the muscle. The gash from the sword was red around the edges and swelling so that it not only hurt to move, but itched horribly.

"It must be burned. It's the only way to stop it from spreading," he said as the surcoat slipped and revealed bruising on her inner thigh. "Gwenyth. These bruises. What else has passed?"

She didn't look at him.

"Nothing, I'll be fine. You should do the burning now. I don't want the festering."

He nodded and rose, calling upon a surgeon to bring his branding iron.

"'Twill hurt worse than anything you've ever felt, woman, but you must withstand it."

The surgeon came through the flap of the tent. He was an old man with gnarled knuckles and long wisps of hair over his tunic. He eyed her and examined the wounds, unrolling a woolen wrapping of gruesome metal tools. Her mouth fell open.

"I don't want to do this anymore," she shook her head and

dragged herself up on the bed.

William silenced her and took her hand.

"Bad'uns they are," the old man muttered. "She'll need more than one go with this. A shame it happened t'such a pretty leg."

He raised a long iron rod like a sword and she shuddered.

"Just get on with it, man. Her looks are not your concern," William replied. "I shall hold her down."

Her heart began to pump again, but with William bracing himself over her, she closed her eyes and tried to enjoy his touch.

"Please elope with me," she sighed. "I don't wish to part from you ever again."

"I've a mind to, Gwen," he whispered back, nuzzling her and smiling. "Would your father ever forgive me?"

The surgeon placed his iron in the fire and held it there, eyeing her and William again.

William caressed her hair. "Be strong a little longer."

She was trembling and when she felt William lift his head, she opened her eyes to see the surgeon standing above her with a red-hot poker.

"Oh, sweet Iesus..." she whispered and pulled away.

"Come, Gwenyth, you can do this," William coaxed, but she tensed in his grip. "All right then. We'll wait a moment."

He let go of her and brushed her hair back as he rose. The surgeon huffed with annoyance. Pushing back the tent flap, he soon returned with Cavanaugh and Thomas who knelt at her side.

"This is Sir Frances Cavanaugh, and Sir Edmund Thomas, Gwenyth. Sir Frances attempted to rescue you."

She nodded, her eyes welling with tears.

"I thank thee for your kindness," she muttered, trying to smile.

"'Twas nothing, My Lady," Cavanaugh replied. "It was my pleasure, and no wonder now that we have met that Sir William cannot seem to think about anyone else," he teased.

"We've heard much about you, Lady," Thomas added. "All of it seems true."

She blushed and eyed William pulling out a flask.

"They'll help me hold you, Gwenyth, so don't panic in their grip. This will be over soon, okay?"

She nodded, swiping a tear away. She felt foolish in front of them, but couldn't help the tears despite her best efforts. William poured a full cup of whiskeybae and put it to her lips.

"Drink this, woman. Drink it all and quick. 'Twill take the edge off the pain."

She took a sip and gagged.

"It smells vile," she curled her nose.

"Take it, Gwen."

She took swallows, choking on each one. It burned her throat and she grew lightheaded almost immediately. William kept coaxing her until she finally threw the last of it to the back of her mouth. She gagged again and leaned over to retch should the urge continue. The men chuckled.

"I take it you don't make a habit of such drinks?" Cavanaugh teased.

She shook her head as her lips burned, but it wasn't clear if she was shuddering or saying no.

"There now. Lie back." He laid her down on her side and straightened the surcoat around her as she shook. "Here we go now. I love you, woman."

"I love you, my William," she whispered.

William leaned over her and kissed her slowly, caressing her face, then took hold of her shoulder and waist as Thomas braced her head and neck and Cavanaugh held her legs.

The iron was reheated. This time, the surgeon didn't waste any time, but plunged the iron onto her skin. She screamed. Her body tensed as though lightning coursed through it. Once the wound was burned shut, the surgeon replaced it to the fire, then pressed it to her other wound. She screamed again and twisted to break free while the smell of roasting flesh filled her nostrils.

The six hands upon her clamped her firmly in place and the pain became too much. Her eyes went black and she passed out to William's whispers.

It was early in the morning when she woke. She was still in

William's tent. Her head ached from the whiskeybae. She stirred, then sat up, feeling the soreness of her leg and pushing back the blanket to examine the wounds. They were welted, crusted over with dried scabs and tender to touch, but no longer festering. Still, they would leave a permanent scar.

She looked around the tent. It was deep red with black stripes upon it. William wasn't there but his shield, banners and all his weapons were stowed beside the pallet. Even his squire's pallet was there, though it appeared that the squire had been sent elsewhere.

The ground was sodden from the melted snow. She stood to find her boots and her bare feet squished into it. Sounds of men breaking camp and the clattering of arms and wagons filled the outside. The tent flap peeled back and William walked in. She yanked the blanket around her and smiled.

"How's your leg?" he said, his voice scratchy.

He made no signs of turning to give her privacy. His eyes were swollen from fatigue and the stink of ale was strong upon him.

"'Twill be well, thanks to you." He made no effort to smile back. She furrowed her brow. "What's wrong?"

He stood like a stump, his arms hanging limply at his sides as though he carried a great burden. Finally he handed over a bundle of fabric. It was a long skirt.

"From the Lady Sarah of Dunstonwoodshire," he clarified. "She sends word that her father has lived and that she is well."

She slipped it on beneath the surcoat as her father and brothers came in. They looked equally solemn, like a funeral procession and reeking of the smell of many drinks. Her father looked old and slumped beneath his surcoat, which had always made him look strong. George's eyes were bloodshot. Loddin, her brother, looked away, his brow contorted to keep back the tears, and Hershel and Gavin both looked down at their hands.

"Daughter," her father began. "What happened to you at Dunstonwoodshire?"

Her heart started thumping faster.

"Nothing I cannot survive, Father," she replied, though her face turned red.

"Butterfly, don't lie. Tell—" Loddin's face twisted and the water in her eyes began to pool again. "Tell me what happened when

Shea Feargach arrived."

She felt herself shaking her head. Tears forming, she looked down the row of her family. William's eyes were welling and his lips were parted so he could breathe, for his nose was clogging.

"Those bruises on your legs, Gwenyth," William said. "How did you get them?"

"I...I didn't do anything wrong," she quaked as though she faced a lifetime in the stocks. "I tried to stop it...I..."

"What did Shea do to you, Gwen?" William's voice cracked as his tears finally bubbled over his eyelids.

She felt her skin going numb as she stared at the tribunal in front of her.

"Daughter, Hershel told us Shea had victory over you. The men of Dusntonwoodshire said...they said..." though he couldn't complete his words.

Her throat tightened shut and she reached the back of her hand up, dragging it across her eyes.

"I fought, Father. I slashed him," her words were soft and her breathing became rapid. "I kicked and I, I cried, and I begged for you, for help...but I could not...I couldn't stop it..."

She fell down to her knees and put her head in her hands.

"Why didn't you tell me?" William came to her and knelt. "He took you to bed? He raped you?"

She trembled. "I prayed to God and Mary, I thought I was dying until I heard you were here, and I escaped. To you."

She looked up and took his hand, but it was limp.

"But he," William stammered. "He made you a Feargach whore."

His words slapped her. She looked up to him, her face going pale. "I..." She did not know what to say.

Her father walked up and placed a hand on William's shoulder.

"William, lad. You and I must have another talk, I think." He too knelt down and reached out to wipe her eyes. "Daughter, when last did you eat?" She looked down and pulled her hand away from William's, twisting the loose threads of the surcoat. "Daughter? Gwenyth, answer me."

"Two days ago, My Lord," she muttered.

"Gavin, find your sister something to break her fast. After that, you return to Ballymead with George. 'Tis best that way."

"Where will you go?" she whimpered.

"I go with this army," he replied, "With Loddin, Gavin and Hershel. We offer our services to the crown."

She looked at William again who had braced his forehead in his hand. He could sense her stare and lifted his head, gazing at her deep, brown eyes.

"My army leaves today," William muttered. "Shea—" He choked on the word, closing his eyes to get it out. "Shea flees back to Dwyre. I go to deliver his death sentence and free my sister."

"Your sister?" she asked.

"I'll give the both of you a moment to say *goodbye,* then after that you eat and leave, Gwenyth, and William, we will discuss this," Loddin interrupted.

"What is it you mean to discuss?" Gwenyth questioned as her father and William exchanged another grim look. "Please tell me it's not what I'm thinking," she begged. They both looked down. She felt as though she was going to be ill. "I did nothing wrong... Father, William, this wasn't my fault—"

Loddin raised a hand to silence her, nodding and reaching out to her to give her a badly needed embrace.

"Of course it's not, Gwenyth. You're not to blame. You cannot help being the beautiful creature that you are." He held her in his arms, but she was so stiff and cold he finally let go.

He left and her brothers followed. She remained there and William rose, turning from her. He ran his hand through his hair.

"Why didn't you tell me?" he asked again.

"I was going to, but—"

"When? After you convinced me to elope with you and your belly is swelling with his demon? You would deceive me?"

"I didn't think you would judge me," she muttered. "I thought you were different, I thought you would love me—"

"God, Gwenyth, I do love you. I just, I can't..." He turned and looked down at her, taking hold of her arms and lifting her chin. "Christ, why? Why *you*? You were supposed to be mine."

He brushed a wisp of hair from her face tenderly, slowly, as if memorizing the way her skin felt beneath his fingertips.

"I wasn't a virgin when you met me," she reminded him, staring at the mud beneath her feet.

"No, but at least you were married. William Feargach's honor might have been in ruins but yours was not. But now..." He let go of her and turned away again. "Now I cannot marry you."

She stood frozen, knowing he would say those words but never expecting to hear them. Finally when he didn't turn to her again she moved in front of him and looked into his face.

"William." She placed a timid hand upon his arm. "What are these sad words I'm hearing—"

"God, Gwenyth! He's made you his whore! A Feargach whore! You are ruined for me now!" He wrenched his arm free as a tear fell down his cheek. He wiped it stubbornly as if he was the angry boy he used to be. "*God* I knew something like this was too good to happen to me."

"Shea was right..." she whispered in disbelief.

"Don't you see?" he whirled around again. "He did it on purpose and you couldn't stop him!"

She felt her blood pool down in her feet as his words shattered her heart into a million tiny pieces in her chest.

"I tried," she mouthed.

"Why could you not have tried harder?" he pleaded.

She backed away from him, shaking her head as the water continued to bubble like a spring from her eyes.

"You will never know how I tried."

She clenched her teeth, then turned away and spotted his banners again. Limping to them, she grabbed the end of his Cadogan hawk and pulled her dagger from her boot. William whirled around to the sound of ripping.

"What are you doing?"

She turned back, staring coldly upon him as though he were her enemy, as though she saw him through those distant eyes with which he had discovered her.

"My honor."

She held her name outward for him to see, then dropped it into the mud and stomped her foot upon it, grinding it into the soggy soil.

"You fought in my honor and I have none," she fumed. "I'm worthless now. I disgrace my father's house."

You disgrace my house with your presence, William! "Stop it, Gwenyth," he commanded, reaching to her.

"*Do—not—touch—me!*" she cringed as she closed her eyes.

"Gwenyth, you know not how difficult this decision was for me—"

"For *you?*" Her voice rose with incredulity. "How difficult it was for *you? You* did not get raped, Sir William Cadogan! Your life is not over! Don't speak to me of difficulty, for *I* am being punished for a crime against me by the *one man I trusted!*"

"Don't speak to me in such a way," he warned. "If you'll allow me to explain, you might understand my position—"

"I might be a *worthless* whore," her words were full of sadness as he shook his head.

"Gwenyth—"

"But I am not *your* whore, William Cadogan! And I don't have to do as you say!"

"Perhaps those were the wrong words, but—"

She didn't stay to hear him, ripping off the Bainick surcoat as she marched away and dropping it in the mud. The flap fell shut.

The army was all but packed. Tents were collapsed and rolled up. The field was trampled over the rolling hills and turned to mud from hooves and excrement. Smoke rose from smoldering campfires. George waited in the saddle with a spare horse tethered in his grip.

"Gwenyth, I *must* tell you something," he begged as he chased her. "It has to do with who my father is. You might understand why if you'll only let me explain—"

"Will you eat, Sister?" Gavin asked, returning with cheese and bread.

"I would rather starve than eat this man's food," she breathed, trying desperately to dry the tears from her eyes as the soldiers passing by stared.

Limping to George, she grabbed hold of the saddle and reins of the spare mount and lifted herself up.

"I'm ready, Brother."

George wrapped a cloak around her and they kicked their horses into a walk. William grabbed hold of her bridle while Gavin remained with the food still in his hand, confused.

"Please, woman, come back inside and let me explain."

She looked down at his sore eyes.

"Unhand my mount, My Lord."

"I'm begging," he whispered.

She turned the horse from him but he still held it.

"Sir William," George intervened. "My sister bids you let her go. Unhand her."

Reluctantly, he let his hand drop.

"God, Gwenyth, I *must* explain."

"'Tis a sorry lot to be a woman in a man's world, My Lord," she found her voice once more. "You're lucky, for every maiden in the land would love to be your wife. You'll meet someone new but my life is over now for I may as well be dead. And you are now dead to me. And no one will ever love me again. Whatever your reasons, they're of no consequence," she whispered. "I *trusted* you with all my heart...and that was my gravest of mistakes."

With that, she tapped the horse. He jumped before her.

"Don't go yet," he implored, his hands trembling, sensing he had made a terrible mistake. "Please stay, please..."

But she and George pushed past and trotted away.

William called after her, but she kept her eyes forward as they put distance between them.

"He calls for you, Sister. Should you not stop?"

She shook her head as her hair caught on the wind, but did not take her eyes off the hills in front of her. His call grew faint until it stopped altogether.

"Do you not wish to say goodbye to Father?"

Again she shook her head.

"Lady Gwenyth!" another man called as he came towards them. "Do you leave us without saying goodbye? I had hoped to check in on you and see how you faired with the whiskeybae. I wasn't sure if it was that or William's swooning which eventually knocked you out," he chuckled.

They slowed to a halt.

"She goes home to Ballymead, Sir Cavanaugh," George answered for her.

Cavanaugh's smile disappeared.

"You don't look well, Lady. Do your wounds fester again?"

She couldn't speak, feeling hiccupped cries rising with determination in her throat despite her efforts to suppress them.

"My sister's leg is fine and we thank thee for your help."

She looked down at her hands gripping the reins as more tears flowed. Sir Cavanaugh looked at her, then at George, then back at her again.

"What has passed to make you so unhappy, Lady?" Cavanaugh inquired, reaching up to take her hand.

She didn't let him have it, but clenched the reins so tightly her whole arm was trembling. George took a deep breath.

"Gwenyth no longer holds Sir William's favor," he clarified. "Come, Sister. You go with me now."

She couldn't look at the knight and kept her eyes lowered.

"I bid thee well, Sir Cavanaugh," she whispered, and nudged her horse onward.

William's squire began gathering his implements out of the tent, planting them next to Titan who stood in full assemblage. He hadn't moved, but trembled all over. Finally he noticed that some of his men stared. He quickly rubbed the soreness from his eyes and ducked back inside. Over and over again he watched her disappear below the hill without stopping to look back.

"I'm dead to her now," he mumbled to himself, bending down to pick up her name from the mud.

He felt over the letters, rolling his thumbs across them as if it was her skin, the skin that Shea had bloodied and bruised, the skin he had longed to touch and kiss. He hadn't gotten to her in time. He had failed to protect her. Shea had won. He marched over to his Cadogan hawk and ripped the rest of it off the pole.

"Jonathan!"

The squire hastened in and bowed his head. "Yes, My Lord?"

"Put this in the fire."

"My Lord?" The boy looked at the banner shoved into his hand. "This is your crest!"

"Do as I command."

"But sir—"

"Do as I command and do not question it. Burn it now."

The boy bowed and took his leave.

You failed, he berated himself. *I'll kill him. I'll carve him open like a piece of meat. Forgive me, Father Kearney, but I haven't slain dragons, I have become one.*

He held her name to his forehead and closed his eyes, not moving from his spot as the flap of his tent flew open once more.

"What have you done?" Cavanaugh barged in.

"What do you mean?" William retorted.

"The Lady Gwenyth leaves in tears, man, what have you done to her?"

"Nothing. Shea raped her and I have told her I cannot marry her now." He shook his head. "She's been made his whore."

"And you said this to her?"

"I had no choice. I'll be the king some day and it won't do well for me to marry her no matter how I wish it. The scandal could ruin the monarch."

"Come off it. She has all the qualities of a queen. Grace, beauty, bravery—"

"*Believe me*, Frances, I'm not happy about this," he choked on his words, stifling the tears that threatened his eyes. "But none of what you say will replace her honor."

Frances threw his fist and knocked William's nose so hard he tumbled backward.

"What the hell was that for?" William growled, sprawled on his back in the mud as his nose gushed with blood for the first time since boyhood.

"You're a dolt! She has been injured in the worst way and you decide now is the time to prove yourself a typical man? To hell with your code of chivalry. Since when did you care of customs? If you did, you would have taken a wife by now and you wouldn't use crossbows!" Cavanaugh fumed and William lay stunned.

"She must have been in hell to have fought so hard to leave, and you were the heaven she sought. You should be humbled by that, man. If ever she lost her honor, she earned it back on that battlefield! I haven't seen heart in any soldier like I saw in her and I've never seen you ache for a woman. Yet with her..." he shook his head and searched for words again. "I cannot help but pity the frail woman I have just seen leaving now. You've shattered her. I consider you my closest friend, Will, and I've always respected your decisions, but you'll regret this one, man, for she's no whore. She was your match and you're a God-damned fool."

William started to get up when Cavanaugh, exhaling with frustration, punched him once more and sent him back into the mud. This time, William scrambled to his feet and grabbed Cavanaugh, wheeling him around. He returned the punch and sent Cavanaugh to the ground. Grabbing his surcoat, he yanked him up and gripped him at his throat.

"You assault your commander and you're lucky I don't crack your skull in."

"Oh shut it. You know what I think?" Frances continued as he rubbed his chin. "I think you're angry with yourself, not her. Sir William the *Brave* never fails and yet you've failed. You've *lost*." William loosened his grip. "Well now, you really have lost, and what you've just done is your biggest failure."

William glared at him but knew it was true, and instead of engaging further, stormed out.

36

"Take me, William." Her words were silky. Her hair fell from the pins that held it fast and shimmered in a curtain around her. "I forgive you."

William sat propped upon his bed. "Come to me, woman."

The linens had been freshly changed by his attendant and a silken canopy was tied open. The fire was fresh and filled the darkness with warmth that wavered on the walls and on her skin.

She walked forward and reached to his feet, pulling loose his boots. They were still muddy and cached with battle, and his surcoat was as crusted and bloodied as his face and beard from those he had killed. Then she reached to his coif, pulling it carefully over his head so as not to pinch his hair in the links.

Her finger reached to the scar beneath his eye and she smiled at it, rubbing a smooth finger across it. Then she kissed it, her moist lips pressed against his eye so gently that he thought he might melt beneath them.

"Don't stop, woman," he sighed, letting his hands find her waist so that they slid over her gown, up to her breasts. "I'm at your mercy."

She let him and smiled.

"You will make a fine father someday, my love," she crooned.

She turned from him with a grin on her lips, slightly parted, and full of desire to kiss him with more deeply. He shifted upon the bed and made to stand, but ached for her so badly he knew his legs wouldn't support him.

Reaching behind her, she began pulling the laces of her green dress, slowly, so that it loosened with pops of enticement. With a glance over her shoulder, she smiled again. Her eyes glowed like black jewels and she hunched her shoulder to hide her mouth, coy, paralyzing him, as though she knew how beautiful she was.

"Prove to me how much you really want me, William."

Her words were like a song and she let the gown fall to her ankles. William breathed in at her bareness. She turned around to face him, her hands sliding along her hips and stomach, up and around her small, perfect breasts. She pushed her long locks away to reveal her body to him.

"Elope with me, my love..." He was nodding his agreement. "I need you," she whispered. Her eyes became sad. "Will, please..."

"Then you shall have me, woman."

He threw the flaps of his surcoat aside and ripped himself loose from his trousers. Pulling her forward, she smiled again and straddled him, bare and tight and perfect. She wrapped her arms about him and draped her hair around his neck.

Her breath in his ear was like wisps of wind and her breasts pressed to him.

"William..."

His arm fit snuggly around the curve of her back, sloping onto her buttocks, and he reached beneath her to guide himself in...

"William...William..."

Thomas was shaking him. "William."

He sat up from his slumber beneath a tree, freezing cold.

What have I done, Frances? You're right. Day after day I have proven myself as cruel as the bastard I chase.

He didn't want to be there in the winter grayness. He wished to be back in his dream and rubbed his eyes with his thumb and finger to stave off a headache.

It was late in the day. He had stopped his army at the little hamlet in the Northeast Pass to rest. It was nearly midwinter and in the spirit of fraternity, he had volunteered his men to rebuild the village, which was celebrating to the goddesses despite their misfortune.

"What is it, man?"

"The men burn a Yule log with the peasants and bid you join them."

"I'm weary, Edmund, and there's nothing to celebrate."

"You're still their leader and you must act the part, no matter how sick your heart is."

William nodded. "You're right. I pity myself."

He hoisted himself up and rolled up his blanket. It had been just a sennight. Already they had reached the hamlet.

How I dallied in returning her home. This trek is only a fortnight at best. 'Twas here she knew she could trust me.

The pain made his heart feel as if it would implode. He could envision her dancing around the fire like she had that night, laughing, and flashing her smiles upon him.

"I should like my wine," he mumbled.

"More wine is not what you need," Thomas admonished. "Besides, it's souring."

"I want it all the same."

"Then I'll see to it that Jonathan brings it to you."

Cavanaugh had not spoken more than a few sentences to him on the journey, and every time he closed his eyes, he saw the battle, saw Cavanaugh scolding him, or saw Gwenyth. Sometimes she cried, sometimes she stared at him with those distant eyes, or else she seduced him, causing him more than one embarrassment.

"Shea destroyed these people's lives, man," William shook his head as they walked through the slush, back into the mess of men. "They were kind to me and Lady Gwenyth," he muttered. "That man over there lost his fingers fighting to get to his woman as they raped her. It was their wedding we happened upon."

"And yet, he still loves her and they rebuild and give thanks. Shea has not killed their souls. Man's spirit is strong indeed, is it not?" Thomas added with the most depth of thought William could attribute to him.

"What do you know of love aside from the women who lie beneath you? You've not even a wife, man," William chastised. "I don't see how they can find happiness in their sorrow."

William nodded a greeting to his men, spotting the men of Ballymead carrying the new Yule log to the bonfire. Thomas shrugged.

"Perhaps they're closer to one another now because they suffered together, for surely she doesn't see him as weak despite being

297

maimed, and he doesn't see her as a whore when he knows she did nothing wrong. Look at her smile. And he has pulled her close to him," Thomas noted as they scrutinized the couple. "They rejoice in each other's lives which God spared so that they can remain together. They don't pass judgment upon one another, for that is God's task alone."

William thought on those words, the words of Father Kearney if ever he had heard them, and wondered if God was in fact working through Thomas. He shrugged the thought away and arrived behind Loddin and his sons who stood with backs turned, arms folded, deep in conversation.

"Ballymead is surely ready for the festivities by now. It's a shame we will miss it," Gavin noted.

Their father smiled and took a skin of wine offered to him.

"Now that Loddin and Gwenyth are home, it would have been our first Christmas together in quite a long time."

"Except for Mother," Hershel noted.

Lord Loddin smiled again. "Do you remember how nervous your sister was when your mother told her she would get to wear the holly crown and pass out ale to the men?"

His sons chuckled.

"She was only three and ten. Dropped the whole tray," Hershel laughed.

"Remember? She drenched William and Mathew so badly, we could have gotten drunk from their tunics," young Loddin added. "It's the one thing Mathew Whitcroft can still tease her about."

"She always was the winter maiden. The other lasses of Ballymead have been forever jealous," Gavin chuckled. "No wonder you were always beating the suitors away, Father."

William smiled as he eavesdropped, imagining Gwenyth's hair laced with red berries.

"Aye, especially Mathew. That lad was on his path to debauchery with Gwenyth." They all laughed. "It's good we found Marta for him when we did, for I was certain I would have to send him away."

"Do you think she will be well again, Father?" Loddin asked.

William turned to his nearest men to pretend at a conversation.

Their father sighed. "Only time will tell. She was brutalized in the worst way."

"She did well once Gavin took her as a squire," Hershel remarked. "She certainly fought well on the battlefield. Perhaps she might fare well if we make her continue, for it will build her strength."

"Aye, but son, she had a future with Sir William to help her through it, but now…It's a shame what has passed, for she was so set on him…Oh lads," I sighed, his voice shaking. "I fear there's no future for your beautiful sister now."

William, washed over with shame, looked at his hands.

"Do you think he was wrong to reject her?" young Loddin pressed as they passed the wine skin around. "For I must admit, I've grown to love Mary dearly, but back then, I wouldn't have wanted her had I known she had been spoiled by another man."

"I will always feel that Gwenyth deserves special treatment for she is my lass, but William suffers as well." Loddin shook his head and sighed again. "I don't hold his decision against him. 'Tis what many a man would do, though such boldness in *his* character I cannot help but think strange. There must be more to his decision than what he tells me. 'Tis a shame nonetheless, for I don't think he'll ever know how much she trusted him. She was *so* innocent. Such a beauty, she had so many prospects." He took a deep breath, looking into space. "She needs her mother. My sweet Lady Amaranth was strict, but she would know how to comfort her daughter in ways none of us will ever know."

"We shall then support her, for she'll no longer be suitable for marriage," Gavin remarked, taking the wine and swallowing hard.

"No, she won' be," Loddin folded his arms and passed on the wine, "and I won't marry her to a low liege for she deserved the best. Perhaps the convent would give her life purpose again. Dear God I cannot watch your mother's only lass grow into a spinster. My heart will be made sick by it."

"But what of little Louisa?" Gavin continued. "She would stay with Gwenyth, would she not? And it wouldn't be fair to commit her to a life of nunnery because of her foster mother's disgrace."

Loddin shook his head. "She is no disgrace to *us*, son, despite how many men may think. And don't ever let her hear those words for they are pure poison to a troubled heart. Shea Feargach is the disgrace."

"I'm sorry, Father. I only speak of the way others consider it. I meant nothing."

"I know you didn't," Loddin smiled, patting his shoulder.

"I always imagined her going on to be the pride of another lord's house. I never thought this could happen to us...to her," Hershel wiped his mouth.

"We shall make sure Lord Feargach is as dead as his seed before leaving Dwyre if Sir William doesn't butcher him first, for there is anger in that lad unlike anything I have seen." Loddin smiled and nudged his son. "And you, Gavin, when you are married, it will be up to you, George and Loddin here to give me many grandchildren, unless I can get Hershel to remove his monk's cowl long enough to take another wife." He furrowed his brow astutely and Hershel's expression grew sour. "It's up to you to pass on *my* seed. I want at least twenty grandchildren running around my feet."

His boys laughed.

"That's a steep order, Father," Loddin amused. "But Gavin here has had much practice loving women, so it shouldn't be hard for him to do his share."

"Don't remind me of Gavin's trysts," their father laughed. "Perhaps I have my twenty grandchildren already. Speak of a *disgrace* to Ballymead."

Gavin gave a proud grin.

"I intend to give the Lady Sarah only the best service, and for that I must practice often at my craft."

"Lord have mercy," Loddin rolled his eyes. "Perhaps the hope of my blood rests on poor George's shoulders. Just ponder a moment, son, on why you shouldn't be a disgrace, but your sister is—"

Hershel perked up with the sight of William. He nodded in his direction and the men of Ballymead turned.

"Sir William," Loddin called.

"Good evening, My Lord," William turned and bowed his head.

"Come share some yuletide wine," Gavin jested. "It's mulled with the sweetest sweat of men at battle and surely is a vintage all its own."

"How do you fair, lad?" their father asked.

"I'm well."

"You don't look it," Loddin noted, handing him the skin. He

obliged and took a long swig, wiping his mouth with his sleeve. "Did you not rest well?"

"That's impossible on journeys such as these." William looked at Gwenyth's brothers, attempting to find cheer after all that had happened, and turned back to their father. "May I speak with you, sir?"

Loddin nodded and walked with him, his limp pronounced as he slid on the snow. They made their way outside of the ring of soldiers gathering around the fire until they were out of earshot.

"I have been thinking, sir, that I've made a grave error."

Loddin nodded and turned to clear his throat, hiding his smile.

"What error is this, man? Have you made a misjudgment in battle? For I would have to argue that you were quite brilliant."

"Oh no, it's nothing of war."

William rested his hands on his belt and the two stopped to see the fire taking hold from afar. The men below burst spontaneously into song.

"I wish to…well what I mean to say is…well you see, Gwenyth and I didn't part with the best of words—"

"Do you wish to make things right with my daughter?" Loddin spared him the humiliation.

"I do, sir, if she'll forgive me. I was too blinded by my anger to think about her pain and I believe I have wronged her terribly."

"Will you quit talking in your civil ways and speak plainly of your thoughts?" Loddin teased.

William shook his head.

"You don't wish to hear my thoughts right now, sir."

"But I do. 'Twill put your mind at ease. You can wake refreshed on the morrow and will no longer look like last week's supper."

William thought a moment longer and decided that if he ended up flattened on the ground again like Frances had done, he would deal with it.

"I think of her constantly, even when I should be working. When I'm not dreaming of killing the Lord of Dwyre, I dream of her. She's there every time I close my eyes."

"What is it you dream?"

"Sometimes she's crying for the pain that was dealt her, other times like today," he looked up carefully and took a deep breath, "she is seducing me like a temptress, and I'll not speak of what happens in these dreams for you are her father but she is always there, and I wake up in wanting of her more and more."

Loddin belted laughter and slapped his back. "I prayed you would change your mind! Ah, that's the way we men are for a beautiful woman. 'Twill be our demise. I'll leave it to her to offer forgiveness but when I return home, I shall talk to her and send you word by messenger, how does that sound?"

William fell down on one knee and exhaled. "I would be grateful."

"Then it will be done." Loddin patted him on the shoulder and chuckled. "I was afraid I would have to send her to the convent."

"Not Gwenyth, sir. She's too free-spirited to be a nun."

"That I know." Loddin helped him to his feet.

"Then will you allow her to be betrothed to me once more?"

"Is this what you want, William? For she has been married and now has been—"

"Please, man, I pine for her," he cut him short, bowing down his head to hide his embarrassment.

Loddin nodded. "Then yes. You may be betrothed once more. If you both so choose you may take her hand by springtime, for seeing you two at Dunstonwoodshire, I believe a year was too long a time to make you wait."

"Do you mean it, Loddin?" William asked.

"Let me talk to her, and I'll then receive your betrothal contract. Marriage may ensue by May, if that's agreeable."

William smiled his first smile since holding Gwenyth on the battlefield.

"And what of this child you spoke of? Louisa?"

Loddin raised his brow.

"So you have heard us?"

"Only fragments, sir. I wasn't eavesdropping."

Loddin's eye twinkled. "Right. If you marry, then this matter will no doubt affect you. She fosters a babe, a daughter from Dwyre that was smuggled out for fear of safety."

Loddin watched him to see his reaction.

"To whom does this babe belong?"

Loddin proceeded carefully. "It's the daughter of the Lady Janis." He paused. "The fourth wife to Shea Feargach."

William's brow furrowed. "How could you allow such seed in your house?"

"I know," Loddin nodded. "I nearly sent away the man who brought her with a knife in his back. However, Gwenyth begged to keep the babe, for the Lady Janis was her only comrade there. They befriended one another and it is the Lady Janis who gave her much understanding. We honor such a person by accepting her babe."

'You should know that Louisa befriended the Lady Gwenyth when no one else would. It was at her request, knowing how you suffered as a boy, that I send you to get Loddin's daughter...'

The king's words rang clearly in his mind. He thought only his sister had befriended Gwenyth and found himself confused. The babe's name was Louisa.

"Will this bother you? A foster daughter from such stock when you march to execute her father? She would have, after all, known much harshness from such a father."

"Never," he whispered, remembering his own father, then smiled. "Never. Gwenyth has a kind heart."

"And I don't wish to dwell on the obvious, son, for it keeps me tormented at night, but there is always a chance that, that Shea has infected my daughter as well. Louisa would then be kin."

William looked away and exhaled. *The only thing worse than being raped and beaten would be to bear the man's child. I've shown her no sympathy.*

"I know it."

"Does this still not sway your mind?"

He closed his eyes as a breeze blew over them. *This was not her fault. Remember that love she felt only for you and move on.*

"It's all right, lad, if you decide no—"

"Foster or blood, Gwenyth's children will be welcome to me, I swear it."

"Come. You lead an army and must strengthen yourself." Loddin slapped his back. "It's not yet Yule but we celebrate to the goddesses anyway, Pagan customs or not. Gwenyth is lucky to have the favor of such a man as you. Oh, but William?" he paused.

William turned to him. Loddin's face had grown firm.

"I esteem Gwenyth as though she were a princess, as any man ought to look upon his daughter. This is your final chance. Don't wrong her again."

37

The festivities for Yule were well underway when Gwenyth rode into the bailey with George. She had forgotten all about celebrations and Yule logs, and was unable to fathom cracking a smile let alone being the winter maiden to the men.

"You're back, Lady!" Mathew Whitcroft called from over the portcullis.

She looked up but didn't respond. His smile faded when he spotted the damage to her face. She dismounted with the help of George, and Michael came to take the reins.

"You've lost my trousers," he noted, before getting a warning shake of the head from George.

The boy stared at her face and sealed his mouth.

"I'm sorry," she hung her head. "I shall make you a new pair and will never take them again."

Michael watched her with wide eyes as she disappeared up the steps into the great hall, warm with holiday smells. The sprigs of pine that her father had said were necessary in any household, Christian or not, were hanging for the celebrations. The women sat at the spindles in the corner, engaged in the never-ending gossips that accompanied making yarn, and all seemed to be the same.

They jumped up to greet her when George once more bade them leave her be and go back to their work. William beckoned her to his side and stood to hug her.

"Have you suffered, Gwen?" he whispered, feeling her weak embrace.

She didn't answer, but burrowed against him for he had always been understanding and gentle.

"Will you tell me?"

She still didn't answer, but took comfort in his warmth. His fingers traveled over her scabs, lingering on her face, but he didn't ask.

"Have you eaten recently?"

She shook her head against him.

"There will not be a Christmas boar this year," he continued as he seated her next to him and served her wine. He felt for his cup and did the same. "Father isn't here to lead the hunt. We will slaughter a pig in its place and you shall serve the men ale."

"I cannot be the maiden this year," she replied with feeble words, sipping her wine. "I'm not one."

"It doesn't matter, Gwenyth," he replied, pouring some for himself. "It's more a custom for a pretty woman to do it, and you have always been that. It cannot be anyone else."

"Beauty...Is that all I'm good for? I should like to make myself scarred so no one looks anymore."

"It's an honor, Sister. All the women try to be beautiful and the men go to pains to boast their looks as well. It's a celebration."

"There's nothing worth celebrating," she shrugged.

He heard the despair in her words and held her hands.

"What happened, Sister? What's beaten your spirit?"

"Will you excuse me? I should like to see Louisa and rest. I'm weary."

She vanished into the solar.

She remained hidden in her chamber, refusing food despite William's constant worry. George had told him all that had happened. Mary fretted over her so much that she wanted to scream. Yet they meant well, and she could not muster the strength to complain.

Mary knocked upon the door and when no answer came, she pushed through uninvited and set the midday meal next to her uneaten morning meal. Gwenyth looked up from the passages of Hershel's bible and her sister-in-law pushed her stringy hair behind her ear for her, clicking her tongue.

"May I *please* coif your hair?" she asked. "'Twould give me great pleasure to do so."

Gwenyth conceded and marked her page.

"Aye, Mary. 'Twould be nice to do something sisterly," she said and stared out the window.

"You mean it?" Mary squealed. "You never agree to such."

"I do. Perhaps afterwards you and I could work at embroidery? Or perhaps sewing? I owe Michael a pair of pants."

"Of course! If you should like. Don't you wish to ride Luna instead?"

"I believe the time has come for me to grow up," she replied and rose to grab the basket containing her ribbons.

Mary and one of the maids separated her hair into two thick chunks and began tugging loose the tangles. Gwenyth winced.

"My Lady? What's wrong?" her maid asked.

"My head is still sore," she muttered.

Mary found the scab from Maccus's blow and inhaled.

"Oh, Gwenyth. I'm so sorry." Gwenyth shrugged, toying with her nails. "Sister, what happened to you?"

"I beg you not ask," she whispered.

Mary held her arm for a moment, then she and the maid took to work with the combs again, gently braiding it then looping it up and around, making a crown of braids upon the back of her head. Decorated with little ribbons of dark red, Mary was quite pleased and so enthused, she insisted on selecting a matching gown, which swooped across the shoulders with a border of spirals like volutes on an ancient column.

Gwenyth stood mute as she was stripped down to bareness, and neither Mary nor her maid uttered a single word at the faded bruises on her body and between her thighs, or of the hideous wounds from battle and the scars from the wolves, though Gwenyth knew they noticed.

Finally, Mary smiled and held a bronze mirror to her face.

"You're still very lovely, Sister, despite what you might see in your reflection."

Mary set down the mirror and scurried off to get her embroidery.

"You may leave me now," Gwenyth said to the maid who also

left.

She moved across the room to her trunk. *Mother wanted me to save these*, she thought, digging through her embroidery threads. She pulled out her old sewing. It hadn't been touched since she had stitched flowers for her dowry. She could hear Mother fussing at her like she had when she was young for not taking it seriously, showing her how to end each color and how to make patterns on the cloth.

Guilt for disregarding her mother nagged at her. *To have one more chance to spend that time with you, I would give anything...I'm sorry, Mother.*

Gwenyth lifted the basket out of the trunk and onto her lap as she sat. Finding her frame and needles, she pulled out a square of her mother's fabric and laid it across the circle, clamping it into place. She let her fingers smooth the fabric as her eyes became sore, nestling down into the chair as though it was the breast of her mother and managed to catch her tears before they came.

You will quit crying like a fool, woman.

"I'm back, Gwenyth," Mary called through the door and scurried in once more with her needlework. "How nice to spend a peaceable day together. I have wanted this so much."

Gwenyth summoned a smile. "Then we will do this often and I will try to be a good sister for once."

They worked at sewing for the remainder of the day, until finally Mary took her leave to oversee the scullery's dinner preparations. Gwenyth sighed and set aside the needle, pushing Louisa in her cradle.

"My Lady, your brothers request you join them at board this evening," Beatrice called through the door. "You haven't shared food with them since you arrived home. Will you come sit with the family?"

I'm not a lady.

Staring out the window, she quit rocking Louisa and stood. Cracking the door, she looked at Beatrice.

"I won't take supper this evening but thank them for me."

She began to close the door when the maid stopped it.

"I'm worried for you, My Lady. You've grown so thin. Are you ill?"

"Yes, Beatrice. I'm ill and should like to be alone. Please tell my brothers to stop asking for my company."

She pushed shut the door and went back to Louisa's side. She stared at another one of her trunks and decided to go to it. Removing the lace on top, she unbuckled the straps, straps that had not been opened in some time.

The leather was stiff. She pushed up the heavy lid and propped it against the wall. Inside were her wedding linens. Slowly at first, she began to pull out each item, unsure of how to hold them. Her mother had kept them all after the wedding. Every single item was there.

The gown she wore of deep red was on top alongside the belt with woven zigzags, then the ribbons and beads that had been braided into her hair. The bronze circlet that had been specially made was beneath it. She dug deeper, thinking of William Feargach and pulled out each item faster as if trying to dig out of a hole. Her eyes became determined. Soon she was throwing everything onto the floor as she felt his hands holding her on their wedding night. She heard herself crying at the pain of losing her virginity and ripped the slippers out next. She felt Shea's hands pinning her to Sarah's bed and pulled out her wedding necklace, throwing it against the wall.

Then it was William Cadogan. How she had trusted him with all her heart.

He's no different! She fumed, and tore her shifts out of the trunk. *He just throws his punches with words instead of fists!*

Everything lay strewn about her now as she wept. Her dream of him was shattered.

I will never feel the favor of his gaze again. I'm a whore! I'm not worthy of his affection! If only I had tried harder. I tried as hard as I could! I tried to be strong and failed and it's over! I'm ruined for him! He is honorable for killing men, and I am dishonored because I could not fight hard enough...it's not fair. "It's not fair...it's not fair it's not fair it's not fair!" she cried and grabbed the linen in front of her to bury her face. "It's not fair that I be punished like this..." *I cannot forgive him, ever. I trusted him so, oh, how I thought I could trust him for he was there for me when no other man was...*

She was shaking so badly, shuddering as though she might fall apart into pieces and looked down to see she cried into the linen of her wedding night, the dried, brown blood of her maidenhead in a big, proud, faded splotch, crumpled in her grip.

She dropped it as if it were poison and pushed it away, horrified by it. Her honor, the honor she used to have. In a swoop of rage, she grabbed it once more and took it to the hearth, taking her dagger and puncturing it as though it were a deer carcass as she ripped slices off and threw them into her fire.

There was another knock on the door.

"Go away!" she screamed.

Louisa stirred. The door opened instead and George and William came in, followed by a frightened Beatrice.

"Beatrice says you're ill..." George began. "Sister! You destroy your wedding garments! Why?"

He raced to her and grabbed her wrists, removing the shreds of fabric still bearing her blood.

"I hate them!" she screamed. "I never want to set eyes on them again! This!" she shook a shred of cloth in his face. "*This* was my honor! I'm filthy now! I cannot ever get clean, not ever!"

William reached out and held her steady and then pulled her to him, wrapping his arms about her as she shook so violently her knees buckled. Mary crept into the doorway and George nodded for her to close it.

"You're not disgraced in our eyes, wee sister," William whispered, peeling the dagger from her clasp. "If Father doesn't kill Shea, then Loddin will, or Gavin, or Hershel or Sir William. He will die for this and we will see that it's not a merciful death."

"William doesn't care anymore!" she sobbed. "I hope he returns to the capital and I never hear his name again."

"You don't mean that. He's hurt, 'tis all."

"He's like all other men and is only hurt when his pride has been hurt."

"You do care, Gwen, I know you do—"

"I don't! He no longer wants me. He said so. I should like to forget him."

She buried her face against him, mastering her speech and allowing her emotion to drain away. William turned to George.

"Will you leave us, Brother?" But George hesitated. "It's all right. Gwenyth will be fine."

Reluctantly, George motioned to Beatrice who curtsied and left, and then followed her out. The door latched shut and William pulled her from him.

"Will you please talk to me?"

She didn't say a word, but drifted to the hearth and sat upon the rug so that the heat radiated onto her face. William followed and plopped down beside her.

"Sister, you bring great pain upon yourself by keeping all this silent."

She hugged her knees. "I wish Mother were here. I wish she hadn't died. I miss her so."

"I know," William replied. "But I'm here, blind as I am."

"I know."

She laid her head against his arm.

"Do you ever wonder how different things might have been," he said, "if Father had waited a little longer for a suitor for you?"

"What good is that? Wondering?" she whispered. "None of it can be changed. Shea might have lost at Dunstonwoodshire, but he has still won. Look at us."

"I know," William muttered. "But I wish you to know that I would do it all over again. I'll never take a wife and I'll never be a father, but I would have gladly given my life to save yours."

"For what? Father needs sons more than daughters." She rose and paced to the window. "Your sacrifices are noble, but they weren't worth it," she shrugged. "For I will not marry, nor have children either, nor make the name of Ballymead proud. I shall end up a spinster or enter the convent. Those are my only hopes now. All of you would have done well to just leave me with William Feargach."

William also rose and walked up behind her, this time defensive.

"You speak falsely," he bit out. "We could never have left you there is good conscience. You know not the grief we all felt, nor the rage that sparked in Father. You know not how Mother begged and cried at night for God to keep you."

"Please leave me," she said.

"Come now—"

"William," she turned to him, but he held his hand up for silence.

"Over here." He took her hand and pulled her back to the hearth. "Take these last few shreds, Gwen."

He handed her the torn linens that George had not taken with him.

"Go on," he continued, and nodded towards the fire. "We shall burn what remains of William Feargach. Like you said. Your chastity doesn't matter anymore, so why do we need the proof?"

He took a piece and tossed it into the flames. She did the same, until only one piece remained. Looking down, she hesitated, then began to drop it in when she stopped. Instead, she rubbed it gently, then folded it and laid it back in her trunk.

38

Janis mouthed the Pater Noster. Shea's army was arriving, in much smaller numbers. She held the missive she had stitched him with her needlepoint. Not once had she been allowed to venture from the room. No word of her daughter had come either. It was as if Aindreas had slipped from the face of the earth.

She heard the great hall open and tensed. Boots clopped in and many men's voices rang out. A discussion followed, but the voices were too distant and muffled for her to understand anything.

Thumping began to rise on the stairs. She held her breath. The footsteps grew closer and she retreated to the nook where she had kept her ink and quill. Sitting down with her back to the door, she began to pray that she would feel little pain.

The boots thudded down the corridor and stopped outside of her chamber. It was Shea. He would kill her. She continued to whisper the Lord's Prayer as she closed her eyes and folded her hands. The bar on her door was slid out of place. She clutched the little embroidery.

Her door was opened, slowly. It creaked on its iron hinges. Then it shut, and a bar came across it from the inside. Feet walked behind her, closer and closer, and she waited for the blow to come.

Shea moved in front of her, still decked in full battle costume. His face was angry. That was not unusual. But his eyes showed hurt, as though perhaps the little heart beating in his chest might be capable of breakage.

"It's odd indeed that Bainick knights seemed to know my every move." His words were barbed with spikes despite how softly he spoke then. "Sir William Cadogan marches after me with many more men. My metals trade has been barred again, my numbers dwindle. I cannot reclaim what once belonged to my uncle. My only two sons are dead. My grandson is dead. I had a fighting chance but now that hope is gone."

He didn't move, but pulled his hands from behind his back to reveal her quill, ink and wax in one hand, and a dagger in the other. She gulped, but did not look up at him.

"The only victory I can now claim is that I have bedded Gwenyth of Ballymead and hope that her belly swells with my seed in nine months' time, but she has fluxed, and that is unlikely. Yet I feel certain she is no longer of value to the Bainick knight and I will die with that small pleasure."

Her mouth dropped. Gwenyth had not escaped him either.

"It wasn't supposed to be like this," she whispered. *Oh, William, how could you turn her away? Nothing has worked, nothing.* Her heart felt broken as she imagined Gwenyth and Shea. She pictured her brother as a boy curled upon his pallet, trembling from the many lashings their father had dealt him. What kind of man had he really become? Perhaps she had imagined him as good. Perhaps he had really turned into a brute, like their father. *And now it doesn't matter.*

"Who are you, woman?" he asked, barely letting any sound come out.

"I'm your wife, My Lord," she answered.

"You're not the Lady Janis of Stratmoor, are you? Don't lie to me, woman, for I know you and Aindreas conspired against me."

"No, My Lord, I'm not, and yes, I am."

"I will ask one more time, who you are."

She was surprisingly calm for it being the hour of her death.

"I was baptized Louisa Cadogan, My Lord, before the Lord of Stratmoor took me in upon my mother's death and renamed me."

Shea's eyes widened and he actually looked surprised.

"Cadogan?"

"Aye, My Lord. Sir William Cadogan of King Bain's army is my half-brother."

Shea was dumbfounded.

"He's your half-brother...through your father, no?"

"No, My Lord. We share our mother with our two older brothers and our two younger sisters."

Shea pondered a moment.

"And yet he carries your father's name. Odd. Your mother had an affair?"

"Aye, My Lord."

He stood silently with his eyes still wide.

"Then who is his true sire?"

She gulped.

"King Charles Murron of Bain, My Lord." She paused and noted his mouth had parted. "He is his bastard and the rightful heir to the throne."

"Those are rumors."

"I meet my death this day and have no reason to lie. 'Tis truth, I swear it. The king took my mother in secret. But my father always knew and hated William for it. My father had ways much like yours, My Lord."

"Bold of you to talk like that to me—"

"Like I said, I die today. For once, I shall speak my mind and if you wish to hear no more, you know how to silence me."

Shea stood quietly and stared at her.

"He ruled over us without mercy," she continued, "and nearly killed William more than once with his beatings. It was my mother who finally wrote to the king and begged him take William away."

"And that's how he came to be a Bainick squire?"

She nodded.

"He and I wrote for some time, until I went to live with the Lord of Stratmoor and I was pleased to hear him boast of glad tidings. He was tutored, trained, and lived the finest life in the House of Bain."

"Is it any wonder?" Shea muttered. "How did your brother end up with Gwenyth?"

Janis gulped again.

"I...and Aindreas. We were already sending letters to the king of your plot, and told him of Gwenyth's abandonment. I requested my brother be sent to retrieve her."

"And why would the king care of one woman? How would he know where to find her?"

She breathed deeply.

"You ordered her abandoned, My Lord, but Aindreas cared for her and went back for her. He kept her well hidden in the pass for she was too far along with child to travel home. It seems Loddin of Ballymead was already begging for her to be found and you punished. We told the king where she was. I knew my brother was the king's son, and I knew he refused to marry. I also knew he would be one of few men who could understand the brutality she suffered at the hands of your son, much like he did from our father—"

"My son was just. She was insolent."

"Your son was cruel and she lovely, and deep down I think you know it's true for not even you could resist her."

Shea clenched his fingers around the dagger. His hand began to shake.

"I beg you show me mercy and kill me swiftly." Now she began to tremble. "I beg you accept that despite my wiles, I did not marry for betrayal's sake. My foster father arranged my marriage in good faith. It was only once you began your plotting against Bain that Aindreas and I found it in our souls to do right by our king and share of your plans. I began to love you, My Lord, for I knew you loved me."

Shea set down her writing supplies and reached to her face, lifting her chin. *Here it is, woman, he will slit your throat now.* She closed her eyes as a tear streamed down her cheek and her lips quivered.

"Please cut me quickly," she whimpered. "I'm ready, My Lord."

She waited for some moments, but the knife didn't meet her skin. Instead, she felt his lips press to hers. She sat as still as a corpse and returned the kiss, eyes still pinched shut in case he was tricking her. She heard his dagger clank to the table and then both his broad hands took her arms and lifted her to her feet. He pulled loose her gown and pushing it from her shoulders.

"Lie down...Louisa."

Her knees knocked one another as she clenched the little embroidery. She found her way to the bed despite the water blurring her eyes. Shea removed his sword, surcoat, mail, gambeson, boots and trousers. Then, dripping on the floor without regard, he took a washrag and poured water into the basin, lathering his hands with the scented soap of mutton fat and wiped down his body. Taking a pinch of mint, he chewed it into the pockets of his cheeks before spitting and rinsing with wine.

He finally picked the dagger back up and came to the bedside where he climbed on top of her. She parted for him, tears still streaming down her face. He brushed one away from her lips, then kissed her again and pushed himself inside of her. She turned her head, gripping the embroidery as she watched the point of the dagger next to her eyes.

Please do not drag this out any longer! she prayed.

But he moved gently for the first time, pushing and pulling on her and she soon realized he cried a tear.

He climaxed within her. The dagger trembled in his grip and she could tell he was scared to kill her. He rested against her for a moment as he breathed, his forehead pressed to hers, sucking air in and out quickly.

"I can't let you live," he whispered.

She closed her eyes. "Please," she begged so quietly that it was hard for him to hear. The water ran from her eyes down her cheeks and onto the pillow. "I beg you not make me suffer in waiting any longer. I am frightened. I am so frightened…"

He brushed her cheek and kissed her one more time. "I loved you, woman. You'll be at peace now."

The knife burned on her neck. She felt her throat collapsing and warmth running down her skin. She opened her eyes and looked at him as he brushed her forehead. Her vision blurred, then spotted, then nothing but light consumed it. Blood gurgled from her mouth, running down her face and mingling with the blood that pulsed from the heartbeat in her neck. Her feet and hands became cold. She reached with the last of her strength to his hand and clenched it, for his fingers were warm.

"I'm cold, Shea."

He didn't move at first and cursed himself for being too weak to control his tears. Finally he stood. She was blue and dead. He laid a blanket across her and as he tucked her arms in, found the embroidered cloth in her clasp. He pulled it loose and sat back down beside her. As he read it, he hung his head and cried.

"She has gotten the better of me."

"That is Dwyre," Loddin pointed. "The main gates are just

beyond these woods."

To their backs were the flickering lights of the Bainick camp and to the front lay a tiny keep rising from within its fortress. Loddin's tone was normal, though William could see his fist was tight around the hilt of his sword.

"Just before these trees below, that is where they took my William's eyes and damaged his leg so badly it was I who had to saw it away before the festering spread upward."

He stared forward with his teeth clenched, his sons and William's commanders looking onward with him.

"It's wrong indeed for a man to have to do such a thing to his son. I was *so* proud that all my children had grown in good health without maladies...and then my wife died, my sweet lady finally died without having seen her daughter though she begged for her to come...William Feargach refused to let her go. And now my wee lass...my wee lass..."

He shuddered and then he cried, soft, husky puffs of air, dropping his head into his palm as his chest convulsed.

Gavin rested a hand on his shoulder. "Be strong, Father."

"I shall see this man off to Hell." Loddin gritted his teeth, then limped away through the soggy ground.

The king was right, William pondered. *Loddin is no soldier. He doesn't have the strength to hate, so I shall do the hating for him....* "We don't leave, men, until we have seen his dead body at our feet and his blood on our metal," William muttered. "It's been ordered by the king."

Frances and Gwenyth's brothers nodded. Sir Thomas, after some thought, turned away and strolled back to camp as well.

"We assault at dawn, Frances, without warning when the sun rises. The House of Dwyre shall burn and we shall not spare a life that does not fall at our feet to beg for it, save the women and their children."

The night was long, perhaps because William could not sleep. He blamed it on the hard ground beneath his blankets but knew that it wasn't the real reason. Finally he gave up and sat up in the darkness, waiting for the hint of dawn so that he could get on with his quest.

His rage was thumping through him like a drumbeat, having mounted to the point of breaking him. He didn't break his fast, but adjusted his tunics and gambeson over and over again, then waited in the quietude for the rest of camp to awaken.

By the time the eastern sky was barely lightening, the camp was already roused and prepared. He pulled on each gauntlet that his squire handed him, slowly, taking the time to push in his sleeves, adjust his belt once more around his hauberk. Taking the reins from the boy, his breath escaped in puffs upon the air. The camp was rustling with silent movement as his army fell into lines with their weapons ready.

William took up his shield.

The moment I've been awaiting is upon us. And yet now he knew it wouldn't be enough to ease the pain.

He raised his sword, as did his commanders and they began to make their way to the slope through the woods. His crossbows and archers moved silently through the trees on either side of them like two long wings hidden by darkness. They broke through onto the sloping plain towards the main gates, the sun barely breaking the horizon.

A guard saw them from afar.

"Bain! His army is here! Bain's army is—"

A crossbow ended him but the alarm was sounded. They began to scramble for the attack and William hastened forward.

"Release all the crossbows! Take those sentries off the wall now!"

He waved a finger and Sir Thomas lifted the flag.

39

They began their onslaught. Titan stomped and pricked his ears, feeling William's impatience coursing through him as he tugged the reins. With every breath he took, William tried to steady himself.

An arrow sailed at him and he lifted his shield reflexively, snapping it off to watch as Dwyre sentries were felled like dry saplings.

"Foot soldiers!" he shouted. "Breech those walls!"

Cavanaugh ordered them forward. Battle cries filled the morning air and they swarmed down the hillside. Ladders were flung against the walls. Dwyre soldiers tried to cut them down, bludgeoning them as they reached the top. Scalding water met with screams, rocks and hot tar fell through the crenellations. Ladders were thrust backwards. But the crossbows kept shooting and overpowered them.

Bainick soldiers finally climbed onto the walls and drew their swords. Men fell off screaming. Finally, Bain's flag was waving and the main gates were pried open. William nodded.

"Cavalry! Thomas! Order them forth!"

Thomas ran along the trees with his flag lifted.

"Cavalry! Cavalry!"

His knights lumbered up to attention. William turned to Loddin and his sons behind him.

"Ride in with me, Ballymead. We go for our blood justice." With that, he kicked Titan. "Cavalry! Forward!"

The knights thundered into line and marched down from the trees through the main gates. Villagers were crying, fleeing up to the Dwyre battlements.

Just then, a swarm of horses appeared above them.

"William! They come *now!*" young Loddin shouted, pointing his sword.

Dwyre knights were flocking down from the hills, clashing with Bainick foot soldiers. Shea Feargach was galloping at full speed. They spilled onto the hills, war screams on their lips.

"Get into line! Formations now! They don't wait, men! They don't wait!" William bellowed.

He kicked Titan into a run and raised his sword. His men began clattering and Cavanaugh and Thomas galloped away to carry the message farther down the line.

"Cavalry!" he hollered with all his lungpower. "Chaaarge!"

He dropped the metal forward and the thousands of horses' hooves began rumbling to meet Dwyre, shaking the ground as though it threatened to split open.

Titan charged, anger locked on William's brow. He set his sights on Shea. The men of Ballymead flanked him. The two sides clashed. A knight attacked him. William swung his sword against him, shoving him off his mount. He held Shea in his vision.

Another swung his sword. William ducked. The sword came again and he thrust his shield out, knocking it away. He then lifted his and swung it, but the knight did the same and William's sword was knocked from his grip. The Dwyre knight smiled as he lifted his sword once more.

"You're dead, lion!" he shouted.

William held forth his shield and knocked away the blow. As the man tried to recover his swing, William thrust his shield to the ground and leapt from the saddle, pummeling the man off his horse. They fell with a thud and wrestled together in the muddy snow, the wolf rolling on top of him. William struggled beneath his burly weight. The knight dealt him a blow. His nose began to pour and his eyes filled with water.

He reached his gauntlet to the man's throat, held him in place and sent a closed fist upward beneath his jaw. The knight was stunned. William kneed him between the legs, throwing him aside as he fought to get on top. The wolf pulled his dagger and swung but William dodged it. William punched him and straddled him. The knight swung it once more, catching William's face with a gash.

But as he stabbed it again, William gripped his arm and twisted it. The man cried out and the dagger fell. William, snatching it, grabbed the man's head and ripped it backwards. He sent the blade to his exposed neck in a slash, throwing the man backwards as he found his footing again.

Grabbing up his shield and sword, he grappled for Titan who was whinnying and rearing amongst the bodies.

Shea...where is Shea...

He searched the hills and sprang into the saddle, smearing his face as he tried to wipe it.

His eyes found Loddin's green surcoat in the distance, charging after the Lord of Dwyre as he retreated with several knights. Titan grunted as he sank his spurs into his sides.

"Hyaa! Titan! Hyaa! *C'mon*, man!"

Together, they bolted forward. The soggy fields were doused with oil and set to flames beneath the midwinter dawn. Dwyre foot soldiers were withdrawing into the bailey and the portcullis dropped with a crash. William's soldiers began to climb the walls, but the guards atop the inner battlements were making their arrows count.

I need more men, I need my crossbows!

"Damn!" he cursed, watching Loddin and his sons engaged with Shea and wishing he could join them.

He wheeled Titan around instead. They charged back through the burning fields.

"Lions! Lions! Forward to the keep!" he hollered as he flew past his men who had not been felled.

Another knight charged at him and William hunched low, leaned off to the side and swung his sword. The knight's horse was sliced from beneath him and tripped forward, sliding upon the mud. The rider was thrust into flames.

"Edmund! Edmund!" he shouted. "Get our crossbows in here! Now, man! Now! Up to the keep!"

Thomas abandoned his fight and ran his horse to the outer walls. Suddenly, a Dwyre foot soldier lunged forward and Titan reared. William was thrown from the saddle. Twisting in mid-air, he tossed his shield to brace himself and landed hard on his shield arm damaged at Faulk.

He bellowed in pain, feeling his arm crack. The pain was

blinding and he rolled back and forth. The foot soldier was above him, his sword raised. William rolled away as it landed, catching his surcoat with a rip. His shoulder was throbbing and limp. The man swung his sword again. William rolled onto his back. His ball mace stabbed into his back with its spikes. He threw his body to one side as the sword sliced a lock of hair, pulling his dagger.

"Give up, pathetic lion!" the soldier snarled.

"I'll be damned if a bloody foot soldier kills me!" he retorted.

William sent his boot to the man's groin as he raised his sword again. The sword fell and the man staggered backward. William scrambled for it, dragging his arm. The man reached for it as well, both of them fighting for it. He sent a punch to William's side and with a grunt of pain, William swung his sore arm and knocked his fist across the soldier's face, who reeled but didn't relent. Both men gripped the hilt of the metal. He sent William another exhausted blow.

Before William could counter it, Titan rose above them, rearing high. His hooves landed upon the man's back, flattening him into the mud with a shriek. His bones crunched. Titan stomped him again and again until no sound escaped him.

William grinned and spared a split second to pat the horse's neck before retrieving his sword and shield.

Once again in the saddle, he grimaced with each bound as his shield tugged upon his shoulder. His crossbows had made it inside and were taking out the guards upon the inner walls. Bainick foot soldiers were making their way to the top, climbing onto the wall, but the portcullis had not yet been raised.

He spotted Ballymead crests amongst his knights as they gathered outside of the walls. Running Titan hard, he arrived up the fields.

"Where's the Dwyre Lord?" he demanded, pulling the reins to halt.

"He retreated inward!" Gavin replied. "They lifted the port for him and his other knights!"

"Lovely face, man," young Loddin remarked.

"Let's pray your sister doesn't find me hideous now," he countered. "No doubt I'll have an ugly scar."

"It's opening!" Cavanaugh called.

"Onward!" William demanded.

He dug his heels into poor Titan once more. William in the lead, he and his knights flooded through the gates and into the bailey. The screams of peasants and women rose as they fled into the keep. Children were crying, babies wailing. William and the Loddin men swung down from the saddle. His knights overtook the yard and they began to climb the steps to the keep.

Shea looked down at Louisa's body, now two days dead, and listened to the end.

The sound outside was loud. His bailey was overtaken and his men massacred except for the smart conscriptions who begged surrender and mercy. He glanced back out the window.

With one final look at her, he took her little cloth and dashed down the stairs as the women and maids huddled in the corners. His daughters were amongst them. He didn't care.

Bainick knights would never harm a woman unless she posed a threat and my women have done well to know their place. They'll be looked after.

His sword and daggers still stowed, he grabbed up his shield and slid through the back portal as the front doors were thrown open.

The women screamed and clustered even closer.

"Where is the Lord of Dwyre?" William demanded.

No one spoke.

"Search this keep," he said as the wind caught the back door and made it creak. "No...wait."

He strode forward and examined the door, still open.

"Has he gone out?"

Again no one answered, but the way the women eyed the door gave him his answer.

"Stay here!" he hollered to his men and dashed through the door.

He ran through the snow despite his heavy chain mail. The back entrance to the yard was still propped open and the prints in the snow gave Shea away.

"What do you know!" William yelled, standing in the gateway. "He flees from me again like the coward he is!"

Shea turned around, alone on the far slope behind his estate and heading for the woods. William charged forward. Shea continued to run, but William was faster and gained on him.

Shea turned and lifted his sword. "Don't try me, *lad*," Shea insulted.

William lifted his sword as well and squared himself in front of him.

"Don't try *me*, old man. It's not my army's blood that soaks these soils."

William began to prowl in a circle and Shea did the same. He darted forth but William met him. Their swords locked and Shea shoved him off balance.

"You're but a cocky bastard. I shall walk away from this," Shea fumed.

William swung this time. Their swords exchanged clanks and became locked again. William braced himself and pushed Shea off him with a grunt. But Shea whirled around quickly and brought his sword down. It hit William's shield, tugging upon his shoulder. He winced and buckled to his knees, his shoulder burning.

Shea seized the chance and kicked him. William tumbled backwards and Shea laughed.

"A fledgling foal. Bain has employed a weakling for me to cut down. You would not believe the pleasure this gives me."

He brought his sword down once more and William blocked his face with his shield. The wood split down the middle.

"Good riddance. You die now," Shea grinned but without warning, William swung his boot and wiped Shea's feet from beneath him.

Shea tumbled over and William sprang to his feet. By the time Shea had recovered, William thrust his sword outward, catching Shea's fingers on his hilt. Shea grunted and released his metal. William marched forth and kicked it away.

He swung his blade again and again. Shea blocked each blow with his shield. Then he lifted his sword high and Shea lifted his shield to block it, but William kicked his exposed knee inward instead. Shea stumbled once more with a cry. William brought the flat of his sword down upon his shoulder. He buckled, allowing William to pull free the shield.

Casting aside his own sword, he leapt upon Shea and began pounding him with his fist until Shea was dizzy, then ripped loose his coif, punched his exposed face and head, seeing the face of Andrew Cadogan, over and over again as his anger surged through him. It took all of is self-restraint to stop himself. Grabbing his hair, he wrenched the man to his feet and shoved him forward.

"We return to the keep," William panted and resheathed his sword.

"You don't finish me?" Shea slurred.

"I'm not the only man with a right to spill your blood. You go to face Lord Loddin."

"I'll not go," Shea said and tried to run but William pounced upon him and punched the side of his back.

Shea groaned.

"Now you'll be pissing blood, man, at least while you live."

William dragged Shea to his feet again, shoving him forward. Loddin still stood in the doorway, flanked by Thomas and a handful of other Bainick knights by his sides with the burning timbers of the gatehouse behind them. William hauled him inside, releasing him into the center of the great hall.

"The grounds are secure, Sir William," Cavanaugh announced as he breezed through the portal.

The cry of victory was rising on the air. William ignored the noise and stared into Shea's face.

"Cavanaugh, secure that port in the back," he pointed, "lest we provide the Lord of Dwyre with another chance at freedom."

Cavanaugh moved swiftly across the floor as more Bainick knights entered and moved along the walls.

"Ladies," William started. "Are there any more womenfolk in this estate?"

No one answered. He looked at them all closely, a frightened huddle around a cluster of children.

"You there," William pointed to a noblewoman, barely six and ten. "Don't fear me, Lady. Will you answer my question? 'Tis important that you're all accounted for."

She shook her head timidly as though the wrath of God might land upon her if she uttered a sound.

"No, My Lord. We're the only ones here."

"Do you know Louisa Cadogan? I was told she lived at Dwyre," he continued.

Shea's eyes glimmered and William caught it. The young woman shook her head.

"No, My Lord. I've never heard of such a woman."

"Have any of you?"

His question was met with silent shakes of the head and whimpers.

"What's your name, Lady?" William continued.

"I'm Caris...Caris Feargach, My Lord."

William took a deep breath. "Feargach...is this man before me your father?"

"He is, My Lord."

"Are you his only daughter?"

"No, My Lord. I have four sisters here, My Lord," she shivered as she clung to the hands of the other maidens. "Two more who are married and one being fostered, and a babe who recently died."

"Come to me, ladies," Sir William continued, his gaze still resting upon Shea.

The women remained frozen with fear.

"We beg mercy, sir," Caris began to cry again and fell to her knees. "Please don't harm us."

"You're safe in the care of King Bain's army, ladies. You've nothing to fear and will be protected," he held out his arm in good faith. "I don't harm women, and neither will my men."

He motioned again.

"Please, daughters of Lord Shea," he continued.

Slowly, like frightened animals, they crept forth and stood by him to face their father while the other women guarded the children.

"Do you have anything you wish to say to this man?" he asked gently, breaking his stare as he looked down at their pale faces. They held their eyes at their feet. *Just like Gwenyth when I found her, scared, untrusting...*

"We're not to talk to him, My Lord. It's his rule."

"With all due respect, Lady Caris, he's no longer your lord. You are free to speak if you wish. Any words at all?"

They kept their eyes downward, gripping each other's hands.

"I won't lie to you, ladies. This man faces his death. This is your chance to express your love."

Caris and her sisters looked onward at Shea, then back at their feet.

"No, My Lord. I have nothing to say. I don't know him. I only know his anger."

The others muttered similar responses and William felt pity overtake his heart. He forced a smile onto his mouth as he lifted the girl's trembling chin and took her hand.

"You're very brave, Lady. You're right to fear us, but you needn't, and from this day forth you'll be treated fairly. Do you understand me?"

She nodded, but kept her eyes lowered.

"Lady Caris, look upon me," he spoke softly, lifting her chin once more and wiping a tear as Loddin studied him.

My Butterfly needs this man, for he will handle her with the care in which she was raised.

She allowed her eyes to glance up at William.

"All of you. You have the deepest promise of Sir William Cadogan of Bain and all his men, that you'll not know harsh treatment in my charge, ever again. Understand this."

Caris gave a feeble smile and nodded her head.

"Thank you, My Lord," she bowed.

"Sir Cavanaugh," William continued. "Escort the fine women and children of Dwyre to the safety of the stable and ask Sir Thomas to stand guard. See to it they're given proper food and warmth as needed. They mustn't witness what is about to transpire. And Sir Cavanaugh?" Frances turned. "No man is allowed to take liberties, is that perfectly clear?"

Frances bowed his head and held an arm out to guide them to the door. With quiet patters, they scurried away with the children in tow.

"Men, I bid you leave me and the Lord of Ballymead with his sons. You'll do well to rest outside and wait should we fall into trouble."

His knights consented and exited after the women. Once the door was closed again, William turned back around. He stared once more at Shea.

"Shea Feargach," William said in the most commanding voice he could muster. "You launched a revolt against your king. You murdered thousands of proud Bainick soldiers on this Eastern Front and are guilty of high treason. By order of his Highness, King Charles Murron of Bain, you are hereby stripped of your title, and you are to be killed." He tried to keep his words even as he held Shea's eyes with his. "And..." His chest began to rise and fall. "You raped her."

"And she was worth it," Shea answered.

William sprinted forward but Loddin, despite his crippled leg, moved faster than anyone else. He swung the back of his hand across Shea's face. Shea slammed into the wall.

"Perhaps I can tell you how soft she was, Sir William," Shea continued. Loddin punched his gut and he gasped, but still didn't quiet. "So you may know what to expect in your own bed."

The brothers sprang upon him and Loddin released his fist again, all four men striking him into a pulp. William stood still, fuming.

"Loddin," he said softly. "Loddin, stop."

Gwenyth's father stood up, tears of rage upon his face as Gavin sent one more spiteful kick to his stomach.

"I have rights as a father to see you dead," Loddin growled.

"Then do so, Loddin," Shea groaned from his pool of blood. "Kill me. I've nothing left, no sons, no wife, and no freedom. I can die a happy man knowing that I at least punished that wench for killing my grandson—"

"You are sick!" Loddin swooped down and gripped Shea's neck, lifting him and slamming him against the wall. "I blame you for killing *my* grandson! I blame you for making her so unfit she couldn't carry the child!"

Shea's face turned red. He flailed and in doing so, the little cloth fell out onto the floor.

"Where's Louisa Cadogan?" William interrupted.

Loddin loosened his grip. Shea coughed, but did not answer.

"I know you know her. Answer me."

Shea smiled. "She went by the Lady Janis of Stratmoor."

"The Lady Janis is your wife," Loddin croaked.

Shea continued. "*Was*."

"Louisa...My sister, where is she?"

"I killed her."

William shuddered. Gwenyth's brothers watched him with sympathy.

"You may go up to her chamber and see for yourself...*Your Highness*."

"Wh, what?" William sputtered.

"That's right, *Prince* William of Bain. I know of you," Shea continued. "And so did your half-sister. How many others are you deceiving right now?"

Loddin and his sons actually looked surprised.

"Why? Why did you kill her?"

"She was a spy. No hard feelings," Shea smirked. "It's just good politics. King Bain would do the same."

"And now we kill you," Loddin breathed. "All of us. Sons and son-to-be, come and claim the payment owed to your sisters and my crippled son, *my* William. Your seed is gone, Shea, and Bain is free of you."

"You still raise my daughter," Shea choked.

"Don't worry, man. We will spare sweet Louisa of your memory," Hershel growled.

"She'll never know your name," William's eyes watered. He thought of Louisa as a little girl and saw her crying for him as his father whipped him. *A niece, my niece in the arms of my Gwenyth...* "But she'll be proud of the name Cadogan and she'll be proud of her brave mother. And she'll be beautiful like my Gwenyth."

"Look at the dear brother, weeping for a damn woman—"

Shea's quip, meant to insult, hit William like a boulder. Feeling emotion and love was what would make him a better warrior than any other. It would always remind him of what he stripped from others as he bloodied his sword. He didn't feel shame from the tears in his eyes, but conviction. William let his hand crack across Shea's face. Shea reeled backwards. He sent his boot to his chest and Shea tumbled over once more. The sons of Ballymead pulled off his surcoat and his hauberk so he stood before them in nothing but his gambeson.

Without a word spoken, as if they understood the timing as one, the men of Loddin and the third son of Cadogan plunged their daggers into Shea's belly and jerked them hard. William saw Andrew Cadogan again. He jerked his dagger again as Andrew's face began to gurgle with blood. Shea's eyes widened. He convulsed, coughed, and sputtered blood. William backed away as Shea fell forward, staggering until his knees buckled. He wished the raging would stop within him though it just pumped faster.

"You," Shea gasped, "may all...go...to...Hellll..."

"Then I will see you there," William whispered, and Shea died beneath them, without ceremony, without remorse, and not a single man who stood in the great hall mourned him.

In all his years of fighting, Andrew Cadogan's face had finally disappeared.

They waited in silence as if he might rise again. Young Loddin climbed the stairs to the solar, slowly opening the doors until the others heard him gasp. He returned shortly after.

"What was her complexion?" he asked.

"Black hair, and...and black eyes," William sputtered.

Loddin nodded grimly. "I'd say a couple days."

William turned away, his eyes bubbling with water so much so he was embarrassed to be seen.

"William, lad," Loddin placed his hand upon his shoulder. "Do you wish to retrieve your sister's body for burial?"

William wiped his eyes, making his vision more blurry. His breathing became rapid. Then without warning, he roared and sent his fist into the board. The wood splintered. He struck it again and again, pounding it until his knuckles were bloodied. He picked up the pieces and hurled them against the wall, kicking the fragments and sending them skidding across the rushes.

I didn't get to her in time... "I didn't get to her in time! I have failed them both..." *the only women who cared.*

His chest heaved and he collapsed to his knees. Gradually his pulse slowed. Loddin and his sons waited.

"I'm sorry for my incivility, My Lord—" he rasped.

"You're entitled, lad," Loddin nodded. "We've all thrown our fits."

He reined in his anger and stood.

"I don't wish to see her. She rests where she lies, for if I look upon her she'll only become another ghost."

He strode to the door.

"William!" Gavin called. "Wait! Look at this!"

Gavin reached down and picked something up. William turned around to see him holding a little embroidery. Loddin and his sons were gathering around him to read it.

"What is that?" he said.

"It seems to be a letter of sorts, from your sister. Oh *Lord in heaven,* I thank thee Almighty for small favors," Loddin replied.

William came back and snatched it from Gavin's hand.

Dear husband, I have a confession. I have sent Louisa away. She didn't die, and she is not of your seed for I betrayed you. She's the rightful daughter of Lord Aindreas de Boscoe. A gentle man and kind lover, his mark on this world has been left in the hands of Gwenyth of Ballymead, the best of me I have to give, delivered to her by her father himself.

"He knew. He wasn't going to tell us," young Loddin said. "He would leave us thinking Louisa was his child out of spite."

"A tiny bit of glad tidings," Hershel mumbled. "To know that Louisa isn't cursed to be of his stock after all."

William read the cloth again and again, then held it to his forehead. He took a deep breath.

"Perhaps on the morrow I'll be able to smile about it," he mumbled, advancing to the door. "We burn this unholy place."

He heaved it open with his good arm and descended into the bailey as his men watched him.

"Burn it. Burn it all!" William waved a hand outward as he strode past. "The conquest is won and we return home to the capital!"

The Bainick soldiers cheered.

"Cavanaugh, send our messengers ahead with the news. We are the victors and we bring women and children."

"Are you well, man?" Cavanaugh asked.

"My arm is broken and my sister is dead. Of course I'm not well. Get our surgeons in here, for many of our men suffer. Salvage what ale exists on this worthless plot. Our men deserve the spoils."

He had long since lost feeling in his shoulder. Grabbing up Titan's reins from his squire, he swung onto the saddle without looking back and trotted outward to the main gates with the flames of the House of Dwyre taking hold behind him, lapping the sky.

40

"She doesn't come down, Father," George said as Loddin washed himself at the well in the freezing cold.

He put on the woolen blanket that Michael offered and hobbled up the steps. They entered the great hall, still adorned with Yule decorations despite the solstice being past.

"I've tried, but she only sits at board if I order her."

"You *order* her? She's not your maid, son."

"She wouldn't eat otherwise, Father," George defended. "If we leave it to her, she'll starve."

"She's changed, Father. She's taken to proper womanhood," William added as he thumped behind them to the hearth to warm up. "Her spirit is burnt out."

"What do you mean?" Loddin took a goblet of mulled wine from Michael.

"She sees herself as a disgrace to all of us, does not feel fit to be in our presence. Yet she coifs her hair each day and wears fine gowns in a way that would have pleased Mother greatly," William answered. "She'll not talk to or confide in anyone. I have no idea what's in her mind."

"Won't talk? Not even to you?"

"I've tried more times than can be counted," William lamented.

"She made me new trousers and has not once tried to pinch them," Michael added, making the men smile troubled smiles.

"This is all that's left of her wedding linens, sir. She burnt the rest of it and this was all I could salvage, for she was very upset." George produced a strip of cloth with part of a stain.

"What? Burned her maidenhead?" Loddin leaned onto the board and scrunched his brow. "Whatever for? Why would she do such a thing?"

"'Twas the memory of William Feargach, and Lord Shea that she wished to burn," William clarified. "And I think it reminded her of why Sir William rejected her."

"She should know better than that," Gavin frowned. "And now we have no proof she was a virgin."

"She couldn't be bothered with Yule except to help the servants prepare the food," George continued. "Making her be the winter maiden would have been impossible. She wanted nothing to do with it. And when she's not delivering the morning bread with Louisa or helping rack the mead, she is sparring with the quintain, quite well I might add, or working at needlepoint. She refuses to take Luna for rides but will do anything without a complaint if she is ordered to do so."

"Is she here now?" Loddin asked, taking the fresh tunic offered him.

"She's been in her chamber, sewing. She spends much time there."

"I have good news to share with her. 'Twill turn her spirit to be certain." Loddin looked proud and stood. "William Cadogan has changed his heart and wishes to take her as a bride by spring. He's also, as we have just found out..." he began to grin. His older sons beamed.

"What is this news that makes you smile so?" George asked.

Loddin puffed his chest out, resting his hands on his belt. "He's the heir to Bain's throne and will soon be the crowned prince."

George and William gawped at him.

"Close your mouths, lads, you show me what I looked like when I heard him called, *Your Highness*," he teased, and climbed the stairs to the solar. "Your brothers will no doubt explain."

"This will surely turn her sad heart!" George exclaimed.

"Aye, it will," Loddin smiled.

Gwenyth's door was closed and her father knocked.

"Butterfly, we're home and bring glad tidings."

There was no answer so he knocked again.

"Gwenyth?"

"Come in, My Lord," she replied.

When Loddin entered, he found her chamber decorated with pillows like tapestries on her bed. The fresh smell of rose water perfumed the air. She was sitting on a rug by the hearth, Louisa asleep beside her in her cradle as she stitched. Her lips were completely healed and no bruises remained to show of her trauma.

"I wished to have seen your fair face greet us at the gate," Loddin said as he moved to her chair and sat in front of her. "You look lovely with your hair netted like a proper lady."

She did not look up.

"I'm sorry for not receiving you, My Lord. I must have been too preoccupied."

"It's of no consequence, Butterfly."

"I should like to be called by my given name, sir."

Her father ignored the remark and reached to her face, lifting it. Her eyes were black and empty as she stared back at his, the eyes that she and her brothers had all inherited.

"Your mother would be proud of your appearance, though it must be difficult to ride Luna in such restricted clothing."

She made no indication of answering. Loddin grew serious.

"We have killed him, Daughter, I, your brothers, and Sir William. Your honor is vindicated with blood."

She didn't say anything and it was as if she had not even heard his words. As soon as he released her face, she looked back at her embroidery and began to pull the needle again.

"Your brothers say your spirit is low. I know you've been hurt, but you must know that we don't blame you. We love you."

Gwenyth continued to pull her thread markedly.

"I'm fine, My Lord. You have news you wished to share?"

Loddin exhaled, then found a smile and pasted it on.

"Sir William Cadogan wishes to take you as his bride. He begs forgiveness and hopes you'll wed him come May."

She set her needle down and gazed into the fire.

"Well, Daughter? This is most pleasant news because—"

"Please tell him I refuse, My Lord."

Her words shocked him and he furrowed his brow.

"But he loves you, Daughter. He knew his mistake just moments after you left and I've already given him my blessing. Surely you can give this man another chance."

"Please refuse, My Lord. I'm disgraced."

"Come, Butterfly, don't think of it like that. Consider this man, for I know something very important. He is truly the son of our king..." He waited to see if those words would spark her attention. "And heir to the throne. Do you *hear* me, Daughter? King Bain wishes it to be known to the land. Your William is his bastard."

He's not my William, she thought, staring back at her needlepoint.

"I don't want to send him unhappy tidings when he's expecting your forgiveness."

"Are you saying I must marry him, Father?"

"Of course not. It's your choice, I just thought it might make you happy. Did you know that wee Louisa is his niece?" Loddin smiled down at the sleeping babe and tried to make his voice bright in case it should rub off on her. "The Lady Janis was his sister. It's as though you both already have a fam—"

"Does he wish to take her from me, My Lord?" Gwenyth continued to work the needle and placed it into the center of a black figure of a horse.

"Lass, what's wrong with you?" Loddin shook his head. "He...of course he does not. He's overjoyed that you foster her and hopes to know her as his daughter come May."

Loddin removed her needlepoint from her fingers and lifted her head again so he could see her lifeless eyes.

"What is *wrong* with you, lass?"

"Everything..."

Her eyes finally began to water, the first sign of life she had expressed in days. He reached out and pulled her to him so that she leaned on his knees and wrapped an arm around her shoulders.

"Don't make me send him a refusal. Consider this request and share your answer with me at board tonight."

"I already refuse, Father," she whispered.

"Sweet lass, I wish to help you. Are you saying you don't feel for him, Gwenyth? Not even a wee bit?"

He held her face in his hands again.

"I don't feel at all, Father. If my answer is what you seek, then I've given it. Otherwise, I'll do as you say, as is my duty."

She reached out and retrieved her needlework, and Loddin hung his head.

"But he is the *prince*, Daughter."

"He is a man, Father."

She didn't look up, nor did she make any sign that she remembered his presence as she found steady work with her fingers. Loddin rose and walked to the door, lingering there.

"Are you *absolutely* sure? Because I have a mind to accept on your behalf. I like this lad—"

"Oh, please don't make me marry him!" she exclaimed and wept into her hands.

Loddin stood dumbfounded and searched for his voice, though he didn't know what he could possibly say. He dashed to her and fell to his knees to hold her.

"I beg you, My Lord," she breathed.

"There, Daughter, shh. I'm sorry to upset you so." He held her, feeling her stiffness, unlike the carefree embraces she had always offered. "You won't have to marry him if it truly be your wish. I just felt certain you would want him back, for he's miserable without your favor."

"He's dead to me," she wept. "If you must marry me to someone, let it be the church, let me go to the convent, I beg this of you, Father. Please don't give me to that man—"

"Very well, Butterfly. If this is truly your answer, I shall draft a letter."

She did not move, but kept her face well covered in her hands and her father rose. He moved to the door and stopped.

"Gwenyth, are you sure?"

She folded her arms on the seat of the chair and laid her face in them, her chest convulsing as she cried silently.

He shook his head and closed the door.

"How did she take the news, Father?" young Loddin asked as he held Mary on his lap and kissed her.

"I can't believe we're going to be kin to royalty," Gavin remarked.

"'Twill be nice to see her smile again," said George. "Gwenyth will be Princess of Bain. Where is she? Why doesn't she come down to share in the tidings?"

Loddin sighed and picked his wine up without answering.

"You don't bring good tidings, do you?" William muttered.

Loddin didn't smile at their expectant faces. Instead, he took the whole decanter of wine with him, turning towards the solar again.

"I'll be in my chamber should you need anything."

"What's wrong?" Hershel asked.

"I must draft a letter. She has refused him."

41

"The army has returned!" came cries from the guardhouse as they neared the city gates. "Send a messenger to the castle! Prince William and his army have come home!"

"*Prince* William?" Thomas turned to him as a rumble of questions surged through his ranks.

What? He's already announced it without my presence? William looked over his broken shoulder, now snug within a sling, at the procession of jingling horses and muttering.

"My Lord Prince! We heard the news!" came the guards again. "Hail Prince William Murron of Bain! You return to us alive and well!"

Damn it, man! William huffed and clenched his teeth.

"How did *this* happen?" Thomas asked.

They passed beneath the gatehouse. All the sentries bowed down to him. William shook his head, but found a smile and waved despite it all.

He sighed reluctantly. "It's quite simple. The king whored my mother and I was conceived."

Had Sir Thomas had a drink in his mouth, he would have choked. Cavanaugh snorted.

"There's something to be said for blunt, William." Thomas shook his head.

"Aye, and there is something to be said for being a bastard, as I am, and apparently, now the *entire* kingdom knows. And there is *also* something to be said for home wreckers, as our king is, though I cannot say what that is for it is treacherous...*Damn*, he picked the perfect time to tell. I can hear it now. 'My only son toils in battle! I admit to my scandal, but he could be killed! Pray for his safe return, the heir to my throne, the protector of your life and safety, the protector of our kingdom! Sir William the Brave!' What do you bet that he actually said that bit? He counters his scandal with sympathetic supplications."

"Hey, that's not a bad imitation," Cavanaugh teased. "Like father, like son."

"Well then I inherited his art of twisting words."

"Winning strategies, Will," Cavanaugh continued. "He 'fesses up to his crime, dodges shame, gains sympathy, *and* glorifies his son all at once. There's a reason he is the king."

"Did you know of this, Frances?" Thomas asked.

Cavanaugh laughed. "I was the only one who knew until now."

"Well I'm thankful he is as trusting of me as he is of you."

"Oh Edmund," William sighed. "Frances just meddles more, like an old woman."

The three chuckled and William decided not to argue anymore. Instead, he raised his sword.

"We have victory!" he declared, tossing out coins to the peasants who had gathered to cheer.

A cry rose from his men too. Shouting followed them as they clattered up the frozen road beneath the banners of Bain. They passed through the city gates. The townsfolk clustered along the roadsides, creating a human corridor for the horses to squeeze through. Shutters were thrown wide open from the half-timbered buildings as women waved their kerchiefs and men waved their hats. Children dropped their chores to run alongside them.

"Hurray! The army has won!" they called, as the knights searched through their purses for more coins.

"Do you still need a bride, Prince William?" came the call of a prostitute from her window.

Cavanaugh laughed at him and he turned red.

"Why no, woman, though I thank thee for the generous offer!" he called back.

"I do!" Thomas yelled.

"Then consider us betrothed!" she laughed, tossing her hair aside. "Come by tonight, Sir Thomas, and we shall be married!"

"Is that what we are calling it now, Anne?" Thomas laughed.

The crowd roared.

"It seems Edmund has been married many times before!" Cavanaugh announced to rows of laughter.

Reluctantly, William succumbed to the happiness too. This cheering had always filled him with pride before. He waved at the crowds as children scrambled for their coins and begged with smiling faces for more, as the tavern wenches threw kisses and called of free ale.

"If in spite of this scandal," Cavanaugh began once more, "the citizens of our kingdom accept you so openly, then perhaps this won't be an embarrassment you'll have to live down. Listen to them, man. It's just like when we returned from Lispagne with King Bain, except 'prince' is now the word on their lips."

I have brought home the victory, as always. I haven't failed completely, and Gwenyth will be my wife. I am still the First Knight of champions, he smiled, though he thought of his sister once more. *Without her, this could not have been accomplished. 'Tis her victory.*

He thought of his niece and what it would be like to be a father. He thought of Gwenyth and how he would hold her in his arms once more and offend her with his jests. She would steal away on Titan for her countryside gallivants. He would chase her down and spin her in his arms while those long tresses became tangled around them both.

He couldn't wait for that life to begin. Things could not be much sweeter, save the day she was delivered to him before God and church. He would make good on his fantasies of her and they would create many more. He would give her healthy babes, unlike the one she had lost, and God willing, he would sire a namesake.

Their procession wound towards the castle, snaking so far behind it was impossible to see the end. Finally, the outer bastions rose above the rooftops and they exited the city quarters. Passing through the guards, they thundered across the drawbridge as the iron portcullis was cranked.

King Bain, flanked by rows of servants, nobles and guards, stood waiting on the steps. They threw cheers upward as William and his officers lumbered their warhorses to a halt. William swung his leg over and dismounted with a jump, unable to brace himself with his worthless shoulder while his men trailed into the bailey.

His younger squire dashed forward to take Titan's reins and fell into a bow beneath him.

"On your feet, lad," William frowned.

The boy looked up and furrowed his brow. William leaned over and ruffed his hair.

"So what if I'm Prince?" he whispered.

The boy's face broadened into a grin and he scurried aside with Titan.

"Sir William!" Bain called. William looked up. "Approach me and tell me what news!"

William stared at the king staring back and slowly began to make his way up the steps. The servants bowed as he passed, excitement thrumming through the air. He climbed to face King Bain and fell upon his knee.

"These men have fought valiantly, Your Majesty, and deserve your highest praise." His words had lost their cheer and he felt nervous. "It's with pride that I claim victory for you and your kingdom. The sedition is quelled and Lord Feargach of Dwyre has met his death under my own blade and the blades of Loddin of Ballymead."

Bain placed a palm upon his head, resting his fingers on William's coif and held him fast for a moment.

"Rise, my son," he said softly and William stood.

Cheering rose up again, filling the bailey, as the ladies waved their handkerchiefs. Cavanaugh's wife raced forth and he swooped her up into his saddle to kiss her.

The king stared deeply into William's eyes and gripped the side of his face.

"You fought proudly, and you have kept my throne secure. But you were wrong about something, William."

"My Lord King?" he questioned.

Bain lowered his voice even more.

"I *was* proud to have a son, all those years. I was just weak, for I was afraid you would hate me as you hated Andrew Cadogan. But every battle you have fought, I have held my breath until your safe return. Every achievement of yours, my heart has smiled. And all those years of your youth, when I knew you suffered silently, I embraced you, if only in my heart. I too have fought to keep my throne, hence my own scars. And your battles ensure not just my throne, but yours when I die. I'm proud of the man before me."

William felt his eyes water, but quickly mastered himself.

Now..." The king's mouth curled into a smile. "Enjoy your victory." He raised William's good arm high. "My son lives! And he claims victory for all of Bain! We feast tonight!"

Thunderous cheering swelled upward. Hats and kerchiefs were tossed high as the jesters and musicians began pounding. Bain turned to William once more and embraced him, cupping his hand around William's head. He shuddered once, and William felt certain it was a stifled cry.

"Please allow me another chance to be the father Andrew was not. If you do nothing else for me, give me that one chance."

William suddenly gripped him and held him tightly.

"Aye, if I can have a chance to be someone's son."

Bain gripped him in return and slapped his back, nodding all the same. He then turned William outward and made a sweep with his hand.

"Look at your subjects."

My subjects...

"Listen to their cheers, and when you ascend to the throne, keep those cheers. For as long as they cheer, you'll be secure."

I've heard this cheering before, William thought, but never had it been so gratifying.

He listened, his name on the lips of his army and the loyal subjects of Bain. The king was smiling.

Never has a man wanted to claim me. "My Lord," he bowed his head once more and whispered. "May I call you, Father?"

King Bain beamed. Before he knew it, Bain pulled him into another embrace, slapping his back and William returned it.

"Yes, son, I wish it very much," he whispered back. "I would be *most* proud."

William was drilling his squire by the knights' barracks when the messenger from Ballymead was admitted through the portcullis. He saw the green and gold sun from afar and sheathed his sword.

"Let's take a rest, lad," he said. "Better yet, let's break for the day."

"But My Lord, 'tis only mid-morning—"

"Don't question generosity," William smiled. "Or I might send you to the armory with a bucket of piss for polishing."

"No sir! I shall take the day as you suggest!" the squire grinned and hastened out of the bailey with his equipment.

He strode through the arches toward the gates and shoved between the rumps of all the horses.

Trials today. 'Twill be nice when the nobles clear out on the morrow.

After nearly a month of anticipation, the news was finally here that would perfect him like sugar dusted on a cake. The messenger dismounted and seeing the royal medallion about William's neck fell into a bow.

"Your Highness."

"Rise, friend of Ballymead," William clapped him on the back. "I shall never be used to men bowing in such a fashion and beg you only to do so when it's a formal setting. Otherwise I'm simply Sir William."

The messenger smiled, as did the guards.

"Lord Loddin has sent a letter to you. He felt it urgent you received it as soon as possible."

"This is good news, I take it?"

"He didn't share with me the contents. His only request was that I see it into your hands and make haste."

"I bid him thanks. Please make your way to the buttery, man, and find yourself some ale and a hot meal. There's room in the barracks, any empty pallet you wish."

The messenger bowed again and strolled away. William looked at the parchment sealed with the stamp of a sun crest and hastened to the main doors, squeezing back through the horses again. Winding through the corridors, he climbed the stairs to the room of the High Council. Trials were still in session and the king, in crown and full regalia, sat upon his throne hearing grievances.

The guards bowed to him and opened the port. He slipped onto the last bench and waited for the trial to conclude.

"I then understand Lord Bryn to have stolen twenty of my sheep since he *still* blamed me for poisoning his well!"

"It's clear to me that you didn't poison Lord Bryn's water, man, but I cannot assume he stole livestock to retaliate with no proof," King Bain sighed, looking down the scroll to see how many more grievances he had to hear.

He acknowledged William with a raised brow and a nod, then stared back at his scroll.

"Is this proof, My Lord King?" The little liege held forth a wad of bloody wool, unclean as though it had been ripped from the carcass. "*He* does not keep sheep! And this, along with the corpses of several others, was recovered from inside his fences!"

He threw the wool down upon the council table and it bounced with comic fluff. Stifled laughter surged through the room and Lord Bryn jumped to his feet.

"He calls that proof? Rothcoe could have picked that up anywhere!"

"Well I didn't have time to commission a painting of the crime!" the little man snapped.

"Perhaps, Your Highness, his animals strayed onto my property through his ill-repaired fencing and died of water from my *poisoned* well!"

Again, laughter rumbled through the room.

"I brought witnesses! One of which comes from *his* fee!"

A man stood up and Lord Bryn scowled.

"You're wasting this court's time!" Bain bellowed. "And I've a mind to fine you both."

"But he wronged me, Your Grace!" insisted the little lord. "I want compensation for my slaughtered livestock, for it is that which would have turned my profit in wool sales and helped me pay my taxes to *your* crown! Now, I must take this loss from my budget for winter grain for my *entire* fiefdom and he walks away with naught but a slap on the wrist! And now I must spend even more to replace what he has stolen!"

"My Lord King," Bryn huffed with a smug look and adjusted his belt. "This has been a grand waste of time and I have lost valuable workdays by voyaging here. Like you, *I* am put out. He has no proof, and I am ready for you to rule in my favor."

"Don't make presumptions about my intentions, Lord Bryn," Bain warned.

"If there is no justice here today, then I say this crown is corrupt!" assaulted the first lord.

Bain waved a tired hand and rubbed his eyes, muttering to his guard next to him.

"This is enough. Lord Bryn, you are hereby ordered to pay forty pieces of silver to Lord Rothcoe, for stealing his sheep, and will compensate for the cost of twenty new head."

"But, Your Majesty—"

"*If* you don't think it's fair, then admit your part in this scheme this minute, and I shall decide a fairer punishment. One of his witnesses has come from your fee. Shall we hear his statement?" Lord Bryn sealed his lips and sat down. "Apparently you are more involved than you would like to admit," King Bain muttered. "This is my final decision. One sheep is worth two pieces of silver in taxes and Rothcoe is missing twenty, therefore, you pay forty, plus the cost of replacing those you slaughtered. You will settle this debt before leaving today."

"What if I don't have such money on my person, Your Majesty?" demanded Lord Bryn.

"Then you may work it off here by going to prison!" King Bain boomed, jumping to his feet. The room gasped and everyone fell to the floor in bows. "Trust me, man, you'll enjoy life much more outside of my dungeon towers."

Lord Bryn had frozen and slowly reached for his purse.

"I shall pay it then," he croaked.

"I knew you would see reason," the king fumed, motioning to a guard. "Take them to the upper hall and see to it the proper amount is handed over under writ of contract. Then release them to their fees, and in the *future*," the king huffed as he checked his lists again, "do *not* waste this court's time with childish problems! Refreshments *please*! And a recess, men, if you don't mind."

He rose as his officials broke to take a goblet of wine.

"Prince William," Bain called.

William walked down the aisle of benches to the front and bowed.

"My Lord King."

"Rise, son. You seem pleased."

Charles smiled as the room around them fell into chatter.

"I am, sir, for a letter has just arrived from Ballymead."

"Have you opened it?"

"Not yet, I wished to share it with you when you're finished."

"Well go on, we take refreshments and relax for a spell. I have a spare moment."

William ripped through the seal and pulled loose the parchment with a grin. Slowly, his face fell, and he felt his heart began pounding. He shook his head and then looked out through the window, past the officials who poured their wine and laughed, past the scribes who fought to catch up on scribbling.

"I was so sure..."

"She has said no," Bain muttered, resting a hand on William's shoulder.

William reread it, then reread it again before looking up and feeling his heart drop.

She refused me. Gwenyth refused my apology... "But Loddin said he would talk to her," he finally managed. "He said he would apologize for me."

His throat tightened and he felt his fist clench around the parchment.

"Get on with your day, William, and we'll think about this on the morrow," Bain said. "Perhaps I ought to send a request this time. I am your father and a betrothal might be best handled between Loddin and myself."

William thought on it but didn't budge, and saw Gwenyth's face all over again as he told her he couldn't marry her. *She teaches me a lesson.*

"William," King Bain guided him to a more private niche of the council room. "What did you do that you should apologize to this lady?"

William shook his head but didn't answer directly.

"Her honor matters greatly if I'm to be King, does it not?"

"It does, son, very much so if she is to enter the House of Bain. Why? Do you find hers in question?"

"What does it matter now?" He looked back at the letter. "I don't think another request will sway her, for if she's anything, she is determined. Her answer means what it means."

His heart felt withered and he slapped the parchment across his other hand. Bain sipped his goblet and thought.

"You say Loddin apologized for you?"

William nodded and forced a smile, for he could see the other men in the room watching them.

"Perhaps then, William, if your words have hurt her, then only your apology will heal her. For I can arrange a marriage, but only you can earn back her favor. Besides, Loddin and Edward's letters of her capture while you were away were most distressing. She might still be suffering from her ordeal."

She suffers from more than capture, My Lord...

With a slap on the back, the king guided him back to the others.

"Go, lad, this is not the end. Betrothals are often met with rejection at first and are only worked out with negotiation. I must get back to my grievances. It seems I must hear disputes over hunting rights and trespassing next. Do you see the amusement you have to look forward to? Oh, but son?"

William looked up.

"It might be wise to solicit a contract with another lady, in the event that...well you know."

"Right," William mumbled, none of it seeming real. "Whoever you wish, I don't care."

After hours of riding Titan and attempts to rest, William stripped off his regalia, threw on an old tunic, and quietly ducked down the corridors and out of the castle into the darkness settling in.

"You're out of costume, My Lord Prince," a guard noted as he attempted to pass through the gate. "And unescorted. Shall we call for a party?"

"No. I thank thee. I've my sword and daggers."

William tried to pass, but the soldier stood fast.

"My Lord Prince, is it your wish to be unaccompanied?"

"Aye it is. The maidens don't make up their songs of Sir William the Brave for no reason." They chuckled together. "I'm more than capable of warding off assassins."

The guard, laughing, stepped aside, and William roamed into the town beyond the castle gate.

42

He walked through the narrow streets of the city that dissected the buildings. Weaving into hidden alleys, he trod on the cobblestones, sidestepping rubbish piles thrown into the road and wandered into an inn.

I should like to drown in ale, he pitied himself, hoping to find a corner to stand in where he could drink and drink. *Gwenyth will refuse me again, she will. It's pointless to try again, dear Father.*

He found several men already there. Their heads already sloshed like tankards amidst the din of chatter. William ducked beneath the beams. The room was poorly plastered with the wooden timbering exposed, and dirty rushes were strewn across the flooring.

"Sir William!" a soldier called. "My *Lord!* It's like old times, you mingling with us commoners!"

He lifted a hand to wave but couldn't summon a smile to his mouth. If his soldiers didn't shut up, they would give him away. It was good indeed that many folk didn't recognize their new prince in person.

He walked to the counter and threw a coin down to the wench, ordering his ale as he thought of Gwenyth. The woman, her bosom busting upward from her bodice, slid a tankard across the wood and took the coin, smiling at him.

"Here you are, sir knight," she added, flashing him a bat of her eyes.

She's blonde like Gwenyth, he thought, his mind clouded. *How could she have rejected me? Surely my apology was enough for her to know I saw my error.* He stood alone and downed the ale, guzzling like a calf suckling milk and ordered another.

Two of his men walked by and slapped him on the back. He returned with a meaningless joke at which they laughed, then picked up the second tankard from the wench's grip. She looked up at him and smiled again, letting his fingers touch hers before she released the handle.

"They call you *My Lord*, even the knights," she said. "You are high ranking."

"Aye, that I am."

He took the tankard and stared at the woman, young before him, dark eyes and light hair tied to the back of her head as the tops of her breasts swelled. She moved away but glanced back over her shoulder to see him running his eyes up and down her backside.

Gwenyth recaptured his mind. He thought of her face as he spoke his words. *He has made you a Feargach whore...*

The little wench eyed him again. He waved his hand for another.

"You're thirsty, My Lord," she smiled.

"Just keep bringing ale, woman, and I'll keep giving you coin," he replied.

The noise of men grew louder as night settled in and work ended for the day. Many of his soldiers crammed into the room now, laughing together, pinching the serving women as they went by who returned their flirts with smiles, giggles, and occasionally an invitation.

For a price, William told himself.

The little woman brought him another ale and held her hand out to him. He placed his coin into her palm and she closed her fingers on his.

She's no virgin, William thought as he pulled his hand slowly back, staring at her mouth. *She's already a whore and was never a lady.*

He began to nurse the third tankard.

"Come'ere, wench," a man slurred, yanking loose his purse.

He pulled the woman forward and grabbed her buttocks, forcing her against the wall. She giggled as his hands roved over her body and up to her breasts.

"Eh, eh, man," she wagged her finger. "You must pay me first."

"Aw, be *kind* to an achin' soldier," he muttered, grabbing her breasts again and biting at her neck. "I carry a heavy load, woman, and need those warm lips of yours to unburden me." He smothered her lips in his and again she giggled, letting her hand stray to the front of his trousers.

He smiled and bit her lip. But she pushed him back and he groaned defeat.

"How much this time?" he mumbled, taking her hand and replacing it to his trousers.

She leaned up and whispered in his ear, then pulled open the top of her bodice. He dropped his coins in.

It's that simple, William thought. *He gets his pleasure and then it's over...*

They slipped away from the casks and the man swooped her up into his arms. William watched her go and grew jealous for reasons unknown, except that she resembled Gwenyth. She threw William another look, inviting him to be the next in line, then threw her head back and laughed. They disappeared under the stairs and pushed closed the curtain.

He ordered a fourth tankard, then a fifth, then a sixth, then a seventh as his eyes lost the edge of clarity. He watched the curtain, waiting for the woman to come back out so he could grope her with his eyes some more. Then, perhaps, he could take her himself and see what his men jested about.

What does it matter? Gwenyth doesn't want me, and she's right. Many women will gladly squabble over what she discarded. It's her fault. She's to blame that my thoughts stray. She could have accepted me. She could have agreed to marry.

The man finally stumbled out from behind the curtain. Pulling his tunic down over his trousers, he laughed and fell back to the counter for another drink. The little woman arrived moments later, adjusting her bodice and wiping her mouth with a kerchief before refreshing herself with drink and a pinch of mint.

She smiled sweetly at him.

"I see you're still here," she muttered, noting his empty tankard before returning to work.

He knocked back the last swallow, mumbling a drunken jest to the knight next to him who laughed and draped an arm on William to keep from falling. The sun had long since gone down and the little lattice panes of glass were growing smudgy. She approached him and reached out a hand, placing it on his arm.

"You stare at me, My Lord," she smiled.

"I want another, woman," he muttered, staring down at her breasts.

"Is that all you want, man?"

She flashed her eyes at him and he smiled.

"I would like for *you* to serve it to me," he flirted.

"Not another woman?"

He thought of Gwenyth and shook his head. "No. You. And perhaps from the bottom cask." *Then, either way you bend, I'm rewarded*, he thought.

She gathered this right away and indulged him with a long, low bow that caused her bosom to practically spill into plain sight. He grinned.

"You have a nice smile. Surely many a woman has loved those lips."

She served him the tankard and went about her business, allowing the men to taunt her and place coins down her bodice as she eyed him again. He stared at her and neared the dregs of his ale. She grinned, coming back and leaning forward so that her breasts were squeezed together.

He couldn't help but stare and reached a hand out to touch them, before stopping himself.

"Am I so hideous that you need to drink a whole cask before you have the nerve to proposition me?"

"No, woman, you're fair indeed."

"I am *fair*," she raised her brow. "And you're *proper*. Come with me, *kind sir*, and I'll show the honorable knight a proper time."

He swallowed his ale as though it were water and slammed it down, allowing her to drag him away. His soldiers began shouting and laughing.

"Is that true what those men are saying?" she whispered, having pulled him through the back door and out into a close.

It was soiled in urine and festering with peasants. He braced her roughly against the wall and let his hands take the liberty of grabbing her waist, shifting her in front of him.

"Is what true?"

He began to slide his hands to her bosom.

"That you've never taken a woman?"

"Aye, it's true, but that doesn't mean I don't know what to do."

His words ran together but he didn't care as he bent down, so drunk from sucking down ale he had no will to stop. He tasted her lips, allowing his tongue to push into her mouth as he held her head close to him and pressed himself between her legs.

"Why have you saved yourself?" she breathed between kisses, brushing back his hair.

His grip on her tightened. He could feel the stab of rejection all over again.

"No questions, woman," he murmured and paused in his kissing. "I shall pay you to be my first, 'tis all."

"No, I won't charge you, My Lord," she whispered, sensing tragedy in his words. "Consider losing your virginity a gift."

She reached to his trousers, sliding her hands in and felt the front of him. He was ready, and as she slid her hand up and down, he exhaled and pictured Gwenyth, her breasts so small and perfect for his hands. He had always been ashamed for wanting her but now all he could do was imagine her beneath him like she had been at fireside, with her hands rubbing his back and her legs wrapped around him. How he wished he could have bedded her, just once, so he had a memory to tuck away for his lifetime.

"You boast a healthy size, My Lord," she found words from beneath his lips.

"Lucky for you then, woman," he groaned as he pushed the sleeves of her bodice down.

He pulled forth her breasts so that they were fully nude, large and bulbous, feeling them and welting her lips.

"And you certainly know where to roam, My Lord. You'll no doubt be a favorite of mine."

She lifted his tunic so his chest was nude. Slowly, she squatted, kissing down his stomach until she was kneeling before him. He held his breath, bracing himself against the wall over her as she pulled him loose from his trousers. She grabbed his hips and took him in her mouth. The feeling was so ecstatic he nearly collapsed, feeling her moist lips sliding up and down him.

She could feel him trembling and smiled, rising to face him

again. His tunic fell and she grabbed his neck and held his face to hers as his hands began to hike up her skirts. Again he pressed his front to her, so lost in inebriation that all ability of deciding right and wrong had lost him. His fingers moved across her thighs, plump and soft, and he imagined Gwenyth's, tight and slender. He imagined the river trickling over her, his hand beneath her shift as he caressed her while she released soft sighs of pleasure from his touch.

Then it hit him. This woman was nothing like her. He didn't even think her pretty now that he compared her with Gwenyth and felt revulsion, yet was too far engaged now to quit. His hands slid around her buttocks and grabbed her stockings, which he yanked down. She parted her legs for him and he slid his hand between them to feel the moistness of her center.

"William?" a voice sounded behind him, but it didn't register and he bore down on her lips again.

Then a hand landed upon him.

"William! What the hell are you doing?"

He turned to see who interrupted him and found Frances Cavanaugh, nearly as drunk as he with his arm around another knight for support.

"What does it look like?" he slurred, adjusting his trousers.

"You don't want a prostitute, man, they're filthy. You wait for the Lady Gwenyth."

"He doesn't seem satisfied waiting," the woman smiled, pulling William's face back to hers.

"No, I'm not," he murmured and went back to groping, pressing his mouth against hers as she giggled.

Frances pulled him off of the wench and her skirts fell. Angered, William whirled around with the grace of a dizzy camel.

"Gwenyth doesn't wish to marry me, man!" he rumbled, ripping loose his letter and slamming it against Frances's chest. "Read for yourself! She rejected me!"

"Well you were an ass and she a fine lady! She bids you work a bit harder to make up for your insults—"

"Is there any harm in taking another woman? I don't have to marry this one, for marriage seems like nothing but a game of entrapment, one in which Gwenyth does not want besides. I can bed the wench and leave."

Frances swayed on his feet, then took William by the arm and tucked his letter back in his tunic for him.

"Does your father have any idea what mischief you play at this night?"

"No. I'm my own man and don't ask permission to drink."

"Why should his father even care?" the prostitute snapped.

Frances chuckled. "Believe me, wench, he would care greatly. Come, William. Let me get you another drink and we'll talk. There will be other nights for other women if you're bent on it. But your cock will be diseased come the morrow if you whore this one. Then no lady will have you, least of all Gwenyth. You'll have to import a bride from Lispagne."

The wench screwed up her face. "The man can decide his own mind for himself!"

William braced an arm on the wall to keep from toppling over, falling into a chuckle.

Frances burst out laughing. "I would argue, woman, that the man cannot even decide whether to stand or fall!" He rolled his eyes. "Away with you, wench. I speak for the man when his mind shuts down, and he chooses much higher quality."

Pulling out a coin, he flicked it off his thumb at her. She folded her arms instead and let the coin bounce away. It clattered against the cobbles, ringing out amongst the muffled sounds of drink, men, and spontaneous arguments that sprang from the back alleys. A peasant crawled forth from the rubbish and snatched the money she rejected.

Without another glance, Frances grabbed his knight with one hand and William with the other, dragging him back into the inn and paid for another round.

His men hailed him.

"Only a few seconds, he lasted!"

"She probably didn't feel it happen!"

The jokes continued until the disappointed wench stormed back in.

"No, no! He didn't take her, men!" Frances announced like a noble proclamation. "He had a moment of judgment and decided that he hadn't yet had enough drink to make her beautiful!"

William snatched up another tankard as the men threw taunts

at the wench. She scowled at them all and stomped her foot, *like Gwenyth, as she stomped her name into the mud, poor Gwenyth... 'You fought in my honor and I have none! I'm a disgrace...a disgrace...' '...you disgrace this house, William...'*

It was late when he and Frances were admitted into the castle. They stumbled into the quiet yard, laughing, so tanked with drink that neither could walk properly. Each fumble of the foot tripped the other, causing them to snort and snigger. Finally, Frances managed to haul him to the main doors where guards stood watch and pretended not to stare.

"See this good man to his chamber, gentle men," Frances slurred. "I must go home to me wife, for I'll certainly get a tongue lashing, and I'd rather hear it when I'm drunk!"

They admitted William who stumbled along the halls and up the stairs until he came to his door, pried it open, and fell inside. He barred it shut and leaned against it, feeling the coldness of his new chamber. The bluish moonlight flooded through his window and cast lonely shadows across the tile. His bed sat waiting for him with covers turned back. The fire that had been set for him had long since turned to embers, and he thought of Gwenyth's cold eyes staring at him as she built a wall between them and mounted to leave with George.

Staggering forward, he fumbled to the chair by the hearth and attempted to sit, falling onto the rug instead. He decided to lie down in that spot rather than fight for sobriety anymore.

Gwenyth was no whore at all and the severity of his words flooded his mind. *There is no worse a label for a lady than to be deemed a whore, and I have called her it. What have I done to you, Gwen?*

"Forgive me, Pater. Help Gwenyth's heart to forgive me, for I want no other," he muttered as blackness claimed his vision. "Thank God Frances found me, thank Christ he found me..." His hands found the letter from Ballymead inside his tunic and he pulled it out, clasping it, and fell into a deep sleep right where he lay.

He woke on the floor to pounding, which he mistook for pounding in his brain. The sun was already high and cast a painful ray upon his face that made his eyes squint.

I shall be sick this day, he groaned.

"Prince William! Your presence is requested!"

The banging continued and he rose, his head throbbing as

though he had slammed it into a wall. He staggered to his feet, looking at the letter that lay wrinkled on the floor, and shivered.

With great effort, he made his way to the chamber pot, releasing his water in a long stream that seemed to have no end. The banging became even more vociferous and he finally made his way to the door.

"What is it?" he snapped as he pulled it open.

His pageboy stood erect in front of him, blinking with offense at the stink of alcohol that wafted from his breath.

"His Highness, King Bain, requests your presence at board, My Lord Prince."

"Has he given a reason? For I want to sleep. I'm ill." He rubbed his eyes, envisioning his pillow beneath his head.

"He said you might say that."

"And?"

"And he said he doesn't care. He requests that you don't make him wait any longer to break his fast, My Lord Prince. He's not in good humor."

William huffed and leaned on the door.

"Very well. Send in my attendants."

His servants, waiting all morning for him to open up, swooped in with a flurry. They filled his wine decanter and noted his bed, still not slept in. He was stripped of his clothing and scrubbed clean with soap, redressed in fresh undergarments while another scurried away with his chamber pot.

"If you please, My Lord Prince." His pageboy bowed and opened a box. "'Twill help greatly to refresh you."

He held mint out to him and William took the hint, taking a pinch and chewing it into his cheek.

"Do I smell that poorly?" he jested as they combed through his hair.

"I have smelled sweeter roses, My Lord Prince," the boy smiled.

Once freshened, he took a goblet of wine offered him and downed it, praying that it would take effect on his sore mind soon. He made his way through the corridors and down the stairs to the great hall. The fire crackling in the giant hearth was inviting, Yet Bain's face was anything but. The servants bowed. Bain, frowning, stood up and grabbed his shoulder.

"You look like hell," he remarked, shoving him into his chair before he had a chance to bow.

"I feel it, sir," he mumbled, wincing as a bowl clattered to the floor.

"Lord," King Bain turned his head from his breath. "There isn't enough freshener in all of Bain for you right now. Did you douse your stomach with an *entire* supply of ale?"

"I believe I tried, sir, though I cannot quite remember."

"Judging by the spectacle my guards reported last night," his tone was honed with well-sharpened words. "I would say it's a miracle I still have an heir. I'm surprised at you. Such behavior I never would have imagined from Sir William."

"I'm ashamed of myself, Father." He took the meat offered him with a nod of thanks.

"What have you to say for yourself then?"

The last thing William wanted was a royal inquiry, but answered nonetheless.

"I was angered by Loddin's letter and allowed my judgment to be clouded. And I'll never get used to having no freedom. I'm accustomed to being my own man."

Bain shook his head.

"My God, you're more lovesick than a girl for a puppy. You haven't done anything regrettable, have you? The House of Bain needs no more making of bastards."

William shot him a scathing look. "*Indeed.*"

Bain sighed and his face softened. "'Tis not what I meant. But if we're honest, when I bedded your mother, I caused a string of consequences. I wish to spare you from repeating such hardships with a babe of your own. And so? You've done nothing regrettable? For if you have, the time to intervene is now."

"I almost did, but was dissuaded at the last moment... thankfully."

"How close is *almost*, William?"

William looked around to make sure no one was nearby, then back at his food.

"I was already beneath her skirts and I would have finished what I was starting, too, if Sir Cavanaugh hadn't stopped me."

The king leaned back in his chair, exhaling loudly.

"Cavanaugh dissuaded you?"

William nodded.

"Perhaps then I should cancel the notice of discipline I have ordered sent," he muttered.

He rested his head in his hand while he rubbed his forehead as if he sought patience to grace him. Just then, his youngest daughter scampered to his side in tears.

"Look, Father," she pouted, her lip sticking out as she held up a finger.

"Not now," he muttered, scooting her away. "One child's problem at a time. Where is her maid?"

"Come over here, Grace," William coaxed as she walked to him, her green eyes welling with water.

He lifted her onto his lap and smoothed the wrinkles from her gown as she clasped her finger with a reddened sore.

"What have you done to your finger?" he asked.

"Mary poked me with her needle because *I* wanted the green fabric to embroider." She let a tear roll down her cheek. "It's the only piece of its kind and I wouldn't let her have it, for she's selfish and always gets what she wants."

"That wasn't nice at all, was it?" William smiled as he lifted her stubby finger to his mouth and kissed it.

The king looked at him and watched, then smiled.

She shook her head. "No, it wasn't. Now my finger will turn black and fall off."

William stifled a smile as Bain grunted and picked up his goblet.

"Not after one of my kisses, it won't," William scolded.

She looked up at him in puzzlement.

"Did you not know?" he said. She looked blank. "Well now my heart is hurt."

"Know what, Brother?" she begged. "Are your kisses magic?"

He frowned. "'Tis true, girl, the kisses of big brothers are magical, but only if you believe it, and now I fear my kiss has been wasted."

She threw her arms around his neck. "No, William, I believe it, I do!" she pled.

He grinned and set the child down again, shaking a warning finger.

"Then your finger shall be better soon, but only if you promise to divide the green fabric and share it. Else it *will* fall off."

She nodded and smiled, then ran away. Bain watched her go and sighed.

"You've a way with children, son. You'll make a fine father someday."

You'll make a fine father someday, Sir William, when you finally choose a bride... "If only I had a fine wife to help me sire them," he mumbled.

"Well you'll not have one if your debauchery continues. Was it a whore you almost bedded?"

William answered with a nod though didn't look at him.

"*Christ,*" Bain muttered. "You'll not do so again, William. You'll not tarnish this monarchy. Today you work, for life continues despite your troubles and let this be a lesson. I don't care if your head swells into a pounding smithy today! I have taxes to collect and it will be *you* with the assessors who go to gather them, today and the rest of this week."

William consented with a nod.

"Then, I believe you have squires who have sat idle all the morn. They won't be as ruthless as their master if you let them grow lazy." Again, William nodded, dreading the work his muscles would have to do. "Consider it my sanction for behaving like a fool and praise be to God for making the sun shine today. It will surely beat reminders into your head every time you look up at it."

William frowned, and pushed away his trencher. "Are you quite finished?" he grumbled. "Or will I be peeling carrots in the scullery before the day is through?"

Bain paused a moment, then chuckled. "You're not married yet. If you choose to sleep with woman it's on your repentant conscience, just do so without the drunken foolery, hmm? And at least

362

save your royal seed for someone better than a wench. The last thing in the world we need is a bastard peasant. On a different note, I've drafted this contract. What thinks you?"

He placed a sheet of parchment before his son.

Lord Loddin of Ballymead.

This contract hereby proclaims the intent of the High King, His Highness Charles Murron of Bain, to request the marriage of his son and heir to the throne, the High Prince, His Highness William Murron of Bain to your daughter, the fair and gracious Lady Gwenyth of the Noble House of Loddin. By signing this with your mark, you agree to enter your daughter into wedlock of the highest honor of the land, the Royal House of King Bain, Your Lord and Supreme Sovereign. The requested dowry is one horse named Luna, and as a token of the honorable intentions of the High Prince, please accept this silver lunette to seal the betrothal. He would be most pleased if she wears it. 'Tis Prince William's sincerest hope that the Lady Gwenyth reconsider his proposal and accept his apologies. Your reply is awaited in urgency.

The letter was stamped with the king's royal crest and it made him smile.

"What lunette, Father?"

"This one."

He held forth a solid silver lunette with engravings of lions around the rim that matched the chain William wore.

"Did you have this crafted for her?"

His father shook his head.

"I had it crafted for my queen. It sealed our betrothal to one another and she wore it each day until the birth of Grace took her from me. I would be honored if my daughter of marriage wore it when she stands beside her husband. For it's only fit for a queen, and the Lady Gwenyth seems only fit for you."

43

"It's Lord Edward approaching! Raise the portcullis!" a messenger from the main gates called.

The entourage from Dunstonwoodshire made its way up the road to the keep. Mathew Whitcroft saw the red and gold banners and sprang from the brattice. Loddin was in the meadery re-racking the mead with George while William wiped out the slime that had settled in the casks.

They sweated despite the chill of February that plagued the highlands, as if to say spring would never return. Loddin wiped his brow and stuck the tube into a newly opened barrel of mead, sucking on the end until the golden liquid came rushing through. He aimed it into the empty cast beneath him and the mead flowed out with splashes.

His sons laughed.

"How much did you drink last night, Father?" George teased.

Loddin looked down and chuckled.

"You mean this isn't a chamber pot?"

"For a giant, mayhap," George replied. "So now I know why this mead is so special."

"The secret ingredient, lads," Loddin grinned. His sons laughed. "Don't tell the vassals what it is they really crave when they come for orders in the spring, for the joke is on them."

"'Tis the right color too," George snickered.

"That's vile, man," William snorted as he groped inside the cask with a rag.

"George, seal that one and place it on the far shelf. It's a testy batch. I fear the draft is too cold on the front rack to save it."

George sealed the lid with a mallet and rolled the barrel away on its rim.

"Lord Loddin!" Mathew barged in. "Lord Edward from Dunstonwoodshire arrives with all his children. Will you greet him?"

"*All* of his children?" Loddin said.

"Even his daughters?" William added, turning suddenly red.

"Both of them," Mathew replied.

Loddin smiled and grabbed a rag to wipe his hands as he set the tube against the cask.

"What is his reason for coming?"

"A visit of good faith, sir. I believe to discuss the wedding details for Gavin and the Lady Sarah"

"Of course, of course, please bid him come in. Oh, and Mathew?"

"My Lord?"

"Find a maid to chaperone the Lady Sarah. Once Gavin sees her, he's likely to grow careless and try for liberties unbecoming of a maiden, hmm?"

"Aye, sir, I'll ask Gwenyth's maid."

"Take this, George. I must go and wash. Come join us once this one is full. We will finish our task on the morrow."

Loddin exited into the wind coursing through the bailey.

"Edward, man! A happy surprise! How goes your health?"

They clasped wrists as Edward dismounted.

"I'm well," he sighed, patting his stomach. "Still sore but the bastard didn't damage anything important."

"Good to hear indeed. And Lady Sarah," Loddin remarked. "I do believe Gavin will be most pleased to see your pretty face."

He helped her down from her saddle, her cheeks rosy from the cold, and kissed her hand.

"My Lord," she bowed to him.

"But who is this fair thing? Amber, is it? Or should I now call you Lady?" Loddin remarked as Edward's two older sons dismounted and handed over the reins to the stable boys.

The few guards who had ridden along found their way to the buttery, clasping wrists with Ballymead sentries. Amber smiled as she clenched her reins.

"Allow me, Lady," Loddin smiled. He reached to her waist and she braced his shoulders to be brought down. "My, you've grown up since last we visited. And have become fair like your sister, no? No doubt the suitors will begin calling soon."

"You're too kind," she smiled and bowed as Sarah reached to her to guide her inside.

"Come inside, please" he added. "Mary and Gwenyth will be most pleased with your company."

"How *does* your daughter fair?" Edward asked as the others were led in ahead.

Loddin lost his smile and shook his head.

"I don't know. She won't speak. Over a month has passed and I felt certain time would help her but instead it has turned her inward. She's not herself anymore, refused marriage as well," he added, raising his brow. "I'm considering the convent for her, for she's soon to be eight and ten and needs to have her future secure."

"Who sought her hand?" Edward pulled off his gloves as they entered the warmth of the keep.

Loddin exhaled. "You won't believe this,"

"I'm interested now, friend."

Loddin continued to shake his head as he pushed shut the door against the wind.

"She had a suitor, Sir William Cadogan, the leader of Bain's Army. He was sent to retrieve her from Dwyre last autumn and they fell in love. You should have seen them. Completely besotted."

"But he's the new prince," Edward exclaimed as Loddin ordered meals to be prepared.

"Aye, that he is, and Gwenyth has refused him. After Shea forced her..." He pursed his lips. "They had an exchange of harsh words and now she won't speak of him."

One of the women poured wine and handed them goblets.

"I'm still so burdened that I didn't protect her, Loddin."

"I don't fault you. You took a knife for her, which proves your loyalty. God has allowed it to happen, though I pray each night for answers as to why he should make my lass suffer so." He huffed. "Marriage to William would have been good if only she could have seen it, for the lad is smitten with her."

"You shouldn't let her make this choice. She's your daughter and duty bound. Marriage into such stock would be wise politically. And a royal alliance would be good protection for someone like you so far from the capital."

"I know it, but if she would be miserable, I cannot condemn her to it."

"You're soft, man." Edward took a sip as his daughters were unbundled and his sons clasped wrists with the sons of Ballymead. Gavin wasted no time sidling up to Sarah to kiss her hand while Hershel, carrying little Hershel on his back like a sack of roots, descended from the solar. "She would learn to love him and besides, marriage with our kind is not about love. It's political. Love is for a bard's tales."

"I suppose you're right, and I would if the chance came again for the thought of her as a nun is wrenching, but what's done is done now. I sent her refusal."

Mary came down the stairs with a grin upon her face.

"Where is Gwenyth?" Loddin asked.

"She'll come down momentarily, once her coif is finished, My Lord," she bowed, then turned to Edward's daughters and embraced them. "Welcome, sister-to-be and Lady Amber," she smiled. "Will you pardon my rudeness? For I was not expecting you and I have news I must share with my husband."

They furrowed their brows but nodded. She scurried to young Loddin and pulled him aside.

"What is it, woman?" Loddin asked. "We've guests to greet."

"I must speak with you, husband, for I was already on my way." Loddin stepped aside with her.

"All right, out with it," he urged. Mary frowned at his tone and Loddin softened. "I'm sorry, woman. You're radiant right now and I ruin it."

She smiled again and grabbed his hand.

"I feel radiant, My Lord, for I have just discovered news and pray you will be pleased. I cannot wait in sharing it."

She reached up and whispered in his ear and Loddin's face

dropped.

"Is it true?" he whispered, his own mouth broadening into a smile.

She nodded and blushed. "It's three sennights overdue and I now begin to feel the sickness. Mrs. McIntosh says I have all the signs. Loddin, please say you're happy."

He grabbed her around the waist and twirled her, laughing.

"You're a blessing, woman!" he exclaimed as he kissed her. "I am more than pleased! I am overjoyed!"

The others stared as George and William came inside from the meadery. Their father rolled his eyes.

"Is this how you greet our company, son? *Mercy*, Edward is going to think his daughter comes to a house of fools!" his voice boomed.

He ignored his father and set Mary down, kissing her again and placing a hand on her flat belly.

"May I tell them now, wife?" he whispered. "For your man bursts with pride."

She nodded and clung to his arm as he turned to the others.

"Loddin, you make us appear rude," his father scolded.

"Mary tells me she's with child, Father!" he beamed.

Loddin's face fell from sternness and the room erupted with salutations.

"You grace me with another grandchild?" he said.

"I hope to not disappoint you this time, My Lord," she dropped her head.

"Oh, Mary, you were not to blame for losing the last one. It was God's will and with his grace this one will survive and make us proud."

He hugged her tightly and turned to his son.

"I'm most pleased. Well done, Loddin, well done." They clasped wrists as young Loddin glowed, surrounded by the guests and servants. "I am proud of this. Another grandchild. 'Tis about time you motivated your lazy seed...where's your sister?"

He looked around. Gwenyth had not yet come down.

"Beatrice, go and fetch Gwenyth and tell her that her presence is requested. She must share in her brother's happiness." Beatrice nodded and left Sarah's side, which proved to be a mistake, for Gavin moved in and took her about the waist. "We celebrate tonight!" he announced. "And with Gavin married to Sarah, I hope to have many more blessings."

"Well, man, the details of their marriage are only part of my reason for visiting," Edward began. "I have something to request. It will seem odd indeed, for the man is supposed to do the seeking, but I should like to discuss a matter with you. In person."

Loddin nodded and led Edward up the stairs as Gavin squeezed Sarah, making his expert move to steal a kiss.

"What do you wish to ask?" he questioned out of earshot.

"Loddin, you'll know that my daughter Amber was made blind by fever when she was just ten years."

"I remember, man. 'Twas tragic for us all."

"I don't wish her to be a spinster, yet you'll know that her prospects are low, for no one of standing wishes to marry a blind woman." Loddin looked down from the solar as Amber sat in a chair so as not to be trampled in an unfamiliar house. "I haven't told her what I hope to gain by coming here, but what I am about to ask of you is a very large favor."

Loddin began to nod.

"Do you mean to ask if my William would be interested in taking her to wife?"

Edward exhaled and rested his hand on his paunch.

"She would be ready for marriage by autumn time, when she reaches six and ten. But it's much to ask. I won't lie, man. Marriage into your family is good considering the clout you have with Bain. And I figure if the lad's sight is also gone, perhaps they might be good together. She's a good lass, Loddin, and would work hard to be obedient to your boy, I know it."

Loddin rubbed his chin. "I have no doubt, man. I'm certain she would bless us. What of her dowry?"

"I have dray horses for labor and silver on reserve. Sarah would help her with her cloths and linens, for right now she makes her own for Gavin."

"I would need to request a servant or two as well, seeing as my house would swell in numbers. My staff alone would become burdened, and I suppose the time has come to allot a small fee to each of my sons."

Edward nodded. "I'm prepared to send a sister and brother from the village. Any particular age?"

"Oh, I'd say around two years past ten, young enough to learn our ways and be fostered, old enough to do the work and be strong against illness."

Lord Edward watched his daughters, Sarah blushing as Gavin whispered in her ear and Amber sitting quietly by herself.

"She'll be alone without her sister by summer and I dare say that marrying William would then have a double benefit, for she would still have her sister, plus a good marriage."

Loddin thought some moments longer. "I wondered why you packed up your whole family to ride here. 'Twould be William's choice, of course, and I'll need to talk to him, but aside from a daughter's duty, I hope you'll respect that I wish Amber to also want him. Living with the lad is no easy task. His pride is sore because of his lameness, and as of late, he's felt very little of a man worthy of a woman's affection."

Edward nodded. Loddin caught Hershel's attention as Gwenyth slinked unnoticed down the stairs and moved to the shadows.

"Aye, Father?" Hershel said as he came up the stairs.

"I'm doing an experiment."

His son raised a brow. "Speak plainly, please."

"I wish you to take William to the Lady Amber, talk with them both, perhaps let my grandson loose upon them for children always ease nerves."

Hershel looked down upon the room, William standing by the hearth, alone, Amber sitting, alone, and little Hershel climbing with determination into a chair as he reached to the berries being laid upon the board.

"What for? He can find his way if he chooses."

Loddin sighed. "I wish to see if they show signs of fancying one another."

"What? Why"

Loddin and Edward chuckled together.

"Are you being serious, Father?"

"I am indeed. I wish to see if William takes kindly to her company. It will help me make a decision."

"William is too proper to make advances, you know that," Hershel remarked. "Even if he did fancy her, he'd be embarrassed to show it."

"Aye, but he'd mention her later, perhaps talk of her when he's with his brothers?"

"He's never mentioned a lass before, ever, even when his eyes worked and he could see them."

"Just *do* it, son," Loddin fussed. "It's not my fault your heart has shrunk to the size of a walnut."

Hershel scowled. "You'll never let up on me until I find another woman myself, will you?"

"No, I won't," Loddin jested, knocking his shoulder while Edward snorted. "You were the best husband a wife could have asked for and your bride would want you to live on. But since you choose celibacy, I shall tease you."

"All right, I'll get William to talk to her if it will satisfy your *experiment.*"

Hershel rolled his eyes, muttering as he went while Gwenyth sat beside Amber.

"How goes it, Amber? It's me, Gwenyth." She took her hand.

"Oh, Gwenyth, you're well indeed," Amber sighed, smiling as she gripped her hands in return. "We were so distressed over your lot when our home was seized."

Gwenyth's face remained straight. Her trauma was a distant sorrow that was somehow separate now.

"You made a perilous trek to come here in such weather, and yet your auburn hair is quite pretty indeed. How did you manage?" Gwenyth continued.

"Father insisted we come. 'Twas bitter cold and I don't wish to return yet, for sleeping by campfire thrice has made me terribly sore. But I'm very happy to visit you and the others, Lady."

For the first time in over a month, Gwenyth thought of her campfires with William, curled together, his arms around her, *in such blissful comfort as if it were meant to be*, and those lips, those soft lips...*which betray their sweetness with such hurtful words.*

"It is my hope you can spend some days here in our manor then whilst you recover. The female company is most welcome."

"Are all your brothers to be married now?" Amber asked.

"George is being sent away soon. Father insists he visit a vassal south of the capital and choose a woman there, and William of course has not married."

"William was always sweet," Amber remarked. "But he teased me horribly and I was certain he must despise me."

"It couldn't have been more the opposite," Gwenyth smiled.

She looked at Hershel walking to William, standing alone and quiet, so unlike the gentle and funny brother she had known before his sight and leg had been ruined.

"Brother, you're rude to stand apart. Come," Hershel said as he guided him by the arm.

"I wish to stand here," William replied.

"*No*, you do not," Hershel said, and William could hear him roll his eyes.

"What is it?" he fussed as he threw his brother's grip away.

"Just come. Father is scheming something," Hershel said. "It's utter nonsense, but go along with it to humor him."

"What does he do?"

"You won't believe it. He plays matchmaker, like an old hag," Hershel laughed.

"What do you mean?" William hesitated.

"He wishes to see if *you* fancy the Lady Amber. No doubt, he and Lord Edward want to force the two of you upon one another."

William stiffened. "The Lady Amber is blind, is she not?"

Hershel shook his head and huffed. "I know it's not ideal. Just come and be polite to her so Father will let it go."

"I cannot," William replied, grounding himself like a tree root.

"Why not? She's our guest. 'Tis hardly strange for you to greet her. Don't make me yank on you like an ass, just come on."

William turned bright red and shook his head. "No. I'll talk to her another time."

"Don't pick now to be stubborn...What's wrong, Brother? She

won't bite. She cannot even see to bite you."

"Your jests are cruel," William fumed. "She's kind and you poke fun at her."

"Come, man, I only tease…what is it?"

Hershel watched the expressions on William's face that he could not see himself. His brow was sweating and his cheeks were pink.

"She would never be interested in me, man. 'Tis a bad idea. I'm crippled. I could never care for her the way a husband should."

Hershel's mouth fell open. "Husband? Who said anything about marriage? You…you *do* fancy her, don't you?"

William burned brighter than before and stepped back, shaking his head.

"Of course not, Hershel. She's too young, besides." His voice trailed away.

Hershel looked up helplessly at the fathers.

"Go *on*," Loddin mouthed with a shoo of the hand.

"I'm trying," Hershel mouthed back. "Well she's not too young anymore, she's nearly of age."

"Please don't take me to her," William whispered. "I should like to talk to her later, when I'm ready."

"I cannot do that. Father glares at me as we speak. Where is my son?" Hershel scoped the room and spied him. "Hershel! Come here, lad. Do you see your Aunt Gwenyth with that pretty maiden?"

"Stop, Hershel," William fumed, though his brother ignored him.

"Run and announce to her that Uncle William wishes to come speak with her."

"With the pretty maiden, Papa?" he asked.

"Don't to it Hersh," William begged.

"*Aye*," Hershel corrected with a frown. "Tell your aunt he *wants* to greet her."

The boy scampered away to relay the message. It was clear immediately when Gwenyth's head shot up that Hershel had followed his father's order. Amber blushed bright red and looked as if she might cry. She clenched Gwenyth's hands, trembling so badly that the whole room could see.

"I did it, Papa!" he yelled, prideful as he ran back.

"What did you say, lad?" Hershel scooped him into his arms.

"I said that Uncle William wants the pretty maiden, Papa! Is that right?"

The men burst out laughing so hard their sides split and William threw his head down in shame. "Dear God, dear God," he muttered, his face hidden.

"Aye, son! You've done well!" Hershel belted as tears formed in his eyes. "Go and tell your grandfather what you've done!"

William recoiled farther into the wall, his face so red his brothers almost felt bad, and Loddin and Edward began to roar from the solar.

"Come, William!" Hershel snorted, slapping him hard. "It seems you must now apologize for being lewd!"

"I'll not forgive you, man," William seethed, pounding a fist into his arm over and over again as Hershel ducked and wrestled with him, still laughing. "You're lucky I cannot see you to place a proper punch!"

Hershel guided him across the room and Gwenyth bolted to her feet as though fire was beneath her.

"Hershel!" she scolded. "Your son's mouth should be washed with soap! What a horrible thing for him to say!"

"Why Sister, you're alive behind that solemn face after all!" he taunted.

Gwenyth looked fit to spit.

"Lady Amber," he began, reaching down to take Amber's hand. "I apologize for my son. He was mistaken. What he meant to say, most incorrectly, is that my brother William wants to greet you. Will you speak with my youngest brother?"

Amber was still trembling and her words quivered.

"I suppose, My Lord."

"Good. Now I must discipline my child. Hershel!"

"Aye, Papa?" He came running with berry juice on his lips.

"That was naughty of you to embarrass the lady so."

The child looked confused. "But Papa...you, you said to tell the pretty maiden with Auntie Gwen that Uncle Will—"

"Eh, eh, eh!" he wagged his finger as the men began snorting with laughter again. "I know what I said, lad."

"But Papa..."

He dragged Hershel away. Gwenyth took William's arm. He was so embarrassed she could not help but giggle herself.

"Are you all right, Brother?" she whispered. He nodded. "Is it true, you wish to talk to her?" Again he nodded, glowing red. Gwenyth clenched his hand. "You should know, Will, that she fancies you."

"Where is she?" William whispered, clutching her arm.

"Right in front of you." She took his hand and found Amber's. "Here, Lady Amber, allow my brother to show his greeting."

She placed their fingers together and backed off to give them space. Despite their distance, the room still watched. They groped clumsily for a moment before taking hold. William pulled her fingers to his mouth and kissed them, then contorted his face into a grin.

"Do you still tease me, sir, after all these years?" she quaked.

"No, no. I'm sorry, Lady," he whispered, sitting before her. "I'm ashamed of my brother's prank. This was our fathers' idea to match us."

"I see...This must be why my father made me come...Please don't be angered," she whispered in reply.

"I hope it's not too bold of me to say that I'm pleased by it... if you are," he added.

"Oh, My Lord, I'm pleased."

He pressed her hand to his mouth again.

"I have no eyes like I used to have, Lady," he whispered. "And my leg is gone. Why would you consider me?"

"Is it true that you lost them fighting for your sister?"

"Aye, 'tis true." He hung his head. "There's not much left to like."

"Oh, but sir, there is. You would lay down your life for a woman without a thought and that's noble, and, well..." she seemed to falter on her words. "'Tis romantic. I should only wish that you—I mean, that a man would do that for me."

"You only boost my pride, Lady." He kept his head hung,

though he smiled and the others could see it even if they could not hear. "May I see what you look like?" She nodded and he seemed to feel her body move. "Will you put my hands on your face then, so I don't jab it with my fingers?"

She giggled and blushed again, but moved his hands to her face. He began to trace her features, running them over her cheeks, nose, eyes, forehead, and she soon lost her giggle and did the same with him, looking upon him in the way that only the blind could see.

"You're lovely, Lady," he whispered.

She reddened again. William could feel the heat from her skin and smiled.

Loddin walked up behind his daughter. Her eyes watered as she watched her brother lose his heart and suddenly she felt saddened. *Even he is not too crippled to find love. 'Tis only me.*

"God made William blind for a reason," Loddin sighed. "And I couldn't see it. Do you cry, Butterfly?" he asked, so pleased she wasn't looking like a stone.

She sighed and he pulled her to his chest.

"William has always fancied her," she muttered.

"Has he? Why did we never know?"

"I have always known," she smiled. "He told me many times that when she reached six and ten, she'd be lovely and he should want her despite her eyes."

"You and your brother, closer than two peas in a pod." Loddin shook his head. "And I had no idea. How is it I was so lost?"

"William is stubborn, but he's also shy. Let him marry her. It would make his heart strong again...and for the sacrifice he made for me, he deserves this and more."

Just then, the great hall opened and Mathew Whitcroft blew in, sending a draft that made the room fuss.

"My Lord! A messenger from the capital with a letter from the High King! May I show him in?"

"Certainly, man," Loddin replied, his brow scrunching. Gwenyth's face dropped and she backed away. "I'm a man of popularity!" he jested. "For the world has chosen this eve to visit!"

The wine and black surcoat swept through the doors with the proud silhouette of the lion upon his chest. He bowed deeply and then stood tall.

"Are you Lord Loddin of Ballymead, sir?" His words were curt.

"I am."

"I have a parcel from His Majesty the King of an urgent nature, which he wishes for your hands and your hands only."

"I will take it then."

The messenger handed over a bundle of cloth and a letter sealed in wax, then stood dutifully.

"Go, man, through there to the kitchens and find a warm meal and drink. You may rest here in the barracks before you journey home—"

"My Lord, you will know that I'm ordered to return with that same letter in hand, with your mark upon it if you so choose. I shall not return to the capital without it, with all due respect."

"Of course, man. Do you know what this is regarding? Have I fallen out of favor?" Loddin asked.

"It's happy tidings, sir, though not my place to say."

The messenger stood expressionlessly. Loddin glanced at the others, then shrugged and broke the seal. He read deliberately, over and over again, then held down the parchment and nodded.

"What is it, Father?" Loddin called.

The elder Loddin looked at Gwenyth. She shrank farther away.

"Gwenyth. Come here, lass," he requested.

She moved from the shadows as her heart began to thump, her cheeks turning the color of her gown. Loddin slowly unwrapped the parcel and opened a chest, exposing a shining lunette. The room sighed.

"This is for you. From the High Prince of Bain."

She took the necklace and stared at it, unsure of what to do.

"Lady Gwenyth," Sarah and Mary scurried to her side. "'Tis a treasure you hold. Put it on!"

Her fingers were lifeless and held the lunette dumbly.

"What," she began, but her mouth felt like chalk. "What does the letter say, My Lord?"

Loddin was dumbfounded. "Your William won't accept your

refusal."

"He's not my William," she mouthed as Mary became too excited and snatched the lunette to put it around Gwenyth's neck for her.

"He wishes to be," Loddin remarked. "This is a formal betrothal contract, issued from our High King to me."

"William wouldn't exclude me from this decision...or maybe he would..."

She grew angered.

"Perhaps he hopes I might give him a better answer," Loddin scolded. "By accepting that lunette, you agree to marry—"

She ripped it from her throat faster than Loddin could think and shoved it back into his hand.

"Then I don't accept it!" she cried, and turned to dash away.

"Gwenyth!" Loddin shouted. She froze. "Come here!"

She crept back beneath his command and dropped her head.

"You'll not flee to your chamber this time. I cannot turn down this request."

"What about the convent, Father, for surely marriage to God is just as noble—"

"No. You'll think on this and you will come to a reasonable conclusion, by the morrow."

"You mean *your* conclusion?"

Loddin tightened his lips. "Do not contend with me, lass."

"Have I no say in this?" she pled. "You have always given me that freedom—"

"Not this time," he reprimanded. "You're sought by the prince of our land and I'm not daft enough to refuse it again. I've been blessed with a second chance. He *pines* for you, Daughter. Sends you fine gifts—"

"He *buys* me with them! Collars me with his lions! Do you not honor my wishes anymore?"

She seemed to crumble before him and he softened, brushing her cheek.

"Gwenyth, this time you obey me. I'm your lord and I say it must be so. Go and think on this, and we will speak when we break our fast."

Numb, she turned away as her brothers stared in disbelief.

"Sister," George came forth. "This is good news for you. You should be pleased. Sir William is a good man."

He attempted to hug her.

"Get away from me," she whispered and recoiled into her own grip, "or am I ordered to embrace him too, sir?" She turned to her father. *Go and think on this! Marry him!* What else must I obey? For I am nothing but a woman and a whore and only fit to do a man's bidding! I have no rights!"

Loddin grabbed her and shook her. "Now listen! You act foolish! Such wicked words you speak!"

"I'm sorry, Father…" Wisps of words escaped her as she cowered beneath him. "I shall marry him, it will be as you say…"

Loddin saw her eyes pinched shut and realized she feared him in that moment, as though he were William Feargach ready to strike. William placed a hand on his father's arm as Mary reached for her.

"Father, she's frightened. Let her go."

"Please, My Lord," Mary whispered.

Slowly, Loddin released his grip and looked at the silent room, then turned toward the messenger though didn't look at him.

"You are welcome to warm food and a pallet. Allow Mathew Whitcroft to show you. You'll have your parchment come the morrow with my mark. It's my promise."

Mary attempted to comfort her but Gwenyth bolted to the door, running out into the cold. She threw open the stable door and dashed to Luna's stall. Jumping upon the beast bareback despite her gown, she grabbed Luna's mane and backed her out. They charged through the open gates, slowing just beyond the battlements to a halt where she leaned onto the horse's neck and wept.

The tears froze to her skin and loose strands of hair were made messy by the wind.

I'm being forced into it. William no longer cares if I love him or not. He is a lion, just like his father, and conquers whatever he wants…

"There are worse fates," a voice spoke to her.

She whirled around.

"Brother, you risk getting lost," Gwenyth dried her eyes. William rode alongside her and felt for her hands. "How did you find me?"

"I followed the sniffling."

William dismounted and helped her down.

"Come here, Sister. *Talk* to me of what plagues your soul," he pled. "I won't share it, I promise."

Their father hobbled around the gate but stopped short and backed up to watch.

"Father is saddened by your grief and knows not what to do," William continued. "But you can tell me, Gwen, you can tell me anything, you know that. Please don't keep this locked inside for it will eat you away, I beg you tell me."

She pressed herself to him, holding him and thinking of how he had always cared for her when Mother could not. He kissed her head and waited patiently.

"It hurt so badly." She let the memory trickle from her lips. "William Feargach hurt so badly. Every time he hit me, took me to bed…William, I cried, for he was rough, and I would bleed and I had no one and I missed you…"

William clenched her, smoothing back her hair. Loddin felt tears well in his eyes and listened. She gripped William so tightly now, she risked breaking his skin through his coat though he made no sign of caring.

"What else, wee sister," he whispered. "Let out these demons."

"He called me a whore. He called me Shea's whore and pushed me from him. My husband called me a whore, some of his men called me one…but Sir William…I never thought he could think something so cruel…"

"Gwen, he couldn't have meant it."

"Of all the men in the world, it means the most from him. I trusted him, Will."

"Keep going."

"I cannot, it's all locked within me," she breathed.

"Please, Gwen. I will not tell a soul."

She didn't answer, but clenched him still, seeking refuge in his embrace.

"Then you must share it with William if not me, for it's *poisoning* you."

"He will always haunt me. Every time I hear that name, see a wolf, think of marriage and children, think the name William, the ghost of William Feargach hides behind my every thought. I cannot give my heart away, Brother, I cannot, for all he will do is trample it again."

He held her until the shaking gave way to shivering.

"Marriage is frightening to a woman."

"Then I will always be gentle with Amber," William replied. "And *you* will find happiness with William again. He's your match and he knows it. He pursues *you* when he could have any other. Sister, look at me."

William tipped her face up towards his as though he was actually seeing her.

"Listen to me well, for it's advice Mother would give." Gwenyth watched him. "Not all men are evil like William Feargach. Some men simply make mistakes, and this was his, and there will be many more but you must forgive him, not punish him for another man's wrongs. If you won't trust Father this time, trust me, and do as *I* say. Marry him."

"I will do as you say," she nodded. "I will do it."

He forced a smile onto his lips, though she could tell he wasn't happy.

"Come. Let us go riding together like we used to, and spend this time well before we are duty bound to others."

He released her and groped for his reins, and Loddin, still eavesdropping, looked down at his hands.

"William?"

"Aye, Gwen?" he paused and turned back.

"I missed you most of all."

"And I missed you, more than you'll ever know."

When she entered the great hall again, the sun had long since left the sky. With William beside her, the room hushed. Dinner was all but prepared and platters of roasted venison were being carried out. She hesitated and William urged her forward. She walked to her father and bowed before him.

"Please forgive me for my loose words, My Lord. They were disgraceful and they embarrassed you in front of Lord Edward—"

"You were forgiven before you even spoke them, Butterfly," he croaked, brushing her cheek though she stepped back out of his reach. Loddin's hand fell. "I've been insensitive. Have you anything else to say, sweet daughter?"

"I accept this union, as you wish, and won't argue it again."

"Then we should celebrate!" Gavin called.

"To Loddin and Mary's child!" called one of Edward's sons. "To Amber and William! And to Gwenyth!"

Cheering rose up and Gavin ordered another cask of ale tapped but Gwenyth bowed her head once more.

"Will you excuse me from board, My Lord? I feel poorly."

Loddin nodded and she scurried up the stairs. He looked at William who was shaking his head.

"Son, come here." William obeyed, and the room fell into chatters once more. "What passed between you two?"

"May I be blunt, sir?"

"Aye, be plain."

"You know that spirit she used to have?"

"Aye?"

"Well now I don't think you will ever see it again. Congratulations on making your royal alliance. I hope it was worth your daughter."

With that, he hobbled to the cask and served himself ale, walked to Amber and kissed her hand, then climbed the stairs to his chamber.

44

William threw his feet up. His page served him wine despite his complaints that they were coddling him. The sennights had been exhausting, especially this day, and the king had done his best to keep William so busy he would not have time for ale or self-pity.

The work seemed never ending. Taxes were reviewed and quantified. Trials were heard. Soldiers were sent to strengthen the Eastern Front, a particular matter where he was placed in command. Visits to various fiefdoms were made. Shipments from the Land of Spices were examined for their oils, herbs and silks, and Grace was given a whole bolt of rare, green fabric from her brother, though one extra was saved for his niece, Louisa, if he should ever meet her.

"Was it a difficult day, My Lord?" his page asked as he arranged William's garments in his trunk.

"No, just long, and I must still tend to my squires this eve. They've had less training than I would like."

"Shall I send in servants to pour a bath?"

"It's not necessary," William replied.

The page refilled his decanter and brought him a clean tunic.

"Did you levy more taxes?"

"No. Toured the workhouses, the royal granaries. Be glad you are an apprentice here and not there," he chuckled.

He spared the details of the fullers who toiled in vats of piss to soften the royal wool. The toxic smell had turned his stomach.

"Think on that next time you get a new tunic, and remember the peasant whose life is cut short for your comfort," Bain had remarked as they returned to the castle. *"On second thought, they do have the cleanest feet in all of Bain."* Their entourage had laughed heartily.

William and his father had ridden beneath the royal banners, escorted by armed knights.

"It is senseless to employ so many soldiers for this outing," a guard had muttered. "Prince William is protection enough for us all." Again, chuckling rippled.

It was then that they passed a familiar inn. Two stories high and lopsided, it hung over the road with plaster barely holding the timbers together. A blonde wench pushed open the lower door and dumped a chamber pot into the road before seeing who was about to trod on it.

King Bain huffed. "Foul, that is," he shook his head and sidestepped the excrement.

She recognized William right away, her eyes widening when she saw the golden lions before finding wits enough to bow like all the others. William glanced at her but made no sign of comprehending.

"I am shamed for this," he muttered under a stern brow.

"Is this the one?" the king muttered.

"There will be talk of what royalty tastes like tonight," William huffed, humility preventing him from being able to look anywhere else but ahead.

"Good heavens, son. You were feeling poorly indeed. 'Tis wise that you've refrained from drink, if that's where a drunken mind takes you..."

"Is there anything else you require, My Lord?" the page said, interrupting his thoughts.

"Nothing at all. You may take your leave."

The page lit his candles and scurried from the chamber. William grabbed a catalogue upon his table and re-opened the boring task of memorizing the vassals' names and lands. It was so tedious, he rubbed his eyes and contemplated a nap instead.

Lord Edward of Dunstonwoodshire, two sons knighted in Highland Order of Chivalry, Lord Faal of Parthshire, has four sons, two of which are his lower lieges knighted in the Order of the Cross, Lord and Lady Hathaway of Brighton Hill, a fostered son knighted in the Order of the Cross, Lord and Lady Heaton...

He yawned and caught himself as he nodded off.

Baroness Kincaid, benefactress of Byron Manor until the knighting of her eldest son, Lord and Lady Lennox of Lennox Wick, eleven sons, two of which are now deceased and four daughters...impressive, practices more husbandry in his bed than in his stables, he chuckled. *Lord Loddin of Ballymead...* "Loddin," he muttered out loud and his smile drained away.

No response had come from Ballymead. He slammed the catalogue shut and shoved it across the table. Closing his eyes, he began planning his squire's exercises for the morrow and pushed Ballymead from his mind.

"If only sleep would claim me now."

Yet now, sleep would not come. He was wide-awake. Instead, he pulled out a faded scrap of fabric from within his tunic and felt over the letters sewn upon it.

Gwenyth.

He could not bring himself to throw it away despite having accepted life without her. It had been over a month and the king's messenger should have returned by now, unless he had embarked on poor weather or tragedy. He had convinced himself that the news was poor and that the king had spared him the message.

His journey through the Northeast Pass seemed now like a fleeting gallivant, nothing but a brief interruption in his life. Their meeting at Dunstonwoodshire was an unexpected moment that could have been perfect, but was adulterated by Shea and spoiled by his own lack of judgment.

"You won't ache for her if you don't think of her," he scolded out loud, but her face was waiting beneath his eyelids. "You'll let your father arrange a marriage of his choosing and that will be that."

His eyes grew heavy once more as he dozed in front of the fire, basking in what little daylight remained. Slumping in his chair, he was just breaking the edge of sleep when a knock came on his door and roused him. Groggy, William stood and opened the portal. The pageboy looked excited.

"What is it, lad?"

"His Highness requests you in the great hall. He enjoys a tankard of mead and says one waits for you as well."

"I'm resting. Does he need my help with drink? For I don't need to be taught to enjoy it amongst all my other duties."

"We all know, My Lord Prince. You've proven that lesson learned," the youth giggled.

William cuffed him playfully.

"You're lucky I don't make you hold your tongue," he threatened. "Did he tell you what this regards?"

"He did not say."

But the boy looked excited all the same.

"Well, *come on,* lad, I don't give you extra coins for nothing," he teased and ruffed his hair. "What kind of sleuth will you be if you simply steal my money?"

"A good one, sir," he smiled.

William rolled his eyes. "I'm too soft with you. Speak, lad, what is happening?"

"I don't know if this is related, My Lord, but a messenger just rode in with a letter and a cask in tow bearing the brand of a sun crest, which Our Lord King has received. He has opened it—"

"The cask or the letter?" William joked to hide his excitement. *Loddin has sent a gift of mead.*

"Both, and he smiled when he read it, My Lord."

"Did the messenger bring anything else back? Any parcels, about, ye-big?" he gestured.

"No, My Lord Prince, only the cask and the parchment, nothing else."

"That means she took it!" He gripped the stunned boy and shook him. "Well done! Well done! I'm on my way!"

He left his door open, abandoning the page on the spot. He walked, then jogged, then ran down the corridor and twisted down the stairs to the great hall, which was filled with the king's close friends.

Bain looked up from the board and his face lit up. The guests in the hall began to clap for him as he entered. He bowed.

"You requested my presence, Father?"

"I have indeed." Bain attempted to look severe. "Rise, son...I expect my first grandson in a year's time."

The whistling and clapping continued and he knew a stupid look lay on his face.

"Loddin sends his blessing, William, and sends his daughter, *and* this fine mead which I dare say I will enjoy getting for free, for he charges no meager price. Give my betrothed son a tankard!" he boomed and a servant obliged.

William raked through his intellect for a voice. "Then the necklace worked? Gwenyth hasn't refused me again?"

"Well, Loddin hasn't refused you. Any man would be mad to hold such riches as a silver lunette in his hand and reject it."

"What about Gwenyth?"

"Loddin is a business man, son, and this is merely a smart trade..."

William looked down at his tankard while Bain talked on, suddenly having no appetite. *Is that what I'm doing now? Trading a lunette for a woman? Like trading sacks of grain for a cow...*

"...and Loddin may come off as a country highlander, but he is no fool," Bain continued, chuckling to his nearest neighbor. "Drink up, man, drink up, this is a proud day! Not to worry, son, you have the girl. It's what you wanted, is it not? I told you these things take negotiation...what is it, William?"

William was shaking his head. "Is there any message from Gwenyth?" he asked. "Anything at all?"

The king nodded and walked around the table with the letter folded in his hand. Placing an arm around his shoulder, they strolled away from the others.

"I am pleased for you, even if you're not. I don't want the others to hear this, and I'm not sure I even wish to tell you, but—"

"But what? What has passed?"

"Don't become upset, William, for I was quite shocked when I heard this. Lord Loddin has always struck me as a gentle soul."

"I must know of what you speak," William mumbled.

"You'll know that this decision was not her choice. My messenger reports that when Loddin told her she must marry, she argued quite boldly, and that Loddin grew angered and physical with her to make her comply..." Bain watched William's face drop.

"Loddin would never..."

William pictured it in his mind, Gwenyth cowering for fear of violence. It was no wonder she agreed, for William Feargach had trained her to be fearful.

"He didn't strike her, did he?" William whispered, every ounce of joy now gone.

Bain shook his head. "I understand it never went that far. He

---

387

shook her forcefully and shouted. I also understand Loddin to have been pained by how he had handled her, but she fled from him before he could make it right."

William strode forward. "I must go to her."

Bain grabbed his arm. "Don't be irrational."

"Irrational? I need to explain it was never my intention—"

"In due time, in due time." The king held his arm fast and William flopped helplessly against the wall. "Your Gwenyth is of strong character, is she not?" William nodded. "Do you still wish to have her?" William nodded again. "Then this matter cannot be solved by contracts between fathers. What you two need is time together, not apart, to have a long talk."

"I wanted her to be happy when she arrived. I wanted this to be behind us so that our meeting could be joyous. I'm forcing her into this."

"One doesn't put problems behind them until they've faced them. You know that. Just like war, women are no different. When you met this girl, was it joyous?"

"No, sir. She was dying and she was scared of me."

"And she learned to love you because you proved you could be trusted. No doubt, the honor-bound knight was chaste and polite?"

"She was untrusting but she did warm to me with time."

"Of course it took time, but once she fell for you, it was more than sweet I bet," Bain nudged him with a sly grin, "knowing that the favor of her gaze rested on you. I'm sure you had moments of closeness, perhaps shared of your deepest thoughts? Perhaps shared sweetnesses? And your adventure made you rely on one another for security, for companionship?"

William nodded again and thought of their campfire chats, thought of her dancing, thought of her embraces. He pictured her killing the wolf that tried to kill him, jumping into the river to save him, fighting trained men on the battlefield to get to him. *God, her trust in me was stronger than a fortress and I discarded it, I threw it into the mud.*

"We did," he croaked.

The king looked down and saw the fragment still clenched in his grip. "What it this?" He pulled it from him, eyeing it suspiciously.

"It's my old Cadogan banner, her name, the honor I fought

under."

"What's it doing ripped?"

"She did it. I spoke harsh words to her, for sir, she was—" He cut himself off.

"What is it, William?"

"She was raped, sir."

Bain's mouth dropped open and his eyes widened. "Raped? You haven't spoken of this."

"By Shea, man, he brutalized her just like your rumors said he would, beat her like her husband did, and I didn't think I could have her anymore and told her...something to that effect." He couldn't bring himself to repeat his exact words, for they were as shameful as his tryst with the wench. "She cut it off and said she had no honor for me to fight for. Dropped it into the mud and left me. That's how we parted."

Bain set down his tankard, then turned toward the window and looked out upon the gatehouse that protected the portcullis. He didn't speak. William finally decided to drink his mead. It was sweet, like the descriptions Gwenyth had given.

"Your silence is bothersome. I cannot marry her now, can I? Do you think she has no honor? Sir, I cannot bear the thought of sending a rejection now that I've pursued her so persistently." *I should have kept this bit of news to myself*, he thought, as he watched business as usual in the yard.

"This is serious. She was right to refuse you. If the nobles hear of this, it could result in more scandal. Princes don't typically marry whores."

"I was not a prince until just a couple months ago. And she's no whore."

"And I believe you. No child of Loddin could ever be one, but that's not what the nobles would think."

William slumped back against the wall again, setting down his tankard.

"So your answer is yes, you think she has no honor?"

"I didn't say that." Bain shook his finger. "Honor is earned in many ways. Certainly this complicates things, but..." Bain sighed. "Lord, why can things never be simple with you, William? Forgive me for sounding like a senile old man, but what are your reasons for wanting this woman? Deep down, why do you pursue her still when there are so many others, *virgins* at that, that you could have? After all, a royal marriage is not meant for love, but meant for making heirs and alliances."

William's warmest memories of her flooded back, her Latin words, her stories, her playfulness, her passion, her understanding of his pain. Soon he was smiling and did not realize it until Bain cleared his throat.

"She's incredible, Father. You would see it if you knew her."

"Then my next question is one to be thought over with your head in place." He put his hand upon his son's shoulder. "Do you think she has the strength to be the queen of this land when I die? To withstand this criticism and many more should this come to light? Do you think she is capable—"

"I would bet my life upon it, sir," he interrupted.

Bain folded the fabric as though it was fine silk and tucked it back into his hand.

"Then what *I* think, is that you hold her honor captive, and perhaps you ought to give it back. We shall send for your bride without delay."

"Then this wouldn't bring scandal upon your house?"

Bain sighed. "*Our* house, lad, and *I* don't care about these social customs. I only care of the nobles' gossips and fixing problems that could have been avoided. It would be so much easier if you would find a virgin. But Lord knows I've already been working to repair my reputation." He shook his head. "Intercourse is intercourse, no matter how the church vilifies it. It can be a bad decision which creates nothing but problems, and it can be good as it was no doubt when Loddin seeded your Gwenyth. But what's clear is that this wasn't her doing." Bain let his smile return. "My First Knight always has the best reasons for what he does. If you'd bet your life upon her strength, then I can only trust your judgment of her character. We'll weather this when it becomes a storm."

45

"We've been graced with more good weather today," Hershel said as he shoveled dirt over their campfire, smoldering it.

"Good for traveling. We'll surely get there by midday," Loddin replied.

Mary began to pack the food while Sarah gathered the linens and Amber, sitting in the cart, folded the napery. Loddin looked around.

"Where's Gwenyth?" he asked, pulling on his gauntlets.

"She's by the burn, My Lord," Sarah replied.

Loddin looked through the trees and saw her sitting by the stream, holding her knees to her chest with Louisa beside her in the grass.

"Has she spoken?"

"Still not a word, My Lord."

Gavin finished helping his brothers load their tents into the cart and waited for his father to turn his back before he took Sarah about the waist. She giggled and Loddin looked back.

"Gavin, I'm warning you," Loddin frowned.

Gavin threw his hands up. "I'm sorry, sir, 'twas just a kiss."

"Lady Sarah, you're dismissed to help Mary."

Sarah scurried away and Loddin grabbed Gavin's tunic.

"You'll not deflower that girl before your wedding!" he growled. "'Tis with great trust that Edward sends his lasses to help Gwenyth. You're a grown man and will keep your trousers fastened for once! So help me, if I even *think* you have dishonored

Dunstonwoodshire, I will make sure you know pain for the first real time in your life—"

"I won't, sir, I swear it," Gavin begged.

Loddin softened and loosened his grip. "I'm sorry. I have grown cruel."

Gavin shrugged himself loose and backed up.

"Just because you're angry at Gwen doesn't mean you have to punish us."

Camp was finally broken. It had been nearly a fortnight on the highroad.

"Sister, we're leaving," young Loddin called.

Gwenyth returned from the water and handed Louisa off to Mary. She stood by Luna and her brother lifted her into the saddle.

"You look lovely, Gwen," he smiled. "You'll make us proud when we reach the capital today."

She simply gathered the reins and nudged Luna forward. Parting with Ballymead had been pure anguish, yet while her heart cried to leave Mathew and Marta, Beatrice and the other ladies and guards, she had neither cracked a frown nor looked back.

Loddin lifted his banner and the party moved onward, all five of his sons wearing the sun crest and their decorative swords that they had earned from knighthood. His daughter, wearing her finest green gown, was belted with golden threading of suns with a swooping neck that rested on the slopes of her shoulders. Her cloak flowed around Luna's rump and her hair was blinding in the sunlight. The skirts and crenellated reins of green and gold on all the horses completed the splendor. Around her neck was the silver lunette.

He's reeling in his lead the closer we get, she thought.

It was midday when the castle upon the hill came into view. The carts, loaded down with casks of mead, creaked as they approached the outer gates of the capital.

"The sun crest! Ballymead! How goes it?" called a guard from the gatehouse.

"A joyous day, man!" Loddin called back.

They could see the tail of a messenger as he galloped away toward the city gates.

"We've just dispatched the glad tidings! An entourage shall

meet you at the city gates to escort you! Good day to you all and welcome!"

They passed through the stone portico and marched by little clusters of huts full of peasant faces peeking out. The dense thatching and tiles of city rooftops crowded around the castle on the summit in the distance. Gwenyth soaked it in.

Loddin turned to see if any expression would move her face. None did. She could have been thinking of bread making for all he could tell.

"What do you think, Butterfly? Not so bad a future, is it?"

"No, My Lord," she answered. "'Tis most impressive."

He nodded but frowned at her emotionless tone.

"At least she speaks," muttered young Loddin.

"I spent part of my boyhood here with King Bain who was naught but a pampered prince in those days," Loddin laughed. "More than once the tutors slapped our wrists with their straps."

"Not you, Father, you were always perfect, were you not?" Gavin teased, turning around to see Sarah peeking out of the curtain of the cart and winking at her.

She blushed and hid her face.

"If only you knew how capable of mischief I was. It wasn't until I met your mother that I knew I must grow up and be the first son, and barter for her as my bride."

My mother was bartered for like I am, Gwenyth thought.

"You'll know a fine life here, Daughter, and you deserve it too. For William to send for you so promptly, he must be anxious to begin that life together."

"I'm certain I will be well-tended, like rich crops, My Lord."

Her words were icy and Loddin heard it clearly.

"You'll be well-*treasured*, Daughter," Loddin corrected. "Do try to think of it that way?"

She didn't answer, but continued to trace the image of the capital in her mind.

"What are you thinking of, Gwenyth?" he asked.

"My thoughts are not important, My Lord."

"I don't agree. You've spoiled Will, here, with your secrets," he added. "He keeps them as tightly as you do. But I wish to know your thoughts. Certainly being treasured by a man is not an *insult*, is it?"

Her brothers chuckled.

"Certainly being a treasure is no different than being a fine crop, or a cask of select mead for that matter, for no matter the object, they're all used to another's liking as I will be again. And therefore, Father, I must admit that my mind is confused, for I was taught to think and read and feel for life, and yet none of it really matters, except for my beauty, which earns me a place in such a fine house as Bain despite being ready to bed down with my third man at the age of eight and ten."

The brothers glanced at Loddin to see if he would react.

"Forgive my tongue. It's vulgar."

Loddin didn't try again to excite her.

"You may always think freely with me, Daughter, but you must hold a civil tongue."

"Then I apologize for my uncivil mind, for I said I would enter marriage and not argue it again, and I won't. Yet I admit I feel like nothing more than my father's right to boast of royal relations."

Loddin nodded and thought, as though arguing with a fellow scholar.

"Aye. To be blunt, you're a woman, and women are property in the eyes of the law. And we use property to gain alliances. Any man who won't admit that is a liar. But I know you are human and have wished you to know it too. Mayhap it was a mistake, raising you in such a way. However, I would argue that it's made you the strong lady that you have become. And your beauty has not earned you a place in a royal house, but your spirit has won the heart of a champion."

"And I would counter, that princes or peasants, champions or criminals, they're all men of the same physical make and willing to do what's necessary to subdue their women when it suits them. I rejected William and in doing so, must have challenged him, so he had the king bribe you with treasures and you fell for it."

"Prince William must *adore* challenges, for he gets one now," Gavin jested.

"There's more truth in that than you know," William spoke up shrewdly.

"All he has to do is silence me," Gwenyth replied, "for he is to be my new lord and master in three days' time. Nothing else matters, not even this debate right now."

"I have only once gone against your wishes, and that time is now," Loddin concluded. "Yet I've forced your brothers to do many things that they didn't want to do, which proves you've been given far greater liberty then they."

"You've trained them to rule over their own house and family. I'm but a prized servant to a lord. I fail to see how their lot has been so terrible."

"But they must still marry, same as you, regardless of their wants."

"Were they allowed to pick their wives?" she continued. "Because making them marry who they choose and forcing me to marry who *you* choose are very different."

Loddin sighed.

"She has a point, Father," Hershel added. "You've raised a woman scholar."

"I know it, but I cannot change the law. We all have roles in this world. We can fight them, or we can make fine mead out of honey. If you think marrying you off brings me joy then you're wrong, for I send you away knowing I'll never be your protector again. But if you think that sending you away brings my heart grief, then you're also wrong. For you go to a man who wishes you to be the other part of his soul and for that, I'm joyous."

"With all due respect, Father, this isn't about your heart," she whispered, daring a glance at him. "*Your* heart went to Mother."

He set his gaze forward and didn't look at her.

"It's about yours. You will know," he added cautiously, "that I'm forever shamed for sending you to Dwyre, and not a day passes when I don't sit penitent before God for my lack of judgment."

"Oh, *My Lord*, you could never have known—"

"I take *full blame*, lass," he said harshly, "and will die with that guilt for failing you. But I vowed to never put you in danger again. I've fought with Prince William, and spoken with him like a son of mine. He avenged you with every strike of the sword and avenged you as he thrust his dagger into Shea's gut, and he trusted me to tell of how your sadness tormented him. Had I done these things with William Feargach, I would have known right away he was not the one for you."

He nodded to himself. "I can say that here, in the House of Bain, with your William Cadog—William Murron, you won't be well-tended like a crop, Butterfly, you will be treated with the dignity and love that you've always known at Ballymead."

"I still would have preferred the convent."

Loddin sighed but made no more argument. She turned her gaze to the approaching gates that led into the city and began to feel again, nervousness and fear, but at least she felt.

"Finding you marriage is my role as a father, and I fulfill it. Entering marriage is your role as a daughter. Accept it."

The passersby on the streets gathered to watch the strange procession as guards from the castle arrived to greet them. The Bainick knights eyed her carefully.

"Sir William is quite the lucky bastard, is he not?" one of them jested. "Wish I was in his shoes. Not bad indeed."

"Lord Loddin!" the other exclaimed. "Welcome! Allow us to escort you!"

Gwenyth could feel the stares as the throngs admired her. She saw her father smile proudly at the comments of their display and at the beauty of the lady sitting aside the saddle. They passed taverns and merchants, inns and markets, men and ladies, children and prostitutes, drunks and peasants, all of whom cleared the way for the royal soldiers leading the flood of green fan fair to the main gates.

"Perhaps we can share stories of Prince William's sweetnesses!" came a sudden call.

Gwenyth turned her head. A blonde woman, clad in an old bodice was leaning out of a tavern door while a gathering of wenches cackled.

"Come by this eve, M'Lady, and I'll tell you *all* about him!"

Loddin and his sons exchanged looks, then glanced at Gwenyth who tried to ignore her though her face was turning pink.

"He's built like a *stallion!*" The giggling continued. "A rare treat among men!"

*He didn't wait for me either...all his promises were lies...*A tear streaked down her cheek.

"Can you shut that wench up?" Loddin grumbled to a guard

who fought his way through the crowd.

She looked straight ahead as the heckling continued.

"You may thank me later, M'Lady! For giving him practice for your wedding night!" More laughter followed. "I take payment in gold coin, thank you!"

Finally the guard reached her, shoving her inside as the door slammed shut behind them. The insults ceased. Gavin moved up beside her and patted her arm.

"Don't think a thing of it, Sister." She couldn't hear him. "It means nothing at all with a prostitute," he tried again, though still she couldn't respond. "Believe me. He wishes for a real lady. Besides, she's trying to rattle you because she's jealous, 'tis all. Dry your tears. You'll be greeting the king soon—"

"Are those words supposed to make me feel better?" she snapped incredulously.

"Gwenyth, try not to be bothered. He isn't married yet and—"

"Coming from the expert!" she hissed. Gavin froze, no longer knowing what to say. "How many women will be shouting such insults at the Lady Sarah?" she continued. "Do you wish to see her arriving to you in tears?"

"Of course not, but—"

"How many women will Sarah be wondering have warmed your bed before her? I can tell you now she thinks you to be pure and she's most excited. It's the most sacred of acts between a man and wife, and yet you give it away at will and *jest* about it! Don't talk to me. Your words are stupid!" She said no more, but clicked to Luna and urged her ahead.

Their horses and carts thundered across the drawbridge, over the ditch that encompassed the castle walls. Looming above them stood guards patrolling the gatehouse beneath the banners of lions. Gwenyth could see the main doors in the distance, the portal standing wide open through the frame of the portcullis as it was cranked on its chains.

In the doorway stood a party. Guests filled the bailey. Servants and ladies in waiting flanked the door down the stairs. In the center were two men, decorated with gold that sparkled in the sun, one man fair and one dark, both tall and lean beneath their Bainick regalia.

It was William. The whole event became real like a slap to the cheek. She stopped Luna in midstream.

"Sister, come," George stopped beside her and smiled.

She coaxed Luna onward again. As she drew closer, she could see William's face, marred by a long scar. His eyes were an exact match to the king's and they shared features in their faces that proved their relationship.

They lumbered across the bailey and were seized by responsive squires, including young Michael who was now ten and three and anxious to show his worth to the Bainick court. Gwenyth looked down and tried desperately to control her eyes but could feel William's stare moving over her, could feel the king watching her.

Her father lifted her from the saddle. She allowed him like a proper lady. He tried to wipe a tear, though she leaned away.

"That wench was nothing at all, Butterfly," Loddin whispered. "You're lovely and hold Prince William's favor."

"Lord Loddin!" boomed the king. "A handsome family you boast! You must be most proud!"

"My Lord King," bowed Loddin, before standing tall and clasping the wrist offered him. "I'm very proud indeed!"

His sons bowed as well and Loddin escorted Gwenyth up the steps. She fell gracefully into a bow without looking up. Bain took her hand and kissed it.

"She is like a faery," she heard a little girl say from behind the king's fur-trimmed cape.

"Welcome, Lady Gwenyth. I'm truly humbled by such a radiant sight."

"You're most generous with your words, My Lord King. But 'tis I who am truly humbled," she responded, though he could feel her hands shaking.

"She's crying, Father," the little girl said before another wrenched her away.

He released her hand into William's. His touch sent excitement coursing through her. William squeezed it for security, begging her dark eyes to look upon him. She remained downcast.

"Rise, Lady," the words were scratchy on his lips. She obeyed. He reached his thumb out and wiped her cheek. "Why do you weep, Gwen?"

She didn't answer.

"Nothing but a heckler in the city, a prostitute shouting insults, 'tis all," Loddin replied tactfully, though he stared at William with a stern brow. "Made such preposterous claims as to have known you. I feel certain there wasn't an ounce of truth to her vulgar claims."

William felt his mouth go dry and squeezed her hand, then fell on bended knee. He pressed his lips to her fingers and held them fast.

"It's not what you're thinking," he managed to whisper, staring up at her. *The prostitute...the damned prostitute!*

Her hand remained rigid until he finally let go. Loddin was still watching him and Gwenyth's eyes were still watering, so she kept her head down.

"You must be tired, Lady Gwenyth," Bain intervened. "Go with the women to rest and refresh yourself and we'll look for your company at board this eve. A private chamber awaits you. Loddin, man," Bain turned to her father and clasped his wrist once more. "Come. Let us partake in drinks of celebration! How goes it, man? William, did I ever tell you Loddin and I were tutored together? How did your land fair through the winter..."

They disappeared through the door, all the men of the court following as the ladies in waiting helped Mary, Sarah and Amber from the cart. A fuss rose from Louisa and a maid whisked the babe into her arms. Louisa reached her hands to Gwenyth.

"I shall take her," Gwenyth intervened, tucking Louisa's hair back beneath her bonnet.

"My Lady, we're here to serve—"

"Nonsense," she interrupted. "She's my foster daughter."

Gwenyth exhaled upon the men's departure. The attendants ushered them inside and swept down a corridor by the banquet hall that led to a staircase. Gwenyth stopped and glanced out at the torchlight flickering, the jovial laughter of men and clinking of drinks echoing, and didn't see William.

You're silly to look for him. He beds his whores and takes his wife, like any normal man. No need to seek him out sooner than necessary, she thought and walked ahead.

William crept out of the shadows to watch her, feeling lowly for spying, yet wishing to see her all the same. He smiled at Louisa in her grip, right as he backed into a metal shield upon the wall sending it crashing to the floor.

The women whirled around and Louisa let out a cry.

"Damn it!" he whispered, jumping into a shadow as Gwenyth held a wary look over her shoulder. *Damn it, man!*

"My Lord Prince!" a guard exclaimed. "Are you well?"

He moved out of the shadow, his face glowing red, making the scar stand out. Many of the women giggled. Gwenyth simply stared at him.

"Of course, I just, em, I'm fine." Despite his embarrassment, he couldn't break her gaze. "Gwenyth, I—"

"Come, ladies," Gwenyth directed. "I'm weary and should like a bit of privacy from the men," and with that, she turned away from him.

46

The knocking came all too soon for her liking. Her attendants whisked in like ants, pulled her from bed, doused her with refreshing water, and began redressing her while her coif was expertly repaired to look fresh. She was still groggy from sleep when her door burst open with no knock and a child with golden curls scampered in, followed by her two older sisters who tried to catch her.

"Away, girls! You intrude without permission!" the maids fussed.

"I'm sorry!" the oldest exclaimed. "But Grace knows not her manners and we try to stop her!"

Their maid scuttled in behind them, bonneted in a wimple and looking flustered beyond containment.

"Girls!" she scolded, patting her brow. "Out this instant!"

Gwenyth snapped out of her shock and looked at the girls, the oldest no more than two and ten, hanging their heads in shame.

"Who might you be?" she asked, bending down.

"They're the daughters of His Majesty and ought to be ashamed, My Lady. I'm most sorry for this intrusion. They have been full of curiosity about you all day."

Amber, Sarah and Mary were brought to her door with Louisa who gurgled and bounced.

"Then they'll be my sisters soon enough."

"And you shall decide the proper time to meet them, My Lady," the maid said with satisfaction.

"I should like to meet them now," Gwenyth replied.

"But the men await your company," she began.

"And men are experts at entertaining themselves. They can wait happily with their ale. What are your names?" Gwenyth asked.

"I'm Annamaria, this is Mary, and Grace is our youngest sister. You're the lady betrothed to our brother."

Gwenyth looked down and knew her smile had vanished. She quickly fixed a fake one on again. "Aye, I'm to be his wife."

"Do you fancy playing with dolls?" Annamaria asked.

The maid rolled her eyes. "She's a grown woman and plays not with trifles, girls."

"I admit I've never had one," Gwenyth smiled, ignoring the sour woman.

The girls' mouths dropped open. "Never had one?"

"I grew up with older brothers and many squires. I mostly rode horses or played with lads. Do you like horses?"

"*Horses*," Mary scrunched her face. "How is it that you're so *beautiful* if you know not dolls?" she asked dreamily, reaching to touch Gwenyth's hair.

Her hand was quickly slapped away by the maid hovering behind them.

"It's okay that they be curious, Madam." Gwenyth's tone was curt.

"I like horses," Grace smiled. "My father has given me a pony to ride."

"Then we will surely get on well together."

"Are you happy here?" Grace asked, tilting her head and twisting back and forth as she clasped her hands in front of her.

"Of course," Gwenyth whispered, though now her smile was gone again and she didn't try to recover it.

"You don't look happy."

"Shhh!" scolded Annamaria.

"What's wrong?" Grace continued. "Is your finger sore?"

Gwenyth furrowed her brow. "Why would you ask that?"

"Well, I had a sore finger, but William kissed it for me and said his kisses were magic and they could make anything better."

Now Gwenyth smiled. *You have a way with children...*

"But how would that affect me, sweet Grace?"

"Well, mayhap if you're feeling poorly, his kisses could make you feel better too—"

Gwenyth blushed and the maid threw her hands over her mouth while the chamber fell into giggles. Her older sisters began scolding her while her maid dragged her away.

"You are shamed, girl! I shall tell the king what you said!"

The maid did not waste any time either. By the time they entered the banquet hall, all of the men at board sprang to their feet. So surprised, Gwenyth and the others quickly collapsed into bows.

"Rise up, rise up!" Bain called. "Lady Gwenyth, I wish to apologize to you."

"Whatever for, Your Majesty?" she kept her head bowed.

"I was informed that my youngest embarrassed you."

"I'm not offended. She was curious, 'tis all."

"Nonetheless, little Grace owes you an apology."

Grace came out before the room and walked to Gwenyth, tears in her eyes.

"I'm sorry, My Lady, for saying my brother's kisses would make you feel better." Stifled laughs rumbled throughout the hall and William began to grin. "'Twas most rude," the child sniffled.

"Oh, dear Grace, 'tis nothing at all." Gwenyth knelt down, pushing back her curls. "My Lord King?"

"Yes, Lady?"

"I'm embarrassed such a scene has been made. She did nothing wrong, and therefore I accept no apology. She only spoke of a brother's magical kisses and how they are most successful at mending sore spirits."

"Actually, Father, I said that if William kissed her, then maybe she wouldn't feel so poorly," the girl cried.

The room laughed louder now. William looked down to hide his grin and Gwenyth did her best to hide her blushing.

"It's my wish that she be forgiven," she finished.

"Then it is so, Lady," Bain smiled.

She turned back to Grace who grinned and threw her arms around her neck.

"You will visit me and we'll go riding together," she whispered.

Grace nodded. "He fancies you, Lady," she meant to whisper, but the secret was spoken loudly. "He always turns red when he talks of you to Father—"

"Grace!" William chided.

"*Enough*, child! Go to your supper and leave the poor Lady Gwenyth be!" the king fussed.

Gwenyth dared a fleeting look at William who was, in fact, red in the face.

"Come, ladies, we await your company with urgency, for there is only so much men can talk of before they miss the women!"

The ladies were ushered to their seats. Gwenyth was led to the head table and placed at William's side. She locked her gaze at her feet, though could feel his closeness like rushing rapids through her veins.

He saw her seated, then lowered himself next to her. She could see her brothers clustered together with Mary, Sarah and Amber, and longed to join them. A bard began with his harp and gentle stories, and delicious food sat in heaps, savory smells wafting up to them. Gwenyth didn't want to ruin its beauty.

"May I serve you wine, My Lady?" came William's voice by her ear.

She froze. Goosebumps rose up and down her arms. She knew she was being watched but could not help becoming as rigid as a pole. A single nod was all she could muster, for fear of what sound might come from her lips if she spoke.

She watched his hand, decorated in a golden wristlet and ring, his nails cleaned and polished. Yet no amount of pampering could conceal the scarring that marred his skin. He tipped a decanter into a silver goblet notched with lions, then placed it in front of her and waited, his hand on the stem until she reached for it.

He allowed his fingers to mingle with hers as she took it, then turned to his own trencher being piled with food. He didn't try to speak to her, though she could tell he was nervous for he couldn't form proper sentences when talking to the king.

"Daughter-to-be," Bain began. "I understand you're an expert horsewoman. Your father boasts that you've delivered foals, tamed wildlings, and can turn the meanest horse into a dove with your gentle hand." Gwenyth smiled, but didn't answer. "I too adore riding and

404

would like to invite you out on the morrow, you and me, a father-daughter outing. Perhaps you may ride Titan, for I believe the word is he has missed you."

"Of course," William agreed without looking at her. "She's most welcome."

Gwenyth searched for her voice. Being cornered by the king of Bain was not a welcome gift she wanted.

"My father sings my praises too kindly. But I'm afraid you would be disappointed, Your Majesty."

"Come now, Gwen," Loddin said. "That isn't true."

"It was merely a child's past-time, Father, and nothing more," she insisted.

"Are you then refusing?" Bain asked.

Gwenyth felt herself pale.

"Of course not. It's as you wish, Your Majesty."

"Good," he nodded. "On the morrow then."

She felt as though she had failed a test. Bain sat back and she stared at her goblet to steady her mind. As the room fell into chatter, she seemed momentarily forgotten. She noticed her brother William whispering and laughing with Amber. Gavin was sitting across from Sarah at her father's wise discretion, though he tapped her feet with his as if no one could see. Loddin was laughing, throwing his arm around Mary, her father at the king's side was engaged in childhood reminiscences, and it was then that William slipped his hand onto hers.

She froze, expecting him to make some sort of move, but he didn't. He leaned over to her so his lips were right beside her ear. She could feel his breath and it was intoxicating, for she thought of his roaming lips sliding across her neck.

"May I call upon you this eve, Gwenyth? I should like to talk with you, in solitude."

She didn't answer, but felt her eyes well and she suddenly sniffled so loudly the king turned to look at her.

"*Dear Lady*, are you all right?" Bain asked.

William jumped back and the room hushed.

"I'm fine, just very tired. I think I need some more rest."

"Of course, you're quite pale, Lady. Go and sleep. I shall see you on the morrow."

She scurried as quickly as was still ladylike away from the torches and staring eyes. Once around the corner, she fell against the wall, breathing in heavy spurts. She wanted him to touch her, but it would mean reliving the nightmare that had made him push her away and until now, she had done well at burying it.

*My brother was right. This nightmare is poisoning me...*far more than Shea had done.

"Are you well, My Lady?" a deep voice came, and for a moment she thought it was William.

She jumped as a guard who stood in the shadows stepped forward. The corridor was dark and he was large. She felt fearful and held the wall.

"I...I'm fine..." she managed.

"May I be of assistance?"

Despite his bulk, he offered a kind hand. She took it warily.

"I search for the ladies' quarters, sir," she breathed.

"This way."

Guiding her through the maze of stairs and halls, he escorted her to the anti-chamber where a female attendant sat. She sprang to her feet to open the door.

"I thank thee, sir," she bowed her head and the guard backed away.

"My Lady," started the attendant, plump and aged with the look of a spinster. "Do you not wish to dine tonight?"

"I need more rest. Will you see to it that I'm not disturbed?"

"Of course. Even by the prince should he come looking—"

"Most of all him." Gwenyth looked down and restarted. "What I mean is I wish to sleep, and choose solitude from all others."

47

There were no disruptions as she had requested but now a fire was relit in her hearth and her maid was quietly scurrying around the room.

"Oh, you wake, My Lady. His Highness has requested your presence at board. I was about to rouse you."

More people... "It's early, is it not?" Gwenyth muttered.

"Oh, yes, Lady Gwenyth. The sun has yet to rise."

She didn't elaborate.

"I'm not certain I can handle any more excitement," she muttered, rubbing her eyes.

"You needn't worry about fanfare, My Lady. It's a quiet affair this morn," the maid explained as she readied the mint and washrags and pulled back her canopy. "His Highness says he has engagements with you today."

"Aye. I had forgotten."

She traveled through the corridors to the great hall. King Bain rested at the board sipping from his goblet. She was so quiet, her father and brothers remained in their conversations as she dropped into a bow.

"My Lady," the king sputtered through his goblet. "You're as silent as a mouse. I didn't hear you."

"I'm sorry to startle you."

She began to tremble, knowing her face was as blank as it had been all the day before.

"Rise, Daughter-to-be. Being startled by such beauty is most easily excused. Come and break your fast. I imagine you're famished."

She made her way to the board beneath their stares and could feel her heart race. Loddin rose and took her hands.

"Daughter," he whispered. "I worry for you. None of us could check in on you last eve. Your attendant turned us all away and we have news for you about William. He didn't do anything regrettable in town...you look tired, lass. Are you well?"

She sidestepped him without a reply and Bain pulled out William's seat next to his.

"Please sit, Lady."

"Does William not come?" she questioned.

"He declined to join us this morn," Bain replied softly, seeing her seated and served with wine. "I imagine he will be occupied for most of this day as well as the morrow."

So I have succeeded in pushing him away, she thought.

Bain patted her hand and left her to her food.

"Are you certain such a gown will be suitable for riding, Gwen?" George teased. "Those aren't your typical riding clothes."

King Bain scrutinized her appearance with her hair in three sensible rings.

"Quite becoming for a woman, though, I should say," he remarked.

"She's known, My Lord King, for taking to the hills bareback with naught but a pair of trousers and a tunic," Hershel added.

The others grinned and Bain looked at her again as his brow furrowed.

"Trousers?"

"Hershel, please," she whispered, keeping her head bowed, and thankfully her brothers heeded her embarrassment.

She forced her stomach to accept the food upon her trencher.

"Would you like for me to show you the outer pastures? Perhaps the hunting lands? There is ample room for cantering and the dangerous wildlife should be minimal."

"I'm certain that whatever you wish to show me will be most wonderful, Your Highness," she responded, summoning a smile to her lips.

She allowed herself to look upon him. He looked much like

William, but with creases of experience on his brow.

"You're quite lovely when you allow a smile to grace your lips, my dear." King Bain patted her hand again and looked upon her trencher. "Are you quite finished?"

A sudden sneeze caught their attention. The men looked around and a servant rose to examine the noise. The sneeze came again. Lifting the linen upon the board, Loddin spotted Grace in her nightshift, clutching a toy figure of a horse at their feet.

"Dear lass, whatever are you doing under there?"

Loddin scooped her to her feet and turned her towards the king, smoothing out her robe.

She stuck out her lower lip. "I want to go too."

"You cannot go, Grace," Bain began. "Lady Gwenyth might want a peaceable day—"

"Lady, I want to ride my pony with you and Father."

She pattered around King Bain, making her ringlets bounce and without asking, climbed onto Gwenyth's lap.

"Grace, this is quite enough," Bain scolded. "For the last time, leave the lady be."

Gwenyth smiled and gave her an assuring hug.

"Do you not wish for me to come, Lady?" Grace pouted, allowing her eyes to well. "You did say you'd take me riding."

I should like very much if you did come, child. 'Twill keep your father from interrogating me about William.

Bain looked at them both and rolled his eyes.

"It's hard to say no, Charles, is it not?" Loddin chuckled. Bain shook his head, picking his goblet up and gesturing for more wine. "I can remember the same looks upon my Gwenyth's face—"

"Father!" she whispered.

The Loddin men chuckled.

"Grace, you must go back to your chamber this moment. No doubt your maid is searching for you."

"Oh, *please*, Papa? *Please?*" she begged, cuddling into Gwenyth's lap.

Again Bain looked at Gwenyth.

"She is most good at making pitiful faces, Lady, it's her talent. You need not be fooled," he laughed. "William is fooled enough for us all. Wrapped around her finger, my son is."

Gwenyth giggled. "I don't mind her company, My Lord. She has spoken of her pony."

"Oh *please*, Papa? Please may I ride with you and the Lady Gwenyth?" Grace begged.

He sighed and Gwenyth could tell he was irritated.

"You know, Loddin?" Bain conceded. "It *is* hard to say no." The men laughed. "All right, Daughter. You may come along."

"Oh, *thank you*, Father!"

She launched herself from Gwenyth's lap into his. He juggled the wine as it sloshed, sighing with exasperation as he succumbed to embracing her.

"You'll not do well to ride in your nightshift, girl," he complained. "Go and have your maid dress you."

"Come, Lady!" Grace yanked her hand and Gwenyth began to rise.

"For *mercy's sake*, child!" Bain thundered. "What must I do to make you leave her alone?"

"I bring her with me, Father, so you cannot leave without me!" she giggled, and dragged Gwenyth willingly away.

They passed beneath the arches and came upon the knights' barracks. Gwenyth held Grace's hand. The yard was dotted with squires in training, lounging, or running to and fro on errands while servants and launderers bustled about their business.

"Bad form!" a knight hollered at his squire.

His opponent, another squire, smacked his blade away and looked to his own Master for approval.

"Closer to the body, lad! Those clumsy swings leave you wide open! Christ!" the knight continued. "You're fighting like a *damn* woman...oh, My Lady!" He bowed as Gwenyth guided Grace nearby. "Forgive my uncivility. I didn't see you and Princess Grace."

"'Tis of little consequence, My Lord," she muttered as the men stared at her.

Grace pulled her onward, bubbling with excitement.

"You know he's right?" the other squire baited. "You *do* fight like a damn woman! Probably about as good as that maiden there! I bet I can level you again, right now! Em, no disrespect, Lady!" he grinned. Gwenyth slowed and glanced their way despite Grace's tugging. "Just wait until Prince William's squire spars with you! You'll be eating dust from his sole!"

He darted forward and became engaged again as metal clinked when the first youth was shoved away once more. He stumbled backwards across the yard as he tried to regain his balance, but slammed right into Gwenyth. She tumbled to the ground beneath him.

"My Lady!" the knight exclaimed.

Every able man bolted across the bailey to help her as she pulled herself to her feet.

"Lady Gwenyth!" Grace exclaimed, then rounded on the squire. "How could you! You ought to be ashamed! Knocking down the lady! I shall tell my father!" she shook her finger.

"Damn it, lad!" the knight boiled. "Can you ever forgive me, My Lady? I shall see to it the lad is duly punished—"

"I'm fine. Please, sir. There's no need to make such a fuss."

William walked around the stable with his squires trailing behind him and saw the commotion.

"Ha! He takes his falls like a woman too!" the winning squire smirked.

Stifling a glare, Gwenyth dusted her dress and picked the pebbles off her palms. William began to stride down the steps when she turned to the first boy, his head hung so low she was certain it might roll away.

"I think I know your problem, lad," she smiled. "Come here."

William stopped. Gwenyth removed her cloak and handed it to Grace, placing her upon a bench.

"My Lady?" the young squire questioned.

"Here, let me see that sword and shield...may I?"

"Eh...what?"

She motioned for it again and he held forth the hilt, hesitating as he did so. He then held the shield for her to lace her arm through.

"Do you mind, sir?" she turned to the lad's knight who bowed his head.

"He takes training from a woman too," the other smirked.

"He'll be stitching flowers before the day is through!" a knight jested.

Again William thought about going to her aid. The boy dropped his head again but Gwenyth smiled and took his arm.

"And yet! He is the one with a woman on his arm!" she jested. This was met with more laughter. She turned to him. "Don't mind him. He's full of talk because it upsets you. My brother once told me that whoever has the power to intimidate is in control. Should you let him have control?" The boy shook his head.

She took her position.

"Now, you must catch his sword in such a way that the blow is forced down to the hilt, like so," she demonstrated.

He froze and watched.

"I've already explained this, Lady! The lad is thick!" his knight called, making the others laugh.

"With all due respect, My Lord, perhaps what he is in need of is encouragement, rather than insults!" she replied.

The knight heard the edge to her words and didn't answer.

"Okay, lad, hold it closer to you, like your master said. Shall I show you?"

The boy stood quite still, unable to answer one way or another. She turned to the other boy as King Bain himself came out of the stable and walked up next to William.

"If you would be so kind as to assault me?"

The squire's jesting stopped and he gawped at her. He turned to his knight for an indication of what he should do.

"This isn't necessary, Lady. If you were harmed, we would be in trouble indeed," his knight intervened. "To be honest, none of us are sure what you aim to prove."

Again, chuckles followed and Gwenyth felt her face burn.

"Do you fear that I would be injured, sir? Or that I might be the victor?"

The knights in the yard began to chortle. William grinned as

King Bain eyed her. Finally the knight consented.

"It's her neck," he shrugged. "All right, go easy, lad. I'd hate for little Grace to run off to His Highness with tales."

He stepped forth, a boy of four and ten and already the muscle of a young man.

"My Lady," he began "I don't want to harm you."

"Of course not, lad." She smiled a beautiful smile that he could not help but stare at. "But I don't wish to show off by sparring, for I have had little training and you would surely win. Just come at me, all right?"

He did so without warning. Gwenyth spun out of his path and slapped his rear with the flat of her sword as he fell past. The bailey filled with laughter.

"Careful, lad!" came a call as the knights congregated. "I saw Sir William's woman at Dustonwoodshire! She's no weak target!"

The boy regained his balance as the weaker squire stifled a laugh.

"My Lady," he whirled around as if she had lied to him. "Is it true? You're the one that Prince William boasts about? You are to be his wife?"

Gwenyth looked down. "I suppose if he boasts, that's his business, but I do think I was the only woman fighting in that battle, Aye. Clumsily too, like your opponent here. I should be easy pickings. Come again."

"This is the woman you wish to marry?" Bain whispered.

"Aye, Father, it is."

"She *is* incredible, as you say."

William nodded. "'Tis a shame she no longer wants me."

The squire wasted no time trying to redeem himself and charged forth. He swung at her legs and she blocked him, but he spun on her again. Swinging his metal up and over, she took a high guard and caught it, their swords locked together at the hilt until she shoved him back.

Again, laughter rose. He set his face and frowned, coming with a quick sprint. The spar continued and once more he was unsuccessful. He scowled, then his face lit up.

"You say you *fought* at Dunstonwoodshire? What *I* heard, is that Sir William had to *rescue* you," he spat. "*I* heard he rescued you from the bed of Lord Shea Feargach of Dwyre!"

She froze and the squire's grin broadened.

"What was Lord Feargach like, My Lady? Or do you deserve a different title? Tell, me, are the rumors true—"

"That's enough!" William boomed, storming forward.

All the knights backed away and dropped into bows. The squire fell down on his knee, shaking.

"I'm sorry, My Lord Prince, I didn't see you—"

William grabbed his tunic and yanked him up so that his feet dangled over the ground. "You disgusting excuse for a squire! I'll see your arse horsewhipped for your wicked tongue!"

"Stop it, My Lord," Gwenyth murmured.

"I'm very sorry!" the boy quaked in William's choking grip.

"It's not I who deserves the apology! Well? Say it!"

"My, My Lady, I'm truly sorry," he wheezed.

"William, stop," Gwenyth said again but he ignored her.

"You break your vow of chivalry in this moment! Her title is, 'My Lady,' always! And—"

"Please stop," Gwenyth said once more.

"I'll not let this halfwit or anyone else insult you—"

"Stop it, William!" she whispered. "I don't need your pity!" He looked at her and loosened his grip. "I don't *want* your pity."

Fuming, William stared at her, then at the boy, then her again and released him. He looked at her and scowled, then back at the squire and jabbed his chest.

"I care not what the lady says. You're being trained for my army. *My army!* And you don't need to be my squire for me to see you returned to your family in disgrace." With that, he backed up again.

"My Lady?" the knight said. "Do you wish to withdraw?"

"No!" she snapped. "I have a point to make now. Come."

The squire looked helplessly at William who was himself sulking, then back at her, then him again.

"You heard her. She doesn't want my pity. By *all* means, attack," William gestured, and when the squire saw no sign of stopping, came forth with a holler.

She met him again, blocking his blow, sidestepping him as his swings became more desperate. Her dark eyes narrowed and with each blow of the sword, she heard the dreaded words ring in her mind.

A Feargach whore! You're ruined! I'll show my wife what it means to be a man's whore! A Feargach whore...

She found her teeth were clenched angrily and the boy was tiring. He swung and their swords became locked once more.

"There, now!" Gwenyth called to the other boy. "I could push him away!" she strained. The boy braced himself for the shove. "Or I could turn his sword under..." Now he tensed his arms and wrists, "Or I could...oh!"

Suddenly she faltered.

"My Lady!" the squire relaxed his grip and William launched forward. "Are you all right—"

With no warning, she flicked her sword, knocked his away and rammed the shield into his chest so that he stumbled and fell.

The bailey erupted with laughter. After a moment, she reached down to help him up.

"You feinted," he scowled.

"Aye, that I did," she seethed.

He ignored her hand and got up himself, dusting his rear.

"Women are filled with wiles," he mumbled.

"Any enemy would have wiles. But don't blame me. You let your guard down, squire, and 'Lady' or 'Whore,' whichever title you prefer, I'm still a woman and you still lost."

He glared at her as the laughter continued and she turned back to the other boy.

"Now you try! Come, for surely if a simple woman can hold her own, then it shouldn't be difficult for a boy of your size!"

The boy grinned.

"Lady Gwenyth, you were wonderful!" Grace squealed, jumping off the bench. William managed to grab her and hold her back from the swords.

"I believe I fight like a damn woman," she said to the boy's knight. "Apparently that's an insult?"

"I've been most humbly corrected, My Lady," he bowed.

She looked to William, still watching despite his anger.

"You know not the damage you do when you speak such awful words to the lad. But he'll improve and make you proud if you only guide him kindly."

She dropped the weapons at his feet and walked away, pulling Grace from William's grip as she went.

William wanted to chase after her but remained still. King Bain stepped forth and patted him on the back.

"Yes, William...incredible."

48

"Quite a spectacle in the yard this morn, Lady Gwenyth."

Bain rode next to her while she sat aside Titan who was rearing to run. The countryside was lovely and the sky had decided to let the sun shine so that their skin was warmed. Far above them on the summit, the steep walls of the castle stood.

"She *was* wonderful, Father!" Grace beamed. "I should like to be able to do that—"

"Oh, sweet Grace," Gwenyth said. "I'm certain that's not your father's ambition for you."

Grace pouted, bumbling beneath them on her pony with a poor attendant on foot holding the lead.

"I'm sorry, Your Majesty," Gwenyth replied. "I let their taunting upset me."

"No need for apologies. I don't know a woman who would have the nerve or the strength to challenge it. No doubt they've learned a valuable lesson about their future princess and queen."

She sat silently as her face burned.

"I had hoped to get to know you better, without my dear daughter in our midst," he remarked.

Titan thrashed his head and tried to break loose into a trot.

"William's steed seems inclined to run it seems," Bain continued. "No doubt it's taking expert hands to control him."

"Oh, he's mild and it is no trouble," she said as she strained with the reins. King Bain raised his eyebrows at that. "I'm not quite what my father boasts about, My Lord King."

"Well if not your father, then William. He speaks highly of your skills."

"No doubt, he's impressed that a woman knows of horsemanship at all. But as you know, I *was* raised in the country with naught but a household of brothers and squires, and a father who spoiled me silly."

King Bain chuckled.

"It's no wonder that you act so freely with my men then."

"Father, may I run my pony?" Grace asked.

"No, Daughter. You must be older first."

"But I've run him before with William," she argued.

"Grace, I said no," Bain sighed.

"But Father," she began as her green eyes fill with water.

"I shall tell your attendant to lead you back home if you cannot ride quietly, girl," he huffed.

Gwenyth giggled.

"Lady Gwenyth," the girl ignored him. "Do *you* not think I ought to be able to run my pony?"

"*Dear God,*" Bain complained as one of the guards chuckled. "I rule over an *entire* kingdom yet I cannot make a little girl obey!"

"Sweet Grace, what I think is not of concern. Your father's word is law of this whole land. I fear you're putting him off, child."

She stuck out her lip as her eyes reddened around the rims.

"Oh, *please*, Father?"

"I'm not fooled by your tears, girl—will you take her home now?" he asked the attendant who began to steer her away.

"No! No! I'll ride quietly, I will!" she exclaimed.

Her tears miraculously vanished and Bain suppressed his grin.

"May I at least hold the reins, *Your Highness*?" she enticed him with the title.

He rolled his eyes. "*All right.* You may hold the reins."

They rode onward in the quietness, their entourage of guards flanking them from behind. Titan snorted and tossed his head again. There was a ridge coming up with a wood to their side. A doe walked secretly amongst the trees while her spotted fawn wobbled behind her. Spring birds flitted here and there.

"These are the royal hunting lands, Lady. Do you hunt?"

"I admit I have a softness for animals. I find it difficult to do the killing unless I must."

King Bain nodded.

"I brought William hunting with me many times, even as a squire. He was always good at hiding his feelings and yet, even then, I could see he was giddy," Bain chuckled. "Couldn't believe the king would want his company. He was a natural hunter. There seems to be little he does not excel at, though, if I may be so bold," he cleared his throat. "He seems to make quite a mess out of love."

With me or with his mistress? she thought, and felt her heartbeat speed up. *Perhaps there have always been others and he simply lied to me...and why not? He was First Knight.*

The very thought of him with another woman made her want to cry and she looked down, chiding herself to get her tears under control. Bain watched her.

"There's a river beyond that ridge. It's quite a drop and makes for good defense...May I ask you a question, Lady?"

"Of course," she nodded.

"Why do you resist William?"

Gwenyth turned bright red.

"I...well, I..."

"I told you she was unhappy," Grace added, making Gwenyth blush more. "That's why William needs to kiss her—"

"Grace Elizabeth Murron!" Bain exclaimed. The girl bit her tongue. "My Lady, that was sudden and unfair. Forgive me," he added. "I only ask because I see he's quite miserable."

They began to round the edge of the trees. Titan suddenly stopped and raised his tail. The other horses snorted and began prancing.

"What is it, Titan?" she asked, trying to nudge him onward.

He wouldn't go, but pricked his ears and snorted.

"What's wrong, beast?" Bain began and nudged his horse again. "Come now, let's move on—"

"Your Majesty! A bear!"

"What?" a guard exclaimed.

A massive animal lumbered out of the trees.

"Protect the king!"

The guards scrambled into formation around Bain and Gwenyth.

"My daughter!" Bain shouted and drew his sword.

Startled, the bear let out a cry. Titan began dancing. Grace started crying.

"Hold still, child!" A guard rode forth to grab her reins.

But the bear rose upon its hind legs and roared. Grace screamed. Her pony bolted.

"*Daughter!*" Bain bellowed and kicked his horse forward, but the bear attacked.

The horses spooked and Titan reared. Gwenyth nearly tumbled off. She let go of the reins and grabbed his mane. He began to thrash. Grace was screaming still. Her pony ran onward.

"My daughter! Save my daughter!"

Bain was thrown and his horse dodged out of the way. The guards surrounded the beast as it swung its claws.

"Damn it! Get my daughter!"

A guard began to make chase but the bear struck the king. He staggered, then swung his sword. It slashed the animal's belly. A paw lashed out again and knocked a guard over.

Titan stomped in circles. Gwenyth grappled at his neck. He whinnied and reared but she managed to swing her leg over. Both feet in the stirrups, she grabbed the reins once more.

"Come now, horse, relax," she crooned. "Come now, Titan."

Grace was still screaming in the distance. Bain tried to get around the beast once more, but it roared and attacked again.

"My little Grace!" Bain hollered.

Gwenyth wrestled with Titan, crooning and finally making him manageable.

"Hyaa, Titan!" she called, and sank her heels into him.

He shot off like a sable firework while Grace barely held on.

"Help me!" she wailed. "Papa! Help me, *please!*"

Titan streaked across the meadow after the pony, Gwenyth

hunched over his neck with her knees tight into his side, her arms moving back and forth with his gallops.

"Come on, Titan! Come on, man!"

Her gown billowed like a banner and the rings in her hair bounced loose. The pony was nearing the ridge.

"Help me!" Grace sobbed. "Papa! Help me! Papa!"

"Hold tight, girl!" Gwenyth called. "C'mon, Titan, c'mon!"

She glanced under her arm back at the bear, which was lying in a lump. Bain was in his saddle again and chasing after them, guards right behind. Titan's long strides covered the ground in a blur. Gwenyth guided him next to the frightened pony.

"Lady!" the little girl screamed.

Her arms were cinched about the pony's neck. Gwenyth wrapped her hand around and around Titan's mane and leaned off the side.

"Grace! Grab hold!" she hollered, reaching out her hand.

"I cannot!"

They were nearly upon the ridge. Titan jerked back and Gwenyth shook loose. Her body fell and she clung to the horse's neck. Her legs slammed into his forelegs. She kicked loose her slippers, trying desperately to keep herself from becoming tangled between his hooves. Her feet dragged upon the grass and knocked against a rock.

She screamed out and clenched her eyes.

Her skin burned, her hands, her feet, and her arms burned. Clasping his neck, she summoned her strength and swung back up into the saddle with a grunt.

"Lady!" Grace shrieked.

"Steady, Titan! Steady, horse!"

Bain was in pursuit and gaining.

"Daughter! Damn it, horse!" he bellowed, willing his mount to go faster.

"Come now, girl!" Gwenyth shouted, leaning clean off Titan's side. She cinched her legs around him and gripped his mane. "Give me your hand!"

"I can't!" she sobbed.

"You must! Do it!"

"Lady—"

"Do it *now!*"

They came upon the ridge. Grace reached out a terrified arm. She jostled loose and fell, Gwenyth barely catching her. She wrenched the child away and dragged her onto her lap, yanking back on Titan's mane. He whinnied his disapproval and his hooves skidded as he attempted to stop, sending pebbles spraying over the drop. But the pony tripped, tumbled, and plummeted off the ridge. She grappled one-handed for the reins and turned the horse, peering over the cliff in horror. The pony had smacked upon the crags below.

A shudder rushed over her.

"God in heaven!" She shielded Grace's face as the girl convulsed in her arms, burying her cheek against Gwenyth's breast. "You're safe, lass, you're safe!" she exclaimed.

Titan snorted and cavorted in place, and Gwenyth kissed her head then turned back the horse.

"You're safe, wee Grace."

"*Daughter!*" Bain shouted, galloping to them.

"Papa!" Grace choked, her face stained with tears. "Papa!"

Bain swung down before his horse had even stopped and ran to their side. His arm was sliced from the bear and blood was smeared across his tunic. He looked up at Gwenyth and his eyes welled. He staggered, then fell to his knee.

"My Lady, I am forever indebted," he choked. "You saved my daughter's life!"

"My Lord King," she breathed, her face flushed from the excitement. "'Twas not a thing to think twice on. Any man would have done the same."

Bain rose and rested a trembling hand upon Grace's back. He took Gwenyth's fingers and pressed his mouth to them.

"No, Gwenyth," he stammered. "You are indeed incredible. Of all the battles I've faced, not once has my heart been as frightened as it was just now. Your skills are unparalleled… unparalleled…your father, William…they've not boasted well enough."

"Papa…my pony," Grace wept.

The rest of the guards walked to the edge and Gwenyth turned away. Bain peered over and grimaced.

"Dear Christ, that could have been my little girl. I cannot believe it, I simply *cannot* believe it. We celebrate in your honor tonight, Lady. I wish the kingdom to know your bravery." He turned to her again and smiled. "A heroine. Every word he spoke was true. Truly a *worthy* and *honorable* match for William if I've ever seen one."

"I am not honorable," Gwenyth breathed before she could stop herself.

"Lady?" King Bain furrowed his brow.

"I am ruined for him," she whispered. "You bestow your compliments on me too kindly."

"Why would you say such a thing?"

She felt tears coming on and pried Grace from her grip, handing her to Bain's waiting arms.

"I'm sorry," she whispered. "'Tis nothing."

"No, Lady," Bain sounded stern. "You'll tell me why you say such an awful thing."

"Please, My Lord King. I wish not to."

"Gwenyth," he commanded. "Don't make me wield my authority."

She breathed deeply as she heard William Cadogan call her a Feargach whore again, reliving the sting of William Feargach's strap.

"'Tis just something William told me once," she exhaled, "For I...I've been disgraced and shouldn't be here!"

"Gwenyth—"

Without letting him answer, she kicked Titan into a canter and hurried away, leaving the entourage behind her.

Wine and ale was poured. The nobles feasted and the men of Ballymead stood proudly. The music was jovial and the juggler was fascinating the ladies. Roasted lamb and deer were served, seasoned with saffron and garnished with berries and seasoned roots.

"Where is she?" Bain fussed. "All the other ladies are accounted for. Go and ask of her."

A servant bustled across the banquet hall to Mary. Bain turned to William.

"I tell you, the most incredible sight. I'm still in shock. Had she not been there, Grace would be as mangled as that pony is now."

"The story has already circulated amongst my men, sir. She's become a topic for gossip, though the youth she sparred with earlier is still cross," William said.

"How did your squire fare against him?"

William grinned an arrogant grin. "He whipped him, of course, as always. Would you expect anything less?"

"Then you're no longer cross at her?"

"I admit, Father, I'm more angry that she pushed me away."

"My Lord King," the servant returned.

"Well?"

"She remains in her chamber. Claims fatigue from today's excursion."

"I'll believe that when the sea dries up," Bain muttered. "No one with skills such as hers fatigues from a midday ride."

The servant remained inclined and stared at his sandaled feet.

"That is what the Lady Mary has said, My Lord King."

"That won't do. We celebrate in *her* honor. Have the Lady Mary come forth."

William frowned and swirled his wine. "It's because I'm here. Perhaps I should leave—"

"No. This has gone on *long* enough," Bain fumed.

Mary pattered across the floor and bowed beneath them.

"You wished to see me, Your Majesty?"

"Lady, why is Gwenyth not here?" the king huffed.

"She is fatigued this eve, sir." Mary held her head down and folded her hands across the front of her beaded gown.

"Dear Lady, I don't mean to sound frightening, for you have done nothing wrong. But if there is more to her claim, I wish to know her real motives. Did she speak of today's incident?"

Mary swallowed and shifted so that her auburn hair swung behind her. "She did, My Lord King."

"What did she say?"

"Only that she was frightened and that her feet are sore."

"I do hope you don't lie to me, Lady," Bain pressed.

Mary began to burn red. "I'm sorry there is cause to think that, My Lord King," she squeaked.

"Father, this isn't necessary. Let Mary and Gwenyth be," William said.

"Is it because she fears facing my son?" he pressed, paying William no mind.

Mary swallowed. "I hope Your Highness will respect the confidence that exists between sisters—"

"I order you to repeat what words she spoke," his voice was firm. "Or I shall order her forth whether she likes it or not."

"Father, stop this," William began, but Bain held up an arresting hand.

"Does My Lord King wish to know that it wasn't words she spoke, but tears she cried?"

Mary was clearly offended and raised her head to look at them both directly.

"I'm waiting, Lady Mary."

She inhaled and set her brow.

"Since I'm not allowed to remain polite, she was most distressed over *your* prying demands, if you *must* know and feels too embarrassed to be seen. This whole voyage has been traumatic for her to endure and you did *not* make it the easier...with all due respect," she added with a curt bow of the head.

"What did you say to her?" William demanded, slamming down his goblet.

He stormed away and wound up the stairs to the ladies quarters. The king followed him, causing a surge of muttering throughout the banquet hall.

"I said that she was *honorable*, that's all!" Bain said as he grabbed William's arm on the stairs. "For if we are to speak of harmful words, *you,* dear son, apparently spoke the worst of them."

William whirled around. "What is that supposed to mean?"

"She is ruined for you?" Bain raised his eyebrow.

William paused.

"She isn't..." He shook his head. "I, I spoke falsehoods out of my own anger, and—"

"*Bloody hell!* What a mess!" Bain huffed. "I lied! Women and war are not the same! War is much easier! I return to the banquet. *You* may wish to contemplate whatever else has happened that has turned something as simple as a marriage into a damned fiasco!"

William dashed to the door of the ladies' quarters only to meet with the severe attendant who stood to guard his path.

"I must speak to Lady Gwenyth," he said.

"I'm sorry, My Lord, she isn't seeing visitors."

She planted herself against the door.

"I beg you rouse her. 'Tis most important I see her."

William reached to the latch, but the woman folded her arms and grounded herself.

"It's the lady's wishes I must protect, and she has requested solitude, again."

"Like last night?" William sighed, feeling his spirits drop.

"Exactly, My Prince. You would do well to quit exhausting yourself by running to this door."

He backed up.

"As she wishes," he mumbled. "Please tell her I came again."

The woman gave a bow and he shuffled away.

Gwenyth curled her knees more tightly to her chest as she heard the attendant turn him away. *Let out these demons...*

Her brother had begged she speak to him. She was feeling as though she might burst. Finally, she tossed aside the blanket and grabbed her cloak, exiting into the corridor.

"My Lady?" the attendant rose.

"I am well, I just need some fresh air," she breathed, and hustled away.

49

Every corridor she came to, it seemed she was more and more lost. She twirled the cloak over her shoulders and pinned the brooch as she came upon an unfamiliar corridor. Turning yet again, she hastened back the way she had come, passing the guards that stared at her, though they didn't move. Finally she found the stairs.

The banquet hall was loud with festivities. She froze. Torchlight was bright, and music was loud. She crept forth and peered around the doorway like a lowly spy. William had not returned to the party. Her father and the king were conversing. She could see her name being spoken, even though she couldn't hear.

"My Lady, it seems you're most distressed," came a low voice as a guard stepped forth. "Are you well?"

It was the same man that had helped her the night before. She whirled around with surprise and he allowed his face to crack a smile while clutching his spear. She dropped her head.

"Are you lost again?" he continued.

"I believe I need your chapel, sir," she muttered.

He bowed.

"Allow me to escort you."

He guided her through the corridor and out into the night. Apart from his implements clinking, all was still. The stars extended across the sky and they finally arrived at the arched doors of the chapel, climbing the steps. The guard heaved back the door.

"My Lady," he bowed and ushered her inside.

It was more silent in the narthex than in the bailey and the supports rising in columns up to the timbered roofing were like a forest at nighttime. The masonry was immense and she moved humbly across the floor to the baptismal perched upon a wooden stand. She craned her neck to see stained glass high above like pointed fingers in a row, which she had only heard of but never seen, dark with night. Candles flickered in the niches and beneath their shrines, emitting a soft glow.

She crossed herself, the calm of the church moving across her skin, then moved over the paving stones through the wooden screen and down the steps into the nave.

This is called a chapel? she thought.

The darkened galleries stood above her on either side and to one wall were confessionals. Looming above her in the front hung the crucifix in solid gold. She walked down the aisle, passing through the choir to the altar where she closed her eyes and began praying.

She peered up at the mournful face of Iesus Christus and her thoughts flooded her mind without control. Overwhelmed, she let her body fall down upon the kneeling pad where she gripped her hands in prayer, thrusting her head down.

"Oh Pater, please help me, I'm so afraid..."

Her prayer was a rambling of mouthed words, not forming any one sentence but filled with faith and emotion. She didn't notice that the priest had come to stand before her. He waited. She kept her head lowered in supplication and convulsed with silent sobs no one could hear.

"My child," his words were soft and she didn't hear them at first. "Child, look upon me."

Her head moved upward, noting as she went the sandaled feet, white alb, and vestments of a priest. His hands were folded in front of him and he smiled.

"Father," she whispered.

He knelt down next to her and took a seat on the step, much to her surprise.

"Father, you, you sit..."

"I'm tired, so I sit." He smiled more. "I was hoping I would get to meet the maiden that pierced Will's armored heart."

"I'm no maiden, Father."

"That I know, Gwenyth... may I call you by your Christian name? Formalities of 'lady' and 'sir' don't bode well with me."

She stared at him before she realized she was being rude.

"Of course, Father."

"I would know you anywhere from his description, but I fear he's quite wrong about one thing."

She waited for him to explain.

"He said you were light-spirited, talked of your intellect and how it humbled him. But what I see is a burdened soul, heavy with chains of sadness and it troubles me."

"I don't know what to say," she whispered.

"You were speaking freely a moment ago. You have come voluntarily to church, Gwenyth, and you have chosen well for this is indeed a place for healing of wounds. Would you like to talk, child?"

"I'm afraid I cannot remember how," she said, her cheeks still damp as she stared at him.

"We're alone, Gwenyth, and all things are known before God, for he is ever-present. Are you happy to be marrying our prince?"

"I never knew him as such, and," she paused, "there was a time when I believed I wanted it above all else, but now, I fear him."

"He would never strike you," Father Kearney replied. He rested his hand upon her shoulder, then lifted her chin to the crucifix looming above her. The sculpted blood of Iesus Christus dripped down his forehead as he looked upon her.

"There is no greater fear than what He felt as He learned of His fate, and no greater suffering than what He endured," he added. "You can speak of your fears, Gwenyth, you have the strength. He has lit your soul with the light to speak honestly of your sorrow."

"I know not where to begin," she hesitated.

Father Kearney wiped her cheek and smiled, making his wrinkles crease so that he looked wise. "Cum larvis non luctandum. Just begin, that is all, and the rest will follow."

Her story trickled out, slowly at first, then freely as she allowed every detail of her horrors, pleasures and fears to spill upon him like a knocked over pitcher. She had trusted Sir William the Brave more so than the rising and setting of the sun. She spoke of her babe, her adventure with William and how his tender lips were like rays of sunshine making her skin burn, how he protected her and vowed to love her, of her kidnap and rape, of her fantasies of lying with William even though it was a terrible sin, her battle and the murder she had committed. None of it flowed, yet all of it was there.

She spoke of beatings and humiliation and blood and scars and how she had never known such horrors at Ballymead in her life. How her mother was dead, her brother maimed, and the pain of a man inside of her. She cried of her father's betrayal of her wishes and how she had set her mind to go to the convent. Father Kearney listened and nodded, wiped her tears and motioned her to join him on the steps where she sat at his feet, pulling her knees up to her chest to rest her chin atop them.

Despite attempts to rest, William tossed and turned until he sprang back to his feet. He walked to his chests and pulled forth a piece of parchment, proceeding to fold it into a square, then stormed out into the corridor. The halls were darkened except for the necessary torches and he wound back down through the banquet hall, now cold and dark. His pace took him up the stairs on the other side to the ladies quarters once more.

"She is still indisposed, My Lord," the attendant huffed before he even opened his mouth.

"I wish to speak to the Lady Gwenyth now," he demanded.

"I'm sorry, My Lord Prince," the woman replied. "But this is an old discussion. No man is allowed in."

"I'm to marry the woman and I must speak to her!" he answered, and moved to bypass her. "I'm the Prince! Go and get her, or I shall enter of my own accord!"

"*Please*, My Lord! You mustn't! I have instructions!"

"Damn it!" he cursed like the soldier he truly was.

He pushed past her and barged through the door, surprising the ladies in the anti-chamber as they gossiped before the hearth.

"Your Highness!" they all sprang to their feet.

"You mustn't go in!" the attendant chased him.

"Where is Gwenyth? Which chamber is hers?"

"My Lord, she isn't well," Sarah answered.

"I don't care!" he thundered.

"She has requested privacy," Mary said as the ladies eyed Gwenyth's door nervously.

He followed their gaze and strode to it, knocking loudly. There was no answer and the vigilant attendant thrust herself in front of it. Again he bypassed her and pushed it open. The chamber was dark and empty.

"Please, I'm begging you," he said, his voice scratchy. "I must see her. She won't speak a word to me, won't look at me..."

Mary came to him, taking his hand.

"She isn't here, My Lord. She went to the chapel to pray."

"Why won't she talk to me?" he begged.

"She is frightened, My Lord. She feels you have forced her to marry, trapped her like her first husb—"

"It's not true."

He tried to leave, but Mary was bold and held him fast.

"Please forgive me, My Lord. But you'll only make her fears true if you push yourself upon her. If you love her like you profess, please leave her be. She will have to face you soon enough."

He sighed and nodded.

"I thank thee, Lady Mary. I'll leave her be as you request. But will you give her a gift for me?"

Mary bowed her head and let go of him. "Of course, My Lord. What is it?"

He reached into his tunic, pulling out the folded parchment.

"I stole this from Gwenyth, much to my shame, and I wish her to have it back. Please tell her *those* words, My Lady, those words exactly."

She curtsied. "I will see it done."

Gwenyth and Father Kearney sat on the carpet stretched across the pavers. The chapel no longer seemed large and menacing, and as her story unfolded, the tranquility of the candlelight beneath the Virgin Mother seeped into her, calming her.

Finally she stopped. There was nothing left to say. The time had passed so quickly, she wasn't aware how late it was. William crept into the shadow of the screen and watched her. He craned his neck to hear. Father Kearney looked up discerningly and saw him, but didn't give him away.

"I see that spirit now. You have strength, child," Kearney smiled. "And a fluent tongue, for not even most of the nobles speak such beautiful Latin. Find your solace in prayer, but above all, share your heart with William. A good marriage is built on honesty and you won't have that with him if you lock your heart. One thing is clear to me." She looked upon him. "He does not know how to right his wrongs or else he would have done so. But you must forgive and honor him, for he will be your husband.

"Do you know," he began, shaking his head. "William used to debate with me incessantly. If ever there was a misplaced scholar's mind, it was in him, for even as a boy he could justify the most irrelevant things in the most poetic ways that even *I* would question my own teaching."

Gwenyth giggled.

"It—was—*infuriating*," he marked each word and rolled his eyes. "He would have me angered for days after making scenes. The other boys I tutored would fall into fits of laughter and the entire point of my lesson was then lost."

William smiled in the shadows.

"On a more serious note though, I knew it was all a cover and perhaps that made me angrier, for if he jested, he filled his angry heart with false pleasure and no one could see how empty he was. To watch him train and take pleasure in brutality when his soul was versed in Latin...that lad..." he shook his head. "He's tormented by his past still, Gwenyth, for his father was a beast. I could see in his eyes when he first spoke of you that you had resurrected childhood memories that he had long since buried, as you try to do with your memories now. And he has failed at it, as have you."

He looked to see if William was listening and could tell that he was. *Good, for these words are not just for Gwenyth's ears.*

"You must purge these fears from your heart, for they are foreign to such a free soul. 'Tis like tethering a falcon to your wrist when all it wants is to soar on its own wings."

Alis volat propriis. She heard her mother's exasperated reprimand as she tried to ground her flighty daughter.

"Your suffering has detached you from men, and women are a man's complement, not his enemy as many strict men of the cloth would argue. Rape is a sin, and men justify it. But I don't agree that it's your shame, child. The man that did this to you, *he* is shamed. It is he who now sits in judgment. If your body saw fit to cleanse itself, then you mustn't fear a babe.

William heard these words and exhaled with relief, a breath he realized he had been holding since Dunstonwoodshire.

"I'm not one to thump fear into the minds of God's children, and would much prefer it if we could all enjoy wine in the garden while basking in sunlight." Father Kearney smiled. "In this world, there *is* a place for just you and William, not one man with one woman, not one warrior with one damsel, nor even one prince with one lady, just *one*. When you described how he made you feel," the priest smiled and she blushed, "there was much more than just attraction. There was trust so deep, that even after being violated by your husband, you allowed William to touch your heart. 'Tis not a sin, 'tis God's blessing that you found that *one* with him, and he was meant to find you and lift you up, as you must let him do again. Go, child, and think on this."

She rose as he did, bending down again to kiss his hand as he patted her head. She breezed down the aisle and William backed behind the screen so she wouldn't catch him spying. Returning to the guard who waited for her outside the chapel, she left.

Father Kearney looked steadily at William as Gwenyth swept past. The candles wafted in the breeze from the doors closing, and he motioned William to a pew.

"How is she?" William asked.

The priest smiled, shook his head, huffed, and gazed to the iconography on the wall though not really looking at it.

"You've picked wisely, lad. We spoke the whole in Latin. What a noble woman. 'Tis a shame she doesn't see it but I have faith that she will again, with your help."

"What do you mean?"

Father Kearney sighed. "It's private, what passes between God and his lambs, and I must honor that confidence."

They sat together a moment longer, then the priest smiled and rose, patting him and waited a moment longer as if he wanted to say something else, but changed his mind. He strolled away with his arms behind his back and left William alone.

When Gwenyth arrived in the anti-chamber of the ladies quarters, all had gone to bed, save Mary who was sleeping in a chair before the embers of the waning fire. The door closing roused her, startling Gwenyth.

"Oh! Sister. Why aren't you with Loddin? 'Tis late."

"He knows I'm here." She rose with the parchment in her hand. "Prince William came for you earlier. He was most distressed." Gwenyth dropped her head. "He was disappointed for he wished to give this in person."

She slid it into Gwenyth's hand.

"What is it?"

"A gift. He wouldn't say."

Another gift, she thought.

"I'm to tell you his words exactly. He has stolen this from you, much to his shame, and wishes you to have it back."

"What could he have meant by that?"

"I didn't question him," Mary shrugged.

Now she was confused. *What has he ever taken from me? Perhaps a lock of hair when I slept? A trifle I once held?*

"I go to Loddin now." Mary clasped her hands and kissed her. "Good night my dear sister."

Gwenyth walked to her chamber, pushing the door shut behind her. A fire had been lit but was dying and her covers were turned down. Her maid was fast asleep and puffing soft snores in the next room and she decided not to wake her.

She set down the parchment and pulled loose the lacing of her gown. Her talk with the priest had been soothing. In her nightshift with her hair freed and hanging loose, she wrapped herself within a robe and moved to the hearth where she poked the fire to rouse a flame.

Sitting next to it, she took the parchment and unfolded it. Expecting to find a letter, a piece of cloth fell out at her feet. She picked it up and looked at the parchment but it was blank. Instead, she unfolded the rag. Her forehead wrinkled. The dirty letters on the fabric became clear and she held her breath.

You fought in my honor and I have none...my honor, he gives it back...oh William! You're impossible!

She slipped out of her chamber once more and into the hall. The attendant at the door looked at her curiously.

"Which way to Prince William's quarters?"

"My Lady!" The attendant bolted up. "You wear naught but your sleeping garments!"

"Oh, it's not what you think. I must speak to him."

"At such an hour?"

The woman seemed more rigid than a churchwarden.

"It's most crucial that I do so *at this hour.*"

"A lady has her reputation to consider."

"'Tis my reputation, madam, and if you listen to the gossips, you already know it to be in tatters," Gwenyth replied.

The woman eventually relented and told her the way, and Gwenyth padded softly down the hall, knowing there would be more gossip come the morrow. She moved past the guards and down into the great hall, dim and dark. Climbing the stairs opposite, she soon came to a corridor lined with banners and statues of former kings, and finally came to a set of doors. She stood, puzzled.

"My Lady?" came a voice and she whirled over her shoulder.

A guard stepped forward.

"Oh, em," she breathed. "Which door is Prince William's?"

"My Lady?" he looked down at her clothes.

She clenched shut the top of her robe.

"I will be his wife soon and need to see him."

She stood straight and fixed a stern look upon her brow. The guard scrutinized her once more and then pointed. She nodded thanks and turned to knock.

"You'll not find him there. He hasn't yet retired for the night."

"Where...where might I find him then?" *Please, not with his mistress...*

"He has gone to the chapel, My Lady."

She bowed again and walked away, breaking out into a run as she paced down and out into the bailey.

William was hunched over at the altar, his eyes closed and his hands clasped together. Gwenyth pattered across the narthex and through the screen, running silently down the aisle. She stopped short a few paces behind him, knowing that the scandal the next day would be more delicious than the morning meal with all who had seen her flitting about the castle in her night shift.

He looked so peaceful, deep in prayer, that she didn't wish to disrupt him. Absorbed in his mutterings, he remained bowed. His knight's hair had grown long so that it flipped over his ears and hung into his face, and the scar upon his cheek was bright and fresh. He finally sat back on his heels and rested his hands on his knees as he looked upward at Iesus Christus.

As if he could sense her presence, he turned over his shoulder.

"Gwenyth?" he croaked. "My eyes fool me." She shook her head. "You come to me? I prayed you would."

He sprang to his feet and reached for her but she stepped back and held out a palm.

"I must speak," she stated.

He stopped and watched her.

"Please let me touch you, Gwen," he whispered. "I'm tormented and need your affection."

She lost all nerve, wishing to pry her feet from the floor to run. Taking another step back, he reached out, catching her hand and pulling her close. She did not fight it, but stood so ridged she could have been a standing stone. Yet her heart quickened. His touch was exhilarating. Energy pulsed through her even though he squeezed harder than he ever had.

Bumps rose along her skin. His breath was warming her shoulder where her robe had slipped. He pressed his arms around her waist and shoulders so tightly, she was buried in his muscle, her own hands pinned against his chest clutching the fabric.

"Tell me that you still feel this betwixt us...you must. I'm pleased you're marrying me," he whispered again, then pressed his lips to the side of her head.

Before he knew it, he was smothering her, kissing her face, her cheeks, and then her lips and her mind flooded with tingling from it. He slid his hands up and down her back; his lips searched her face for her to return his affection. She wanted to embrace him, yet she couldn't seem to do it.

"So long as you're pleased, My Lord Prince," she breathed.

Slowly, he released her and furrowed his brow as he took her face in his hands.

"These aren't the words I want to hear you say to me, not after these months," he replied. "I wish for you to be pleased too."

"My father disciplined me," she began again, trying to keep her voice steady. "He made me vow to accept it. So I'll be as good a wife as I can be. It doesn't matter if I'm pleased. I'm duty bound."

She tried to turn away to hide her face but he didn't let go.

"I don't want a typical wife," he began, sliding his hands down her arms to her clenched fingers. "I want you to tell me what to do, for I cannot interpret your thoughts. Tell me what to do so you'll look upon me with favor once more."

He guided her to the steps of the altar and pulled her down to sit. She shook her head and tried to pull herself loose, but still he wouldn't let her go.

"You have done nothing wrong. You only spoke the truth. Everything you said was true."

He shook his head. "No, no, I misspoke—"

"Nay, you didn't. I told you once I wanted to bring my honor to our marriage, and I cannot do it now. I have lost it all."

"It's not true, Gwen."

He leaned in to kiss her again, holding her face to his so she couldn't pull away. She began to cry, yet he did not stop kissing her and let his hands slide around her once more.

"Please let me finish—"

"No, Gwenyth. I wouldn't want you if any of it were true." He bore down harder on her lips and his visions of her in his dreams flooded his mind, her intertwining herself so willingly. "Everything I said was wrong. You're no whore."

He thought of her by campfire. She had let him hold her breasts. It had been so easy to make the wench do as he wanted and he ached to take those liberties once more. She had described his touch to Father Kearney. She had said she felt pleasure with him. Here she was, right next to him, and it had been too long since he had touched her.

He lay her back on the altar steps. She resisted, yet he lay her there all the same. His hand began to travel over her as he locked his face to hers and slowly, he allowed it to push aside the top of her robe.

"You could never be a whore, you're nothing like those women, you're much sweeter and I've been wanting this—"

"Please, My Lord." She began to squirm to get free. "I wish not to be like your mistress!"

"My mistress?" he chuckled. "Who told you I had one?"

"I saw her," she breathed. "In the city, at a tavern—"

"Did your father not explain? She's a prostitute, Gwen, a common prostitute, she's nothing like you."

She tried to twist herself loose once more but he held her fast and braced her back down.

"You'll be my wife, Gwenyth. It's what we wanted. I want you to accept me like you once did. It's always been you that I wanted. I was just so angry you rejected me. Don't reject me again."

She sniffled and fought to free her mouth so she could breathe, catching the crucifix above her and locked eyes with Iesus.

"Please don't do this," she whispered as his hands grazed across her breast. But they continued downward and began to slide under her shift and over her knees. She froze. "Why are you doing this?" she cried. *You're not like this, William. You wouldn't force yourself upon me. You are gentle and kind.*

But he wasn't stopping. Yet she couldn't bring herself to hit him like she did Shea. She couldn't bring herself to kick or fight. She could feel him pressed against her. He climbed on top of her as he allowed his lips to rove across her skin. She breathed heavily and tensed. He pulled her robe completely open and squeezed between her legs. She tossed her head to one side and tried to push him away.

"William, you frighten me. You're scaring me. I beg you stop," she sobbed.

"Why don't you want me?" he asked. "You used to want my touch."

Angered, he began to try harder, as if more force would make her desire it. She pinched shut her mouth and eyes and got ready for it to happen. His hand was beneath her shift, holding her bare skin around her waist.

She quaked, but was too scared to cry out. Finally, she relented and her whole body went limp.

"What does it matter anymore?" she whispered. "You treat me as the whore you call me. Do what you will then." He slowed and looked at her face, hopeless and scared, eyes squeezed shut. "You would not be the first man to rape me..."

He stopped and stared at her, cheeks shining from tears and body limp, prepared to weather whatever assault was dealt.

"Christ in heaven, what am I doing?" he whispered.

She unscrewed her face and looked up at him. He remained over her a moment longer and they kept their eyes locked, then he sat back on his knees.

"What am I doing?"

He pushed her legs together and straightened her shift over them as she pulled herself up on the steps. Shaking, she fumbled with the robe. He wrapped it shut for her as she wiped her eyes, raking his hand through his hair. She clasped it, bundling herself within it as if it were a protective shell.

"Gwenyth, I'm sorry."

He sat before her and laid his forehead on her knees. Without thinking, she wove her fingers into his hair and rested there. They remained like that for some moments, and the trembling finally stopped.

"You had intercourse with a prostitute, My Lord?" William sat up and looked into her eyes. "I suppose I shouldn't expect you to be pure when I'm not, but I—"

"No, I didn't, Gwen, I swear it never went that far. I received your rejection and spiraled down a bad path that night, and all the while I envisioned you and my future without you." His lip trembled and he pursed them shut, rubbing his eyes dry. "Damn it! I made a grave error, woman, for I almost went the whole way with her but I didn't bed her. I waited in hopes I could change your mind. I hoped your father might've shared it with you, but I can see he has not." He grasped her hands. "I beg you forgive me, for I seem to be making one blunder after the next."

He stood and helped her up, but she scooted around him and backed away as Father Kearney, having heard the commotion, walked into the nave.

"I'm so wanting of your forgiveness my judgment is muddled."

"I'll be your wife soon enough, My Lord," she whispered. "And you'll then have your rights. But you'll never know the horrors in my mind. You know not the sort of pain I carry."

"Please," he tried once more. "I want to know. I wish you to tell me."

"Why should I trust you again? I used to long for *this* with you, dreamt of it. How different I thought you were. But you show me how you really see me, with your deeds, and your words—"

"Surely you cannot hate me forever for saying a few lousy words at Dunstonwoodshire," he complained. "They were misspoken and I take them back."

But he knew right away that he had said the wrong thing.

"William? Gwenyth?" the priest began.

"A few lousy words, My Lord?" she scowled.

"That's all they were. Surely you can forgive me?"

"Those words... Had they come from any other man wouldn't have mattered nearly as much."

"Then perhaps, Lady, you're weak for letting them injure you."

Her face turned to fire and she set her eyebrows. She shoved the piece of cloth against him. Father Kearney moved swiftly forward.

"What has passed between you two?" the priest asked.

They paid him no mind.

"I came here tonight because I thought you were serious about what you told Mary, but you're a liar, for you attempt to take whores to bed and make me one as well. I came here to unburden my mind, for I'll have to marry you and honor you—"

"Honor me? Is this how you show it?" he snapped. "By calling me a liar?"

She shook her head. Father Kearney tried to take their arms but William shrugged it off.

"William," he began again. "Gwenyth, come now—"

"You're just like William Feargach," she interrupted.

William scoffed, folding his arms and rolling his eyes. "I see. What every man hopes...to be compared to his bride's first husband. I thank thee for honoring me thus. So I've beaten you and left you for dead?"

"You have fooled my father."

"I don't fool anyone. But you frustrate me, woman! For you used to favor me, but now it's as though you hate me! I don't want you to shut me out! I wish you not to push me away!"

"You've fooled my father and I'm forbidden to go to him to

argue...a few lousy words..." She shook her head. "Don't patronize me with your piece of worthless fabric, *My Lord Prince*," she burned, tears flowing again. "You didn't steal my honor, as you most *poetically* said. Shea Feargach was the *lucky bastard* and he can never—give it— back!"

She turned on her heel and stormed back up the aisle.

"Gwenyth!" He threw his hands up and made chase, but Father Kearney stepped in front of him.

"William, you'll stop now."

The priest's words were unyielding. He braced William's chest with an outstretched hand.

"She doesn't make sense, Father!" William fumed, watching her disappear through the screen.

"William, listen to me now, for if ever there was a time for you to listen and not speak, that very well might have been it."

"But Father! She comes to talk, but then won't talk!" He threw his hands up again.

"There are damages to repair, lad."

William glared at the priest. "You don't let me finish."

"That's because your tongue spits anger. You'll never get through to her by exerting your brute force."

"I don't care anymore."

"That isn't true, or you wouldn't be so frustrated—"

"It is!" he growled. "I try to love this woman and she rejects it! So I'm done with her now! I'll marry her, seed my heirs, and keep this throne secure as are my duties and *nothing—more!* And God willing, there will be many battles to fight before I die so we can keep our distance!"

He shoved by the priest and strode out of the church, slamming the door as he went.

50

'Can I be the bride now?' Amber begged.

'Nay. It's Gwenyth's turn again," Sarah said. "Besides, the bride is prettiest with fair hair.'

Sarah pulled the veil from the basket and then fixed the crown woven of flowers onto Gwenyth's head as they sat upon the fields of Dunstonwoodshire. Gwenyth jumped up and spun around, throwing her head back to catch the sun as the coif fell off.

'Gwenyth, you're messing up my styling!' Sarah scolded as Amber reached into the basket and dragged loose a string of garland, which she threw about her shoulder. She then dug out a cowbell.

Gwenyth scrunched her nose. 'That will never do for church bells!'

'Well I haven't anything else,' Sarah pouted.

'Oh, Sarah, I don't want to marry Sir William the Brave.'

She frowned at the dog, dressed within a scrap of fabric with a wooden waster tied to his back, his oversized tongue lolling upon the grass.

''Tis only for pretend,' Sarah huffed, placing her hands upon her hips.

'Well, when the ceremony ends, can we ride horses together?'

'Ride horses?' Sarah laughed a preposterous laugh. 'That isn't what a lady does after getting married! You must have a baby and work embroidery.'

Amber was holding up a doll by the arm, the 'baby,' and giggling.

'If I cannot ride horses, then I choose not to marry William!'

'Gwenyth! You're spoiling it!' Sarah chided. 'It's just pretend!'

Gwenyth laughed and ran to the crest of the hill.

'...and Father has said that your dear sister must marry him,' Sarah was back to being the make-believe mother when Gwenyth walked back as Amber sat obediently by her, 'even if she complains—'

'Let Amber marry him,' Gwenyth sighed and placed the veil upon Amber's head. 'Sir William the Brave and Lady Amber the—'

'You're ruining the whole game!' Sarah whined, but when Gwenyth gathered a bouquet of flowers and handed them to Amber, Sarah sighed and joined in.

William, tall and barely eight and ten, rode up just then as they were wrapping Amber in a shawl of leftover linen.

'I've been looking for you. Father says Lord Edward is serving supper soon...Who is that ugly beast?' he laughed at the dog, eyeing Amber dressed for marriage and jumping from the horse.

"Tis Sir William the Brave, the Lady Amber's betrothed!' Gwenyth giggled.

'Sir William?' He furrowed his brow. 'You mean, Sir Hairy? Looks more like a hairy, lazy slop than a First Knight! How could Amber's father condemn her to such an ugly creature?' Sarah and Gwenyth looked scandalized and chased after him as he dodged their path, laughing. 'What Amber needs is a handsome warrior.'

'But we haven't any lads to play. They would rather toy at archery...Wait, Brother,' Gwenyth began. 'You're about to be knighted. Why don't you marry her?'

They all fell into giggles again and William grinned, picking up the cowbell.

'But My Ladies,' he bowed dramatically. 'I would make a poor husband...for I would want to spend my days pulling her braids!' he lunged forth and gave Amber's hair a tug, then Sarah's, then Gwenyth's as all three girls squealed and ran away. He shook the cowbell after them.

'Come here, Sir Hairy!' he called. The dog jumped up barking and the girls laughed and ran. He grabbed Amber's hand and pulled her onward. 'Come claim your bride! Come on! Come on...'

The bells continued to ring, many bells, not just St. Andrews but throughout the capital. They filled the silence in Gwenyth's chamber. She stared down upon Grace and her sisters playing in the yard, and her daydream faded away.

She went to the fireplace and knelt by the flame. It was warm and she was growing nervous. William hadn't bothered to find her again. Each time she arrived at board, he stood abruptly and left, and in the stables with his squires the day before, he had ignored her completely when she came for Luna, striding out the opposite door.

She wished her mother could tend her like before and fuss at her and weave the country ribbons in and out of her plaits.

A knock came at the door.

"Enter."

Her maids had arrived. They laid out all their implements like a well-rehearsed act, pulling her gown and slippers from a chest. They then began stripping her so that she stood naked. She was dabbed with rosewater. The air made her skin shiver. She stood perfectly still like a pillar, knowing they were staring at the horrible scars. They doused her with spiced oil, and a silken shift was dropped over her head, cascading down her body.

Her hair was worked through with ivory combs and with the help of her maids, her tresses were woven into plaits alongside her head, then laced and crisscrossed with silver beads, shining like white gold. The ends of her hair were adorned with silver bobbles that clinked like faery dusting as she moved.

The gown was slipped over the shift. They looped the eyelets with ribbons and wrapped the belt embroidered with gold and silver threading around her waist where it rested on her hips. The creamy fabric, detailed with the sun crest, shimmered in the daylight glowing through the window.

A golden circlet was placed upon her head, the point resting on her forehead. The maid looked at the scar beneath her chin and clucked her tongue, though there was nothing to be done about it.

When all was through, they hauled a bronze mirror in front of her. To see herself was like seeing a stranger. She had only seen her face, never the whole of her. She let her fingers move to her neck where they traced the lunette that William had given her, *my necklace, my collar...my ownership. My world ends again this day.*

Her heart began knocking her chest.

"My Lady," a maid bowed. "We all agree that Prince William will be most satisfied."

444

Gwenyth reached out to the young woman.

"I thank thee," she whispered. "If I can only walk now, for I fear my legs are going to give out."

The servant grinned and squeezed her hand.

"You'll do well. When you're ready, My Lady."

They scurried to the door to heave it open. Gwenyth took a deep breath and placed one slippered foot step in front of the other. Led by the others, she began walking the long corridor before her that stretched out like a path of eternal pilgrimage with her ladies in waiting behind her. It was silent. The guards on the walls held perfectly still though she knew their eyes followed.

She arrived at the stairs and wound down to the hall. Her father and brothers were clustered at the bottom in their finest Ballymead green.

It was a servant who saw her first and dropped into a bow. Soon all others had done the same and the Loddin men turned to see her. They smiled and Loddin reached out and took her hand in his.

"They have created a vision," Gavin said.

"She looks like Mother," young Loddin added.

Her father's chin quivered. "There are no words to describe you."

She could sense he might cry. Her eyes welled with tears and before she knew it, she fell into his arms with no regard for her gown and hair.

"Oh, Father! Is there no chance you'll change your mind?" she cried. "Please, sir, I don't want this! I beg you take me home!"

He held her a moment longer as if he might never hold her again.

"Gwenyth," he murmured. "I won't change my mind, and all will be well, you'll see."

"Sister."

William held his arms out and let her come to him. Gently, he felt her face, her hair, and the delicate feel of the designs sewn onto the sleeves.

"You look more perfect than I ever imagined." He kissed her head like her mother would have done, then held her away from him. "May I escort you with father?"

She nodded. "Aye."

Loddin took a cloth to Gwenyth's eyes. "There, lass. You're the pride of Ballymead. We celebrate. Let us get you to your bridegroom, for he deserves to see this sight before me. Your mother would have been proud to see you this day."

With her father on her right and her youngest brother on her left, Loddin, Gavin, Hershel and George took up the train behind her and they made their way outside. The air was crisp and her cheeks grew pink.

Stone, Gwenyth. You can survive this.

The church loomed up in front of her, two tall spires of dark rock, blackened from rain and weather. The door was closed and attended by two guards, and she closed her eyes to steady herself as her father and brother each took a hand to help her up the steps.

William fidgeted before Father Kearney, making his regalia jingle.

"Are you ready for this, lad?" the priest raised an eyebrow.

William frowned, glanced at his father who sat upon his throne, then out at the chattering congregation of nobles.

"What does it matter? It's not how I hoped it would be."

He checked his clothing once more, shifting his belt and sword upon his hip, which cinched his cape to his waist. His royal Bainick surcoat, the black lion woven with gold edging, hung from his shoulders and a brooch of a lion clasped shut his cape upon his shoulder.

"It never is, William. It will be how it will be. Are you still angered? For that is no way to begin a marriage."

"No." William's eyes remained stern. "I cannot hate her, even though I want to," he added.

"Well, at least that is a start," the priest attempted.

"But I don't care either. So you would do well to let the subject die."

"Oh, I see. Have you met your niece yet?" he continued.

William cracked a smile.

"Yes, and she's beautiful. I shall love being her father."

"Gwenyth has done well tending her thus far."

His smile vanished. "Yes, that she has."

There was a pound on the door and a hush swept through the nave. All heads turned. The doors were pried back and a flood of sunlight poured in from the narthex. He squinted. When his eyes finally focused, Gwenyth was passing through the screen with her eyes down, glowing in her gown unlike any other sight he had seen.

A murmur of whispers rose amongst the guests. He lost all sense of place and watched her make her way forward behind the maidens sprinkling the aisle with rosemary. She arrived at the front and dropped into a bow. He could see she trembled.

"Who brings this woman to be wed?" Father Kearney exclaimed.

Loddin stood tall despite his age. "I do, Lord Loddin of Ballymead!"

"Rise, Lady," William said with little expression, though her scent of rosewater teasing his nose was intoxicating.

He offered his hand and she obeyed, sliding her hand into his while her eyes remained on the floor. Father Kearney readied to begin the ceremony. Loddin directed his sons away.

"Prince William," her brother William interrupted. All heads watched him. "Honor my sister, man. Keep her kindly, for she was once cherished in the House of Loddin. Promise this."

William tightened his grip on her hand and felt himself soften towards her.

"Alis volat propriis…"

Her head shot up. To hear those words made her want to cry.

"I'm merely the gauntlet for her to rest upon. There are no jesses tethering her, save the ones we make before God today."

Then she saw the Bainick banner behind him, proud and new with its fresh dyes of black and wine. It was fringed along the bottom with the lion above the proud name of Gwenyth. The lettering was bold. William could see her staring at it and searched her face for some sort of reaction, her rosy lips, her skin like milk, the tiny details of suns on her gown and his lunette of lions around her neck. He couldn't hate her.

"Prince William Murron of Bain, Lady Gwenyth, daughter of Loddin of Ballymead," Father Kearney interrupted his stare.

They turned to him and knelt. He began his ramblings in Latin chant. Father Kearney blessed them, then the veil was placed over both of their heads followed by a ring of garland that held them fast. The chanting continued and he squeezed her fingers.

"Lady Gwenyth, do you give your obedience?" Father Kearney suddenly asked.

She had forgotten where she was. Her voice was hard to find and when she found it, it didn't want to come out. She kept her eyes fixed on the rich cushions of the kneeling pad.

"I, Gwenyth, give my obedience in loyal matrimony."

William held her fingers steady. "And I receive it," he stated.

"Lady Gwenyth, do you give your honor?"

She almost choked on the word.

"I, Gwenyth, give my honor in loyal matrimony."

"And I receive it," William answered softly, turning to watch her eyes as they welled with water that she blinked away.

"Lady Gwenyth, do you give your body?"

"I..." Now she faltered and when she spoke again, her words were slight. "I, Gwenyth, give my body in loyal matrimony."

William squeezed her hand. "And I receive it..." he whispered. "I receive it."

Father Kearney smiled again, continuing with his chanting until he finally lifted the veil and garland from them and placed them on the altar. They rose.

Cavanaugh climbed the altar steps and handed William a golden ring. He took it and turned to Gwenyth. Kneeling before her, he glanced up into her eyes that still did not look at him, but at the floor between them. Her burning cheeks were the only sign that she knew what was happening. Now he was trembling.

"In nomine Patris," he croaked as he slid the ring over her thumb, then removed it. "Et Filii..." He let the ring, threatening to shake loose from his grip slip onto her first finger, then off again. "Et Spiritus Sancti." With precision he mastered at the last minute, he slid it over her middle finger where he pushed it past the knuckle and let it rest. "Amen. With this ring, I thee wed, with my sword, I thee protect. With thy dowry, I thee accept. With my body..." he took one final breath and looked up to her again. "I thee worship."

Her dark eyes met his and he held her gaze, then rose to stand beside her once more. They faced Father Kearney. King Bain came forward and both knelt yet again. He brought with him a small crown, a ring of gold encrusted with precious stones.

"Rise, Daughter."

She hesitated but did so when the king's hand was extended to her. Bain turned to her father.

"Lord Loddin of Ballymead," he said and her father stood. "I accept your daughter as my own, the wife of my son, the crowned princess of Bain, with all the responsibilities of a father to protect."

Loddin bowed and Bain turned back to Gwenyth. He lifted the delicate crown in both his hands and placed it within her circlet. Then, holding the sides of her head, he leaned forward and kissed her lips.

She bowed again. "Your Majesty."

Father Kearney delivered the sacrament, breaking the bread above them, holding high the chalice of Christ's blood. He blessed them again, crossed them, fed them the blood and body and then they rose.

"Face each other, my children, and hold each other's hands."

They turned to one another, fingers clasped so tightly it seemed neither of them could keep from clenching the other. Her eyes studied the detail of his boots, cuffed and made of fine leather. The priest's arms spread wide.

"You make vows today to last a lifetime. What God has now bonded in holy wedlock, let no man put asunder. It is final."

The nave erupted with cheering and Father Kearney smiled. William dropped her hands, his face impassive.

"You're turning out all right after all. No doubt there are many a maiden crying today, knowing you're no longer a bachelor. And you, Lady, so brave to tame this warrior's heart."

The congregation waited, cheering and shouting at them.

"I believe it's a new custom to seal the ceremony with a kiss, lad. Did you forget? The people want their spectacle."

William shook his head and turned away.

"I don't believe Gwenyth wishes me to, nor do I."

"Tell that to your crowd, William."

He looked out at their shouting faces and smiles, then back at

Gwenyth who waited helplessly before him.

"It doesn't matter if they shout. We go to the banquet?"

"What is wrong with him?" a noble questioned. "Where's your kiss, man?"

"Go on!" Cavanaugh exclaimed.

"He's too embarrassed, or scared," came a snicker. "Perhaps he just cannot rise to the occasion…"

Again he stopped.

"C'mon, man!" Cavanaugh persisted. "She's your wife! Take the spoils!"

Again he looked at Gwenyth, then out at the crowd.

"It need only be a quick one," Kearney muttered, sensing the tension.

"No, man. And you'll not suggest it again. Come, Gwenyth."

He took her hand and began walking down the steps.

"Prince William!" boomed the king. "You've not consummated this ceremony properly! It cannot end without a kiss, otherwise, why have we invited so many people?"

The room filled with laughter once more. He glared at the king who raised his brow unyieldingly. With a huff, he took both her hands and pecked her lips. She looked up at him, her eyes sore around the edges. It pained him to see it and he paused. At one time, she had described how perfect their wedding would be. Yet there was no joy now.

Slowly, he reached a finger to her eye and wiped it. His severity melted and he reached his hands to cup her cheeks instead. He caressed her like he had done during that month they had spent together and her eyes fluttered closed. The din was loud and he was thankful for it. He brought his lips to hers.

"Please give me another chance to go forth in your honor. Your name is on my banner where it belongs, and it shall not be removed again," he whispered.

She couldn't move.

"If anything, Gwen, let's just get beyond this moment and I will leave you be."

She nodded and slipped her arms about his neck. He pressed

his lips to hers, slowly at first, then firmly. He didn't stop and held her to him by the small of her back and the nape of her neck as he bent over her. The guests erupted and finally he parted and rested his forehead to hers.

Sir Cavanaugh and Sir Thomas came forth with the king and slapped him on the back while her father and brothers joined them.

"*Now* we feast!" King Bain's voice boomed. "Carry your bride, son!"

William lifted Gwenyth into his arms and carried her out of the chapel with the throngs around them. The bells began tolling again and soon the bells of other chapels returned the call. She clasped her arms around his neck, watching her brothers and father trailing farther and farther behind.

There will be no going back this time.

The drums and flutes played into the night with the heraldic banners blazing over their heads. Congratulations flowed like rivers from those who passed by. William was forever standing to clasp wrists and Gwenyth thought her hand might be rubbed raw of all its skin from the many men's mouths that kissed it.

Guests feasted on the silver platters of fish, peppered and broiled in oils, delicate meats seasoned with saffron and adorned with crowns of parsley, apples cooked and soaked in cinnamon, real sugar and ginger, berries mixed with frumenty, white breads with bodies smooth like velvet and moist on the tongue. The food was endless and forever being replenished, and Gwenyth could only manage a few bites before the nerves in her stomach protested.

She indulged in more than one goblet of great mead in hopes it would make her relax, remembering how her father had let her sit amongst the casks in the meadery as he siphoned out the liquid to rack it. She remembered him, smiling and letting her taste it, her eyes widening at the fruitiness. *'That is why we need the bees, Gwenyth, and that is why you must help tend the hives for honeycomb and not anger the bees. For this drink is fine, and it's all those who buy it that allow you to live so well...'*

Those days were over.

The dancing was lively and the crowd became drunk.

"Remember how happy you were at that little wedding?" William lounged back with a leg propped up as he spoke in her ear.

"My behavior was childish, My Lord Prince."

"You needn't call me that, Gwen. You should dance now. It might lighten your heart."

"Do you wish me to, My Lord?"

"No, Gwen, it's your choice if it would please you," he answered softly, brushing his hand down her hair.

"Then I should like to stay seated until it's time—" She faltered. "Time to retire."

Her trencher was still full of food and the mead hit her stomach hard. She shivered as she watched the happy guests, her face empty aside from the modest smile she found to thank her congratulators.

Bain leaned forward. "Are you well, Daughter?" he asked. "Is there anything you require?"

She bowed her head and brought a well-trained smile to her lips.

"You are ever gracious to me, My King. I'm quite well."

King Bain nodded and sat back, and as her face turned forward, her smile receded like a wave back into the sea. William looked at her again, completely withdrawn. She wasn't well. She was miserable. He leaned to the king and muttered. Bain nodded and patted him. He then turned to Loddin who also nodded and rose to call the room to attention.

"Prince William requests to take his beautiful bride to their wedding chamber!

"So soon?" came a shout.

Laughter followed.

"Yes, man! It seems he feels there are more important matters needing attention!"

"Whatever could those be!" asked a noble.

The laughing continued as William stood. King Bain helped Gwenyth to her feet and leaned in closely so no one would hear.

"Your husband feels that rest and quiet might do you well and I quite agree. You needn't sit here to be polite."

"I don't mean to seem rude," she said. "I'm just...I..." she didn't know what to say. "I beg your forgiveness," she muttered and fell into a bow.

"It isn't necessary." Bain lifted her and planted a kiss upon her forehead. "You will learn to love William again. Give it time but do try. Let us get these marriage customs over with. Go with your man now."

They rose to their wedding chamber. The drunken celebration filled the halls behind them. Gwenyth, mortified, let William drag her before the throngs. Arriving at their door, the procession stopped. In came the king behind them, followed by her father and her brothers. William gave the crowd one final kiss for their imaginations as the door closed, a tender embrace like he used to give, slow to come, gentle to her skin, with hands smoothing her hair down her back.

The bed had been prepared, stretched linens beneath thick wooden posts and a canopy of fabric that flowed like a gown around the sides. A warm fire was burning in the hearth and her dowry chest sat beneath an arched window. Candlelight flickered through the room, softening the shadows.

They were led behind a screen and the maids began to undress her eyelets. Soon her laces were undone and the gown slackened. William stood silently, watching her as she shivered. They removed her crown and carried it to a pillow on top of a chest. Her slippers were taken from her feet. Then her gown was finally pulled loose over her shoulders and it fell to the floor like a curtain. William inhaled, feeling himself begin to throb, for her shift was more sheer than glass and he could see her body, curving, soft and slender. She dropped her gaze.

"Are you well, Gwenyth?" he whispered as the maids now removed his crown and unclasped the brooch of his cape.

She nodded, but her chest was rising and falling rapidly. His belt was undone and the ceremonial sword relegated to his chest. Then his surcoat was lifted over his shoulders and the fine tunic beneath was taken. He stood bare-chested before her, his scarred skin rippling over his muscles with a thin trail of black hair rising up from his navel. The trousers were then slipped down and he stepped out of his boots and leggings. He now wore nothing more than his undergarments. The attendants left them alone behind the screen, folded the clothing, and placed them in their chests.

"Prince William," the king stated. "Are you satisfied with your wife?"

He looked her up and down and took her hands in his. He found it hard to find words to fill his mouth.

"Prince William?"

"*Oh, yes...*" he replied, lifting her chin so that she looked at him. "Yes. Satisfied."

The men chuckled. "We will be gone in a moment, son."

He turned red but Gwenyth made no indication of noticing.

"Daughter," Loddin asked. "Are you satisfied with your husband?"

She too looked over the length of his body, tall and perfect before her despite how ravaged it was from war. His sloping shoulders were powerful and his waist, slender where his stomach muscles traveled between his hips.

"Aye, My Lord," she murmured. "I'm satisfied."

William clenched her fingers.

"Then this is where we leave."

"Good luck, Sister," her brothers said.

"Gwenyth," came her brother William.

She peered her face around to him. He leaned in and wrapped his arm about her.

"I love you."

She began to tremble again and clung to him, nestling her face into his shoulder.

"Please don't leave me, Brother."

"You don't need me anymore," he whispered in her ear and started to let her go.

"No," she clung on. "Please, Will. I'm scared, I'm scared..."

"I know," he replied. "But you'll be all right, wee sister. This time, you'll be all right." His words were thick and he kissed her head. "Go to your man now, Gwen."

Her husband reached out and peeled an arm from him.

"Don't abuse the new princess, William," the king said. "Lord Loddin, let us tap one more cask of mead with your sons, for it would be a shame if the others got to it first."

"We must leave them some for their honeymoon," young Loddin said.

"Quite right. Good for making sons they say and apparently so, look at your father..."

The king's voice trailed away until it had disappeared. The door closed. Gwenyth stood frozen. William peered around the screen to make sure they were really alone.

"Gwenyth—"

"I'm only good for making sons," she said, shivering from the chill and wrapping her arms about her nudity.

"Gwen," he began. "I only care that my children be whole and healthy, you know that—"

"I'm cold," she murmured, turning away towards the fire.

Crouching before it on a fur rug, she began pulling free the bobbles in her hair and ripping loose the braids. He stood quietly, clenching and unclenching his fingers with uncertainty, then decided to follow. Kneeling behind her, he felt her shaking and held her shoulders. She stared into the flame, hugging her knees upward so her breasts were hidden.

"We don't have to do this right away, Gwenyth. I won't force myself upon you again. I'll take the floor tonight so you may have the bed." He rubbed her arms, then turned her to look up at him. "Shall I get you a robe first?"

"I'm sorry, My Lord—"

"William. *Please.* I'm only your lord in formal settings."

"I'm frightened."

He looked into the fire.

"Go get our bed linens, Gwen, and I'll get your dowry chest."

She looked at him strangely, but rose from the floor. William Feargach had not cared that she was nervous.

He watched her go, the heart shape of her buttocks swaying as she pattered across the tile. He collected her chest, carrying the crate with ease while his muscles tensed. As she returned with the bedclothes, she could not help but notice his physique once more.

He took the blankets from her, spreading them across the rug, then found the pillows and made them a bed.

"There. It's like our campfires, remember?"

She nodded.

"I know you don't care for needlework. I told your father I was satisfied with Luna for my Titan."

"I chose to embroider our napery, no one forced me," she whispered, standing before him, catching flashes of the glow lapping his skin.

"Then sit with me, wife, and show me what you made. For I should like to know what flowers will grace our quarters."

She sat before him and lifted the lid to the chest. He scooted in behind her so that her shoulder was against him, one knee propped up for him to rest his elbow.

"I hope you'll like them, for they're unconventional."

Just like you, Gwen, he thought.

She lifted back the flaps of fabric and he looked inside. Slowly, he reached in to pull each piece out.

"Gwenyth..." He held the cloth and looked at her needlework, so delicate and painstakingly perfect. "It's Titan."

The black horse had been repeated around the borders. He pulled out the next cloth, his Bainick lion with Ballymead's sun crest. The next showed him mounted on Titan in his Bainick colors and her in her green dress sitting within his arms, his chin resting atop her head. Another was of them at the wedding in the pass, her dancing, him kissing her for the first time and another still, showed them by the river when she rode his warhorse. The two were huddled by the campfire on the next, and more showed him at battle, carrying his banners in full knight's attire, with her name beneath his hawk of Cadogan.

"You must have been sewing for ages," he muttered.

One by one he held them and realized that not a one bore flowers as was the habit of women working with needles, but each a separate image and together they told their story.

She still cares, he smiled with relief.

At the bottom, linens for their marriage bed were folded, an image of the two of them, their heads bowed together beneath their veil with the trinity above them. He did not say a word but looked them over again and again.

"I'll make others if these aren't to your liking," she began.

"No...no," he shook his head. "They're perfect."

He pulled the blanket up around her as she shivered.

"Why do you worry, Gwenyth? Why are you afraid of me now?

I have said I was sorry."

She turned and inhaled. All the emotions built up from trying to bury him like a dried up corpse began to push against her lips for freedom.

"I don't wish to talk of this right now—"

"I *must* know what to do to redeem myself, or else our union will be as empty as your eyes when you look upon me." He begged. "I know you refused marriage, I know this was your father's arrangement, I know my words were harsh—"

"Harsh? Did you know how I longed for you to come?" she blurted out, tears suddenly gushing like an open floodgate. She turned to face him. "I *felt* like a whore! I fought and kicked and screamed your name and begged for you to come and save me! *My* William, my *sworn protector!* What a jest that was!" Her face fell into her hands and he pulled her to his chest and clutched her shoulders. "I didn't invite Shea Feargach! I killed Maccus, I killed men to get to you! But I felt as worthless as a tavern wench despite it all and the only thing that sustained me was the thought of you! For I knew in my heart you would love me no matter what! I could trust you like you always promised! And you came for me, in flying colors, banners waving...then you turned around and labeled me a whore, just as William Feargach did, and pushed me away..." Her sobs hit him like tumbling boulders and he buried his face in her hair. "A *Feargach* whore! She is *ruined* for me! As if I were the carcass of a dead mule!"

She inhaled a shaking gasp and mastered her voice, reducing it to whispers.

"If ever there was a blow that could hurt more than William Feargach's hand," she reached up and touched his mouth, "it was hearing those words spoken from these lips, lips that I loved and dreamt about. But you were right. I'm no longer pure, My Lord, no matter how many *baths* I take, *confessionals* I sit, *blessings* I receive," she felt sickened. "I feel poisoned, like a pit for a man's rubbish and nothing more..."

He gripped her. "It's not true, woman, not true at all—"

"Now you have insisted upon marrying me and for my life I cannot figure out why, but I know I'm a disgrace to the House of Loddin, and now I disgrace the House of Bain...and I'm afraid..." she gulped, "I'm afraid, for all men do is hurt...and you're a man..."

He took her face in his hands and let his fingers move across her cheeks, then her arms, then he clutched her again.

"I'm sorry, Lady, I'm sorry I'm sorry a thousand times over...*God* I'm sorry I didn't know the damage of my words. I'm a fool when it comes to this. I did not mean it I *swear* I didn't! I was so angry at myself for failing you and the moment you left I knew I had lost you, *you* Gwenyth, the only woman I ever wanted. And even though I have your body now, I know I'm condemned to never have your favor again and I will accept it."

He held her tightly as he poured out his heart.

"But you're mistaken, for you don't disgrace any man's house and I shall never hear those words from you again. They poisoned me as a boy and they will poison you. I don't pity you, Gwenyth, for you're not a weakling. You're simply the only one I could ever see myself matched with and it took Frances Cavanaugh's fist to remind me."

She looked up at him. "I don't understand."

"He punched me, woman, sent his fist clean across my face when he saw you leaving with George."

"Sir Cavanaugh punched you?"

Her crying sniveled to a halt and she wiped her eyes.

"Aye, woman. Bloodied my nose, sent me to the ground and called me a God-damned fool. I deserved it and more...what?"

She giggled, more with surprise than anything and threw her hands over her mouth. "I'm sorry to laugh."

"Go ahead and do so. I deserve that as well. But you know the penalty for insulting my pride, Gwen," he muttered, brushing her cheek. "The only thing to right the wrong, and I'll accept no less."

"Surely a kiss is too much," she remarked, blushing now and looking down.

"I should say this time a kiss is not enough..."

Before he knew it, he was kissing her softly. She let him this time and slowly, he pushed aside her embroidery and let the blanket fall from her. She returned the kiss as he reached down to her sides and shimmied her shift up and over her head.

Laying her back onto the pillows, he lifted her hair so it fanned above her, then pulled off his undergarment so he was fully bare. He lay on his side next to her, letting his hand travel from her face, down between her breasts and onto her stomach. She grew goose bumps all over at his touch, the length of him pressing against her so that she knew he was wanting.

"How could a body like this be anything but pure?" he said in admiration.

He held her face once more and looked down on her.

"Please accept me for *me*, Gwenyth. I don't want you to see William Feargach when you look into my eyes. William Feargach is dead and *I* am your William now, and with me, woman, you must remember my promise. You will never know rough handling."

She took a deep breath and watched the shadows of the flames leap across him, making him look bronze. The fire calmed them both into a drowsy slumber. Nothing but the crackling of wood filled the room. Nothing but the smell of fire smoke and rose water filled their noses.

Slowly, hesitantly, she rolled on her side to face him, pressing against him, and reached up to his hand to pull it from her face down to her breasts, triggering a reaction that couldn't be stopped, for he began to rub against her as he dozed. She then reached around him and caressed the length of his back, from his shoulders over his scars and welts, down to his waist and brought her fingers around to the front of him pressed firmly against her.

He shuddered with pleasure as she caressed the length of him, letting her fingers slide up his abdomen. His eyes tensed. Feeling her soft skin, he began to slide his hand over and around her, exploring her body. She brought her fingers up to his face, allowing one to run the length of the gash upon his cheek.

"You shall reduce me to nothing with touches such as those," he whispered.

She allowed his hand to run over her buttocks, around her thighs and back to her breasts, which he cupped and leaned down to kiss. She trembled and sighed.

"I'm trying to wait, woman," he breathed. "But it's not easy."

She rolled onto her back and guided him with. Moving on top of her, he braced his elbow next to her head and slid his fingers down to her thighs.

"You let me do this?"

She was shaking, but nodded. She closed her eyes and staved off the tears. Yet he was slow and affectionate as he explored her. Taking himself in his hand, he finally sought entrance and pushed himself inside.

"Oh, Gwen…" he shuddered, collapsing on top of her.

She arched her back, squeezing shut her eyes in anticipation. But it didn't hurt. It felt warm. Slowly she relaxed against him, allowing the newness of a man inside of her to heat her belly.

"Do I hurt you, Gwen?" he whispered, moving as slowly as he could manage. "I'll try to stop if you tell me—"

But she shook her head, her heart melting for him again at that moment. As though he spoke sweetnesses to her in the Northeast Pass. He wrapped an arm beneath her head and the other around the small of her back, holding her firmly to him.

"You don't hurt me, husband…this feeling…" she sighed, reaching for his face to kiss him.

He hungrily accepted her lips with a moan as he eased himself upon her.

"It feels right, Gwen, it was meant to be."

"Then don't ever stop it," she sighed.

"Never, woman, never…"

"I accept you, William." She caressed him and held him desperately. "I forgive you, I'm sorry…Te amo."

God, how I've wanted to hear those words, he grinned, bearing down with sudden release. "I love you too, wife. I love you."

Charles Murron of Bain and Loddin of Ballymead listened at the keyhole.

"The Prince and Princess of Bain, sleeping on the floor like peasants." The king shook his head, then pointed a warning finger to the guard opposite the door. "You'll not say a word about your king and his lord eavesdropping like scullery maids."

"Never, My Lord King." The guard's lips danced with humor as he stood at attention.

They rose from crouching and smiled at one another.

"I believe they'll be all right now, friend." Bain whispered and patted Loddin.

"I'm thankful," Loddin sighed. "Time will heal them now. I'm glad I didn't let her decide this matter."

"All I can say, is it's about time," Bain jested. "Never have I seen two people more wanting for one another. The young don't know anything," he laughed. "From the sound of it, they shouldn't be disturbed come the morrow."

Loddin chucked as they walked away.

"My Gwenyth will need her sleep no doubt, for he makes his moves as slowly as a snail. She will surely have to stay up all night just to please him."

Now Bain laughed. "Yes, he must learn how to please a woman properly. An art to be mastered with much practice, and I confess, the rumors are true. He's had none."

Loddin thought a moment. "She's had none either."

The king nodded and understood. "Then they are both each other's *firsts*, as it should be."

"Let us have mead, Charles, for I cannot imagine what toils you will endure with *three* daughters," Loddin jested, and the two descended the corridor together in chuckles.

And as William rocked against Gwenyth, moaning with newly discovered pleasure and kissing the top of her head with his grazing lips, she smiled and clung to him, burying her face against his chest, for William Feargach rose from the chains in her heart and evaporated into the fire before them.

E. Elizabeth Watson is a writer and mother. She earned her Bachelor's Degree from the University of Texas at Austin in anthropology and her Master's Degree from Newcastle University, United Kingdom in archaeology. The history, folklore and architecture of England and Scotland inspired her to write *Prince of Lions*, originally published as *The Ghost of William Feargach*, her first full-length novel. For more information, visit her website at www.eelizabethwatson.com.

Made in the USA
Charleston, SC
11 March 2016